About the Author

After Art College and a career in graphics, Tom Pierce changed course entering the police service. He attended many high profile murder cases as cameraman and artist, but the images he witnessed left him troubled. He took to writing, a cathartic process that led to a creative urge to write full-time, using his experiences as a valuable resource.

For friends who encouraged, cajoled and gave considered criticism: I thank Eve, Lucy, Diane, Max, and last but not least my wife Josie who helped me through to the last page.

Tom Pierce

The
Sweet Taste of Death

AUSTIN MACAULEY
PUBLISHERS LTD.

A CIP catalogue record for this title is available from the British Library.

ISBN 9781786293718 (Paperback)
ISBN 9781786293725 (Hardback)
ISBN 9781786293732 (E-Book)

www.austinmacauley.com

First Published (2017)
Austin Macauley Publishers Ltd.
25 Canada Square
Canary Wharf
London
E14 5LQ

Chapter one

A young life in passing

The van wheezed, its gearbox floundering in torment, leaving the cool air of evening rent by its metallic remonstrations as it swerved violently across the road. The driver – appearing drunk – failed to control the movements of his dilapidated vehicle, the colour of which had long given way to rust. Colliding with the granite surface of the kerbstone, the quiet of evening was thrown into disorder. Metal ground hard against unforgiving stone, until the substructure of the vehicle gave way; being forced to mount the curb it bounced erratically on. No longer in contact with the earth, with both drive wheels spinning unfettered, the engine screamed a tortuous sound as the battered hulk flew across the rough scrub, careering giddily in flight. Then, just as suddenly, the scream was gripped by a deafening silence, followed on by a sickening thud, as the vehicle, landing on all fours, bit into the uneven surface of the grassy bank. The momentum of speed, rather than subsiding, gathered pace as the tyres, such as they were, devoured hungrily into the rough verge. It careered dementedly onwards across the wide stretch of green that flanked the dark thicket wood.

The driver, ill-tempered and unkempt, although swathed in alcohol was not in fact drunk, but in his predicament considered actions were beyond any calculus as he feared the worst. Cursing at the vehicle's sudden and unexpected movements – it was as if he had no part to play in its momentum; the vehicle acting as though possessed careered onwards across the grass slope. Challenged, the driver wrestled with the steering wheel as it swung violently in opposing directions every time the wheels found a deep rut; then between expletives and grass mounds he managed to regain control of its aggressive movement. Finally succeeding in straightening up the vehicle to travel in line with what was an old track within the rough grass, he managed to slow the skewed metal down to an orderly pace. Gasping with relief he then allowed the vehicle to coast towards the tree line. Under the cloaking nature of the shadows below he remained watchful in the dull light, in order to avoid hidden obstacles of broken tree limbs and abandoned debris. The vehicle finally reached the seclusion of overhanging boughs, where he purposefully brought the much-maligned van to a halt.

Turning the key, satisfied he had regained the upper hand, the ignition was extinguished, but even in its death throes the tortured engine shuddered several times, speaking its pain obstinately before falling silent. Minutes passed before the driver, in deep shadowed obscurity, felt confident enough to wind down the window. He crooked his neck to one side and narrowing his eyes he listened intently. Despite his unease and growing impatience, he forced himself to bide his time, sensing sounds and watching for movements as keenly as any other night creature might. Although it had always been his intention to reach this area, in the failing light he was now unsure of his bearings. With a sharp and significant intake of breath, which matched the anxious glint in his eyes, he struggled to consider his situation and take stock of what still had to be done. Chronically aware of the need for action, whilst licking his lips nervously, he again drew in a sudden short breath, signalling that his mind was made up: that a decision had been made.

Concentrating on the world around him, his right hand wandered along the door panel sensing for the handle, once found he gripped it, pushing it down whilst tensing his body against the door. His sinews tightened, controlling the door against any sudden movement. With eyes now better adjusted to the light he was able to satisfy himself there were no immediate signs of habitation and, glancing sideways into the mirror, he confirmed there were no travelling lights on the road. Cautiously he opened the door just enough for him to slide through the gap, then continuing to hold fast to the handle as if it were a rogue creature that might cry out into the night, he found his foothold on the uneven grass. Turning to the rear of the vehicle, he finally let go of the handle and pushed the door carefully to, not shut: just in case.

Lurching uneasily, he made his way stealthily down the side of the van, working hand over hand for support in the darkness. Keeping away from the roadside and using the van for cover, the driver cursed continuously under his breath as he made his way cautiously to the rear of the vehicle. His predicament was not improved as he struggled in the shadows to find a foothold and his mood grew blacker after failing to note just how uneven the surface of the rutted grass was. Several times he misplaced his foot and the unexpected jolt that accompanied each temporary loss of balance caused him to gasp with pain that now bit hard into his groin. At the rear of the van, aware of possible exposure he paused momentarily; he was a furtive creature used to night escapades but he knew much depended on finishing this business without repercussions. Steadying himself for a moment, having both the nous and cunning, he held counsel, remaining still and silent in the shadows. He was pensive; the uncertainty of the outcome, knowing what had to be done did not make it any easier. The effort to check for unwelcome sounds caused beads of sweat to break out on his forehead. He wiped the back of his hand nervously across his mouth, realising the dryness of his lips as he did so. Hesitation crept in as he sought to judge the right moment then feeling reassured by its issuing silence; the empty stage prompted him into action. Moving purposefully forward he gritted his teeth and with a look of grim determination on his face, his frustration of mixed emotions, fear and anger, forged a bitter hatred for the cause of his predicament, combining to harden his resolve. He wanted nothing more than to be rid of the problem and as far away as possible from this place.

Opening both the rear doors of his van, neglect spoke out loudly with a rasping judder. The dry hinges supporting the battered metal echoed into the night and he winced at the sound of it but still did not flinch from his purpose. No longer faltering at sounds or movements, now totally committed, he moved closer and leaning into the interior of the vehicle he bent forward, far enough to balance and manhandle a large object lying on the van's floor beyond. Pulling hard at the tattered edges of the sodden cloth lying across the bare metal floor, he took up the full strain and grunted from the effort. Finally, after some reluctance, the bundle started to give way and move, sliding at first slowly down the vehicle's indented flooring then gathering pace as he purposely strained harder, pulling the object towards him. The earth below the tailgate was moist, so when the bulk finally parted company from the vehicle it floated above the ground momentarily then quickly dropped and sank with no more sound than a dull muffled thud as it hit the mud below. Adjusting his bitten fingers on the tension of the material he gripped hard to its grimy edge; the once proud Wilton was now badly soiled, having seen better days. The man's face grimaced, showing how much effort was needed to move the object across the waterlogged rough grass; beads of sweat broke out across his forehead, signifying his physical strain coupled together with his highly nervous state.

Away from the cover of the vehicle and overhanging trees, the lone figure was only too aware of his exposure; he was bent double, tugging and pulling with great urgency. During his exertions he continued to look over his shoulder, furtive and uneasy in case he should be caught in mid-flight. He had no intention of travelling far with the encumbrance, just far enough to clear the vehicle. The man gave a final hard and purposeful tug, whilst gripping onto the leading edge, forcing the carpet to unroll, the sudden movement as the carpet flipped open causing it to eject its contents, throwing them unceremoniously across the grass. The exposed bundle rolled twice more across the damp mire before stopping, suddenly causing the man to take a sharp intake of breath. He had been brought face to face again with his misdeeds as he stood momentarily looking down at the now exposed figure that lay still on its back.

He felt disgust for what he had done and despised the sight before him as his eyes circled the crumpled and dishevelled shape. He eyed the form absentmindedly, until he focussed on the face held in a death mask looking up vacantly into the night sky: he shuddered. His contempt was manifest – aware of the desperate straits he was now in – he uttered angrily, "Fucking bitch!" His raw emotions at that moment showed little concern for revealing his presence; the expletives were hurled loudly and with much loathing from his lips.

Turning away quickly he continued cursing under his breath as he angrily closed both the rear doors, this time without due ceremony or concern at the noise they might make. He then stumbled morosely back to the driver's door, hunched and degraded, anxious to be gone. This time, without pausing to consider his surroundings and highly agitated, he fell into the driver's seat and immediately set about leaving, his ugly mood replicated by ill-considered driving skills. Forcing his actions into loud statements of vitriol he was no longer cautious; using noise to amplify his wrath he slammed the door hard, as if attempting foreclosure on what lay behind him. His ill humour provided poor judgement and on turning the key without care the engine missed, the mix of fuel and timing made the thing cough and expire for a further two failed attempts at ignition. Finally, after liberal helpings of cajoling and doubting its parentage he ran to appeasement. He panicked with the realisation the battery was giving way, until finally the ignition caught and sparked successfully. With an engine now firing he was able to unleash his full fury on the vehicle, revving the tired beast's heart without mercy. The sound of grating gears rent the air once more, echoing through the trees as the van lurched forwards. Then, driving with his foot hard down on the floor at full throttle, he ran the van mercilessly and recklessly off the bank at speed. It was many yards of tarmac after violently bouncing onto the road that he finally regained control. With noisy acceleration the disagreeable image and its driver faded from the country lane, disappearing into the darkness towards town, as the night and smoke residue cloaked the world's misdeeds once more.

Chapter two

A vision of hell

Her distress was evident as her form bobbed and twitched uneasily along the lonely path, scurrying and sometimes almost pausing, an inconsistent set of actions that described an overwhelming agitation presently consuming the said lady. The odd sounds, which caused her to pause, might clarify numerous possibilities, but in her case, it was either immediate pursuit or the innocent sounds of night, with her believing the former. The stark picket fence – that marked her passage all the way to the cottage – stared out as a dim, silver ethereal glow. It was as if – despite the countless weather-beaten days – the fence had been singularly tasked with holding back the marching menace of the thickly-bound wood. Although not far to the remaining vestiges of town – from where she now hastened – for her it could have been any place close to hell, at the very ends of the earth in fact.

Until today she had every reason to feel well-disposed and confident whilst treading the pathway towards the cottage; it had been one of those resonant happenings, reverberant in joyful shared warmth. This scene of twice daily exercise, shared together with her dog, had today taken on a quite different complexion. After what she had seen, the trees around her – blackened by night and breaching the air with uncompromising jagged fingers – all of nature assumed a malevolent character. Compounded by the scarcity of another trusted human face, it caused a realisation within her that bleak isolation could become intensely dangerous, one that could change her once familiar haunts from arcadia, to one of doom-ridden remoteness. It was this self-same isolation which she had always treasured and which now by the very absence of a kindly voice persisted in sending a chilling message through her.

The town, despite its relatively close proximity, lay neatly tucked beyond the bend out of sight; intervening woodland hung closely, lining both sides of the country road. The obstruction in effect denied any comfort that she may have received from the warm glow of argon streetlights beyond, leaving her panic-stricken in the gloom, devoid of all visual reassurance. Dora Bartlett's agitation grew with every forced pace forward, each step becoming more tiring, thereby magnifying the distance that still remained. All this conspired to endorse her feelings of terror, on a journey that now, because of exhaustion, had become painfully erratic. Her route – made mechanically – following a line well worn by familiarity was directed with grim determination. The two lonely figures connected by a lead clawed their way towards the haven of the cottage. The brooding darkness of the trees closed in around them from all sides, forming an alien audience as they stumbled nervously along. She dared not detract from her purpose either by stopping, glancing up or indeed even taking stock of the distance remaining to the comfort of her own door;

her unease forced her blindly onwards. With head bowed and fearful – not knowing how closely her pursuer lay – and caring not to look back for confirmation. Dora fixed her eyes firmly ground-wards, concentrating her mind, seeking only for the image of the taut lead and little legs that raced nervously to the fore.

Determining the pace of movement was her dog – companion for six years – who had shared this strip of path twice daily with her mistress, day in, day out, come rain, wind or shine. They had seen many seasons together and on numerous occasions Dora had watched with amusement the creature's antics. To the young Sealyham – bristling to the chase – running barking in hot pursuit after a grazing rabbit, the pleasure of the chase was all. The little creature would bark and dance for affection having returned empty-mouthed, dishevelled and breathless, after seeing off all the wildlife in the proximity. In particular, she had always sensed with pleasure the apparent enjoyment the mutt had shown in snuffling at the smell of new growth, during the joyful turn of spring under a canopy of freshly unfurled green. Today's excursion, however, which had started as any other, had suddenly taken on a new element, containing strong doubt and disquiet. Such apprehension – previously unknown to either of them – had become infectious. As they journeyed along together their combined panic affected each other, further igniting their querulous unrest. A circle of self-replicating fear now forced each of them onwards towards their goal, the little dog urging them forward at its own pace. Which, given the wild unreasoning steps taken, neither would be able to maintain for very long.

Despite the creature's small build, its continuous tugging and straining at the leash had borne hard on Dora's wrist and elbow joints, each fresh jolt exacerbating a now painful arm. This added discomfort prevented Dora from concentrating her mind, when dealing methodically with matters in hand. In fact, it left her unable to consider the course of events rationally; instead, she found herself now dwelling on her predicament and its outcomes, which in turn provoked an unhealthy morbidity. Dora's mind embellished what she thought she had seen, which in turn nourished a vivid imagination. Unable to think in a coherent manner the images nagged at her, surreal and unearthly, producing a dreadful foreboding in her for whatever it was that she thought lay behind her in the darkness. The dog, sensing her turn of mind and distraught behaviour, twitched nervously, jumping and snapping erratically as it reared up at an imagined foe. Panic then in turn gripped the small animal, its eyes bulged and amidst much muzzle snorting and loud yapping – which distressed its owner still further – the leash, dog, and her legs became hopelessly enmeshed. The diminutive creature matched its terrier credentials, as it flared with red-flecked eyes and teeth that snapped the air. Dora, dismayed at the abrupt disruption to her flight, was forced to stop. The lead had suddenly tightened around her calves with a strong intent of throwing her off balance and, whilst not actually collapsing to the ground, she found herself fighting to remain vertical.

Looking down nervously at her distressed pet, her exasperation grew, along with a feeling of helplessness, as she surveyed the maze of over-extended lead that now encircled both her and the dog. Considering Pip, its bared teeth and the creature's possible nervous hostility, she struggled in misery with a double fear; it was either a painful bite as she stood in line to its snapping teeth, or a possible encounter with the unknown horror that lay behind her. Looking anxiously back along the path, unable in the darkness to even clarify shapes, her decision was made for her. As unpalatable as her position was, she gave way to reason and attended to the disentanglement of herself and her pet. In the process she kept a wary eye and distanced herself as far as possible from the receipt of a painful bite, the process withdrew Dora from the mental torture of the unknown. She spoke loudly but not unkindly, as she felt, firmly to the animal and indeed to anyone else that may have been listening, in what she considered demonstrably to be her best voice of authority. Dora – somewhat pleased with herself – successfully kept the pet in order, whilst at the same time managing to finally unravel the confusion.

Bent double over her pet on the path where the greensward had given way to roadside, Dora became aware of a vehicle heading at speed towards her from the rear. She sensed further danger and in her predicament tensed at her own vulnerability. Crouching down tightly in a ball and holding firm to the small creature's muzzle for fear it would give them away, she froze. Listening to the approaching vehicle increased her alarm, it was noisy, and the loud thumping coming from it started a pain within her chest. Glancing backwards she saw the road was awash with a row of bright angry lights, as the vehicle raced through the night towards her. Unable to think as it pulled alongside – the noise obliterating all – the scenario was like Hades, horrendous and terrifying. The engine, loud music and gush of wild laughter from shadowy figures within spilled out from the open windows in a raucous barrage: something was thrown. Dora dared not, and could not, move as the satanic illusion roared by, quickly disappearing beyond the bend. Only the bounce of a thrown object registered the reality, she knew then that something had been purposely aimed at her, which seconds later proved to be a bottle that duly shattered against the kerb. With the moment of freedom offered, the shattering of the bottle acted as a catalyst, sparking an impulse for them both to leap forward. Racing away as if to the starter's pistol, panic-stricken, they both sought the succour of home, and the reassurance of sanctuary that they both shared.

The momentary interruption and the distraction caused by the incident had divorced her from her initial fears; now, with second wind – and her mind cleared – she found new strength and hurried along the path whilst mulling over what it was she had actually seen. She was sure that the darkened shape had been that of a man, there could be no doubting it. She hesitated whilst considering his appearance and yet, she knew it to have been gross. But why, what made him so – yes that was it, the wild eyes; wild, wide eyes that had held her in their contemptuous gaze – indecent, suggestive eyes that had held her to ransom. She trembled at the memory of them, there had been – however brief – a deep look, one of a primeval nature. Yes, that was it, menace and, despite her exertions, which were great, the very thought of it produced a coldness that caused her to shiver involuntarily. Could eyes reflect evil, she wondered? They were certainly charged emotionally. The wretched man had been drinking of course, well as far as she could tell at any rate, and heavily at that. The threatening face was one marked by years of excess, thin red lines and blotches of mauve covered his pock-marked nose and cheeks. But none of this was reason enough for her flight – no! The fear suddenly leapt back at her, she could see him in her mind's eye. He was as a wild animal kneeling over a recent kill, his reddened face – she flinched further at the thought of it – almost carrying traces of blood from his victim, dripping down the leering, wet, decaying mouth. She closed her eyes to erase the memory of it, but nothing seemingly could cloud out the conjured image of depravity.

Now with superhuman effort and pushing herself to the very extreme, she burst into an unseemly display of public outburst; looking towards the heavens she cried out aloud.

"Someone help me! Anyone, for God's sake!"

She shouted out desperately once again, praying for someone, anyone to help. Then suddenly stopped, stifling in mid-stream any further cry, instantly regretting the expression of it and her utterance of the Lord's name. She cautioned herself, for if that 'help' appeared, it might possibly be in the form of further danger, even an accomplice. Better nothing at all she thought, at least the odds were one to one, as terrifying as that might be. Her years were now showing as the effort to get home had locked her to a standstill and the pain in her chest was excruciating, she felt she would explode at the severity of it. To continue was impossible, so with reluctance she staggered to a halt once more. Now moaning to herself between gasps of anguished self-pity – the distressed Dora bleated, *'I can't go on,' 'I can't go on!'* Large quantities of air were ingested as she bent double, hands on her hips, gasping and sobbing at one and the same time. She bobbed up and down, trying desperately to catch her breath and balance her equilibrium. The wild scramble and adrenaline overload had pushed her to the very edge and despite the warm glow of her parlour lights – now visible and a very welcoming sight – it all seemed too much for her. With the vision of the hanging lantern in the porch only some fifty yards or so away – at that moment, her energy almost spent – it seemed an unobtainable goal.

Her lungs heaved in a manner quite unknown to herself, panting uncontrollably and standing doubtfully upright on jellied legs. It was some time – indeed it felt an eternity – during which time nothing moved, and the only sound was her wild erratic breathing, as she rasped desperately for vast quantities of air. The dog stood trembling, moving from one foot to another and giving her an over-the-shoulder look of confusion as it waited nervously for the next move. Rallying briefly after the forced rest – however short – Dora allowed herself just one more glance behind. 'He – it must have been a man', she thought peering into the gloom, uncertain of shapes. Was he still where she had last seen him – slumped over – and the word stuck fast in her throat; she could hardly think it, let alone say it – a body? Had he not moved? The relief was enormous, if not somewhat short-lived. For a sudden squall of chilled air licked the trees and rattled the remaining hardened leaves of summer. The dog, further startled by the noise and movement as loose debris and dead leaves fell, barked uncontrollably. The creature pulled hard on its leash, and standing tall on its hind legs it faced the wood bravely and prepared to meet the unknown.

For one terrible moment Dora believed the apparition of horror had somehow rounded on her, cutting off her retreat, and was even now within striking distance and about to pounce. This moment of truth was confirmed in her mind by the incessant barking of the Sealyham. She launched herself dementedly towards the ever-welcoming front door, an agony of time passed whilst identifying the correct key, during which uncharacteristically she cursed and fumbled at the keyhole. The indolent and indecisive nature of the lock further dismayed her, until finally it gave way, emitting a reassuring metallic clunk. She sighed with relief as the five-lever mortise responded, releasing the door, which now swung open wide as a welcoming saviour. Never had her door appeared so friendly, so attractive and so vitally important to her. Once across the threshold and into her sanctuary she released the lead to her companion, then forcefully pushed the heavy door, slamming it shut behind her. Quickly sliding the chain across the hasp she turned away from the outside world and staggered back against the door, exhausted. Dora gave into her overwhelming emotions, sobbing uncontrollably. Her legs no longer supported her tired aching frame, which now inevitably gave way, and slowly but surely she slid down the back of the door. With legs parting ungracefully on the now sliding hall runner, her bottom finally came to rest, sharply and painfully, on the cold, polished quarry tiles.

In the stillness and silence of her hallway, during which she had no account of time – Dora lay propped unceremoniously behind the portico to her home; her face carrying a stunned, glazed expression – whilst her dog 'Pip', lying exhausted across the floor in front of her, whimpered quietly. The jarring, insistent trill of her telephone, urgently seeking attention, snapped her out of her trance-like state. It was a boxer's awakening, as if cold water had been poured onto her face, she immediately sat bolt upright. By the time she had gathered her wits together and made several futile attempts to stand, silence had again returned to the house. The wretched telephone – a term used often by her – had ceased its incessant trill, but the rude awakening had done its work, Dora's mind was now engaged and racing in turmoil. The ensuing silence held a reasoning logic that in turn spurred her into action, reminding her of the many things that needed to be done. Muttering blame and disbelief on herself as she owned to her responsibilities she started to think, what to do.

'Whatever am I thinking of ... that poor creature out there. What was that hideous man doing to her?' Dora stumbled awkwardly along the hallway – her legs still less supportive than she would have wished – until finally pushing the door open that led into the parlour, she clumsily lunged into the room. Crossing it in an ungainly manner she sought the refuge and comfort of her easy chair. The lady of the house promptly fell into the fireside seat, alongside which the telephone sat on a nest of tables. It was one of the modern innovations that she hated, the new push-button gadgetry. The old dials had always seemed so much more expressive, containing an element of romanticism; but nonetheless with the digit nine prodded three times she was relieved at the immediacy of its response. In turn Dora regained some of her self-confidence, and listening to the choices it solicited, she moved into a more positive mode by organising the voice at the other end.

"Hello ... yes of course it's an emergency. Could you please connect me with the police station... and hurry, it is very urgent. Thank you!"

The calming voice of Hereford law came reassuringly through the wires to her, in the form of a more acceptable, experienced man.

"Yes, madam, and how may we help?"

The policeman, aware of her agitation as she gabbled without pause, coughed gently once or twice; interrupting her animated flow and succeeding in establishing control, he advanced carefully probing further for more information.

"Calmly now! Try to tell me what the problem is, from the beginning if you can. First of all, tell me who you are and where you are speaking from?"

Dora was more than a little irritated by this, what seemed to her, patronising response. The cosiness of which and its friendly brogue for some reason – which she could not comprehend – annoyed her considerably.

"Officer, I need help ... NOW!"

Dora struggled with the passing of time and the need for action.

"Please do hurry."

Despite the officer's obvious patience she was not responding to the simple questions of time, place and identity; her mind flashed the image before her and for a moment she quaked, faltering in confidence.

"I'm fri – frightened – I have just seen, I think a woman – or – maybe young girl, being attacked at the roadside. Err! I saw a man kneeling over Ughh!"

She grimaced at the vivid imagery in her mind.

"It was horrible – what looked like a body!"

Pausing to listen whilst catching her breath, she heard the change in attitude as the sympathetic, but now urgent, questions followed through, one after another. She answered them as quickly and best she could.

"It's about a hundred yards, – yes, yes, the town side of Keepers Cottage. My house, – yes it's where I'm ringing from – yes! Yes!"

Her exasperation showed and her voice rose angrily as she asserted herself.

"It's Dora Bartlett here. Please! Please, do hurry."

The policeman's voice continued unruffled as he addressed her, but now it registered in her mind that it was more formal and concise; his matter of fact manner suggested an understanding that this was not a cat-up-a-tree call. Probing, not unkindly but methodically, for the basic facts, the policeman gleaned all the information he could for the actions to come. Finally, Dora found herself floating in a haze of distanced reality, her aching limbs no longer appeared to be attached to her body. The voice seemed to be acquiescent of the situation as she heard the drifting words.

"I'll be sending a car immediately to you madam – stay in the house and make sure your door is kept locked!"

The meaning and good intention of them was not lost on her but she was no longer able to respond. Remaining in her chair numb and silent for some moments after the officer had finished Dora had not registered the disconnection. She spoke again in a quiet manner; the words however remained within her four walls, this time more to comfort herself.

"Yes – yes – thank you, officer."

Dora, slowly and absentmindedly replaced the handset. Her fingers lingered for a while, touching the white plastic, almost patting it, as if willing the link to be retained between her and the reassuring voice of the police officer. Finally, and reluctantly she let go and sank back into her chair, giving herself up to its comfort and reassuring form. After all the immense effort and the powerful surges of adrenaline, which were awash in her body, she felt jaded as the exhaustion finally caught up with her. Hunched, white-faced and dejected, she gave way to emotion again, sobbing quietly whilst waiting for help to arrive. Somewhere outside the safety of her firmly locked door, in the inky blackness of a country night, lay something unknown and beyond comprehension, which again filled her with deep revulsion.

Chapter three

How others see us

The girl's eyes gazed vacantly skywards, a neat almond
shape accentuated by eyeliner in a deep shade of ginger
brown. She was young, possibly only in her teens, and now
life was extinguished. Her shock of auburn hair – in life her
pride – lay across her face in dank, dishevelled ringlets. The
girl's full parted lips were painted with a hastily applied
mix of cheap, orange-red gaudy lipstick; the livid colour
shone out, accentuating both their fullness and sexuality.
She wore a thickly-patterned reddish folk-weave dress,
plunging at the neckline where the lace edging fully
complemented her partially exposed young rounded
breasts. There was also lace at the cuff and hemline; the
whole impression was one of doll-like creation or turn of
the century burlesque. Her legs, bare, were partially
covered with a dress that had ridden up her thighs, exposing
the ivory skin of well-formed limbs and smooth calves. It
left the eye to contemplate on the abrupt, black leather
ankle boots laced to the top, reflecting a strangely evocative
bygone age. Her youthful rounded cheeks and full mouth,
which had taunted so very recently – now inanimate –
remained frozen in its mask of death. A sad inevitability

hung in the soulless glazed pupils of her eyes; mascara had run at the corners as if she had known her lot at the very moment her time had come. The bright orange-redness of her lips, 'beacons of promise' to her contacts through the long nights of work, was smudged and now appeared leeringly ugly at the corners. Lace frills at the neckline of her garment that framed so much of her soft young flesh – now cold to the evening air – also drew the eye purposefully to the deep, ugly weal marks encircling her neck. The indentations marked her last breath indelibly for others to see.

A large, heavily-built, ill-kempt male knelt between her splayed legs, he pushed forwards and backwards, his rough unwashed trousers chafing against the tender flesh of her inner thighs. The girl's dress was rucked up to the waist, her underwear was missing, revealing her soft-downed bare pubis; he seemed obliviously unaware of this fact. His eyes softened by the moisture of emotion studied the girl's face – as he continued moving rhythmically, whilst stroking her cheek with the back of his blackened unwashed hand. The hand that crossed her face time and time again as if willing her to awaken was huge in comparison to her prostrate, doll-like form, which lay so unnaturally still. He created a bizarre image; he was wearing an inordinately large blue serge overcoat – resonant of the Royal Air Force, which he had pulled tight at the waist with a length of rope. His boots were also tied with odd pieces of string and as he knelt his worn soles showed the card inserts he had placed inside against the weather; breakfast cereals curiously displayed.

Earlier, the wild eyes of the bent figure had watched and viewed angrily as the interfering old woman who, accompanied by her dog, had stood across the road

28

opposite, in his mind making judgements on him. He had purposely glowered at the busybody in order to frighten her away, quite enjoying the effect he had produced and her responding rapid flight. Watching her as she staggered to her home – knowing full well where she lived, he clucked to himself wryly at her stupidity; then dismissing her intrusion disdainfully he had turned his attention back to the tarnished beauty before him. Again his eyes watered with emotion as he knelt viewing the twisted young thing beneath him and, remaining concerned by the girl's blank expression, he looked closely for movement, disappointingly for him there was none. As he listened intently, the man busied himself rubbing her bruised cold neck in an attempt, he believed, to wipe the poor bruised flesh clean. Deeply moved by the vision he pulled away and sat back on his haunches, confused, gnawing emotionally at his knuckle whilst considering the lifeless image before him. Immersed and overwhelmed with melancholy he felt a deep pang of regret at the passing of a young life and in this state of morbid introspection he failed to see the changing situation around him.

He was totally unaware of the vehicle that crept slowly forward at the roadside behind him. It was only with the loud slam of car doors and heavy footfall that he broke his concentration, causing him to look round irritably for the source of the disturbance; he focussed on two black silhouettes approaching at a pace. At first frowning with disdain, the old man's attitude quickly hardened to one of angry glowering at this intrusion, as he narrowed his eyes towards the interlopers, both of whom he now recognised. They closed in on him rapidly through the pulsing blue storm of emergency lights, which had suddenly filled the air; aggression seeped through their harsh, angry voices. A chorus of anger was directed in unison towards him, rising to a crescendo as they rushed towards his kneeling form. One of the approaching figures – irate and offended by what he believed he was witnessing – shouted abuse at the kneeling figure; it was closely echoed by his colleague as they both snarled at the man who knelt in a compromising position over the prostrate female form. Both the officers, now with raised voices, threatened him as they physically manhandled the roadster in their rage.

"You dirty bugger!"

"Get away from her you bastard! – She's a young girl!"

The first uniformed figure to reach him began roughly gripping the old man's shoulders in an attempt to interrupt whatever it was he was doing and pull him away. He stopped abruptly and, with a look of disbelief, his angry voice faded as he pulled back, realising he recognised the kneeling figure. The man in uniform, uncertain of what he was witnessing, called out questioningly.

"My God, it's Philip? What the blasted hell do you think you are doing, man?"

The officer, mystified by the image before him of the kneeling figure, together with the presence of what appeared to be a corpse, found the illusion bizarre and incomprehensible but more obviously somehow proven.

"Well! What have you got to say for yourself?"

Shaking himself out of a moment of doubt, the officer, with difficulty, reverted to a well-polished and time-honoured routine by responding strictly to the book. Addressing the tramp through a now tight-clenched jaw, and dismissing past humours and confrontations, the officer asserted his position as upholder of the law and protector of life. Still suffering an overwhelming feeling of disbelief and confusion at the situation he found himself in, the officer breathed in deeply and stated quietly and succinctly without any enthusiasm,

"You're in for it this time, my boy!"

His colleague's anger had no such control; it spilt out into the black night in a loud fury as his outburst rose in disgust.

"Bastard! Leave her be. – Get away from her! – Stand up! Come on, get up will you!"

All of which was accompanied by a severe slap aimed at the old man's face, followed by a moment of general manhandling. The old man was finally and roughly pulled from the body to stand on the grass in the glare of the headlights.

The condemnatory tone of the officer's voice said it all, as the mumbled caution came and went, the words of which meant little or nothing to the confused roadster. Although the angry words and their tone puzzled him, he was confused, disorientated and blatantly unaware of what was happening to him. Suddenly, and unexpectedly, several blows rained down to the backs of his legs as though he were being kicked. He was aware of hands forcibly gripping him and his arms being twisted painfully behind his back. Following this he felt the fine plastic bite into his skin, causing him to curse as the ligature now forced his two hands together. Both wrists were bound tightly behind his back with a plastic strip encircling them; it was pulled very taut and with some relish that made no allowance for comfort. Philip, bound and manhandled with an arm supporting him each side, no longer a free agent, found his feet dangling as he attempted and fought to stand upright.

The dark uniformed figures, angrily resisting his protestations, continued unceremoniously and without feeling, as they pulled him along in conspired violence, slowly dragging the dishevelled figure towards their vehicle. Once there, he was bundled with obvious disgust through the open rear door and onto the back seat, to be closely followed by an accompanying officer, who positioned himself begrudgingly alongside the travel-worn, unwashed vagrant. The driver busied himself securing the doors whilst looking into the mirror at the prisoner; there was a look of grim satisfaction on his face, verging on a sneer. As they drove the now tired and bewildered roadster away from the scene – a prisoner as he was – his haggard careworn eyes briefly saw the black silhouetted outline of the girl on the ground. Philip, putting his face against the glass – flushed with emotion and his eyes watering – mouthed silent words of distress, which ran in spittle down the glass. Two other beacons of strobed blue light now pulsed the air, echoing in tandem the life-blood that had so recently ebbed away. Cars and officers moved in to seal off the scene from the world's disapproving eyes. Within the drawn up cordon a blue glow caressed the girl's legs that were bent awkwardly backwards, one drawn up tightly to her body with a foot lodged under her buttocks. The position of it raised her back in an arch, presenting her fecundity for passing eyes to see, this time without charge. Her loss of dignity seemed immaterial to the uniformed figures as they single-mindedly set about the initial actions of securing the scene for further enquiry.

Chapter four

A mutual dispute

In a cottage surrounded by tall firs, under which pine needles resting in damp undergrowth played host to white-lanterned and probing Solomon's seal, two figures intent on similar missions were set on a collision course. Doors to the lounge on opposing walls opened simultaneously, choreographed to-a-tee as a figure appeared within each opening. So absorbed were they in their own preoccupations and foolishly assuming that the other would be on hand to receive their proposed wisdom, they commenced speaking simultaneously. It was some moments after they had unwittingly gabbled on, before it dawned on them that their partner was not seated but in fact standing opposite, and speaking at the same time.

"I have just been to town visiting the travel agency …!"

"I have just been to town and found an interesting item in the …!"

The voices stopped abruptly with the realisation of the other's position, both, somewhat nervously, with embarrassment laughed out loud. They found themselves looking around the room to the unoccupied seats where their partner would usually be sitting. Clearly there had been an expectation upon entering the room to find a listening ear; one that would be responsive to the overwhelming enthusiasm about to issue forth.

Beth, now smiling across at him, was excitedly waving papers in his direction. Seeing her in the doorway he stood hesitant, with his mouth open in mid-sentence. Beth waved him to enter and took the upper hand, brokering her thoughts first as they both flopped down into their own easy chair to sit opposite one another as usual.

"As I was trying to say, darling, I called in at the travel agents in town!"

Her face carried a beaming smile, as if she were a cat who had licked the cream. Beth waited patiently for a moment or two whilst he made himself comfortable, expecting a favourable response, but to her surprise there was none forthcoming; puzzled, she quickly followed it up.

"I … I know we haven't discussed plans for future holidays as yet but with the weather and – you know well enough, the ugly memories of such bad happenings. I thought it was the right thing to do, certainly it's the right time!"

She looked away for a moment, somewhat embarrassed and confused by what she had initially considered was a good idea but in fact was proving difficult to relate. More to the point she sensed that it was perhaps not the right moment. Beth showed reticence, being almost apologetic when she continued.

"We both need to lift our spirits a bit and I thought a break in the south!"

She hesitated nervously then continued,

"Sunshine, peace and all that." She looked him in the eye, sighing with resolute conviction. "What a good tonic that would be!"

On her face a smile, which revealed her whimsical thoughts of places afar and happy memories in pine-clad hills of the south. Unexpectedly he responded in an offhand manner.

"Do... do you mean the deep south, south seas... exotic, grass skirts and things?"

She frowned at his childish reference to girls, grass skirts and the suggestive tone of his voice. Her mood changed to one of apprehension, it was not going according to plan and so she remonstrated quickly at his remarks.

"No! No, somewhere safe, where we can relax and **not get into trouble!**"

She looked hard at him as she emphasised the final few words. It was as if he needed to be protected from himself and his incessant skirmishes with danger. There was a more formal tone to her voice now and she struggled hard to be optimistic.

"I thought it was time to revisit the village of Bize once more and that delightful garden. I've..."

Before she could finish outlining her plans, he interrupted her.

"Surely somewhere in the Caribbean or further maybe... I think that would be a good idea. You were saying?"

He was clearly intent on irritating her by his continued issuing of such facetious comments, all of which she felt to be most unhelpful. Having taken the wind from her sails, Beth, feeling very uncomfortable, fell silent. She did not care to respond immediately, feeling saddened if not vexed by his sudden decision to travel to destinations unknown and untried; she gazed forlornly down at the floor. Matthew, who contrary to her feelings was now quite buoyant, jumped in to liven up the proceedings; his manner unseen by her as he spoke carried a mocking smile.

"Oh, I was just trying to say earlier that I had been to the library and have managed to find a very interesting new publication."

Beth, feeling downhearted and despondent, barely acknowledged what he said and certainly failed to comprehend; she remained quietly aloof, barely commenting.

"Oh ... I see."

Beth had no enthusiasm for what he was trying to say, rejecting his buoyancy, preferring to remain hurt and preoccupied by his indifference.

Matthew continued, despite her offhand response.

"Yes, it's a book, one I haven't seen before, on history, castles and the cruelty of the past to its peoples, all within settings of some amazing scenery. I thought, in fact I was hoping, you would be interested enough!"

He studied her face as if gauging the right moment in a devilish way.

"Well go on then, get on with it!" Beth snapped with some angst.

"Well, you see there were these people who were known by their faith as 'Cathars'. It seems there was a strong movement of believers at that time, and it spread rapidly, apparently contrary to the Catholic Church's doctrine."

Beth looked at him with disbelief but he continued unabated.

"As a consequence of this 'New Religion' the Pope condemned its followers as heretics. According to this book, and I couldn't put it down, the new beliefs gained so much ground that the Pope panicked. He joined forces with the King of France – who ruled a smaller country than the one we now know – to rid the church and France of the threat. The King, wanting to gain land and power, and the Pope, seeing his opportunity to put paid to the new religion, sanctioned any acts of violence that occurred in the cause to be justified and thereby absolved the perpetrators of their sins."

Beth finally lost her patience, with him, his book, his inability to understand her needs and his apparent new interest, all of which to her were totally obscure and, in the circumstances of her projected holiday plans, quite obtuse. Angry and with growing impatience she demanded with a loud voice for an explanation.

"What the hell are you talking about, Matthew, history and all that nonsense… I just want a holiday!"

As Beth, whose eyes were now watering at his insensitivity, remained just staring at him, the look of incredulity on her face slowly changed, very slowly fading as a glimmer of memory stirred within her mind. Something registered, the words and the names he had mentioned: bells rang. Rounding on him, anxiously wanting answers, Beth raised her voice, not in anger this time but enthusiastically, aroused by what she thought she might have heard, she challenged him,

"Wait a minute, did you say 'Cathars'?"

Beth looked at Matthew, his face carrying a stupid smile of complicity as gradually a recollection dawned on her, she somehow connected with the words.

"I know that! – I feel I've heard that name before, but where? – France? – Is it? Yes, it is France! In the south, Bize Minervois! – Why you!"

She pouted her lips and, red-faced at his underhand attempt at humour, gesticulated towards him by shaking her fist, whilst at the same time picking up the heaviest of the cushions which she propelled in his direction. Matthew, whose face now creased with laughter at her reaction, registered his amusement at her expense but was well aware of the repercussions of mood change. So already dodging out of the line of fire, he coughed and cleared his throat to respond to her angst in a more serious vein.

"Yes I think it's true we're both down – in the doldrums in fact – it's not surprising considering the circumstances and what happened. But it was you who have taken the initiative and made a firm booking?"

At this point he looked in her direction seeking confirmation; she nodded.

"For which I'm very grateful. It would seem that we have divine inspiration between us, or is it just coincidental? I was led off in a similar direction by a new publication in the library; yes, Beth, a very good choice – when are we off?"

She didn't answer immediately; she was rattled by what she considered as his stupidity and inane attempt at humour. To her mind the plans that she had made were necessary for both their welfares and he had very nearly spoilt the moment. Whilst brooding on his annoying habit of abrasive one-sided humour, she bit the nail on the end of her forefinger, trying to snap out of her displeasure. There was no doubting that he also wanted to go to their favourite haunt, but why the hell couldn't he just be open and honest for once and say so. To her it was important, especially when the last months had been so brutal and depressing. Matthew had an irritating habit of always assuming his humour was universal and acceptable by all, whereas in reality it annoyed her intensely. He, sensing her continued unease, though tempted to interject, remained silent as Beth quietly catalogued the past.

"We had such a bad time last year and when – well you know – poor Ben died and you were involved in more than your fair share of danger."

She continued talking, staring at the wall as she did so as if not to be distracted, there was pathos in her voice as she continued without pause. Her emotions showed raw as she rounded on him vehemently, his antics had brought some of the past trauma too close to the surface and she reminded him of the detail.

"You dived into something far deeper and more emotional than you could ever have imagined. You went in up to your neck – and it very nearly took you with it."

She sighed heavily and continued, "A left-over, you couldn't resist. Pride or what! I don't know. But you just – would not – let go."

Her face was flushed and there were signs of watering in her eyes as she bit her lip, realising she had said perhaps far too much in the circumstances and as a consequence fell silent.

Matthew, shifting uneasily in his seat, knowing that he had forced her into this situation with his flippancy, something he had done many times before and regretted, knew he would find it difficult to extricate himself this time and calm her down. But with a sigh he made the attempt,

"I know Beth, it was very bad. And I freely admit that I went in too deep, but somehow I couldn't avoid it. The death of Ben was bad enough. – No that's pitiful, – it was very bad. But somehow the worst thing of all was the feeling of being shut out from work, after all those years; CID was finally out of bounds to me. Retirement always means letting go, I know very well and I was very willing to accede to the idea of leisure with its pleasures and being with you. But to be taunted by ex-colleagues, maybe that's the wrong phrase – arch-enemies might be more appropriate – was beyond the pale. It wasn't a tuppenny burglary or any old handbag snatch. No, it was the death of innocents, young children and after a whole year of futility, I retired, having failed to bring anyone to book! They locked me out, and circumstances forced me to be involved in an obscure and, I freely admit, dangerous way. Of course I found myself drowning, quite literally, and I'm truly sorry Beth, it was a bad year for both of us. We must of course – and I'm determined to make it so – ensure that the coming year is memorable and most importantly enjoyable. I did mean what I said though, France is just the ticket... a splendid idea."

Now standing quietly behind her he bent over, she didn't move or object whilst he kissed her tenderly on the nape of her neck, whispering,

"Thanks for taking the first step!"

Unseen by him she had coloured up at his sentimentality. Beth had always admired him for his loyalty; a man of strong ideals, whom she had always known would find it impossible to stand aside and watch conflict and danger overtake others. Remaining silent a little longer, allowing time for tenderness to be absorbed,

Beth responded confidently to his close-felt gratitude, judging it now to be the right moment to outline her plans.

"Right, I'll make the other arrangements if you like, the flights are booked, so it's just the car to sort out!"

Matthew, now quite excited by the idea, threw a question her way.

"Okay, what about accommodation?"

Beth, who was on her feet now, determined to look efficient, as though there were other matters to attend to, glanced casually around the room as she was leaving, saying,

"That's the best bit! The old folks want to come back to stay in England during the heat wave and have invited us to look after their garden!"

She bobbed back into the room before he could answer, with a beaming smile on her face, whispering, "For free!"

Chapter five

The Past is disturbed

Nothing stirred on the long hot day, nothing save an intoxication of oils from wild herbs. Only the essence of marjoram and rosemary, drifting down from the hillside on a wistful breeze, provided the melange of heady, syrupy calm, captivating all during the last issuing days of autumn. It was a day which slept blissfully on – as summer, turned late autumn issued golden. The air seemed strangely permanent; a shimmering haze hovered above richly laden fields, where the vines of promise sported the harvest of ripening fruit to come. All the creatures of the parish had succumbed to the soporific persuasion of heat and wellbeing, as they closed eyelids and surrendered unabashed to sleep. Even the flies buzzed intermittently in a quiet, lackadaisical drone; their casual short flights appearing pointless as they flitted along the grey stone walls that skirted around the tightly packed cottages.

The buildings themselves – tucked away behind the curtilage of limestone walling – coyly hugged their inner courtyards, reluctant to divulge any detail. Any outer walls had small windows set within deep recesses; all retained an expressionless facade that left darkened interiors to look blankly on. Above the village the scent of summer passed over and petered out beyond, carrying with it the essence of ozone toward the orange hills, a message carried from the calm lap of a beckoning autumn sea. Holidaymakers had thinned from their masses, leaving local and persistent sun worshippers to continue the tradition of communal oiling, by the turquoise Mediterranean waters. The vast swathes of bare flesh were now, for the most part, much further north; wrapped and cosseted in preparation against seasonal change.

The village of Le Chateau St. Jean, or more correctly *'bastide'*, amounted to a small outcrop of dwellings, where the merest trace only remained of the once turreted porticoes of entrance. For centuries the strength of stone had reassured the persecuted incumbents of sanctuary. The ancient site held fast to the hilltop, clinging to the top of a worn promontory – one of many such retreats, where French tradition held steady and the community slumbered through to eventide. The whole area of fortified, hilltop villages, scattered and isolated, yet purposefully positioned, faced outwards in strength from the founding fathers of mountain peaks, towards the call of the sea.

The lapping waters of blue lay only thirty kilometres to the south, where the land fell dramatically to the shoreline – a fact not appreciated by those constrained by gravity, indeed only to be recognised by the proud wheeling birds of the mountain skies. To mere earthbound mortals, the journey could take some two hours or more of concentrated hill driving. Journeys which epitomised frustration as the beckoning azure waters appeared tantalisingly closer at every turn and yet somehow disappeared frustratingly time after time from the expected view. Until, quite unannounced and dramatically, the coast and its 'Etang, – home to the flamingos' – would suddenly be within easy reach.

The village was an entity all of its own; across the open space at its centre – claimed by summer visitors, eager to stand and look beyond the hills to the majesty of the mountains – was an outcrop of ochre rock and behind it rested one small particular dwelling. Although part of, and in essence attached to, the village – as all were, sitting astride the hilltop – it was at the extreme edge of a group of cottages. The modest building somehow managed to retain an air of indifference, appearing standoffish and quite alone. Reticent within a small copse of firs, the ancient stone of this insignificant and perhaps ostracised dwelling was broken by just one small window. It could be construed that it looked towards the heart of the community in a backward glance, keeping a weather eye on all approaches, whilst on the opposite face there resided yet another window with its adjacent door facing both across the deep draft of the valley floor and the hills beyond. It was as if it reflected the tiny building's aloof and secretive nature – distancing itself from the village and its peoples. The building's aspect of passage was in the opposite direction; it had a commanding vista over the vineyards below, and breathtakingly vivid views beyond to the sharp cut on the horizon of the Pyrenees.

In the silence of the afternoon no creature moved, the autumnal sun warmed the walls and a thick hot air wafted amongst the buildings. The low trajectory of light cast long fingers of shadow across walls and roofs, clutching at the inhabitants within. It was a scene set for action that, as yet, awaited an audience, players and for the story to unfold.

Incongruously, in the calm of such a day, a thin metallic chinking sound could be heard in the wings – if there had been anyone to listen to it that is. It drifted along in the wafting warmth, across the car park by the church, skirting the new public toilets and out beyond to the perimeter wall, where the sound flushed into the breeze down to the vineyards far below. On closer inspection one could have pinpointed clearly from where it emanated and for the moment that was the fear that influenced its creator. Behind the entrance door of this self-same isolated cottage, in the hush of the sleepy afternoon, the sound ceased momentarily, leaving an exaggerated silence and a stone chisel and mallet – perpetrators of the intrusion – hovering inactive and expectant in the air. The implements marked a nervous displacement whilst in the grip of tensed trembling hands. Holding them tightly, absurdly locked in mid-flight, was a slightly-built man who, sweating profusely and at the same time straining with every nerve, listened closely for a response to his labours. Wedged awkwardly, he was crouching on his haunches behind the door that guarded the narrow entrance hall within the cottage.

Henri Douchez was his name – a family name not shared with any living villager. He was not a man of great physical presence and crouching in the dim confines of the hallway his bare flesh, dust coloured and grimed, gave his stance an animal-like cunning in the half-light. Normally he would have been found cajoling tourists within the premises of his shop – the only commercial establishment located within the confines of the village – a *curio purveyor'* of the mock historical together with strong reference to the occult.

He was slight of build and extremely unused to the type of physical exertion in which he was purposefully employed at that moment. Everything about him reflected an insidious, secretive nature; one that an observer might reflect upon as a person concerned in matters underhand. He was of diminutive stature; his hair – a mousy colour – was cut awkwardly short, sitting spikily uneven and lacking direction or discipline on the dome of his head. A moustache that in reality was his unshaven top lip, the unkempt growth that resided there achieved little in prominence. All this completed a persona, with its dispiriting features combining to give the impression of disadvantage. He was indeed an unfortunate man, whose habits and personality elicited disquiet from those around him. His ability to produce continuously wet lips, almost to a dribbling efficiency, caused most to shun him. Though it would be unfair to call him ugly, for the yardstick by which such matters can be determined is elusive, he in fact held himself in high regard. But nonetheless the description would in this case be most appropriate, for it was a significant feature in keeping him separate from the villagers – who in general, regarded him with disdain.

On this particular day, his personal isolation from the village was a distinct advantage, for it allowed him to engage in his own pursuits without unseemly interruptions from curious neighbours; something he indeed relished. Henri Douchez had intended from the outset to be secure by the nature of things, in order to counteract any incident that might become - an embarrassment. He had in fact reasoned correctly that other members of his small community – creatures of habit – would be for the most part at rest, enabling him to continue his exertions in peace; without the fear of prying eyes or wagging tongues. Despite this, the fear of discovery remained with him and conspicuously near the surface as he toiled with convoluted feelings of guilt. His anxious state showed, it was marked by the moisture which flowed freely on his forehead; not as a result of the heat of the day – for the cottage remained tolerably cool – but as a consequence of his nervous apprehension, which accompanied his clandestine occupation.

Beads of perspiration ran down his cheeks and side-whiskers and his normally moist mouth now hung open as he struggled for breath in the alleyway of deceit. His shirt, an early discarded item, was thrown untidily over the back of a chair, the only furniture within the building. His bare chest – which appeared strangely white – was accentuated by brightly coloured red braces that ran across it. Running livid red across his shoulders – that were now stained with his sweat – the braces clung fast to an ill-cut pair of dusty trousers. In truth he felt both immense fear and exhilaration; indeed, the latter was overwhelming, providing a compulsion to continue to the bitter end. Henri was consumed with a personal drive to prove himself, to show his theories were well-founded. To succeed in his mission was one thing, but his shrewd reasoning made him aware of immensely rewarding possibilities.

Secrecy was of the utmost importance; his urgent need to slip away – at a moment's notice which he judged to be safe – from the comforting position behind the counter of his shop, had taken a considerable effort of will. He was gambling with his own wellbeing; there were, as he knew, others who, if they had known of his endeavours, would have taken a dim view. More to the point, a situation could well occur which might jeopardise his welfare, or worse, his life. But it was a task for which he had been frustrated from commissioning for several weeks. His impatience had become manifold, increased by the absurdities of the villagers, who for some inconceivable reason had gathered openly for days.

At first he was curious, there were those whom he knew to be openly hostile to one another, who incredulously he had seen standing in expectant groups around the green, seemingly on these occasions to display a deep fraternal sense of understanding. Muttering to himself in frustration at these strange overt gatherings, he twitched the blinds on the office window at the rear of his shop, straining to gather the purpose. *'What are they up to?'* he puzzled. Showing an increased irritation at the unknown he slowly reasoned what it was that preoccupied such a gathering and realised the import of the occasion. Recalling the little known historical detail of the village which it celebrated so rarely – it came to him – *'My God, can it be? – Why, yes it's the hundred!'* He grunted to himself and considered what he should do in the circumstances; despite being removed from the day-to-day activities by his attitude he was still classed as being one of the villagers. Indeed, his family's lineage was as old as any in the village and soaked, as he was, in the myths and mysteries of the place, especially in his present preoccupation; it made his labours even more precarious. His cultural heritage, as unwelcome as it may have been at that moment, drew his mind into thinking through the strange activities. It was a fact that the festival or 'Hundred' so called, was never within living memory, for everyone who played a part, only lived to see it once and some never.

Henri Douchez had dared not approach the cottage during this unusual period; there were gatherings of people in most parts of the open ground between the shop and cottage and because it was taking place out of sight of his shop it was not possible to observe at a distance: he was at a disadvantage. He knew of course the reasons why, but the occasion had slipped his mind whilst toiling with his own obsession. The fact that the 'Hundred' was celebrated only once in every century to remember the perfect ones who died so long ago was one thing; but how they would celebrate or what they planned to do was a complete mystery to him. Reluctantly over the days of feverish activity he had to be content only with noting the comings and goings, whilst waiting for the right moment. In fact, he felt the need to be doubly sure, so he waited until the fanciful meetings had reached their zenith and concluded, the villagers had returned to work and all activities had subsided. Nearly a week had passed before his frustrations were relieved, when this particular corner of the village had ceased being the focal point of great interest. The gatherings to his mind – without rhyme or reason, had displayed an unusual enthusiasm amongst the local inhabitants, whom he considered to be a disparate collection of ignorant simpletons. He was surprised when on several occasions he had observed the appearance of faces in the crowd who were unknown to him, noting the fervour at such moments had spilled over to almost fever pitch. During these homilies directed by strangers, the villagers had displayed marked respect imbued with open enthusiasm, which left Henri feeling distinctly uneasy.

He had always considered the people of the village to be somewhat strange, his parents, and theirs before, being long-term residents of the village had always assumed an aloof – and as the villagers would mutter – superior stance. Distancing themselves from the others whenever possible, the family had always shown their contempt for the local community; the villagers were, in their belief, common rustics. His parents had always emphasised that the local peasants were illiterate and ignorant; only his family had ancestry that could be traced back to the 13th century. Although he should have known what was about to happen he had not attended a meeting at the hall, for which he knew he would have to pay forfeit. After the week had passed, the meetings ceased and the village returned more or less to its former sleepy self. The whole occasion had however unnerved him, leaving him pensive, harbouring a curious notion that perhaps it would have been useful to assimilate with the others a little more. The need to gain knowledge of what was happening around him was paramount for his own survival.

It was he alone from the village that had attended higher education, a matter considered by him not to be a privilege, but his birthright. His education was however to some degree the cause of his present anxious state, whatever its outcome might be. His acquisition of certain ancient documents, together with his ability to understand their content, had led him to be in his present uncompromising position, struggling in the narrow passageway. His knowledge, when others of the village who were not aware were gainfully employed in the mores of passion or sleeping peacefully, held him in a permanent restless state of anxiety. It was he who had possession of the oldest building in the village. Some said there had been continuous habitation there since the 'Perfect ones', the 'Cathars' of the 13th century and only he it seemed, having studied the church papers, realised the implication of this. His education and understanding of the history and of his locale led him to visit Paris, consult the archives and understand the references to the Visigoths and Knights Templar. The result of this painstaking research – found scrawled onto old soured parchments in vague Latin, and the Occitan language – had suggested that out of all villages and houses in the area, his might indeed have borne witness and hold the key to those inglorious days. More importantly, he felt the distinct possibility that artefacts worthy of such Herculean labours might well still be hidden in the depths of such a dwelling.

He listened intently, both eyes darting back and forth as he sensed – snake-like – that quietness prevailed. His one eye remained partially hidden under a sagging lid – a hereditary family characteristic. It was unfortunate for him, giving him a look of cunning as he strained for any responding sound that his tapping may have evoked. It was a narrow, confined cell of exclusion, the walls were close and the earth piled around him lessened the free space that might harbour dangers. Satisfied with his perfunctory check that all appeared well, he lowered himself down again – needlessly smoothing out his trousers – as he crouched onto a large slab behind the entrance door. Then gingerly raising his tool – his apprehension showing through despite his determination of completing his quest, he struck the first nervous blow with his chisel onto the stone and the tool bounced off ineffectively. Then as if regretting every strike that emanated from his wrist, from the first nervous indecisive stroke and onwards, he strained his senses as he attacked with the chisel, each time with more ferocity. Again and again the blade bit; now gaining strength of will with every stroke, he became engrossed in his mission. Despite his acute sensitivity at being discovered, the tapping of his mallet continued, gaining in confidence as it drove on and downwards into the groove between the slabs as if possessed, clearing dust and debris as it went.

Within the building, the metallic ring resonated on every wall of the small structure, echoing his fear of disclosure. Beads of sweat poured profusely now from his forehead, exertion and fear combined to endorse his desire to be elsewhere and yet greed urged him on. Avarice controlled his mind, as the mallet received an extra strong angry blow from a decisive swing, it was brought to bear as if bringing the matter to a speedy conclusion. Hitting the chisel square on, the force gained extra purchase and finally drove deeper to gain purchase and movement. The change in resistance echoed through the tool as he felt it give, causing the cold metal spike to part from his grip and fall free from his aching hands down onto the slabs. Shaken by the loud clattering ring – his nerves jangling beyond belief – Henri anxiously plunged his hand to smother the tool and stay the noise. In the pause he considered the spike that now lay silent amongst the dust on the slab and what had been achieved. Despite his acute anticipation and coupled with the effect of his recent labours he did nothing for some moments; his reward for an experience of fearful anticipation lay before him. He allowed himself the sweetness of triumph and expressed his satisfaction, licking his lips, his face creased into a begrudging smile.

Realisation finally struck him, the chisel, a potential betrayer, had after all his great effort entered deep into the crevice. This insertion into the ancient bond had caused the slabs to move, forcing them very, very slightly out of alignment.

Moving the tools carefully aside, and laying them onto the dirt to prevent any repetition of noise, Henri, forgetting all distractions, now gave his full attention to the finale. Studying the slab with due reverence he brushed its surface gently as if it were a magic totem, whilst half expecting a sign or inscription of confirmation to appear. He looked puzzled, confused and disappointed; there was nothing to be seen but the rough-hewn stone. Henri repositioned himself carefully – though not well built he knew it was to be his moment – no help would be forthcoming from any direction, nor would he sanction it. He spat onto his hands to give them purchase, eager to avoid any injury from mishandled rock, and bending over the slab he prepared himself for one last almighty effort. Standing feet astride – balancing precariously against the stone wall – he bent double, wriggling and gripping his fingertips as far round the edge of the slab as was humanly possible. Heaving the side of the ancient stone he grunted and strained and pulled with fingers that cruelly ached until – at first imperceptibly – then with confirmation, very gradually it gave way to the persistent pressure and lifted: he could not now go back.

With bent legs pushing hard against the ground, his arms extended and muscles aching with the effort, he heaved. Little by little the contact of centuries broke as the slab slowly elevated up towards him. Gasping at the effort and feeling the need to rest, he kicked blindly around with his foot, managing to guide the chisel towards the gap, whilst taking the strain as he clutched the edge of the stone. Managing this agonising action, he contrived to cause the implement to partially slide under the stone to act as a wedge, blocking any retreat and thereby locking the slab into position. The effort left him wheezing in the dust-strewn air, so much so he felt he his lungs would burst. For one small French shopkeeper it had been an almighty exertion, the world spun momentarily as he fell back on the fresh dug earth giving way to panting heavily with exhaustion.

He remained lying where he had fallen, continuing to suck choking gulps of hard-won air into his frame and little by little his colour returned. The expression on his face now changed from grey exhaustion gradually to one of happy resolution. Brief as the respite had been he forced himself back into action, moistening his palm with spittle once more. He rubbed his moist palms together, then gritting his teeth he bent down with obstinate fervour to finish the task. The slab, having given way to its tormentor, now moved purposefully upwards and, having raised it to stand on one edge, he walked it very carefully to one side over the loose earth and leant the curiously carved slab against the wall. The energy that had been expended in such a short furious time was enormous, so for the moment – satisfied the slab held steady – he let go of determination and will, and sank heavily to the floor for a much needed rest. Leaning against the wall in the confined space – at the edge of the void revealed by the slab's removal – he drifted with the pain of exhaustion, totally unaware of any results that his immense labours had achieved. Dangling footloose above the hole – his mind blank, but sensing success – he did nothing for a while; he just continued breathing deeply with his eyes partially closed in satisfaction.

The silence now pervading the building cautioned him into opening his eyes to consider his next move. Having regained his second breath, his eyes once again became alert. The man's gaze wandered from the slab – admiring both its size and his ability to move such an object – then back down to the hole from whence it had come. His feet hung in the hole, it was deep, impressively so and impossible to see the bottom of it without some form of illumination. Scrambling about the floor in the debris he fumbled for his torch and pressing the button a smile broke on his face at the responding glow, his tongue played across his lips as he licked them moist, emotional and wary in the anticipation of what he might see. Propelling the torch and playing its beam back and forth slowly across the hole, he realised with immense satisfaction that he was the first human to set sight into this ancient construction for centuries. Whilst assessing its size he strained his eyes for an object that might confirm his now impatient curiosity. Then in the bottom right hand corner he saw it, a conical shaped stone that projected out purposely.

In his excitement he threw himself down across the earth in order to lie flat on the floor over the hole, he was now able to put his head and shoulders into the void. Having found it just possible with one hand to almost reach and touch the stone, he concentrated hard and realised he could see also its surface. His excitement grew as his eyes adjusted to the distance, revealing what appeared to be markings or incised letters. The anticipation of success in his quest caused him to cast care aside; straining his whole body Henri forced his arm to its extremity. Grunting loudly with the effort as his joints creaked, the tips of his fingers inched forward until finally they connected with the stone and its strange markings. Fingers that touched the stone's surface, now stroked it eagerly searching for a pliable edge to grip; he managed to push it about and surprisingly he found it moved quite easily. With one final effort he forced himself to stretch to the extreme, right down into the hole with his arm and fingers fully extended. He found to his relief that it was possible to claw a finger on either side of it. With persistence he found he could grip it, just enough to raise it up and retrieve it from its resting place. Frightened of dropping it through the delicate process of retrieval Henri breathed a sigh of relief as he placed it carefully onto the dirt pile; then sitting, legs akimbo, feeling well pleased with himself, he gently brushed and stroked the stone's surface. There was a reverence in his action born out of realisation that he was possibly the first person to touch this ancient stone for some six hundred years. With the palm of his hand he caressed the stone gently, clearing the dust and dirt of centuries from its face. Finally revealing an inscription carved deeply in its rough-honed surface, Henri moved the stone around excitedly in his hand, hardly daring to look, yet anxious for clarification: confirmation of success. His eyes gazed in wonder at the mottled purple brown of the rock, found nowhere locally.

He wiped his forehead nervously with the back of a grimy hand, anticipation bore heavily on him, and his face portrayed the picture of a man possessed. There was a look of incredulity mixed with cunning. Others had tried of course, looking here, there, anywhere. The rumours had also been rife, newspapers and journals had long discussed the possibilities. It suddenly struck him; everyone would have been trying so hard for so long to find something, anything, in this year of the 'Celebration', and yet, he was the one to make the discovery. 'The Brotherhood' – responsible for the 'Hundred' and any matter relating to their shared history – surely they would be pleased. Although he thought not grateful, he knew they should be grateful; especially as he now knew the celebrations were approaching. Zealous feelings of devotion to the cause would prevent them from congratulating or even thanking him, or more to the point financially rewarding him. Self-sacrifice they gave unstintingly and would expect the same from him, as from any of its brothers. He felt the enormity of the occasion, the cottage had been in his family's possession since the time when the conflict began, so surely it was rightfully his and finding it was an omen. Was it not his right, his family's right also, to dispose of his own possessions as and when he chose. The fact that he had been in contact with the *'English'* – a small matter of a holiday home – seemed insignificant, after all was he not still the caretaker for the *'English'* and entrusted to do the right thing. Dismissing the pangs of conscience, a look of reverence settled on his face as he began mumbling softly, reading the finely incised and, as he knew, ancient words on the stone. Over and over again he repeated to himself in the old dialect, "Cathari!' 'Cathari!' 'Cathari!"

It was a simple word, but he knew it meant much to the people of his village and even wider in the region to whom it was once a rallying cry. The awesomeness of the occasion induced a fear in him to be urgently away from the place. He somehow knew he had struck gold, the stone was only the keeper and beyond it he suspected would be wealth, albeit of a dangerous kind. Placing the curious obelisk with its markings into a canvas bag, he attended to the securing of the floor and removing traces of his exploration. After methodically walking the large slab back to the edge of the hole as best he could, without scoring the floor, Henri carefully resealed the ancient joint. Collecting dust from around the floor he seeded it from his fingers along the line where the slabs met, blowing the residue clear. When he was satisfied the floor had regained its ancient guise, he stood looking and checking that all was well. With great care he made his way cautiously from the building by a roundabout route, back to his own business premises.

A tarot card in the front window of the shop moved perceptibly, despite his careful unlocking of the front door – the only entrance. As he quietly slid through, checking over his shoulder as to whether his passage had been noted, he breathed a sigh of relief and moved on through to the back room, where he relaxed a little. By and by within the safety of his own domain, Henri, now smirking, walked back into the shop. Feeling quite jubilant he smiled inwardly with satisfaction, then falling back into role, he checked and titivated around the displays as though he had been waiting patiently all day in order to satisfy the curiosity of a passing traveller or two. His personal interest in matters occult had fuelled his compulsion to open such a curio business. Had he noticed the card that had come to rest upside down, mocking the others of the pack displayed around the glass, his demeanour might not have been so calm. The bearded man pictured in a cowled cloak held his lantern and scythe steady, but the legend and the picture inverted questioned Henri's purpose and indeed his wellbeing for the future.

Chapter six

Legal procedures

Gloom hung in the December streets, it wrapped around
humanity purposely driven, cloaking their individuality;
snarling traffic of late afternoon lay static and the misted
air was sour with exhaust fumes and people. Freshly ignited
engines spat catalytic waste into the nostrils of passers-by
as they struggled to and fro for an early finish on this, the
last Friday before Christmas. Situated at a busy intersection
– which dissected the main commercial area of town – were
a number of professional practices, lodged above the street-
level shops. They sat unobtrusively over dry cleaners,
stationers and the like. In one, sporting an ultra-modern
fascia above the job centre, a lone male figure hovered
behind the glass of the large oval window; he looked out,
eyeing the world absent-mindedly. He looked down
dispassionately at the huddled groups of pensioners below
as they responded anxiously to the audio frequency
directing the public crossing. The bleeping, blessed by
designers to command the attention and observance
towards the green man's appearance, forced tetchy and
shop-weary citizens to cross the road before its urgent
sound ceased, and green phased red once more.

Partially hidden from exterior view by scripted gold blocked letters, carrying the legend *'W.S. Stone & Son, Family Solicitors'* – running the length of two similarly shaped windows – the man's face remained impassive. It revealed nothing of his thoughts as he peered down at the frustrated bundles of humanity trudging wearily in the darkening streets below. He was a powerfully built male in his thirties, one who would judge a doorway with an acute awareness for headroom and passageway for girth. His head was crowned with an ample shock of tight, frizzy, dark hair. His tanned complexion served to accentuate a pair of cold, steely grey eyes that cloaked any emotions that may have lingered below the surface.

The south facing windows were well proportioned and should have allowed the room in which they stood to be light and airy. But it reasoned without the idiosyncrasies of the founder member of the company – although now departed – his influence lingered on. As a traditionalist, he had always insisted upon dressing the room – as he saw it – with artefacts of age and dependency. The consequences of this conservative thinking left the room standing cluttered and dull; with oppressive dark wooden shelving that carried innumerable leather-bound books. These books, dusty tomes of law, straddled cases that lined three walls of the room, leaving only enough space for one large leather-topped table, which filled the centre void. It was behind this unavoidable table – quite disproportionate to the lines of the room – that now sat the ruffled figure of solicitor George Stone.

Not for him the pinstriped greys, or bearing of noble Temple tradition – he was a maverick to his own profession. He was a man who dressed without heed to fashion, good taste or professional bearing. He sat silently behind the defensive screen of his table, scowling in his woollen tie and green-flecked tweed jacket. This was the son of the gold-scripted legend, borne so elegantly on the window for all to see. One who, in truth, cared little for the decor of his father – beeswax or the tinted colour of tradition; he was altogether a different fish. Unconcerned with the rights and wrongs of common man – in general that is – he was more aware of the tangible assets that could accrue from successful legal and sometimes other skirmishes. George Stone was an altogether more devious creature – who, at that moment was very involved with his own particular form of aberrant enterprise. It was such a matter that now gave rise to his heated outbursts of displeasure, directed vociferously towards the only other occupant of the room, who remained standing by the window. But despite his venom, he could not conceal or dispel the mood of apprehension that hung about him or indeed the loathing he felt for the man standing before him.

A door, which contained an etched glass, flourished panel, formed the only separating barrier between the room in which the two men were locked in adversarial conflict and the office beyond. Mavis Foster, the other member of the practice, was busying herself in the role of secretary come receptionist in this area, a space quite definitely considered her domain. She had served Mr William Stone, senior, quite happily for a number of years and had only recently agreed to stay on, after his sudden announcement of retirement in favour of his son George. The old man had chosen Mavis, fresh from college with little experience, and had never regretted doing so; her youthful exuberance and unexpected outlook on life had kept him amused.

Whilst at the same time, loyalty and quickly-learnt secretarial skills had impressed him into a realisation that she was indeed a very useful asset to the company. The loyalty factor was however the principle which now concerned Mavis, for Mr George Stone – unlike his father, Mr William senior – was not everyone's choice of fair-minded boss and as yet – despite her promise to his father – she felt increasingly uneasy about the prospect of serving him full term.

Angry voices could be heard reverberating around the office next door. It had been two hours or more since Mr Stone had become ensconced in verbal discourse with this unknown, unseen male; whose aggressive shadow Mavis had watched apprehensively for some time as it played across the etched glass. As far as she could assess, the exchange appeared to be taking a disagreeable turn for the worse. Heated words that displayed far too much verbal emotion, together with the aggressive, gesticulating movements expressed in their shadows, alarmed her. Although not clearly audible behind the glass of the adjoining door – individual words not being completely decipherable – she knew from the tone that things were not as they should be. In any case it was out of character to the good order of the practice and not the sort of thing that she wished to be associated with. Frustrated by the situation and particularly wanting to finish early in order to prepare for the evening's entertainment; Mavis found as yet that she neither had the courage to interrupt, nor a moment in which to intrude, in order to seek the necessary permission to leave.

For some days now she and her best friend Audrey – a long-term friend and kindred spirit, who worked in similar employ with the legal profession, had been planning a night on the town to celebrate the Christmas season. Audrey was employed to word process documents for the Criminal Prosecution Service. They often – though they were well aware of the illicit nature of such chats – exchanged information together. Working as they did, in civil and criminal law, meant they could mull over both the proclivity and vulnerability of their community, with a host of privileged information, that made for many a juicy exchange. On this occasion however it was the holiday break with its accompanying celebrations, which concentrated their minds; in the long telephone conversation between them references were made reflecting the friend's frustration.

"I know Audrey – but they've been locked together in that room for over two hours. – No! – No!"

She did not like the persistence of her friend's interrogation.

"No! I don't know what they're doing."

Pausing briefly, she listened to her friend's reply then continued in a calmer tone,

"No, I didn't make the appointment! I never saw who it was. He must have arrived when I was out at lunch."

She stopped talking for a moment and scribbled on her pad, it was a crude image of a man, then resumed suggestively.

"I went to 'JULIO'S' today… yeah and their sauces," she made a loud sipping noise with an intake of breath, "are fantastic. And the food arrives carried by this dark looking waiter – yeah I know they're all dark – but this one! Well! You want to see… he's very, corrrh!"

She made several noises to suggest that she would willingly abandon all, to the pleasures of the swarthy male.

Then, picking up on her friend's comments, "I can't just butt in you know... but I don't like the sound of what's going on... it's not the same any more. Mr... Stone... you know, Mr William, old Mr William that is... was a real gent. He would have given me the day off! – Yeah I know – I think after Christmas I'll look around for something else."

The voices through the glass were again raised, a fist was laid to bear on the table top as the extended shadow moved excitedly back and forth across the door panel; she watched with morbid curiosity, considering with disdain the gesticulating shapes.

"Of course I want to come out, I've arranged to meet Steven... you know, the body-builder, have you seen him? Oh he's built like, it's, – ooh! – Beautiful! Well anyway he's good at... No! That's not what I meant! Hey stop it! No don't! That's naughty – nice though. Well anyway... look – I'll try to get in to see the boss when there's a break in this yattering – 'Outside the Odeon' – 'Eight o'clock tonight'. Okay?"

The intercom on her desk crackled into life just before she finished speaking to her friend.

"Oh! Hang on a minute, Aud!"

Her boss, George Stone, was speaking to her in a clipped, tight-lipped voice that seemed to typify him. It was a harsh-sounding voice, with just a hint of a middle northern accent.

"Are you there, Mavis?"

"Yes Mr Stone! – Is there – something?"

"No... but you can make yourself scarce."

It was a typical offhand command, one that irritated her.

"Now if you like! Take the rest of the afternoon off, will you? I'm tied up right now… on business."

"But Mr Stone… have you forgotten? – It's Christmas next week?"

He replied after the briefest of pauses.

"Oh! – Well. – Of course, I suppose it'll be after the holiday then! Off you go now, Mavis!"

Mavis's face lit up at the news and she visibly relaxed, answering in a happy submissive fashion.

"Right Mr Stone – I'm on my way!"

Releasing the button, she returned to addressing her friend, who was still waiting on the end of the line.

"Audrey did you hear that – yeah at last. See you shortly… bye!"

Mavis looked around the room as she gathered her thoughts, collecting up her bag whilst at the same time throwing her coat across her shoulders; she paused for a moment by the door and listened. There was no sound, but before the boss could change his mind or the arguing voices influence her thoughts once more, she hastily switched off the reception light. Mavis took care not to touch any of the other switches, especially not the 'neon' that controlled the glowing facia of the building recommending their legal services. She slipped the latch on the door, and pulling it open just wide enough to ease herself through the gap, the girl disappeared as quickly as she could into the corridor beyond.

oOo

George Stone sat cogitating, pushing a pencil up and down through his clenched fist, cocking half an ear for the closing door as he did so. Seeing the light finally extinguish in the room beyond, he turned back with some satisfaction to address the figure before him. The large black silhouetted image stood framed against the night sky in the window, waiting quietly; the lights of town flashed on and off, creating lurid shapes across the man's face. He stood with his back to the solicitor, his protagonist, seemingly indifferent to the commencement of yet another verbal attack upon him. The solicitor, addressing him with increased volume and excited venom through salivating lips, spat each word out in clipped, concise consonants.

"I'm – not – con – cerned – with – the – how! – De – tails are im – mater – ial to me, – just – get – it – done!"

George Stone's overly large head with its piggy eyes was tinged red as his blood pressure soared, he leaned across his desk to accentuate his delivery. His small eyes narrowed to slits as he spat out a further torrent from his tight mouth; it was in a distinctly Mancunian brogue.

"Get it sorted! If he moves any closer or others show an interest. You'll feel the wind this time – I promise you that!"

A moment's quiet followed the postured threat; despite an obvious difference in the physical prowess of the men – an onlooker might have reasoned the control differently. The solicitor marked the moment well and waited for a response as he sat agitatedly tapping his hand with his pencil. Unlike the standing figure with thick set hair whom he was now admonishing, his own pronounced balding dome gave his eyes the appearance of being even smaller than they really were, with eyebrows that swept up and over his forehead in a badger-like flourish. Whilst delivering his ultimatum, Stone's pained facial expression gave substance to the suggestion that he himself had been on the receiving end of such an outburst and was still suffering from the indignity of it. He lacked the assuredness of strength, which caused him to degenerate into a figure of pathos. The man to whom he addressed his remarks seemed similarly unimpressed, indeed his swagger gave him the appearance of making light of the whole situation.

"Look, how am I supposed to find the old fool after all this time? He could be anywhere!"

The younger man's voice held the thread of a lazy upper-class drawl that lacked humour.

Stone sighed with disdain that the man had the temerity to treat the situation with such flippancy, he bit back, reinforcing his concern with an account of recent events.

"It so happens that I know a lot about him, where he's been and possibly where he is at present!"

His visitor stared back at him, surprised by this admission, which changed his manner by promoting a renewed interest.

"How come?"

There was a thoughtful pause before Stone answered as he shifted on his chair, puffing himself up, aware now of holding the other's attention for once; from under a furrowed brow he now attempted to raise status and issue a credible response.

"I make it my business to know!"

Stone stared him out.

The big man threw in a casual comment.

"But… he's been missing for at least a year… since..."

His voice trailed off as though he would prefer not to consider the details. George Stone weighed up the response and, noting the reticence, continued,

"You don't think I would get in as deep as I have without knowing all the details do you? I've got too much to lose! We all 'ave! – Your family did the signing – don't forget it! And St. Matthew's took him off your hands, kept him locked away conveniently for you! I just looked after the paperwork – legalities... formalities – and things!"

Stone shifted uneasily on his seat, he felt uncomfortable being reminded of past indiscretions.

His visitor stood before him with a face wrinkling into a sneer.

"Don't make me laugh! You did well enough out of it."

Stone, after a short pause, retorted indignantly through gritted teeth,

"I took commission for certain transactions of course!"

Pausing further he reflected on his complicity and found himself feeling distinctly uncomfortable; the realisation of being implicated with such an unyielding and potentially dangerous confederate had not slipped his notice. But nonetheless he was still determined to press on for results.

"That aside, I made sure I kept in contact with the place – and after he was... transferred to Hereford and the centre."

A puzzled look appeared on the younger man's face.

"You didn't say anything?"

Stone quickly interjected,

"I didn't see the need – when he was released, he took to the road with more than a fair share of confusion and seemed to disappear. There was nothing to concern you with… until now!"

The younger man looked puzzled, questioning the solicitor's statement.

"Okay, so what's happened to change things? – The old fool doesn't even know who he is!"

The solicitor knew full well he was in deep, he'd left traces here and there along the way, which would at the least be considered unethical and at worst… well. Too much had happened, he sat cogitating, glowering across the table as he twisted and rolled his pencil between his fingers, attempting to elicit a course of action that was both adequate and would deal with the situation. Neither of them spoke for a while. Stone was nervous – although he tried not to show it – reasoning through the process, what had to happen would be unpalatable and at that moment unspeakable. For the time being they needed each other, one for his brawn and the other for his brains. Stone broke the silence, feeling the need to make a case for the other's involvement to keep him in the fold and pressure him into action. He recounted recent matters in which he had been involved.

"When I put the matters in place to… to tidy things up, all his business arrangements, I also re-addressed his mail to be delivered here. There's not been a letter, bill, or anything of note. Not till this week, that is."

As he spoke, he passed a white envelope across the table for his visitor to see, which at first he was reluctant to take note of, but after glancing at the cover stamps his interest was aroused so he snatched it up. The floral postmark and stamps were both clearly French. He pulled carelessly at the flap and shook out the contents from within the envelope, which was a single thin sheet of paper. Looking at it and turning it over back and forth, a puzzled look came over his face as he exclaimed begrudgingly,

"I can't understand it, it's… it's in French!"

Standing moodily in silence for a moment, appearing to be aware of his own inadequacy, he turned on the solicitor with an insistent angry outburst, demanding an explanation.

"Well? – What does it say then?"

Stone, exasperated, snorted disparagingly through his nose: hog-like.

"No it's not straight French, I give you that. But if you had used your privileged schooling to some advantage, you might at least have an inkling."

The solicitor sighed yet again in obvious dismay, but sensing his advantage over the brawn standing before him, he made the specific point of elaborating on the detail to exemplify his abilities.

"It's in a colloquial form – that's a local way of expressing things. I think, as far as I can tell, it's one used by people of the region from whence the letter came. It's French-Catalan, Occitan to be precise. In basic terms, it seems a Frenchman called Henry Douchez has written a letter, this one addressed to the old man – your uncle."

Stone narrowed his eyebrows in a disapproving way and continued.

"Philip Evans – remember? It's about a cottage that seems to be partly his?"

Stone looked up quizzically at his visitor, attempting to sense whether this was a known fact or not. But there was no betrayal of emotion to tell him either way. It was important for Stone to realise all the factors when making decisive moves.

"He says he's been looking after it for him?"

An edge of sarcasm wafted across the table, to register his displeasure at the new revelation. It was to his mind a dangerous extension to an already complicated conspiracy. The idea of this new element in the widening contacts being made by the boy's uncle, Philip Evans, concerned him deeply.

"I've written to him!"

A moment passed without comment then the visitor's mouth dropped open in disbelief.

"You've what!"

"I said I've written…"

He looked steadily at his visitor, then resumed his conversation and for the first time he referred to him by name.

"It's to tidy up details here. I don't want snooping Frenchmen inquiring about our Philip, neither do you, Mark, I'm sure!"

They both fell silent for a moment.

"Look you'd better know the rest, at first it was just the old man's money and house. Now there's a cottage in France and the joke of it is this Frenchman's on the make as well, or to be more accurate he and Philip are not averse to a little, shall we say, trading? But here's the difference. According to his letter he's been scratching around in the cottage and he's found something interesting in the cellar, which he wants to share," the solicitor carried a strange half smile on his face, "with Philip of course!"

"What do you think? What's it about?"

For the first time Mark Gower, belligerent wheeler-dealer and more often than not on the wrong side of the law, showed signs of a deepening interest, he began sniffing the air of good fortune with a satisfied smile.

"I don't know exactly, he doesn't say but there are two things to be dealt with; if it's important enough to write to England about – and the French man doesn't want the locals to know – then I smell something interesting, money, treasure trove, it's worth looking at I would think. And in any case, it would be best to find this foreign gentleman as he seems to know our mutual friend."

"Are you seriously suggesting a trip to France?"

Gower, who had worked – a loose term – with or for George Stone over a number of years, leaned across the table in an intimidating manner, bringing his face close to the solicitor's.

"Is that before or after I go looking for a crazy old man somewhere in Herefordshire?"

Gower pulled back from his intimidating stance and turned disinterestedly to look out of the window once more, maybe with a degree of uncertainty. Stone hesitated to answer immediately, leaving the air silent whilst he thought it through; he knew this well-built male cared little as to the 'how', when the time came for sorting out trouble. The solicitor moved uneasily on his seat – he was not himself a violent man – yet here he was knowingly active in inviting a response of finality, to cover his own misdeeds of the past. He knew of course, or suspected, there could well be many advantages for him to continue with the project, which included playing along with the unpredictable nature of his visitor. His earnest hope was that somehow he might be able to sever the connection at a later date. This man, his business partner so-called, one who caused the demise of others in unconventional ways – at least that was how Stone believed his visitor worked – was not one to deal with flippantly in fact. The thought of the decisive conclusion being considered against a third party caused him to shiver. The solicitor wanted to end the meeting and thereby deny the association as quickly as possible, he needed a concise plan that could be acted upon, one which would solve the problems of disclosure. There was a time factor as he saw it in which desperate actions were called for. It was now crucial to recover his equilibrium and assume the leading hand, before things got further out of control.

Stone resorted to the obscure safety of a set speech, quite inappropriate in the setting of Machiavellian conspiracies to murder. He divorced his mind from the obdurate nature of his proposal and continued, considering the community and its problems as he might in dealing with the details of any family that might elicit his help.

"Since this Government policy called *'Care in the community'* came in, it would seem there's little or no provision for money, or the follow up care and treatment."

He remembered what he was doing and corrected his drift to consider the subject of his delivery.

"What I'm trying to say is, there's no checking or anything to show the authorities where their patients have gone to. That is, where or what our 'mutual friend' is up to." Stone paused, reflecting on the situation a moment. "He just upped and disappeared – until last month. Luckily, I've a friend or two who keep me informed… there's… been an approach… apparently to a solicitor in town. It would seem that he recently came to the notice of the local police, some involvement in the death of a young woman."

"The old devil!" commented Gower with a sly smile on his lips.

Stone looked over his glasses, frowning with disapproval, giving a cautionary look as if to confirm bad goings on ran in the family.

"He was released I'm told, because they think he stumbled on the body by accident, at least there's no evidence to suggest otherwise. So nothing too serious at present, but anything further and it might be to our detriment. It would seem that the old fool is becoming a nuisance... to everyone."

Stone looked up to emphasise his words and make doubly sure his meaning was understood.

"Time for a long rest – give everyone a break!"

Stone shifted uncomfortably on his seat, aware of the finality of what he was suggesting.

"As to the French connection I intend to ring direct and sniff the air so to speak; I'll arrange a meeting for you."

He eyed Gower with disdain, who replied questioningly, "Over there?"

Stone rose from his seat, hoping to signify to his irascible visitor that the meeting was over and had reached, as far as he was concerned, a satisfactory conclusion. The attempt in essence was to give his statement more prominence.

"For a time, we believed that creative accounting and subtle changes in property ownership was just a matter of paper manipulation and keeping quiet. Well that's not quite the case now... you've got some work to do. He must be found... and by you... soon. He's got no home so there must be documents on him or somewhere close by, something about this new surprise of foreign properties and his caretaker friend. I want them. Get them and bring them here. Then I think you'd better have a little trip to see our holiday cottage and its creative local caretaker."

Stone blustered on, feeling it was now all or nothing.

"So just get out… find him… and..."

The words were left unsaid but the look that was exchanged between the two men needed little explanation.

Chapter seven

Foreign enterprise

The quiet corners of the bizarre interior jangled with the insistent sounds from the period telephone resting on a dust-laden shelf in the corner. The unwelcome sound issued forth and echoed around incense sticks, Buddhas and musty leather-bound volumes, many of which were piled high in every conceivable space. Its large megaphone speaker and corded earpiece demanded instant attention. The phone's authenticity, like much else in the emporium, was questionable; its urgent summons into wakeful annoyance however was very real. This mid-morning intrusion into the jaded calm succeeded in evoking swift action, a woven screen parted violently and through it, slithering into the room, came Henri Douchez the proprietor, in a confused state. His behaviour towards this intrusion appeared unseemly and strangely unaccountable, as he rushed headlong towards the noise with his two hands poised – as if to strangle it. Ruffled by the unseemly sound of his own telephone Douchez snatched the earpiece anxiously from its support, the sudden move restored silence instantly to the musty, incense-laden air of the curio emporium. It left Henri however, shopkeeper, owner and tourist parasite, breathless and on edge, as he clutched the offending instrument close to his chest and stood unaccountably listening to the passing breeze. Nothing stirred outside the broad expanse of the double-fronted cluttered windows, all appeared quiet and the manor opposite, tucked behind foliage, remained placidly still as all its inhabitants went about their business within its dark interior. The furtive darting of Henri's eyes was the only suspicious movement to be seen, as they sought reassurance from the quiet interior of his shop. Finally, appearing satisfied that the fragility of his world had returned once more, Henri cupped the telephone to his ear and interrupted an anxious silence to reassure the would-be caller at the other end.

Licking his lips nervously, he spoke in a low voice – almost inaudibly so – how he could imagine it would project along the wires, all the way to England was a mystery, but somehow it did and a response came quickly to his prompting.

"Allo! 'Objets d'art D'ancien', can I help you? This is Henri Douchez, who is that please?"

"Bonjour monsieur, je m'appelle George Stone, solicitor en Angleterre. That is Monsieur Douchez? – Henri Douchez?"

"Oui monsieur, speaking! Please be brief, but speak with care. I may not be able to continue this call for long."

Douchez wiped a persistent bead of sweat from his brow.

"Is it that you understand what I say?"

"Of course, I will speak quickly. It's about our mutual friend mentioned in your letter, he alas, is not very well!"

Stone appeared to pause, giving significance to this statement.

"I fear he may not survive a further attack... he is somewhat careless in his lifestyle. He is of course a great concern to us all. He takes far too many risks at his time of life, for which his health may in time... suffer. I am acting on his behalf and that of his estate under instructions from a relative – his nephew, Monsieur Gower."

"Oui Monsieur Stone, I am in receipt of your letter and the photograph of our friend's nephew. Please I will only speak for a short while, you understand when I say voices can be heard and sometimes misunderstood."

The solicitor of dubious credentials – experienced in dealings of a delicate underhand nature – understood the message well enough. It fitted in with his assumption that whatever the proposal might be, it more than certainly would broach illegality and thereby offer financial advantage. Obviously the Frenchman was frightened, but of what Stone could only surmise. The portents Stone thought – could well be to their advantage; even if the circumstances were difficult it might allow for a bargain to be struck in their favour. The solicitor was treading carefully into a situation where the circumstances were unfamiliar to him; he mulled the matter over for a moment or so until the Frenchman's dramatic voice broke his reverie.

"Please, I think to mention names, is for the moment too dangerous and somewhat immaterial."

Stone heard the man hesitate then after pausing to clear his throat he continued.

"I have been working on a project within the house of our mutual friend... I think he knew of the project, though not understanding its possibilities, leaving me to attend to all practicalities."

The Frenchman hesitated again before commenting.

"I did not think he would be so distant and lacking interest? – It is a long time since last we met."

Stone's difficult, and sometimes delicate, dealings over the years had equipped him with guile enough to placate the inquiring nature of strangers. He responded he thought in a manner appropriate, but clearing his throat a little too quickly he realised may have alerted the Frenchman.

"Our friend has been unwell for some time and we were not aware that the project was proceeding so fast! Of course you can count on our continued support, but we know so little about what it is you are doing... but interested. Yes we are!"

Stone listened intently, careful not to interrupt, hoping to receive a glimmer of information that might give a clue to the nature of the venture, its worth and commitment.

"That is good because I believe it will not be long before I have some very interesting news. I have made an important discovery, the matter of which you will know more of soon. It will be essential that I can arrange everything with you, make arrangements for us both... mutually acceptable of course and when the time comes hopefully a speedy exchange can be accomplished. My calculations lead me to believe that it will be a most significant consignment – highly beneficial... to us all. It is difficult for me to discuss this matter in detail now, discretion is of the utmost importance."

He paused, and lowered his voice so that it was almost imperceptible.

"There are people, here where I live you understand, who would not comprehend my point of view in this matter."

There was a moment's silence as if to emphasise the gravity of the matter, during which Stone remained silent.

"They would show their displeasure... which would almost certainly be most unpleasant! You understand care must be taken... our mutual friend always indicated to me that he would help when appropriate? If he is not available?"

Stone, aware of doubtful and questioning inflections in the man's voice, quickly interjected.

"Pas de probleme monsieur... Don't worry, we will do whatever needs to be done!"

And quickly as an afterthought Stone added,

"On his behalf, of course."

Stone's irritation at the lack of detail was now perceptible; it showed in his voice as he spoke, responding rather more curtly than he would have wished. The language itself was difficult enough but together with the lack of detail the proposition left him frustrated, he still had no idea how lucrative the deal might be and in turn how much energy was justified in the enterprise.

"I will send instructions – nearer the time – for a meeting with my cousin across the border. There must be no direct approach. It would be too dangerous! Exact details of where to go, the times etc. will be sent in due course. My cousin will contact me after the meeting then we can arrange transactions acceptable to all. I would caution our friend's nephew in this matter."

A sound of rustling from the room divider caused Henri to curtail his conversation, he listened intently, then returned to the telephone, this time speaking in a different vein to suit his now worrying circumstances.

"I have to go now… thank you for calling… the matter will be dealt with as soon as possible… I am sorry for any interruptions."

He very carefully replaced the handset, buffing its surface with a cloth as though it had not been involved. Making a play of moving openly into the well of the shop where his activities could be freely noted and approved by prying eyes he made for the door. With a considerable display of action he stood at the shop's entrance adjusting the hanging sign on which the word 'OPEN' was now displayed. The latch hit the metal with some force as he lifted it up forcefully, ensuring a noisy opportunity of show as he opened the door. With pretence of acclimatising to the time of day, he looked up and down the deserted lane with an assumed air of confidence, before retiring back into the darkness of the shop's interior. The noise of his bustling at the door somehow gave him a queasy feeling, gaining no confidence from the action which just bolstered his unease. After a cursory glance around the shop once more, he sighed and resumed his position behind the counter. Standing idly thumbing through some catalogues laid out casually on top, he awaited the attention of an unlikely passer-by to lure with the shop's curious objects of mystery.

Chapter eight

Philip

The ugliness of the man's gait was not lifted or enhanced in any way by the oversized blue-serge topcoat that hung awkwardly about his frame. Having seen better days, it looked dirty and dejected – after suffering a life of abuse serving its common purpose as blanket, dinner tray and cloaking device. Vaguely reminiscent of its RAF antecedents – now button-less, and tied very tight at the waist with two twists of binder twine – the coat, as if in sympathy with its wearer, appeared tired and unappealing. The overall impression of the man with his greying hair was one of middle years, but his size and bearing belied this fact; for without the surface confusion, he could have struck an impressive stance. He was however unshaven, the unkempt growth of several days on his chin sat uneven and spiky, the hairs stood out, ugly against his ruddy complexion. Fine lines of crimson ran across his nose and through the bright blotches on his weather-beaten cheeks; a visage which betrayed his habit of long standing, an affinity with the bottle which he relished too often and too long. It was a lifestyle to which he had become accustomed since taking to the road. It meant comfort now the bursts of winter-wind pursued him relentlessly around the alleyways he called home. The tiredness of seeking survival amongst whirling papers and dust, reduced eyes to the slits of winter vision, inner warmth was crucial.

His daily scavenging ranged over all manner of bins, and alleyways – he had no preferences – if lucky, a discarded bottle lying prematurely abandoned, might still contain the precious amber liquid he so desperately sought. He no longer concerned himself or cared enough to check the contents, other than a cursory sniff to confirm its alcoholic nature. This done, he would consume it quickly there and then – it was a symptom of the dog-eat-dog mentality – as if another of his ilk might appear and deprive him of its pleasure. Whatever shape or form it took mattered little to him, for the bottles gave much comfort and helped ease his mind; just enough to forget.

In his right hand he hauled a battered, brown suitcase. Tightly secured by a stout black leather belt, it appeared to be burdensome to him, holding it as he did to his rear. He appeared to be both concealing its presence, yet at the same time holding it tightly to announce his total possession of it. Despite the man's size, his anonymity was such that the world passed him by as he stood at the roadside, prospecting among the riches of the gutter. *'The rush hour traffic'* – absurdly stated – slowly pushed itself alongside, drivers oblivious and busy shoppers bustling in and out of the crowds, too preoccupied with their own compact lives to notice just another tramp in their city. He bobbed up and down every so often along his purposeful path, collecting and secreting items into his voluminous pockets. He moved about the gutters and bins, sifting the discarded commodities dropped into the depositories of town. Not all dismissed his presence so lightly however; some eyes, more qualified, watched his slow methodical progress with interest, as he made his way to the end of the broad walk of High Town.

A police officer emerged from an alleyway; his immediate task was to sort out the sprawling mass of hesitant vehicles. Jarred by the sudden change from the quiet of specialist shops and galleries, effusing their ethereal elegance in the confines of Cathedral Cloisters, he found himself suddenly confronted with the rumbustious clamour of unforgiving traffic chaos. The officer's discomfort was obvious as he winced at the prospect of dealing with a blockade of frustrated drivers, amongst a background of throbbing engines, erratic horns and billowing fumes. Sitting impatiently, horn-hovering hands at the ready and feet in clutch-slipping misery, they were all unsuccessfully attempting to woo the static metal pile forward. Taken aback by the complexity of the scene and the volume of sound emitting from it, the officer stood for a moment, confronted by such a vision of confusion he remained perplexed as to know what to do next. Pushing his helmet back on his forehead he rubbed his brow then, sighing to himself, it was – on reflection – like any other day he thought, yesterday, tomorrow and most probably all the seasonal days to come. Shrugging his shoulders with reluctance but aware of the need he moved to enter the fray, catching sight of the collector as he did so.

In his peripheral vision he could see a shape and immediately in his mind's eye identified to whom the shape belonged, groaning inwardly and muttering to himself at the same time. 'Oh no – Evans, that's all I need. Dossers and traffic jams, just about my level.' Sighing again to himself under his breath he expressed a personal opinion. 'Funny old devil, round the bend… they all are.'

Another uniform – snaking in and out of the static queue of cars – caught up with him, approaching from across his line of vision, it was the Sergeant out on his rounds. After a cursory friendly nod, they joined forces and walked along together, at first without speaking, then,

"Sarge, can you see who it is? Isn't that Evans up ahead? I thought he'd been lifted and was safely inside, bang to rights. You know?"

The young officer looked down at the ground while talking, aware that his comments were not being well received, but his strongly-felt sentiments kept him going nonetheless.

"While the team in the incident room follow up their leads on the murder. I gather from my mate he was caught on the job, very much so, found on top of her!"

The young officer didn't like down-and-outs, he couldn't understand the need; a bit like wasps he thought. An opinion and attitude which he believed in fervently; failing to hide his obvious disdain caused him to continuously get into deep water with those who carried a more balanced outlook. The Sergeant winced with open disenchantment at the man's attitude towards roadsters and checked the younger man by voicing his more rounded opinion, together with an assertion of his seniority towards the matter.

"I think," his face creased with disdain at the young officer's comments, "it's highly unlikely that our Philip Evans would sink so low as that. Committing murder is somewhat out of his league. He's annoying, I give you that and not the kind of person to welcome into your home maybe, but he's certainly not a criminal... in the true sense of the word. An opinion I believe that's shared by the team in the incident room. He is out on police bail at the moment, but the general feelings are that he probably stumbled across the body by accident."

He breathed in a deep sigh.

"Anyway it's very unlikely that he was in any way responsible. It would seem – as unlikely as it would appear – that he was, or so he says, trying to revive the poor kid and bring her back to life. Unfortunately for her, and he seems to have been quite unaware of it, he was already too late; she'd died some time before. They think it probably happened in Birmingham – very likely whoever did it drove her out to where she was just dumped and found by the tramp."

The Sergeant stiffened as he turned, whilst studying the young officer's face thoughtfully. Conscious of his colleague's overt cynicism and although time was pressing he felt the matter should be dealt with there and then. With an eye cocked on Philip Evans, realising the image was not helping his case for love of fellow man, he spoke softly and without rancour.

"Evans may appear scruffy, dirty and well, not very wholesome, I grant you that. But it's likely and I quite believe it, he has known better times. It's not for us to judge others, that's not our job, we are here to supply the facts as they are known and if possible, corroborate them. We are not sitting in judgement on others... we don't have that right!"

"No... sorry Sarge, but I just can't go along with that. I don't like him or any of his kind."

The young officer eyed their quarry, clearly expressing his dislike towards him and his ilk.

"Just can't come to terms with them. I don't see why anyone needs to walk the streets and bum off the rest of us?"

Moving closer to the careworn weather-beaten tramp, they eyed his antics – appearing comically to one and to the other demeaning – as he stood, bowed head, locked in his preoccupation of poking around aimlessly in the gutter. They made note of the traffic congestion beyond, both concluding it could wait for a while and then, standing patiently, they both waited at the kerbside for the roadster to reach them. The old man's recognition was not long in coming, the tramp was well blessed enough with the powers of observation to survive and as such, quickly became aware of their presence. Firstly, spotting their shiny boots, the old roadster knew his territory had been invaded and by whom. He responded by turning his head slowly in an exaggerated and perverse manner, pulling a strange stance of burlesque proportion with his hands raised and fingers outstretched as if to question what it was he had discovered. Slowly – with head tilted, and his eyes widened in exaggerated wonderment – he moved his gaze in a less than respectful manner to follow his line of sight and take in the black trouser legs. Then raising his head, he uttered,

"Oh! You know me, don't you?"

It was an expression laced with calumny, born out of so many difficult encounters between himself and the keepers of law. The Sergeant looked hard at Evans and, despite his balanced views on life, still found himself wincing at the sight before him; there was little to be found in the vision, the Sergeant observed, which would enamour him to the world or receive a sympathetic understanding.

Checking himself in an attempt to be more objective – dislike being a powerfully provocative and visible emotion, which could damage communications – he grunted inwardly and smiled towards this shape of humanity pulled together by string that stood before him. Then speaking quietly to the man, showing a tolerant acceptance of the tramp's existence, he said,

"Yes… yes I know you well enough Philip – still collecting are we?"

The tramp relaxed a little and nodded, appreciating an understanding of shared secrets. He spoke in a soft rounded theatrical voice, smiling confidentially as he did so.

"I'm very rich, I am!"

Evans' conspiratorial voice, like a loud rasping whisper, was delivered as he looked about, eyeing the passing crowd suspiciously; then as if to make a point he suddenly raised his voice defiantly.

"Very rich!"

His head dropped again and with a sly, secretive smile he dwelt on his inner thoughts, real or otherwise. For a moment he distanced himself from the intruders, pillars of the law, both of whom he too regarded with disdain and also to be his inferior. Despite the illusion that he afforded to others he considered himself to be a cut above, relishing his own dimly-remembered background of favoured upbringing and possessions, all of which added to give him a false sense of superiority. Nothing was said for a few moments; Philip Evans remained wrapped in his own thoughts whilst contemplating the gutter and its contents – an unconvincing image of wealth. Then without looking up, he addressed them both, but now there was a sad reflective ring in his voice.

"They've taken it… all of it, everything I 'ad… And they won't give it back to me!"

He stood glowering at them, in appearance blaming others and indeed the world for his predicament.

"Yes I know Philip… or so you say! It's a story you've told me many, many times, but we still don't know who **they** are?"

The old man, in a sudden display of anger, kicked at something real or imagined in the gutter; unfortunately for him his foot collided painfully with the kerbstone but apart from wincing, he said nothing.

"You're always telling me that you're very rich, but I don't see any evidence of it!"

The Sergeant jibed at him, then checking himself continued more gently, as if to humour the man,

"Is it in your suitcase then? Maybe?"

Evans, affronted by this personal questioning, pulled the case tightly to his chest as if protecting the most precious items in the world. With flaring nostrils in a mock expression of theatrical distrust, the tramp stood insolently staring at them both, his head framed above the case. He struck an odd figure of pathos in amongst the bustle of town and the officer cautioned himself against goading the sad old man any further. In many ways he felt extremely sorry for the tramp, he couldn't believe anyone would elect to live such an existence willingly. There may well have been an element of truth in what he was saying, but psychiatric welfare was not in his remit and those to whom it was, seemed to have cast the old boy adrift. The old man lowered the suitcase, softened a little and with the lack of immediate threat he visibly relaxed. But keeping his head lowered as if to conceal whom it was he was addressing, he continued, as if talking to the world in general,

"I've been cheated I 'ave. I 'ad lots of money, I was rich – then!"

He gabbled on morosely for a while then after another thoughtful pause reasserted himself, reflecting,

"No I am rich, I own 'ouses, I do… I… I."

The Sergeant and his young officer had by this time turned away to face the angry pall of fumes and concentrate on the job in hand. There was still no movement in the traffic queue, so the two men gritted their teeth with resolve and moved forward, the Sergeant calling over his shoulder to Evans as they went,

"Mind how you go now Philip, we have to get on, can't stand here talking to you all day me-lad, we've got to sort this lot out!"

Then looking back for a moment he surveyed the strange wild figure in the gutter and voicing, not a threat exactly, but more an intimation that the force would be aware of his movements, called out to him,

"I'll be watching out for you! So be good now!"

The tramp's gaze fell and just as quickly he became sullen again having lost his ready audience; he mumbled to himself, looking up every now and then watching with a glazed expression as the officers turned their attention elsewhere. With the sudden awareness of returning loneliness his eyes widened, panic-stricken – with his head turning in every direction – he realised the uniformed figures were no longer interested in his cause and had moved out of vision. The distraught, careworn figure in the gutter looked around in vain for an audience. His general appearance failed now to turn a head or induce a listening ear, either sympathetic or for ridicule to give credence to his over-blown allegations.

Walking along together in silence the Sergeant gave a complicit look to the young man at his side, which spoke volumes; he wasn't so naive as to ignore the possibilities with the old man – befriending him was going too far – but you never knew in life what the truth might be. Philip, on the other hand, shuffled uneasily, he had heard the words and knew the implied meaning: they were always watching. He responded by pulling an absurd face of insolence as he looked beyond to where they were about to disappear, until finally their uniformed figures turned the corner out of sight. Gaining confidence as officialdom faded from view, he re-inherited his own world, Philip raised his voice in defiance by shouting loudly in their direction,

"Watching me?"

But it was obvious, even to him, that his initial command of the world's attention had faded, the general mêlée now turning its disinterested back on him left him to contemplate his own demise. So his final words died in his throat, somehow loudly echoing his own obscurity.

"But you don't… listen!"

Broad Street contained the head of the same snake of metal coiling through from High Town, the young policeman found himself on his own as he moved briskly along towards the Cathedral – his Sergeant having found an excuse to pop in somewhere whilst passing. The officer's thoughts remained occupied by the earlier incident with the tramp, rather than considering the agitated drivers, wrapped in their misery alongside. The drivers were less than complimentary in their thoughts towards him as he walked by, seemingly indifferent to their plight. His thoughts were on the innumerable tussles with the old man and the many occasions he had moved him along. It was on reflection, not a very charitable thing to do, turning vagrants out from their hideaway boltholes late at night. Although the Sergeant's reprimand – as light as it was – had left him smarting a little, he knew their ilk were not liked generally by the law or for that matter by the public at large. The accompanying smell and soiled clothing, reflecting their antisocial style of life and living alongside, on the back of, but never part of mainstream society. It usually precipitated the practice of moving them on, hopefully without the need for physical contact and as long as it was 'onto somebody else's patch'; all was well.

The local police considered him and his like, as they euphemistically put it, 'Yampy', a condition caused by too much of the local coarse cider. It combined with their plight of hopelessness and seemed to induce a light-headed stupidity, which on occasions flared into belligerence if riled by the inequalities of life. At such times they would stand their ground and feel like fighting the world, usually taking on the local police force as their worldly contact and focus of hurt. The policeman shook his head, dismissing the incident from his mind, noted the time and sighing deeply stepped briskly onward towards the river to find the head of the queue and bring what influence he could to bear on the slow parade of metal.

Philip Evans, on the other hand, unaware of the police officer or anyone's continuing interest in him, turned the corner into the narrows at the head of Broad Street. He was pleased with himself, the paper lining he had so carefully placed inside his boots was still intact and warm and the new string he had been given to tie them up held firm; he felt reasonably comfortable but he was very tired.

Sensing the different sounds surrounding him, he stopped ferreting in the gutter where he stood amongst the discarded objects of society and looked up to get his bearings. After tapping his bulging pockets for reassurance to confirm that the morning had been successful, he looked straight ahead to his objective – a side street opposite; then walking purposefully he stepped straight out into the traffic. Cars in the broad main approach road to the cathedral – although moving slowly – braked fiercely to come to a sudden halt. Their highly stressed occupants saw the sudden movement with alarm and, in their agitation, hooted vehemently to vent their frustrated anger at him. He, aware of the sudden imposition of loud noises, stopped and glared back at the traffic. With a face more suited to melodrama, with its overstated jaw set firmly forward and an eye raised in quizzical manner, he looked down his nose at them. The ill-humoured tramp now played to the seated, confused audience – no one in particular – as he moved menacingly towards the nearest occupants.

Stopping by a driver's door he looked down into the window; he could see the passengers and their driver quite clearly as he leered in at them, the driver was feeling distinctly uncomfortable at his close proximity. Far less confident now than when he had brashly sounded his horn singling him out, the provocative nature of the tramp's presence made him twitch in his seat. The intervening glass rather than protecting him had the reverse effect, now instilling a feeling of entrapment. The unkempt creature put his face tight against the glass in order to contemplate the manner of the occupants, his warm breath misted the cold glass and the driver inside immediately panicked, moving as far from the window as his seat belt would allow. A pair of thick lips pushed flat against the glass, showing a row of yellowing, uncleansed teeth. Then in an instant they were gone, all that remained of the encounter was a wet salivated hole in the mist, through which the lolloping image of Philip Evans could be seen retreating to the side street opposite. A cacophony of different pitched horns was now blaring, this time directing their venom towards the occupant of the car that had been visited by this wild apparition. In his discomfort the driver of the vehicle had not noticed the traffic ahead had finally moved off, leaving the road strangely calm and empty ahead.

In the relative quiet of the small unassuming side street chosen by Philip Evans, he looked up and down it taking soundings; finally stopping at what he considered to be the appropriate place. Satisfied with his position in the street and confident that he would not be disturbed, Evans lifted his old battered suitcase up onto a flight of steps, placing it onto the large curved bottom step. This particular flight of steps he had chosen – totally oblivious to his surroundings – rose to front the facade of a prestigious office block. The fact that he had selected this spot on which to stop and conduct his business meant little to him, for marble and stainless steel were not commodities that formed any part of possessions he considered to be precious. On either side of the approach steps where he stood was a curved wall upon which sat large copper lanterns, the whole, then graced an impressive entrance to a suite of offices above. The wall served to funnel approaching clients towards a large, highly glossed wooden door at the top. It in turn was flanked by rows of brass plates, concerned with the intricacies of insurance, its practitioners and the names to whom one could address problems, having first succeeded in entering the hallowed portico beyond of course.

Philip however did not consider the gleaming brass and he remained blissfully unaware of eyes from within that watched his audacious approach. That such an apparition could hover so near to their exalted domain unnerved the two sets of eyes that watched him as he sat down. Philip acclimatised himself, sitting down comfortably on the step next to his case and then warily he unbuckled the belt that held it firm. They watched this disagreeable image as he carefully lifted the lid and looked inside, licking his lips nervously, they saw him plunge his free hand into the pocket of his heavy coat and pull from it the contents, dropping them into the collection that was now almost level with the case edge.

Matches, thousands upon thousands of them, new, used, bent, burnt, broken, piled higgledy-piggledy and after divesting his pockets of their precious cargo he jealously glanced about, guarding the collection with one hand as he closed down the lid with the other with a resounding thump. Reverently he circled the case with the belt and secured his hoard from view; totally immersed in his pleasure. Philip failed to see or hear the big door to his rear slowly open, nor indeed had he noticed the disdainful expression portrayed on the face of the man who had opened it. Standing holding the door slightly ajar was a neat man dressed in a pinstriped suit, who nervously viewed the form of the match collector through the narrow gap. Standing behind him, just visible was the figure of a woman, who was directing his performance by prodding

96

him into action with an extended finger, whilst she stood resolute to the rear, as any good commander should. The prodded man with a supercilious air then spoke his lines in what he considered to be an authoritative voice.

"I say, you! This is private property, be off with you! Go on, be on your way."

Evans slowly lifted his tired frame from the cold step on hearing the words, he barely turned to see from where the voice issued, being well used to such behaviour. Sometimes it annoyed him and he growled back, but today he just muttered to himself, dragged his case up from the step and moved in his shuffling gait across the small street, disappearing out of view into the alleyway opposite. The faces at the door continued watching until they were convinced he had left the area, the man very relieved there had been no unpleasantness. Grateful that a satisfactory conclusion had been reached in the presence of his companion; who now smiled meekly up at him as she resumed her adopted, submissive stance as together they closed the company door.

The collector, satisfied he had gathered sufficient for the needs of his case, turned his mind to the other important and urgent scavenging in his life: food. The alleyway, in which he now stood, serviced the remains and discarded morsels from pristine tables of restaurants beyond. Frequenting the underbelly of alleyway servicing he was unaware of the bright fascias that welcomed the prominent, accompanied by the elegant, as the power brokers of the city dined exclusively in this smart part of town. Philip's only consideration was, that this was the best fare to be found anywhere in the city bins. Whence came the significant and seemingly never ending supply of exotic food was to him, unimportant. Every evening, there were remnants from the party fare discarded within the soft lit, seductive atmospheres of the many four-star gastronomic temples, all of which were out of bounds and inaccessible to him. Most often, the well-heeled – in a ritualistic exposure of being seen with the best at the most expensive – pecked absent-mindedly at exotic plates of culinary fantasy set out before them. The bins in the dark alley behind this bright façade, unseen by these rich grazers gorged with the remains of sophistication, were the recipients of waste and thereby treasure houses for Philip and his kind. Weekend pickings were particularly good. Philip moved up and down amongst the bins, selecting a leg here and crust there from the plentiful supply. After carefully pocketing his gleanings, he returned to the side street gloom. Slowly, Philip ambled through the interconnecting back streets, towards the outer ring of the city, single-mindedly intent on food, rest, and the comfort of his night-time refuge.

This singular existence, in a lonely bizarre world inhabited by the sometimes eccentric behaviour of others, people of troubled minds, aching hearts and confused souls, was by its nature a potentially dangerous realm. Rarely mixing and viewing their contemporaries – roadsters of all descriptions – they viewed one another with a delusory distrust and always at a distance when passing. Having severed their connections with society for whatever reason, it was necessary to be self-reliant and safer to remain suspicious of all people. Philip's size and sudden emotional outbursts had caused others, who might have befriended him, to keep their distance. His changing moods - unpredictable and often violent - proved too much of a challenge for agencies and their goodwill, so he was left to survive by his own endeavours.

Whether it was a sign that age and his rough living were taking their toll, he was less wary than he ought to have been. For eyes, belonging to one who was blessed with more animal cunning than he, had watched unbeknown to Philip every movement he had made from the brightly lit Broad Street into the gloom of side street and alleyway. The steel grey eyes, that watched his progress with cold, dispassionate interest, were concerned only with where he would finally stop his wanderings for the night and pause for sleep. Philip Evans, blissfully unaware of the interest shown in his journey, pulled himself slowly along the interconnecting back streets that echoed with the muffled sounds of impatient traffic a block away. An occasional lock hitting home, securing its connections for the weekend as businesses closed, were the only other sounds to follow his progress through the gloomy streets. The collector turned the corner away from the rows of empty offices that now generally lay darkened and deserted, to finally emerge from this quiet backwater into the chaos of traffic on the outer ring. He walked alongside the main route that funnelled all vehicles towards the new bridge that crossed the river. Hazard lights on vehicles were flashing, headlamps glaring onto meaningless traffic signs. The swirling exhaust fumes licked upwards into the cold night sky; combining into a melange of drama that evoked the very essence of city rush hour.

The cosseted suitcase had, for some two weeks now, spent the nights with its owner in one of three houses, all that remained of the terrace that once had hugged the old wall of the city, watching its passing commerce for over a century. Most of the dwellings were now cleared, secured and prepared for their final ignominy of demolition; but for the moment the seasonal holiday had caused the operation to fall silent. A momentary respite had been given to the remaining cottages and one in particular, in which Philip had found a temporary haven. There was one chair and a dry floor, which was wooden and complete and without the more usual abandoned house odour of human waste or rot; the easily accessible rear door had been left conveniently unlocked. He shambled through rubble heaps that once sported cottage gardens, to reach the side passage and rear entrance. Lights from the snarling, laboured vehicles splashed across the ancient limestone wall that rose above the rooftops to the rear of the houses. Garish shadows danced along the wall and down into the old back parlours as Philip, tired but relieved, pushed the door shut behind him. Finding his way through the gloom, with the assistance of the intermittent lights of town, he sank down gratefully into his chair, a Windsor-backed diner in relatively good condition. Now comfortable and safe he sat for a time contemplative and catching his breath.

Across the road and directly opposite, standing just inside the columns that supported the giant black wrought iron gates of the old cemetery, was a tall, heavily set male. He was dressed in a three quarter length green leather coat and seemingly he appeared to be just idling, but the truth was far different, for his eyes held an obsessive interest in the cottage opposite and its sole resident. Having spent many arduous hours over the last week endeavouring to sight his quarry, he had no intention at this point of losing the opportunity and finalising what had to be done. Leaning against a long neglected tomb almost covered with dark green ivy, the incised numerals of which were now defaced, he idly picked at his nails as he waited for the moment. He stood where it was both discreet and advantageous, there was no fear of being disturbed. Indeed, this was not a place where many would enter willingly as darkness fell, aside from jingoistic beliefs and the association with death, there were others who inhabited such places for pursuits immoral or illegal, all of which gave the ancient resting place an unfortunate reputation.

In the cottage opposite, after a short rest, Philip rallied and attended to matters in hand, lifting the large case up onto his knee. Releasing the belt from its commitment with vigour, he held the two sections of the case excitedly watching the contents disgorge and fall willy-nilly onto the floor, where they formed a large pile of small wooden sticks. The old man peered inside several times to ensure the case was empty – satisfied his hard-earned consignment was safely gathered in. He threw the empty case down dismissively in the corner and bent forward, collecting together handfuls of matches, contentedly spilling them through his fingers onto others that were in the grate already piled high; now the game began. He teased two dry unused matches from his hoard abrasively against one another and to his pleasure both ignited. He played with the matches as any schoolboy might, spreading the flames amongst the scattered pile. Poking, coercing and carrying flames on lighted spills to encourage a glorious glow, his wizened face wrinkled with delight as each in turn ignited, spreading the escaped flame haphazardly about the room.

Philip, now weary, slid down off his chair, landing heavily but untroubled onto the floor. Settling himself firmly down onto the boards, close to the fire with his feet under him, he rested on one elbow preoccupied with digging deep into a patched pocket of his serge overcoat. His grimy fist struggled for that expectant touch in the depths of his pocket, where finally he retrieved the prize of the day. Although the sole occupant of the room he made play of checking to ensure his prize was safe. Always suspicious he might be subject to another's envious gaze, he slowly raised the brandy bottle up to his line of sight and, seeing its welcome shape, relaxed with anticipation. It had fitted easily and safely into his pocket, his face now mellowed to a smile savouring the warmth to come. He stroked the rounded shoulders of the bottle with reverence, its shape, unmistakable for quality, left him wondering at his luck. For once he had restrained himself, saving such a find for later – no one could steal it now, he thought. Holding it up at arm's length against the flames, the amber colour glowed with an exciting rich hue, flickering with desirability. It must have been dropped by mistake he thought, for the bottle was full. Philip made much of the significance of opening a fresh, untouched bottle; pushing his head back he emptied a large consignment of the contents down his throat, as though there were no tomorrows. Although it was only a moderate sized bottle, the equivalent of a dozen nips, its quality assured the drinker of its worth. The warmth of the fiery liquid glowed within his mouth, the sting caught in his throat just enough to induce a sudden closure of passageways until he relaxed to allow its course down his gullet. The mature syrup provided what only such a distilling could, immediate succour to his weary frame. The neat brandy awash in his empty stomach had an instantaneous effect; he was overcome by a mellow complacency. As he sat watching the flames of the fire dancing across the bare walls, his whole being finally seemed at peace. The flickering light played across his collection that edged the whole room, piled high against every wall; thousands upon thousands of matches. The warmth of the precious liquid entering his body continued to evoke pleasurable feelings and, along with the dancing light from the glowing wood, it gave recourse to happy memories. His body succumbed to these feelings as he slithered down to lie flat on the bare boards, his eyes closer to the warmth and dancing light.

Lying half propped on an elbow, Philip casually threw handfuls of matchsticks towards the grate and in the process, unnoticed by him in his reverie, they fell about outside the foot of the glowing embers, leading a trail across the floor. Easing himself across the boards he moved ever nearer to his supplies and, grabbing large handfuls, held them above the flames in clenched fists, gradually releasing them to tumble through his fingers into the heated air. He watched them fall – in his mind's eye float – gently downwards and then as they were caught by the searing heat to burst into flames and then be consumed by the voracious appetite of the fire. Again and again in an increasingly frenzied effort he grabbed at more of his store and trickled, then threw, vast handfuls into the ever-growing furnace; appearing quite possessed. The fire grew and each scattered oddment began steaming and puffing, soon as they became superheated the sticks burst into flame, one after another. Philip in his glee consumed the contents of the bottle greedily until it was totally empty. As the inner warmth of best brandy took hold, the bottle slipped from his fingers to fall unnoticed on the floor. Careless, oblivious and with frenetic fervour, casting more fuel to the hungry flames, his efforts carried the marching fire out from captivity in the grate and across the floor into the room. Evans, already tiring and now frenzy spent, sank back onto his haunches in a happy state to admire the glowing inferno from the centre of the floor. Apparently unaware of the possessive nature of the fire and its dangerous encroachment, he lay back on the warm boards exhausted; with his eyes shut and shallow breathing he drifted. Through the closed lids of his eyes he watched the blurred dancing shapes cavort across the ceiling. His clothes heated and steamed as he fell into a not uncomfortable slumber. Whilst drifting into a comatose state, the flames greedily consumed both the floor and oxygen from the room, seducing him yet further into deep sleep.

Through the warmth that bathed his tired, aching body, Philip imagined luxuriant hills surrounding him in summer light. It caught the lids of his eyes as his mind filled with the images of rich colour from the deep south of Roussillon. He was travelling once again along the twisting narrow lane that hugged one side of the hill in southern France. Onwards and forever upwards, climbing steeply through the vine-clad slopes – across the valley – the partially derelict remains of a chateau, that guarded the valley's entrance from the south, standing spiky on its sunny knoll. The road levelled out towards the top, flanked by ancient stone buildings; a cluster of mediaeval dwellings that had protected the peoples of the hilltop village through the centuries. He felt the thrill, as he always had on the few visits he was able to make, upon seeing the hill from a distance, the hamlet steeped in history and encrusted with age, the wine and the heady clear air of mountain vista. He now felt the sun beat down on his head; it was very hot as he reached the crest. Then again the pleasure he felt driving to the edge of the village where the land fell away to the valley floor below. Parking, in his mind he wandered about, absorbing the memory of his first recollections. The neat rows dotted by vines absorbing the sun, and beyond to the foothills and the majesty of the Pyrenees.

Every time on arrival it had been the same slow ritual, a walk from the car to stand and gaze in awe at the world of savage beauty that rose and fell before him at every turn, until reaching the highest peak. How many times had it been since the first moment, he wondered and that lucky find of heavenly bliss. Being financially comfortable – his mother had left him more than sufficient for his needs – and equipped with a good education he had sought to widen his experience of life by taking more time for travel. It was on such a journey that he had climbed the hill in this wild corner of France to discover the little cottage that stood modestly amongst the trees, on the edge of the village which was to become his second home. Puzzled by the intense heat now troubling him, but unable to respond or move into the shade, concern registered in his mind; he had suffered severe sun stroke once before, when very young and inexperienced. Turning his head to avoid the direct light – it felt so hot – his eyes were now too heavy to open, and his limbs failed to respond.

Unbeknown to him a shadowy figure held briefly against the grimed glass of the window, its hand rubbed ineffectively at the dirt of ages. The intensity of the interloper's eyes – which peered through – held a cruel glint of satisfaction whilst attempting to assess the interior. The figure moved closer to the door, confident enough to enter the room until, startled by the power and intensity of the fire, forced to draw back hastily. A wry smile passed across his face in finding the whole floor being consumed rapidly by fire and there at its centre the prone figure of Philip encircled by flames. He also noted the piles of matches around the walls, which were blackened and smoking, this man who had waited his moment cheered dispassionately for his job was half done.

Pulling his heavy coat up tight to the neck and keeping his head down into the raised collar he entered the building, keeping tight against the edge. As he moved in he grabbed eagerly at the fuel as he went; finally bending down by the wall he managed to topple the vast collection of matches onto the floor. Moving quickly about the room he concentrated single-mindedly on working the tumbled sticks towards the centre and surrounding the immobile figure in a funeral pyre. Then retreating to the doorway, forced back from the crackling blaze, he rubbed at the singed hairs on the back of his hands. The flames lit a darkened corner by the doorway and, spotting the old man's case lying abandoned, he grabbed it in passing and lifted the battered, protesting article steaming into the air. Wrestling with its remains he made a bee-line for the door, the intense heat was overpowering and he felt himself succumbing to its persuasive call. Anxious to breathe fresh air he forced himself out beyond the furnace and, stopping briefly by the door, using the glow of the fire he looked inside the lid.

After a pause his face enveloped into a satisfied smile, the confirmation he sought was there at hand, his mission had been a success. He carefully removed a bulky envelope secured under the lid, held on by several dirty torn strips of sticky tape. There was no time for in-depth examination; merely a glance which confirmed the scrawled handwriting on it was in French. Pausing briefly, he reflected whether to look further, then tapping the envelope onto his palm he realised how the intensity had increased, the blaze was forcing him to leave the room. Standing briefly in the doorway, mesmerised by the inferno, he backed away, absorbing all the detail of the room as he went. Giving some regard to the prone form that was now steaming on the floor, he appeared momentarily lost in thought, as though family and its passing held some personal significance to him. A reflection that was not necessarily emotional but featured a written page of shared history. Then, placing the precious envelope carefully into his inside pocket, he looked back into the voracious flames now engulfing the room and as if to foreclose on the incident he hurled the case into the midst of it.

He shook his head as though to clear his involvement, and turning quickly away withdrew from the glare, the deed and possible discovery. Leaving the door slightly ajar, to re-oxygenate the room, he stole away, slipping into the shadows and security of night. Slithering and cursing, baulked momentarily by the brightness of fire, he stumbled on through the contrasting dark shadows of rubble piles. Making a hasty retreat the man, eager to join the path further on, no longer looked backwards; instead holding tight against the old city wall made good progress in the obscurity of darkness. The flames of the fire, firmly in control, engulfed the entire room and climbed steadily through the building's fabric, climbing up through the stairwell to the upper floor where it illuminated the street outside from the top floor windows. The flames and crackling, desecrating the sturdy walls of ages past, masked any cry that may have been uttered by its inmate. Someone, somewhere seeing the resultant glow had already made the call, the emergency services had been alerted and a siren was already playing its urgent appeal across the city wailing into the night air. The air crackled and spoke as the gathering blue strobes reflected on the billowing smoke stack. Flamed tongues licked the night sky, carrying paper debris, sparks and the last persecuted gasp of a renowned roadster swirling high above the ancient city ramparts.

Chapter nine

Cathar fire

Much higher and later – with the smokestack of yesteryear long since dispersed – a mixed assembly of people with great expectations of freedom and, more especially fun, sat tightly packed in a thin metal tube. The pilot eased back on the throttle control, levelling above wisps of white cloud at 35,000 feet; his reassuring voice broke through on the intercom. His refined laconic tone both reassured and welcomed the passengers to a pleasant flight of some two hours to Girona, in Catalonia. He continued with small details that might be of interest to the nervous, in particular noting a strong tailwind to speed the journey. One passenger, ex-Detective Superintendent Matthew Rawlings, relishing the thought and the need for solace after a traumatic first year's retirement, sat beside his wife Elizabeth, known affectionately to him as Beth.

Matthew's absorption had left him blissfully unaware of those sitting close to since take-off as he thumbed his way happily through a colourful booklet. The detailed photographs and illustrations espoused the attractions of the region, noting its turbulent history, sometimes in finite detail to a point of fascination and horror. It would seem to be a region of France that held deep secrets, in a wild sometime lost landscape where the traumatic beliefs of peoples had flourished and because of it were persecuted to extinction. He noted in particular the demise of a religious fraternity who died in the flames for their belief. Matthew, not a great lover of modern travel, finding the concept of flight a necessity, but also a regrettable intrusion into the realms of holiday and relaxation, found himself vexed at the quality and condition of the proposed flight. Having boarded the plane late, and ruffled by the lack of comfort in the seating, which for the most part was in need of some loving if not remedial care, he was now aware of a greater displeasure; the flight was priced to exclude in-flight food. For Beth's sake he had refrained from commenting, however the high acceleration and steep climb were not to his liking either, so burying himself in the book was a preferable alternative to souring the moment by voicing his disquiet.

The book was proving invaluable in distancing himself from the hustle and bustle and general discomforts of the flight; its contents had totally absorbed his attention. The reality was that the early hour, pre-flight journey and movement had taken hold, numbing his concentration enough for him to fall into a fitful doze. The awkwardly positioned sleeping partner had become subject to Beth's close scrutiny – she had been aware of his initial agitation and it didn't take much imagination on her part to realise what was mithering in his mind. She wished he had fallen asleep with better grace and certainly assuming a better position before doing so, stiff necks and backs were his forte. She watched him drifting into sleep and noted the changing sleep pattern, worried about his comfort; being very aware he may be having a bad dream or nightmare she had tried several times to rouse him without success. The confine of a packed charter jet was not the desirable place for a sudden nightmarish outburst.

o-0-o

Matthew for his part found himself enmeshed in a strange surreal world of graphic images that seemed to control his thoughts and insist that he continued along the journey with them. The images were vivid and uncompromising as he felt himself trapped within this strange bleak grey and unknown world. Tossing his head from side to side he was aware of angry flames licking hungrily at their sumptuous supply of dry wood, the mighty fire throwing great twists of whirling sparked demons skywards, as each heavy log collapsed into its white heart and was consumed.

The smoke-laden air trailed high and lifted on the rising breath of thermals, he watched it grip the rock stack on its upward journey, swirling free at the peak and blending into a blue haze that drifted downwind into what he could now see was a valley. As the plane flew onwards it met with turbulence and buffeted about; feeling the movement he too was flying free alongside great winged birds, the screeching rulers of this high domain. They soared along the valley wall and circled the solitary crag; Matthew, nervous and apprehensive and despite attempting to turn away several times, found himself unable to withdraw from the scene. Restless and anxious, through the smoke and noises below, Matthew became aware that they circled in an intense concentration above groups of people sitting huddled around their own small spluttering fires. This flight of death, for that was the feeling that now overtook him, a symbolic death scene within the ramparts of a castle on the peak itself. It was as if he was being allowed to witness a series of events in a trance-like state from which he couldn't pull back. From their lofty spire the occupants of the castle could see the columns of men, horses and supplies wending their way along the twisting narrow paths of the valley floor below; sounds from the base camp increased in volume with every new arrival. The incarcerated band within the confines of ancient stone had watched for days as the odd horseman then an odd fire here and there had increased in number until now the very earth trembled with the milling scene of devilment.

Matthew, having no power to withdraw or any feeling for the need to extinguish the world he found himself in, was drawn in by morbid curiosity, but more to the point he felt for a given purpose; as if summoned, frighteningly or commanded to watch and comprehend a moment in time. Below many horses could be heard as they whinnied in confusion, metal clashed and smoke from the numerous fires billowed and spiralled upwards leaving a bluish hue in the now chill evening air that rippled perceptibly in circles around the outer wall as if encasing those unfortunates above. The perimeter wall that marked the edge to their temporary sanctuary had been cleverly constructed so that it mimicked the colour and texture of the rock upon which it sat, leaving its very existence a questionable matter to the onlooker from afar. The ramparts of the walls sat on the very edge of the abyss, continuing the line of the peak ever upwards reaching to the sky. Imperceptible from below even the crenulated tops were obscured from the valley floor.

The inhabitants of this fortress refuge on its high peak, in dress and attitude of simple peasants clung desperately to their beliefs as they huddled around their dying fires in the courtyard. They were all too aware now that their cause, way of life and regional identity would soon dissipate when their security was breached, as inevitably it would be. With every increase in activity that echoed around the valley floor, they were reminded of their date with destiny that must surely come soon. They huddled together looking for reassurance from their lord and master; his chosen path of perfection had led them to this lofty peak and the attentions of the knight crusaders below. What had seemed to them to be a perfect refuge, impregnable and too obscure to concern those who opposed them and their beliefs, had become the centre of interest to Rome and the French throne.

Matthew felt their isolation and shook at the sadness of their plight; he moved uneasily in his seat. He could see and feel their despair and hardship; hunger occupied their minds, it had been many days since a meal had passed their lips. Somehow, he already knew their story, its narrative, the players and the dreadful conclusion that would be reached as he watched totally captivated by the drama. Abandoned by all, even '*friends*' who knew the paths and had looked to their welfare so well, now mysteriously they too no longer appeared and the supplies that remained were at a dangerously low level. They were sorely weakened by hunger, and although they were not marching the psyche of their plight told hard in their despair.

The need for warmth had exposed more of their presence with every tree that fell from the surrounding defences. They had gathered together on this peak once before and held the siege, when the hordes below had not the will to wage a war of attrition, but had chosen instead to seek easier victories elsewhere on the plain. This time however the noisy air reflected the determination of the assault and the defenders shuddered, knowing that the Crusaders were strong, brutal and would exert their will upon them, whatever the cost. Horses, soldiers, supplies, the build-up was relentless, it played on the minds of the believers, whose fatalistic acceptance of what was to come now filled them with numbed terror affecting their state of grace.

In contrast the arriving horsemen below sensed victory, the optimism permeated through the camp with its bustling activity, the onset of winter was in the air, they would be glad to be free of this place and back in the lands they knew, among their own kind. Matthew, only too aware of the outcome, wished to depart as he watched the scene unveil – a foreboding rested heavy on him – but he also found himself totally absorbed, somehow he was meant to bear witness. He could see all the people, all the places, and understand only too well what was happening.

Such an obscure refuge relied heavily on goodwill from those who would protect and aid with food and supplies and as the rewards had dwindled and the dangers had increased, so too the supplies had all but ceased. The secret supply routes which crossed the undertow of the rock face and meandered in and out of cave entrances to appear yet higher and on other faces, would only remain secret whilst the believers commanded respect for their beliefs and, more relevant, showed tangible proof of their wealth. The remaining treasure held in trust by the believers had now been buried away from human eye, before the final assault, its whereabouts known only by one trusted follower who had been smuggled away days before the grip of steel had tightened. He carried the sign in the folds of his garment; a golden bee which would elicit help and rally the faithful again in another place. For although the peasantry in the region were for the most part believers and passionate separatists, there were always those who held worldly goods in greater acclaim than spiritual reward.

Matthew's attention was drawn and forced to concentrate on figures around a fire; he was surprised and unnerved to see how close he had been allowed to come, almost touching the leading players, close enough to see and hear everything. The leader of the group stood slightly apart, his gaze centred on the fire and he appeared to be absorbed in thought. Other knights stood in a group together on the opposite side hugging the embers of the blazing fire, one of them called across the flames.

"My liege! This is the man who says he knows." The commander of the knights turned from his thoughts and the warmth of the bright embers; still clutching the remnants of a leg of roasted bird in his gloved hand, he wiped his grease-stained chin with his gauntlet and beckoned the man forward into the firelight. A wind gathered as the man stepped into sight, sparks from the fire spun off into the night encircling him as he stood awestruck in the presence of one held with such fearsome reputation. The knight beckoned for him to come closer – in a manner that suggested to the simpleton that he had the personal ear of conspiracy, then the powerful lord spoke to him, quietly.

"Well, what is it you have to tell? You can tell me, but be quick for I have much to do and I do not intend to fail in my cause, we have the Pope's blessing, it is God's work we are about."

The man's eyes sat wide, he was a simple farm hand from the village, the weapons, armour and language were strange to him, he stood open-mouthed and hesitant at the power of the words. The great knight wearily looked to his staff for the manner in which to deal with the simpleton. One who had travelled far and seen much in the knight's company touched his money belt, the meaning of which the knight knew only too well. A leather drawstringed purse appeared and he opened it; the informant's eyes widened in the firelight as he saw wealth beyond his dreams. There were golden coins, he licked his lips salaciously and could not look away from the gleaming promise as the knight spoke to him again.

"You have travelled these paths and know them well?"

"Aye sire."

He replied with cunning as he bobbed up and down in submissive cowering, a smile formed on his rustic face, as he savoured the rewards in his mind.

"You have seen the chateau above?"

Beaming at the simplicity of the question and being lulled along by the interrogator's ease of manner, his wit was unable to consider the implications of it, so preoccupied was he with a gold reward. He replied with bright confidence, this time without bowing, he remained steady.

'How soon these simple men forget their servility,' thought the knight.

"Aye sire, many times!"

"Yes of course, you helped with food and things. It must have been difficult for you travelling such dangerous paths, being laden so at the time?"

Sensing a twist in the questioning and being aware of them all standing watching him in the firelight – though the changing mood was too subtle for his simple wit – his natural animal cunning and survival mechanism identified sudden danger to him. He shifted uneasily on his feet; he could not leave, but he walked through the motions on the spot. The knight, with a wry smile on his face – he cared not for informants – moved intimidatingly close to the man's unwashed face. A display was made of the blade of his knife, it glinted menacingly as he cut descriptively into his meat and tugged flesh from the bone, eating it with relish. Narrowing his eyes, the knight turned his lips close to the peasant's ear and spoke in a harsh voice, menacing every word.

"If you have fed and watered the heretic, then perhaps you should do the same for the flames of his fire!" The man fell instantly to his knees, trembling and wailed,

"Nay sire, I… I just saw the others, I watched them only. I took no food – or anything, I only saw."

His voice trailed away as the knight raised his gloved hand for him to stop, and in the same movement beckon one of his council forward to deal with this despised creature: informer. Much as he needed the information, the treachery left the knight ill at ease, for the whole crusade was marred by disloyalty. Rivalries, which left him on many occasions wearily forced to defend his rear, whilst at the same time driving forward into the attack. He passed his final comments before dismissing them all to turn to other matters.

"Watch him closely! Nothing must befall – our friend – whilst he is in our employ!" With an ill-humoured sneer he expressed in a loud voice his contempt for the objects of his campaign. "He is the key, to the Saintly Kingdom above!"

Amidst the roar of approval from his followers the knight turned disdainfully away, casting one golden coin into the dirt at the peasant's feet as he did so; his lineage and its future success hung on creatures such as he, the knight knew he would not forsake this place again until full repentance had been gained, or the fires had had their fill.

Strength and reputations hung in the balance on the slopes of this soaring rock. The heretics had fled the plains and towns had fallen to the sword, yet until these far corners had been cleansed, stories would persist and balladeers would sing of the Perfect Ones: uncertainty would abound. The house of De Montfort had travelled far in the great crusade against the Cathar heretic, but the closing acts were proving irksome and difficult and leading to veiled criticism in whispered corners. His final rewards would be high in prestige, with his spiritual leader the Pope and more importantly with the King, having subjugated much land to the throne of France. With confiscated lands that were now considered his own to use as he pleased and the wealth accumulated therein, what was there to lose? Absolution from the Pope covered all the atrocities and necessary punishments meted out by his over-zealous soldiers. Only the time now concerned him, the pleasure of power and authority, so far denied to him, hung on these miserable wretches above. It seemed to him that the end to the whole wretched chapter of history now lay in his hands. The obstinate persistence of such people in obscure corners of inaccessible valleys must be broken and where religion and nationalistic fervour held sway to resist the larger order, then they must fall for a greater nationhood. Troubled by the image of failure and wearied by a long campaign, he pulled his cloak about him and watched the destructive flames, whose pointed fingers reached skyward for their victims; he shivered despite the heat as he felt its anger singe his own flesh.

Chapter ten

Down to earth

Restlessly he tossed his head, the flames obsessing his mind as he became consumed by the passions presented to him so graphically. Feeling uncomfortably hot, his light breathing running to frantic, rapid gasps, with an awareness of tugging on his arm, his body had started to fall. He struggled and lashed out with both hands as the sensation continued. The whining wind was unlike any storm before, its high-pitched note, invasive and penetrating deep into the interior of his mind; he heard his name being called over and over again. Concentrating on the sound, it was a voice he knew and it was getting louder and more persistent.

"Matthew! Matthew! – Calm down! – Come on for goodness sake wake up, we're here. It's time, stay with it! We're about to land."

His eyes opened and in the waking moment the flames were extinguished, soldiers, horses, all were gone; all that remained was the high whine. No longer the wind blistering the rock face and fanning the hungry flames, but instead a constant sound of jet turbines throttling down and the cold whistling wind playing over the aerofoils on the wings' extremity. Aware of the restlessness of people around him, seeking bags and companions, the constant high-pitched whistling stayed locked in his mind as the plane, angled in steep descent, dropped through the darkness of a Spanish night into Girona airport below. Twice the tired plane touched Spanish soil; it kicked and shrugged objectively skywards to return and grip the tarmac with renewed vigour, finally resigning itself to taxiing obediently towards the disembarkation point. The equally tired crew sighed as they prepared to assist their charges with the chaotic jostling of customs and baggage retrieval. For them there would be little respite before the journey back, carrying a suntanned cargo homewards, quietly burdened with the prospect of returning to the realities of life.

Following the hiss from the doors the tightly-packed contents of the bus alighted from the strap-hanging bus connection. Brought to a halt suddenly on the curve, leaving the vehicle swaying indignantly, the multitude peeled out aimlessly into the terminal building. Moving forward by rote as it threaded its way towards the gun-on-hip officials, a sight which always in Matthew's mind confirmed the freedoms of home, they poured onward towards the uniformed security who stood at the barrier. The hour and menial task on hand giving rise to indifference, as their disinterested gaze considered the surge of crazy tourists, who should have been back home in their nice warm beds in England, instead of annoying them at such an hour in the baggage hall. Milling through the gap everyone stood numbly and compliant; their tired eyes peering for prized cases full of risqué dresses and creams to oil the over-exposed flesh. Watching the circling cases as they made their second pass, their prospective owners, sleep-starved and travel-weary, failing at first to recognise the coded ribbons and symbols which identified them, finally grabbed the boisterous cargo, pushing aside fellow passengers as they did so, eager to be on their way.

The monotony of hanging about caused Matthew's mind to drift yet again, his eyes still open but vacant, picturing shapes and images, a hill, horses, fire, where? He closed his eyelids hard squeezing the thoughts out, the pictures were relinquished but something remained, a mood, a feeling, an unease, what was happening to him; his name, there it was, his name being called again.

"Matthew! … Oh for goodness sake grab that one will you? Come on love, Matthew, snap out of it, come back here from wherever you are, I'm just as tired as you! I need a hand."

Beth was standing close by, anxiously pointing to a large suitcase coming into the final straight, there was an angry edge to her voice.

"The big black case with the red label and tassel on is ours. Okay!"

She glared at him hoping for a response.

"When it comes past grab it, it's far too heavy for me to lift!"

The nausea, confusion and anonymity of the night flight left him enfeebled, unable to shake himself back to reality. Feelings of continuous travel persisted, there were strange shapes marking time in his mind, the unfinished page of drama was undiminished, its images vivid yet somehow indistinct as it hovered somewhere close, reluctant to leave. He had been seriously unnerved; it was all too close and too real, but how? Matthew decided it would be in his best interest to keep his eyes open from that moment on, as his wife nudged him again, this time with her elbow.

"There it is, please, now grab it then we can go."

She sighed loudly, mainly for effect, then doing what she was good at assessed the need objectively, by summing up.

"I'll drive, until you come round!"

There was a pause, as she looked hard at him.

"You know only one tablet was necessary, you haven't used them before! Why this time?"

Though he heard his wife's voice and comprehended what it was she was saying he remained silent with no response, too deeply troubled by inexplicable illusions. England was left far behind yet somewhere out there phantoms of the past were massing, it left him very uneasy. Pushing the trolley out, as always across a busy roadway to the car park, Matthew eagerly sought sight of the hire car that would take them over the mountains to paradise. The crowds were now visibly thinning as many boarded coaches whilst others more independent drove away into the night. Using unknown vehicles on strange roads had the effect, initially, of causing the drivers to cling to the white line adjacent to the kerb – gripping it as if a white stick in an unseeing land – until they became bold enough to let go. When the sun arose the following day it would be in destinations exotic, for their fourteen days 'absentia'. Beth had driven in Spain before, so after paper signing, petrol deposits paid, he just lounged back into his seat letting the world go by as his wife drove confidently onto the perimeter road to leave the 'Aeroport' system.

It was a small white, nondescript vehicle, about which Beth commented positively across to him saying 'purrs like a sewing machine', not that she was terribly familiar with such things. He relaxed and was instantly overtaken by the warmth of night as his eyes fluttered, succumbing to sleep, but just as quickly to be awoken suddenly with the uncomfortable feeling of being hurled forwards. The vehicle appeared to be tumbling sideways as it veered dramatically. He opened his eyes wide, his mind alert, just in time to see bushes rush past the windscreen as his wife gasped out loud in anguish.

"Damn the… what the hell do you think you are playing at!"

Beth's distress was obvious as she cursed out loudly to someone or something he could not see. He was aware of her desperately trying to control the vehicle, which had by this time bounced up the kerb and onto the grassed bank. Sitting helpless beside her, not knowing what was happening, he felt the vehicle's movement as it drifted awkwardly sideways for a few metres before coming to rest with a final jolt. The vehicle stopped its travel against the post of the entrance sign 'Bienvenido'; it was their first sighting of a palm tree, sitting beyond the sign unperturbed in the headlights of the car, in the well-tended garden. Matthew shook his head and parted from the final remnants of sleep to look at his wife with concern, quietly seeking an explanation.

"What happened Beth? That was quite something."

"I don't know…"

Beth sat dazed, her speech fizzled out while she considered the incident, then with a vitriolic outburst uncommon to her she registered her disbelief.

"Some idiot in a white car… same as ours I think! Crossed in front of us, wrong-siding us and leaving me no option but to take evasive action. I had to swerve to avoid them… and that's how we landed up on the grass verge."

She was angry with them and herself, always having prided herself as being a safe and capable driver, especially in foreign lands. Then, as if trying to find an excuse for the erratic driving she looked directly at him and forcefully concluded,

"We would have collided if I hadn't!"

Beth looked out into the night, attempting to pinpoint the culprit, but the road had suddenly emptied, leaving her with a feeling of dejection as she mumbled,

"Sorry love."

"Did you see the driver?" enquired Matthew.

"No! I don't think so, it all happened too quickly. There was just a blur to one side; I caught the movement out of the side of one eye. It was all so quick I was forced to swerve then… then they were gone. But they were travelling far too fast, you'd think they'd wait until they had become used to the roads, at least before going for speed!"

Aware his wife was shaken by the experience, he took her hand in his and squeezed lightly.

"Are you okay? – Would you like me to drive for a while?"

Matthew, concerned at his wife's flushed face, sat patiently while she gathered her thoughts; he was himself well awake now.

"No. – No I'm just angry… that's all! But I shall be all right, you go back to sleep, I shall need a break later."

Within a few hundred metres they had joined the 'Autopista' heading for the border and 'La Francia'; the steady purr of the engine and the rocking motion as they sped along lulled him to sleep once again, although fitfully, always waking just before they held him. Whoever they were? He could see shapes again, but the faces remained indistinct. Their costume was very strange, yet, somehow it was more than a dream, they seemed to know he was there; encouraging him to watch and bear witness.

Knowledge of the mountains of the Pyrenees and of their existence, being aware of their physical presence did little to express their grandeur, without visible contact. The thrusting rocks soaring skywards and the awesomeness of them was completely lost in the inky blackness. The darkness of night cloaked the undulating landmass with the headlight beam gripping the tarmac as the car dropped to the valley floor; unhindered they crossed the frontier and headed towards the distant twinkling lights of habitation. The troubled journey calmed with the prospect of respite as they swung onto the slip road with the headlights catching glimpses of the white chevron signs and finally a push box communication panel, 'PHONE HOTEL', the notice was simple and explicit. They were thankful that no voice responded to the call of the pressed button, but were relieved when the long galvanised gate eventually rolled sideways beckoning the weary travellers into its secure domain. The road followed round in a loop through successions of different coloured oleanders, glimpsing here and there the bark of parasol pines, to finally stop at an illuminated entrance on the rise, there was a small car park adjacent where they parked. It was late and the detail of terms and price no longer seemed relevant, only the urgent need for a place to lay one's pounding head, put the wearied mind to rest in order to drift from the journey-worn day, but inevitably there were procedures to be attended to.

"Bonsoir monsieur! Vous avez une chambre pour deux personnes?"

The Frenchman at the small desk with a reading lamp glowing over an opened book looked up and with disdain,

"Quel jour, monsieur?"

The question seemed irrelevant at such a late hour; it must be obvious that they needed a bed now he thought. However, preferring to avoid altercations and wishing to avoid an excited person speaking in colloquialisms, which would have achieved little, Matthew responded to the obvious.

"Pour ce soir. Pardon, maintenant, s'il vous plaît!"

"Ah! Oui monsieur, un lit deux places, ou deux lits?"

Having agreed to one large bed and, through the tiredness peak, to take 'petit-dejeuner' sometime earlier than imaginable that same morning, he bade the man goodnight. His tired frame pulled the two heavy cases along and up the double staircase, it was always up he thought, when carrying excessive weight, there never seemed to be a down or along. His wife followed on obediently and in silence with the incidental hand luggage, coats and flight bags. They moved together as automatons along the ill-lit passageway in order to find rest and succour in this blackened, unknown land. Whilst climbing the stairs their exasperation increased when the auto-timing light closed down on them as they were passing the 'BOIRE FRAICHE' dispenser glowing in the recess. Together they summoned up just enough change to select a single tin, which crashed noisily into the slot below. Disbelief at the cost of such simple fare left them angrily thinking it was probably twice the price of such drinks at home. It was, they knew, equally unlikely that they would have contemplated drinking fizzy orange at one in the morning back home, but their dust-laden throats gave them no alternative and somehow it was just like nectar. The shower was a step too far as they tumbled into bed together and despite their abject tiredness joined as one, relishing each other's generous warmth. It was as if expressing the need for reassurance after a troubled start to their vacation. The world of problems they had left behind for a brief time slowly drifted away as their breathing patterns became gentle and even.

The babble of people discoursing in different tongues, along with the sound of car horns being applied without mercy, broke their reveries of the night. Rolling out of bed at an hour, after glancing at his watch, he considered being indecently early, Matthew peered around the thick curtains. With tired pinched eyes braced for the light he was greeted by the sharp bright cut of southern sun, together with the gentle warmth of early morning bathing across his now closed eyelids. Tired or no he could not resist the swell of excitement of just being there. Through half-closed eyelids he could make out the distant edge of the mountains framing the horizon and the rolling swell of the Corbieres in the foreground, cloaked in forest and vine. He could comprehend the beauty of the hotel's situation for skirting the edges of its hotel grounds green fronds of pine shone bright with colour, their brush-like arms laying texture on the land. A persistent grey haze tinged with blue held the viewpoint, whilst beyond, through the moisture-laden air, taller biscuit-brown rocks of the foothills caught the bright light of day, throwing their contours into sharp relief. He stood mesmerised, unable to pull away from such a beckoning landscape, he knew their holiday had truly begun.

Breakfast – set appealingly on the terrace, within the partially glazed foyer for the hotel – provided an amenable hour of humour and good food, shared alongside two other couples and their young families. One woman, far from self-conscious – doting on the antics of her offspring – revealed a particular adept skill with a hovering spoon. Her motherly intuition gauging play – should the laughing mouth open just long enough – produced strange noises and gurning faces to amuse the little ones at her table and in turn the strangers alongside. Finally, when the anarchy of mealtime was over and the families had departed Matthew sat quietly in the alcove with his wife; it was peaceful and gloriously warm as they relaxed together. Allowing the sun to wash over them they sat contentedly looking across the valley towards the peak of Mount Canigou, impassive on the skyline, a sacred symbol to the Catalan heart.

In less than two hours they were both feeling elated as the little car bounced happily along the country lane to approach the tiny intersection of the crossroads. Just below the rise, at the edge of rough moorland and the first sighting of the morais, which continued for several kilometres up to the Montagne Noire, were two tiny insignificant roads which crossed the main St Pons- Narbonne road. At least that's how the ill-informed would see it, but to those with inside knowledge, the roads were full of wonder and delight as they carried the traveller into the region of Minervois; a land of ripening vine and limestone outcrops. They gleefully turned right, being lunchtime, not a car or person was in sight; it would be another four hours before the land re-awoke from the magic spell of siesta. This was it, so very special, despite the journey, lack of sleep and anxious preparations, all of which paled into insignificance with the thought of paradise approaching. The turning right, which they sought, finally came into view; they turned into the lane that dropped immediately into a boulder-strewn dirt track below. This followed alongside a vineyard to the right and finally petered out into a small field, in the corner of which was a large a patch of watermelons. Only a matter of metres along the lane they turned left into the grounds of their holiday home, driving slowly along the gravel-covered track towards the house flanked by fig trees and exotic blossoms. In amongst the trees, dotted here and there the familiar sprays of water already dispensing the lifeblood of the garden, pumped in daily from the riverbed beyond its lower reaches. Driving slowly forward they savoured every yard, at the end of the drive of fine chip it widened into a parking circle in front of the house, where they finally pulled to a halt.

By the side of the house their friend's old camper van, a relic of the past and now in retirement, sat gathering dust under a lean-to carport supporting a wild profusion of wisteria. The vehicle had served the old couple well over the years on their many journeys around Europe as they gathered memories and more especially seeds and plants, many of which now featured in the packed displays of mature trees and shrubs that the wonderful garden boasted. And the van decommissioned long ago now served as an affectionate memorial, a metal sculpture in homage to their collection.

"Matthew! There's a note! … It says they have left a meal on the table." She sighed with pleasure. "They are thoughtful, it's our first *'salad Niçoise'* of the holiday, all garden produce duly noted of course!"

Beth galloped off to the house, excited to be back. It was a safe haven and well liked by them both, they knew the district, drank the wine in pleasurable quantities, swam in the pool and occasionally stirred to 'sight-see' something new. The village was a sleepy mediaeval hamlet built of greying stone many centuries before, as all the tiny hamlets in the area appeared to be, a strong mentality of 'there's always tomorrow' prevailed. Close to the border with Spain and at one time subjected to its rule the ways of mañana were ever strong. The voices and music that barked from speakers high in the avenue of limes each morning were the only disruption to this near idyllic life and even then, it was usually a message concerning the imminent arrival of food, the fishmonger, baker, shoe or meat vans assembling on the village square overlooking the river. Nothing really disturbed the equilibrium of the village's ancient twisting lanes that weaved in and out between houses erected during the middle ages, at a time when no thought was given to vehicular access. As if an announcement was necessary, each village in the locale was clearly marked by the magnificent avenues of mature plane trees on the approach roads, many resulting from Roman occupation. The giant camouflaged bases stretched out into the countryside forming colonnades of beckoning fingers to welcome travellers into the heart in order to provide succour to their needs with local cuisine and fine appellation wines.

By the time Matthew had reached the house – struggling with the over-loaded case – finally dumping it at the foot of the stairs amidst the strong sounds of splashing water, Beth was already screeching joyfully as she leapt in and out of the pool. He smiled as he looked on, her inhibitions gone as she pranced naked around the pool; amused by her carefree antics Matthew noted her sun-cheated white skin which in two weeks would mellow to a golden coat to match her golden hair. Pulling the door to and wandering down to the pool's edge he sat contented on a stone by the pool, warming to the day and her enjoyment as she swam and played in the sparkling waters.

Chapter eleven

A brush with the past

The blotched pastiche of pastels, biscuit browns, olive greens, cream and greys, intermingled across the bark of the trees; the softly alluring patterns welcoming curious visitors into the lair. Mature plane trees standing solid, edging each side of the narrow approach road, so redolent of sleepy hidden France and its villages and this small corner was no exception. Overhead the great boughs joined harmoniously to spread across the road forming a giant canopy, under which the weary travellers gained brief respite from the heat of day. Wide of girth and bulbous based, the presence – obvious and status accepted – caused drivers to check and slow their vehicles, as the giant sentinels appeared to swell and narrow the gap on the twist of road before the first dwellings appeared in view. Midday had approached – a time when inhabitants of town and village in the deep south rested, announced by the faded shutters – now casually pulled to – coyly hiding the occupants within to retain their privacy from the casual glance of passers-by. The wooden slatted covers dressing all the windows, sun bleached and flaking, held the charm of yesteryear.

An old man sat seemingly contemptuous of the world on a reed-woven chair, he leaned backwards against the cool stone of the wall, guarding his door at the roadside from any would-be intruders. Leaning precariously against the rough rendered wall of his dwelling, the occupant sat shepherding his own duly protecting his domain in the noonday sun. He had acted as watch and guard for the sleepy hamlet for a number of years, protecting the community as if sitting on a rock above, calling when intruders approached. So the old man, face half covered by his beret, despite the fullness of the heat, sat resplendent in his worker's uniform of blue serge; the only compliance to the extreme temperature was the short sleeves of his blue cotton shirt. His face bore a laconic expression, registering life as he saw it and with a shrug of resigned diffidence that reflected his inability to change anything. Across his face the periods of hardship were etched deep into his flesh mixed together with a wry smile, for the moment restful shade excluded him from all demands for an hour or two.

Through the slits of his half-closed eyes, the old man absorbed the oncoming image of an approaching vehicle. Disgruntled by its presence, he shifted uneasily on his seat noting in his mind the manner of it. Driver, male: a thick shock of dark hair; light skinned and tall, but not Spanish; yet the number plate on the vehicle told him a different tale, it was obviously from over the mountain and thereby Catalan. Shaking his head slowly, the old man gathered a contemptuous mouthful of spittle ready to indicate his feelings to the world, but held back from an obviously displayed insult, preferring instead – whilst swallowing down his displeasure – to mutter to himself. It was a time to ruminate on old scores, broken trusts, folklore and to the

134

people of his village, matters of honour. Meanwhile frantic screaming of rubber from an abused grinding tyre bit its path sideways along a granite kerbstone and rent the air with a harsh pronouncement of the vehicle's arrival. The vehicle with its occupant careered wildly, cornering in a fashion guaranteed to raise eyebrows as it entered the square, scattering grit, and forcing dust to snarl upwards as if snorted from the nostrils of some wild beast. The old man again shook his head with disdain – it was confirmation to him that his assessment of the newcomer appeared perfectly correct. One who disturbed the tranquillity of his and this siesta driven corner of France must naturally be a mad outsider and as such was unwelcome. Just as soon as the dust settled down onto the now silent road, the old man – whose bottom had lifted off its seat in expectation of a fist-shaking sudden departure – relaxed his frame and lowered himself back down into place; hoping to resume his sojourn in the noonday sun.

Heated hubs of the dust-blown, hard-driven vehicle released their tension as the engine died from ignition denial and the abused metal box, eager for rest, fell silent. A stiff, un-oiled hinge on the driver's door broke the immediate silence, the raucous loud creaking rent the air as it opened with intermittent jerks, the rebound of sound echoing against the walls in the empty square as it released an encased tired occupant. The driver sat, initially relieved at the silence and then, struggling with the interior of a small car and his disproportionately large frame, attempted to extricate himself from it. His appearance was unnerving; with a face set hard with determination he carried the look of trouble, exaggerated by the unshaven grime of travel. Swinging his left leg out from the driving seat, the man uncurled his large form from the cramped space within. Then, pushing himself up to full height, which was well above the vehicle, he steadied himself against its roof with one hand; he stood looking about to get his bearings.

Stooping back down for a moment the stranger squatted on his haunches and reached across to the back seat, where from a bundle he withdrew a large sweat-stained hat; deliberately tapping the bundle in passing. After dashing the brim of the hat against his arm several times to free up some of the dust, he placed it onto his head where it sat, resting upon a thick mat of unkempt hair. In his younger days – and he was by no means old – he must have struck a formidable figure, but there was something about him now, brought about by age or experience, that questioned his motives. Maybe the eyes, which held an element of desperation tinged with cunning, giving the overall effect of menace. His eyes were large but despite this his appearance though perspicacious, the overall image was one of an appearance tainted by guile. His eyes, accentuated by the darkness of shadows beneath them, were the combined result of playing close to the wind in life and his recent excessively long drive. It changed the would-be humour of his face from goodwill to one of cynical distrust. Pushing his hat firmly down, he eyed the shop opposite; with his face supporting a grimace, a hard warning of intimidation to anyone who might cross his path, he strode out meaningfully towards 'le tabac' across the empty 'Place du Cloche'.

The shattering silence that had overcome the vehicle caused the remaining bundled heap – lying across the back seat – to stir and a dazed form of half-life to emerge. Lifting up with sleep-cheated eyes to peer over the window rubbers the occupant pulled a face of disbelief and puzzlement whilst watching the departing driver, now across the square and entering the small nondescript shop adjacent to the church. Eyes that held his fading image were dark – not quite black – but limpid-pool and large; they were set in an oval, almost colourless, yet flawless face. Through the left nostril – breaking a youthful perfect skin – were two gold rings, which cast a suggested warm glow of colour against the pale skin. Absent-mindedly a hand, with many rings on its fingers and bracelets jangling on the wrist, brushed at the loose strands of hair falling across her face. The action stopped whilst the figure eased itself upwards from the cramped confinement of the rear seat and stretched both arms and legs, twitching the numbed limbs back into life. A covering blanket fell away revealing a petite female form dressed in a crumpled, violet batik'd sweatshirt, which covered, but not quite concealed, an uncluttered breast form. The garment was short and rucked up from an enforced back-seat sleep, the stretching torso revealed at its base a rounded stomach with pierced bare navel. Adjusting her eyes to the light and geography the girl swung her jean-clad legs lazily down, in an effort to search with her toes for footwear. Her feet prodded here and there for a pair of black leather boots. Attempting to find the much-maligned footwear that lay crumpled on the floor, having been kicked off and abandoned the previous day, was proving to be an arduous task for her. Finally finding a toehold, then without bothering to look she struggled to pull the boots up onto her legs, falling sideways onto the seat as she did so. The girl opened the car door in much the same ungainly movement. Boots half on, and swinging her still sleepy, willowy form out of the vehicle she met the ground awkwardly, managing

137

to twist her ankle, enough to cause her to curse out loudly. Her travel-weary body sought its ailing blood supply to respond as she tapped feet and shook arms, anxiously looking around the village square.

Whilst going through the motions of escaping her confined space – having endured an unforgiving, bounce-ridden journey of hundreds of kilometres – she failed to notice that her companion had returned. As she withdrew from the vehicle to stand erect and get her bearings so he had correspondingly ducked and re-entered, sliding noisily across into the driving seat. In the mirror his eyes checked the surroundings for onlookers, then the road for vehicles; they were set in an uncompromising, determined expression. Casting a look rearward towards the back seat, the same eyes narrowed along with a sudden intake of breath, showing displeasure at the absence of his passenger. He slammed his door shut and turned the key simultaneously, igniting life into the tired engine. The girl, still standing dazed heard the noise with displeasure, looked skywards and moaned.

"Oh shit! Mark, where are you off to now? – I need a pee! We've been travelling all night, I'm busting! When are we gonna stop?"

She looked around at the empty square.

"I want food, and I want a darned good soak. What's the bloody rush all the time?"

She stood slouch-shouldered, eyeing the empty square with disdain, there was nothing as far as she could see to satisfy any of her now urgent needs; what made these people so different that they didn't need a loo or water to wash with. No boulangerie either. She commentated about this omission, barking in a tired, agitated voice.

"I thought it was law over here or something to have a *'bakers'* in every village!"

He looked across the car through the side window, which was partially open. Her bare midriff – which was clearly visible to him – with the golden down of hair pushed against the glass as she leaned hard on the door beckoning to him. Her waistline, slim and attractive, encouraged the eye to wander and examine a gold pin pushed defiantly through the tummy button. It was an area of pleasure, the soft down that had lured him into the hidden delights below. Normally the pleasure of such images – promising more in the form of participation than the distant art of voyeurism – would have taken hold and influenced his judgement, yet at that moment the sight of such a promise only annoyed him, causing him to respond fiercely. He spoke at her with a growl, sensing her belligerence; he was in no mood for an altercation, especially with such a young offbeat female.

"Are you getting back in the car or what? I've got business to attend to and it ain't around here."

Emily noting his tone, resisted commenting further but remained looking around in despair, the apparent absence of facilities that she needed – quite desperately now – was influencing her judgement and his manner was insufficient lure to persuade her back into the cramped rear seat of the vehicle. She bit her lip, no she would not be bossed around and certainly not cajoled – at least not just yet. The prospect of bouncing around on mountain roads without just cause was not in her opinion an attractive picture or one that her bladder – in its present delicate state – would particularly relish. She raised her voice, this time with sarcasm.

"Not till you tell me what's going on! I came with you 'cause I needed a break, and you said the Pyrenees... south of France... okay so far... remember? Sounds great! Beaches and things... or did I imagine it?"

Without giving credence to her outburst or physical needs he cut short her goading demands. He was riled and now spoke slowly in a calculated, exact manner, showing his obvious irritation and being openly dismissive of her demands. Continuing to put her down, his manner was harsh, displaying an element of menace in his voice, something, which she was not familiar with. At the same time – expressing his anger and frustration – he continuously revved the small car's engine, whilst fixing his eyes on the road ahead.

"I'm not 'faffing' around here anymore, there's somewhere I've got to go! And someone I've got to see! – If you stand in my way, I won't hang around waiting about, you'll regret it, you'll see! – Forget the beaches and things, until I've finished what I came to do!"

He growled threateningly at her stomach.

"Right! Then maybe we can relax! Are you understanding and getting in or?"

She continued leaning against the car door, both sullen and obstinate, not making any attempt to comply.

"No, I'm not. I want food, I wanna know what's going on!"

She stared at him defiantly.

"I'm not moving from here, till you tell me!"

Despite the absence of sleep and the distress of failing to respond to bodily functions – she changed tack and foolishly tried to look cute – bobbing down, looking through the glass at him, whilst making a lame attempt to pout. She pulled some of her long black hair across her lips, it was a foolish, futile gesture, for his intransigence was not to be broken and truth to tell in her unkempt condition, the allure was far from tempting anyway. Emily's tired eyes were anxious, it began slowly to dawn on her – as she pushed herself upright – that she knew very little about this man. He might well just leave her there. His aggressive attitude for the last two days or so had confused and latterly frightened her. She thought – foolishly now – that on the few occasions that they'd been out together, her assessment and judgement of men would stand her in good stead. But things were far from well, she found herself nervously anticipating being dumped in the middle of nowhere with no possessions. It all became academic as the realisation dawned on her that the vehicle was starting to move and that he was indeed leaving her to survive on her own.

"Oh Shit! Shit! Shit!" She cursed the air in exasperation as the car engine revved and the vehicle gained pace, shooting away from her touch, the door handle painfully knocking her thigh in the process.

"Wait!"

She screamed at him, then open-mouthed in disbelief watched as the car, following the narrow roadway between the pharmacy and the church, bobbed about then disappeared from her line of sight, to leave her in the deserted square overwhelmed, alone and panic-stricken in the silent aftermath.

As the distant hum of the engine became more indistinct, she glanced about, feeling the shuttered windows looking down on her in judgement; the silence of the strange village now closed in on her, leaving her somewhat frightened. There had been other trips to foreign countries, usually beach parties or a villa, not many locals involved, the ethnicity of this place unnerved her. She wondered how many eyes were watching from behind the dark recesses of the shutters. Looking up and down the square anxiously, Emily hastily grabbed her bag that he had thrown through the window at her, the only possession she had with her to survive. She ran hurriedly on in the general direction that the car had taken, hoping that he had just done it out of bravado and that he would be around the corner waiting for her. Emily shouted as she ran, hobbling along with boots still only half way up her legs, the noise was mainly to give her confidence a much-needed boost.

"Mark, Mark… wait you bast…"

Before uttering the final syllables the feeling of presence overwhelmed her, and the word died on her lips as she looked nervously about at the row of stone cottages. The intimidating half-closed shutters were like large ears turned to receive whatever she was about to say, feeding the unseen listeners who were sitting behind in judgement. Quickening her pace, with nervous glances back and forth, she ran anxiously on past the silent dwellings, until well clear of the last house and the village. Finally, with relief, finding she had reached the open countryside beyond the furthest cottage, Emily gave in to an overwhelming desire to collapse where she stood. Clear of the dwellings, she sat on the grass bank, panting and taking stock of her position. The vines hung with clusters of blue-bloomed grapes and although the pervasive silence still hung around her, the beauty of her surroundings softened the panic and gradually she managed to relax and breathe more easily, the bushes nearby would hide her and her call of nature and console her battered ego.

Against the side of the road on the greensward was a large sign. It was faded, as all wooden structures seemed to be, but the legend displayed on it was still legible. Pleasures and attractions of a village called 'Le Chateau St Jean' were still clearly visible, a large arrow encouraged visitors onward in the direction she was walking. Emily allowed herself to relax a little for in the distance she could clearly identify Mark's car, which could be seen hugging the bank as it climbed up the steep, vine-clad slope to the village on the hill. Emily sank thankfully down onto the grass bank and picked up odd stones lying around where she was sitting; her temptation to show violence towards him was relieved by throwing the stones out onto the road one by one; a curse was uttered with each stone as it bounced off the tarmac for the deed of deserting her in the middle of nowhere.

Mark Gower had travelled in many lands, wheeling and dealing as he passed through, exchanging property and currencies. It was his belief in free enterprise – he was not in his considered opinion, criminal – he was ever the opportunist entrepreneur. Most of his deals were at the expense of the host country, which he briefly visited during his enterprise, while denying them of some cultural or historical artefact. The rewards for this precarious occupation were very lucrative, for his customers paid handsomely for the rare, unique and unobtainable. He drove single-mindedly upwards through the grass-banked, hairpin bends that fell away to steep rock-strewn slopes down to the valley floor below. It was not a mountain peak, only rising to some 400 metres, but the lanes were extremely narrow, with few passing places. His haste would draw unwelcome attention to himself, a facet of life that he usually considered with great care when contemplating his survival; strangely this girl had riled him, when normally women did not feature highly in his personal arrangements.

His grip tightened on the steering wheel, concentrating hard on the thrill of swinging the machine into the bends and dropping down through the screaming gears to drive hard into the curves. The new tarmac road had no well-defined edge; it just petered out to grass from whence it fell away treacherously to dangerous drops. Across the valley on a similar hill, close by, stood the ruins of a chateau that once boasted to be the residence of the Fourth Grand Master of the Knights Templar; the driver had given it a cursory glance but failed to register its relevance. The long-suffering, overheated car, having gained the summit, nosed into a farmyard entrance at the approach to the hilltop village; turning off the ignition he sat for a moment, thinking out his next move.

England – where it had all appeared so simple, and the deeds controllable – seemed so far away now. Stone would be tucked up in the sheets, snoring the night away, comfortable in the knowledge that someone else was bringing the catch in. The old man – his uncle – clutching a suitcase full of matchsticks, everyone laughing at him. Stupid old fool, he thought sneeringly, why should I care, he was going to die anyway; he was asleep and didn't know what was happening. Gower was not given to caring or the consideration of process by which he made his gains; only the final outcome remained pertinent, marked as it was simply by his judgement of value gained against risk. He pulled a sheaf of stained papers from his wallet, the badly watermarked and creased papers, that had been carried for years inside the lid of the battered old suitcase, failed to excite the mind in their present state. The papers had been exposed to the elements every time the lid had been lifted and were now stained and in a bedraggled state, but they still signified the rights to possession for another questionable deal.

Mark Gower did however, despite his appearance, feel tired and ill at ease, it was the wrong moment to conduct a delicate business. The small car had cramped his frame for far too long, it had been two days since landing at Girona airport; time spent waiting for a given moment had become irksome. At first they had travelled along the coastal strip wherever possible in order to hide in holiday traffic. Then, although not wanted for any particular reason at present, they had struck a course inland through the Corbieres, it was as well not to be checked or noticed by officialdom en route, especially when involved in such a delicate matter. The day before had been spent on the move around the town of Figueres, a town with much to see and, as Emily had pointed out the land of Dali. But the intense negotiations had taken time, – food, sleep and rest had all become hostage to fortune in the process. He considered the girl's need of food and a damned good bath and conceded that both would be well received by him, but no matter; the smoke screen was now in place to confuse the authorities or whoever; he felt the odds were just in his favour for a calculated risk.

Sat in the vehicle he could see the approaches to the village, or hamlet as it was, for it only amounted to a small collection of stone buildings perched up on a hilltop. The narrow lane twisted left in a severe bend just beyond where he was parked; there was a small intersection with a farm entrance and to the left a rear approach to some dwellings. Beyond, on the curve, was a terraced row of ancient buildings; houses intermingled with an occasional commercial enterprise. Opposite, occupying much of the bend until the road surface petered out to a stone and clay mix – sat an ancient manor. It was formed by a collection of deep red, sandstone buildings, which abutted the road, quite unlike any others in the village. A barn, house and the castellated clock tower clustered together, standing sentinel at the end of the metalled road and guarding the open space beyond, which acted as the village car park. Centrally, amongst variously shaped divisions of dwellings, was a double fronted shop premise, the decor of which set it apart from any of its neighbours. He had agreed in the recent negotiations at Figueres not to directly approach the place, especially during daylight. Gower was however his own man, who gambled on his own judgement and with the wellbeing of others along the way when it suited him. The phone call he had made earlier had not welcomed the visit, in fact it had been positively rejected – but still, here he was!

He stood across the road opposite the front entrance, waiting and listening; the centrally placed door and window fascia held strong echoes of a golden age of 'Art Nouveau', but nothing moved. Their sweeping curves of wood edging the glass would, in normal circumstances, have defined elegance. The finely proportioned frontage however took on a surreal aspect, as the viewer approached for closer inspection, one would feel vaguely uneasy as the merchandise crammed into every corner shouted out with a sinister theatricality. A row of gaudily coloured candles, some depicting figures in grotesque stances, looked out and around the shop, incense sticks lay smouldering. Masks, statuettes and books, all displaying the same air of mystic connection together with complex treatises on Christianity, Eastern faiths and the occult, were piled up on all levels. At the front of the window, displayed individually, as a border around the edge of the glass, were large 'Tarot' cards, the grim reaper, hangman and other characters mocked the casual passer-by of which today there were none. In the quiet of the empty lane, the shop sat silently brooding its menace, daring the passage of feet to enter.

Gower stubbed a fictitious cigarette into the dust, signing the ground as if to mean business, then crossed the road, ignoring the intimidating contents of the window as he entered the 'Objets d'art! D'ancien'. Inside the shop it was gloomy, the smoke of incense increased the claustrophobic nature of the place. A young woman standing behind the counter in an alcove that lay just beyond the line of sight glanced up as if to speak. She smiled but before a syllable could be uttered she was distracted, leaving her mouth open in surprise as the proprietor, Henri Douchez, swept into the well of the shop, somewhat flustered and animated, emerging from the gloom beyond through the hanging screen. He tutted and waved to her dismissively amid gesticulations that she could remain where she was and watch the shop.

"It is alright, Denise, I will attend to the customer."

The uneasy pause was broken and as if to excuse his intercession he continued,

"The gentleman rang earlier – he is from England, you know."

A comment presumably meant to impress. She stood and watched as her employer, Monsieur Henri Douchez –

appearing ebullient – swept the screen aside with an exaggerated movement of his left arm, to indicate in the self-same movement for his customer to go on through. Denise, looking puzzled, reviewed the situation whilst she chewed for a moment on the end of her pencil. The appearance of her boss – in her opinion a small insignificant man – making such magnanimous gestures, was in itself strangely out of character, but to such a large and powerfully-built Englishman it then fell worthy of comment. Looking down at her counter she wrote something on a piece of paper, which she carefully folded and immediately placed into her bag.

Chapter twelve

A pool of ideas

When they awoke, the sun was strong; it shone with intensity, the contrast making whites too bright so that more than a glance hurt the eye, whilst at the same time throwing shadows into deep obscurity. The clear waters of the pool below danced and twinkled with a myriad of sunspots as the swallows screamed downwards, dragging their open beaks across the rippling surface to collect hovering insects. Matthew Rawlings opened the patio doors with relish and joined nature as he drank in the morning, England seemed so remote at times like this, he thought. His wife, sensing movement within the house, called out to him from the kitchen where a meal was well under way. It again was proof that they were away from home as they shouted out loudly to one another, not something to do in sedate England.

"Are you going out to the pool?"

"Yes, I think so, − it looks inviting," he remarked, turning his head in the direction of the house, then absent-mindedly and more to himself,

"I thought I might try the big toe test… at least!"

She had left the house and picked up on his comment as she approached, retorting playfully,

"Well, on the way to your major exertion, be a love and carry the tray out to the table will you, we can breakfast on the terrace. It's pretty well laid up and ready, is that all right?"

He shook his head at the teasing, enjoying the moment of companionship. It was one of many moments of contact lost through the, sometimes, arduous years of being a chief police officer in criminal investigation for the force. Collecting the tray – laden with its selection of compote, steaming coffee and crockery – he was pleased to carry it out to the table by the pool and turning his head as he went he raised his voice a little to reach the interior of the house into which Beth had recently disappeared.

"I think something is missing… you've forgotten the..."

Before he could finish, a movement at the doorway confirmed Beth arriving as on cue – clutching a long warm fresh baguette, together with a knife and board to prove him wrong.

"Some of us were up early," she looked across at him, pouting cheekily, "shopping in the village."

He raised his eyebrows in mock surprise and disbelief.

"Okay, I was woken up by the village tannoy –'Allo Allo,'" she mimicked, squeezing her nose to mimic the sound and then more reassuringly in a softly spoken voice she reconfirmed her love of the place.

"But I so desperately wanted to see the village again and feel part of it… early… you know, doing local things."

She turned to him dreamily.

"Watching them going about their business, shopping or just standing passing the time of day is… well, very comforting. It reminds me that wherever we go – language apart that is and the fact that all of us are different colours and sizes – we are still very much the same underneath!"

Beth bobbed down by the poolside, her skin already responding to the glowing sun as its warmth wafted over her, she sat purring with a feeling of wellbeing. Finally turning to him she gave him one of her broad, warm smiles, meant to reassure him that everything in the garden was very rosy. Having gauged his mood she ventured on, hoping he felt the same, as she voiced her aspirations and plans for the future, but very carefully.

"This place – I don't know – it gets into your soul. It's more beautiful every time we come."

She paused to assess his reaction and felt embarrassed by her lack of confidence, surprised that she even needed to bolster up her courage and yet she was equally pleased, realising that he was quietly smiling and listening to her every word. It was a moment of bonding, very precious to her, her reaction was to lower her voice and assume a more wistful manner.

"Matthew, how long is it since we've been coming here? – Three – four or six years! I can't remember, but why, after all this time, haven't we looked into investing in a little place of our own?"

She lowered the bread onto the table, hardly daring to utter further, Beth quietly wiped the palms of her hands on her pinafore as she looked away, waiting anxiously for a response; it was not long in coming and he surprised her totally by being wholly positive.

"We could certainly consider a second home, after all we have the money. It's ours to spend, as we have no…"

His voice petered off, realising he had unwittingly crossed into troubled waters and, quickly seeking to keep the conversation positive, expanded further.

"It's not beyond our means. If… if you would really like to?"

He continued to speak, fully aware of her warm acceptance and duly noting the coy smile that had crossed her face with obvious approval for what he had to say.

"Perhaps while we're here we could have a good look round and see what the options are… there's a vendor in the village where we could start and… if you still feel the same way at the end of the holiday, we could – just maybe – make arrangements to return soon and take a really serious look at something we fancy!"

Beth beamed; it was indeed what she really wanted.

"Do you really mean that, Matthew? Are you serious?"

"Of course. I agree with you, it's time. After all we come here so often, it's like a second home to us anyway. We know the people in the village, the scenery is perfect and the food excellent and there's still plenty of places to explore, so why not?"

They both fell silent, not wanting to spoil the mood as they held their own counsel on a dream yet to be fulfilled. They exchanged warm smiles every now and then, content to say nothing that would break the spell.

This year in fact they had thought of alternatives, destinations further afield, anything rather than face the obvious that they were both decided and afraid their decision would be met with ridicule. It was only the last minute availability of the villa that had somehow honed their minds to distinct possibilities, a moment of serendipity that could not be ignored. The subject of a holiday home had been much talked about over the years, but never clearly defined. The conversation had always managed to skirt around making positive decisions. The job or some other controlling factor was as always his distraction with a case in the offing, or an enquiry, which travelled with them as a constant companion. To Beth, it left her husband frustratingly distant so that an optimistic opening always finished with the same disappointment. She had always found the conversation exasperating and her agitation at his intransigence, disheartening. Matthew simply became dismissive, electing to stick to a train of thought that was both illogical as it was unhelpful, always stating negatively, 'It's a big world out there!'

Where out there was, she never really knew, it was yet another smokescreen to hide behind. It was true to say that neither of them seemed to have quite the courage – up to now that is – to take the plunge and truly adopt a second base and, with some effort, language. Reality lay in the fact that this southern-most, uncluttered, wild and people-free corner of France was a favourite for them both and perhaps now the time was right when they should be honest with themselves and make a firm commitment. Beth – not wanting to spoil her initial success – encouraged Matthew, using the wiles of women; to subtly change the direction of his thoughts by finding out what it was he wanted to do this trip. Knowing full well that he had a particular interest in the hills of the Corbières, along with its history, she prompted him,

"Do we still go on pilgrimage to the land of the Cathars as you planned? I thought perhaps tomorrow we could jaunt out somewhere? After picking up that guide in England, the castles look worthy of an attempt at least, they are nearly all in this area sitting on the tops of mountain peaks... pretty inaccessible by all accounts. But I think it's still possible to get up to see some of them or maybe most of them. Though I'm the first to admit that a pile of rocks is not a truly absorbing subject to me, I imagine the view alone would make the effort worthwhile?"

Matthew appreciated her compliance with his holiday agenda; noting that she was happy to make the effort, indeed promised to visit as many castles as possible during their stay.

"I'd like that Beth very much, it means a fair bit of travelling though! Are you really up for it? I'm sorry... I mean are you sure you want to travel that much? They're not really very far away, any of them, but there are no straight roads as such, it's all... as you'd expect with mountains, up and down so-to-speak."

Beth could feel indecision looming and was anxious to set the seal on the conversation.

"C'mon Matthew, I said I wanted to go, so let's just plan tomorrow and get on with it!"

Matthew, relieved that his holiday plans were going to work out, moved from the pool and made his way into the garden. It was perhaps the only difference between them at times like these, his character and years of disciplined, demanding work left him with an inability to calm down and relax when the moment arrived. Beth on the other hand needed to totally let go on holiday, to recharge her batteries; there was usually an understanding, which relied heavily on her ability to compromise. He wandered down the gentle slope past three rows of tomato trusses leaning heavily on bamboo canes, the jewel-like cherry fruits he noted desperately needed harvesting, with the canes hanging at obtuse angles. He made his way with difficulty on through the garden to the river's edge, finding the paths of last year were less accessible, the three acre site, now almost edge to edge with trees, presented a profusion of blossom and fruit. The river though, was strangely quiet at the foot of the bank, normally, the water splashed the rocks to continue downstream but there was just a mere trickle. The reeds were parched – no rain for a while he guessed. In previous visits, the district headquarters of the 'Sapeur-Pompiers' across the basin on the opposite bank of the river, just visible through the undergrowth, had been stretched to breaking point. Long hot summers, leaving hillsides tinder dry with their resin-rich pines always eager for flames to complete their cycle making the land vulnerable. Aircraft, flown from a military base nearby, released water bombs continuously over the impenetrable maquis of the hinterland. To cope with the hillside blazes, helicopters would fly in constantly to the small landing strip opposite at HQ, where spotters and fire fighting personnel were flown out to the inaccessible terrain to fight the outbreaks. So far this year there was a sultry calm, no fires as yet, just a sticky moist heat with an expectancy of rain. For the time being, before the storm broke, it was just a very nice place to be. He sat on the bank – his legs dangling down the dirt slope – chewing on a piece of grass. Colourful flashes of bright-feathered birds flitted back and forth as small colonies flew in and out of the tall reeds; it was bliss, no worries, no danger, just perfect peace.

Beth had all but cleared the remains of breakfast as he returned, slowly meandering around the edge of the pool.

155

She was busying herself clearing the remnants; a succession of visits to the south had brought its awareness of long standing food and the problems of insects, especially wasps. With the last bowls and spoons held firm she bided her time, watching him approach past the bougainvillaea in full bloom. Then, calling out to him, interrupting his thoughts,

"Matthew, do you fancy a stroll – before the sun gets too hot?"

He looked up, feeling affable but lazy, muttering a response 'um!' After considering his wife's suggestion, the slow saunter to the village sounded a good idea. Just enough exercise for the rewarding prospect of a warm sunny afternoon of idleness with glass in hand on their return. The early sun was already affecting him; his eyes felt heavy and tired, the strength of the sun's rays in the south needed acclimatising to. He disappeared into the house to find something appropriate and returned shortly after sporting dark glasses; on his head – much to her disgust – an old battered straw hat: his favourite. She clucked, standing with hands on her hips feigning disapproval.

They walked slowly along the drive wrapped in their own thoughts, crunching together on the yellow stone chippings while absorbing the warmth of the sun; it felt very good as the garden cloaked them with its profusion of growth. Over the years – although not theirs – they had come to feel some ownership as the garden prospered. Matthew felt well disposed towards his wife Beth with everything in the garden falling into place. She however was less confident, despite his assurances. True, outwardly his desires matched hers, but she also knew he was prone, after due thought, to change and reason quite to the contrary. The beauty of the place did much to allay her fears; the air was heady as the sun worked its magic on roadside herbs to spill their beckoning perfume. As they left the garden the reassuring soft drone emanating from the pumps somewhere in the undergrowth faded from their hearing, although they had duly noted with satisfaction that their charges were well cared for whilst they walked out. Water would continue to play across the trees and exotics over the three acres until on their return the whole site would gleam green and fresh.

The accompanying sounds underfoot soon changed to the softer sound of padding feet on the dusty lane, they both glanced briefly left seeing the field full of dark green swollen watermelons. All the vines had a fresh clipped and manicured appearance with the season's fruit now clearly visible, ready to begin the long swell to autumn. Matthew casually pointed out the new signs posted among the vines; he counted them idly as they both walked up to the road above, mentioning the nature of the shoot. They were after all warning signs for 'La Chaisse' and it seemed to him there were many more this season.

"Urgh!" Beth muttered – killing was not her forte – and under her breath she continued to comment disapprovingly.

"No wonder we don't see much wildlife here now, it's either shot or in hiding, probably too frightened to come out I shouldn't wonder!"

He passed no comment, just kicked a loose stone on the rise, knowing full well she would delight in eating the delicacy of quail or some other unfortunate victim of the same shoot during their stay.

Disappointingly there was also considerable evidence of new properties; houses seemed to be springing up in every corner. Nothing too obvious or outrageous, in fact quite to the contrary; Spanish styled turreted villas now lay adjacent to their beloved holiday home. The new buildings were of yellow stone, which matched the houses in this medieval village, all reflecting a close proximity to the Spanish border. The appearance of these new developments was not necessarily a matter of concern to him; aesthetically speaking at least, he quite liked the curve of the tower and bold stonework. Matthew realised that others were much further advanced with their plans to settle in the valley, it seemed sensible to him to invest and enjoy the location themselves. They reached the bridge together – which at one time must have marked the boundary to the village, the reed bed had expanded to the width of the stream. A fluttering here and there suggested the birds were still present though: despite the guns.

On the pronounced bend in the road an expansive fig tree hugged against the stone wall. The wall belonged to an elegant town villa that abutted an area of tall shuttered, terraced houses all marking the initial entrance to the village. The walls of the buildings were of yellow stone and greyed with age, an odd glimpse of peeling paint on the shutters adding to the sleepy charm of the facade. The impressionist view of what the English in their droves returned to every year, French village life, with its cosy, easy-paced gentility. Plane trees, mimosa blossom and dapple-shaded squares, places to idle away the hours sipping wine. Nothing stood out in crude form of shape or colour, everything maturing like the fine wine itself, slightly dusted with mellow obscure colour. Numerous window-ledges displaying flowered profusion, along with a backdrop of pine-covered limestone crags, left the viewer quite speechless. It was a world where superlatives were inadequate, they both smiled inwardly; their pursuit of gardens, viewing and assessment of plots of land had taken on a new dimension, since consensus ruled the day.

"What time is it?"

Beth carried the family watch, he rarely did so these days, preferring, when necessary, to ask her the time or not to know at all. His professional life and consequently their private lives had been governed by time, its relentless pace controlling their very being.

"Just after ten-thirty, why do you ask?"

"Oh! Nothing – perhaps a short stroll down to the square then?" he suggested.

"I think the tannoy announcement suggested a happening in the square today."

Nodding in assent she felt more buoyant as they entered the village; they turned right into a further avenue of trees leading them towards the river. The dappled trunks were so obviously a part of the village furniture, filling a considerable portion of the roadway in front of a stylish, yellow schemed, double-fronted old town house. The coloured bark of the trees mimicked the chiaroscuro of the shadows that spread under them and out beyond, towards the pharmacy and adjacent small general store.

There was not a great deal to see at the square, there never was. Just the usual 'beret and walking cane club', the old men in animated conversation and the women bustling in pinnies and headscarves, before the noon-day sun curtailed the demands of the household. There were just three mobile vans parked under the trees flanking the river edging the perimeter of the small public square.

"Baker had a bad morning!"

Matthew, glibly pointing to the pile of part blackened, crusted loaves of bread for sale, smiling at the effrontery of it. The boulangerie in the centre of the village was more than adequate for a village of its size, he couldn't understand why anyone would bother to try bringing bread into the community that was so obviously self-sufficient.

"Yes, it's a shame working through the night for that!" she observed.

Beth wandered over to the last van, it was typical of street traders' vehicles; a converted coach with its sides folded down and pulled out to produce a flight of steps. Potential customers could climb up into the dark interior with its countless shoeboxes and rummage around. Matthew sighed, he had an inkling of what was coming, it was not the money, just the inevitable wait, 'umming and erring' about colour and size and her inability to make a decision.

Bize was only some fifteen kilometres from the major cosmopolitan centre of Narbonne, once Roman capital of southern France. Sitting boldly astride its canals, Narbonne's waters fed down to the coast only five kilometres beyond. Despite this proximity to the chic and civilisation beyond, the village of Bize had remained off the beaten track an age away, locked into history. The medieval formation of close locked houses – fanning out in concentric circles from its heart-blood, the church – had not changed since conception. Many of the roads were accessible only on foot, with hands touching both sides in passing; it was a medieval maze of brick and stone. During their many visits to the South of France, neither of them had quite fathomed out how it worked. Finding the boulangerie at its centre, adjacent to the church in the 'Place du Cloche', was like winning a prize – the warm bread and gateaux more than adequate for this purpose; the return journey was just as enthralling.

Beth reappeared on the top step, having on this occasion declined the samples offered, but it was all good-humoured. *'A bientot'* he heard her say in passing, that's right he thought, they would probably be back the following week. Walking on under the archway they were soon into the enclosed heart of the village, just at a spot where the sound deadened, the houses all mimicked one another. There was nothing precise, greyness with deep shadows at the corners. The lack of people or sounds emanating from the dwellings was strange. It was very quiet, unaccountably so, and for some reason on this occasion it felt claustrophobic, Beth also felt uncomfortable. Despite the sun reaching its noonday height this area was quite devoid of its presence and she was troubled by a premonition of something sinister. Relieved to reach the road where it divided in front of a fish restaurant – the main carriageway – they strolled along, making their way slowly towards the river, neither of them commented on their adverse feelings. At the 'Auberge' the road petered out alongside the hedgerow of tightly clipped box-privet. They were passing the entrance driveway to it when they found to their amazement a large holiday coach wedged into the tight courtyard. It was parked at the door of the premises and a large number of people were spilling out from it. There was no turning circle within the grounds; how it would manage to get back out they could not imagine. Voices from the group filtered across to them, and Matthew turned his face towards her, grimacing with dismay, 'English and Londoners to boot.' There was not an intended antipathy towards fellow countrymen or big city dwellers, but a foreign holiday meant exactly that to Matthew, to wallow in a strange foreign tongue would conjure the mystery of that land: a spell easily broken by the interjection of cockney. This village of Bize was a comparative stranger to the English tongue; it was always testing to the memory or finding the need of a phrase book when wandering through the medieval alleyways. All of which in the past had been a shared pleasure, their 'raison d'être' for being there, suiting them both well. Quickly moving on, still jarred by the realisation that other 'Brits' had discovered and entered their paradise, they walked to the riverside and sat quietly for a while where a group of local youngsters were enjoying water play at the river barrier. Deep enough to dive into, they screamed and giggled as any children might; the happy noise was enough for Beth and Matthew to visibly relax again. The sound of youngsters at play was universal, but at that moment it seemed more fun in French.

Meandering slowly back, they found themselves wandering through the labyrinth of tiny streets that were alive with mingling voices off; villagers in their shuttered homes. From its cage high on a balcony, a tiny bird called, a mother bawling demands for attention from her kitchen echoed around the alleyway. Spending a little time between the tightly-bound houses looking at names on doors they realised the houses, each one of them, carried the name of its inhabitant; how different they thought. Engrossed in this discovery they had not noticed the street appeared suddenly to end at a wall. About to turn back and retrace their steps, they were somewhat surprised to hear footsteps approaching from somewhere ahead of them; the sound came from the dark corner at the end of the street. The closeness and proximity jolted them with surprise, because the area remained ill-defined and in shadow. A figure moved out into the bright sun as if from the wall itself, which unnerved them both for a moment. They were in fact wandering into unknown territory, somewhere they had not previously explored, and the sudden appearance of the figure mystified them as to how it was possible. Dressed in summer whites, including a flat cap, the figure dazzled them in the harsh sun as it strode forward towards them supporting a camera, gun-like in the right hand; the man, who they imagined to be in late middle-age, walked confidently straight up to them. Without attempting a word in French or even a mock pidgin accent he confronted them straight out, as if he knew his quarry and the fact that they were English.

"Allo, this is a strange one, ain't it? You never seem to know where you are here!"

His voice grated on Matthew's ears, it was in a broad London accent, probably strong cockney… the very worst he thought. He had hoped the man – an obvious tourist – was a European national and by that token would have left them in peace, but it was not to be. Beth then confounded him by making an effort to respond courteously to the stranger, smiling and opening a conversation with this man who had taken the liberty of accosting them.

"Are you enjoying your holiday?"

The man thought for a moment as she continued to press without waiting for his answer.

"Is this your first trip to France?"

He pushed his cap back and scratched his head, as though the question might prove difficult.

"No – not really, but the last time I landed," his face creased into a smile, at least that may have been his intention, although in fact it appeared more a leer as he reminisced, "I had to swim in, carrying a gun. 'Course it was a bit wetter and colder then, up north you see?" He hesitated momentarily to see if his audience comprehended what it was he was saying and then as if to prompt, "You know, the war an' all?"

He spoke as if in the *'Up north'* they were still fighting.

"You folks live here?"

"In a manner of speaking, yes, but it's just a couple of weeks each year at present. All the same we value it tremendously!"

Beth annoyingly – thought Matthew – was keeping the conversation going and involving a stranger in their personal lives; he hung back disheartened. The man appeared puzzled over Beth's pronouncement.

"Always to the same place, d'you mean? – Don't you get bored? – I travel a lot y'know, there's lots of places to see and I… erhm. Well… don't want to beat about the bush." He winked at Beth.

"Haven't got too much time left you know, to see it all I mean. Well, none of us are getting any younger?"

Matthew observed the man closer and found that he was irritated by the assumed intimacy, in what he considered to be a ploy to gain sympathy. To add further to his frustration the old man seemed to enjoy the encounter, making light of it as he continued, this time in a livelier vein; perhaps because he thought the listener was receptive – the subject – Matthew felt was being embellished with an edge of sauce as used only in known company.

"And people, what a mixture they are. Up to all sorts of things! You wouldn't believe some of the things I've seen 'em do! Make your hair curl that would, not that such pretty hair needs curling." He sighed as he searched his memory. "And all of it usually for money."

Matthew watched and listened to the man's speech closely and found himself disliking the stranger even more, there was something about him – it was not just his dialect or the casual know-it-all attitude – there was something in his manner that bred doubt. His sixth sense, working overtime, nurtured a strong feeling that the man could not be trusted but it was difficult to put a finger on exactly why. It was not just the fact of where he came from or that he was basically English, although that in itself would have been sufficient to alienate Matthew at that moment. No, it was more than just a surface annoyance. Maybe the offhand nature of his conversation, the little man spoke at length and listened little, Matthew almost felt the meeting to be contrived. After all, why had they been singled out to approach in such a remote road with no chance of avoiding the interception? Uneasy as to the outcome of the intrusion Matthew wished to bring it to a close as soon as he possibly could. So he used the indiscreet nature of the conversation in order to interject. Knowing many things that people did in foreign lands were questionable and indeed not suitable conversation pieces to be held between a total stranger and his wife, he rounded on the man. He was annoyed at this intrusion within the confines of '*their village*' by this little man from London, he intended to be rude and objectionable enough for the man to go on his way and leave them in peace.

"No! – We don't get bored actually! We love this part of France. It's off the tourist trail, so it gives us a chance to unwind and not be reminded every five minutes of home. We can choose with whom we speak and mix."

He laboured the point, hoping the stranger would take the hint. It was not his normal manner to be discourteous, especially not so to strangers and he knew he was being particularly unkind. Being obtuse did little for his own self-esteem; it made him feel distinctly uncomfortable. Beth was not happy with his attitude and he was aware of her reaction; sensing a raised elbow poised to dig him in the ribs, he fell silent. The stranger stood his ground, but his humour, real or otherwise, was less obvious as his manner changed. Appearing to remember why it was that he had confronted them in the first place, he adopted a more conciliatory attitude. Turning his head sideways in an obsequious manner did him no favours, making him appear even more suspicious to Matthew. As he looked up and down the silent street and finally back to them they were left with a distinct impression that all was not well as he broke into their silent thoughts.

"Ah! – You couldn't do me a favour old man, could you? You said that you are you actually staying here, in this village I mean, – um – dare I ask is it for much longer?"

Although addressing Matthew in speech he really projected himself in favour of Beth, sensing perhaps he had the upper hand in his divide and rule protocol. To Matthew's obvious annoyance Beth responded immediately even to the point of prompting him further.

"Yes, another week and a half, is there something?"

Matthew groaned and turned away – *'invite him home for tea, why don't you?'* he thought.

"You see, it's the camera!" the stranger said.

"My video camera, I'm not very good with technical things and I just can't seem to remember where I left my charger. That's the trouble with these sorts of journeys… so many hotels, towns, countries you know!"

He paused and his early smile returned. He appeared to be watching for their reaction; after underlining his wide experience in travel, he faltered.

"I… I can get a new one when we get home, but in the meantime I only have one, camera battery that is – you know!"

He searched their faces eagerly for a response then became more insistent.

"This one's nearly run out! – We're going somewhere special tomorrow… I've only got one to cover the trip and everything else." He paused to gauge the response.

"It will be a shame to lose the opportunity."

Then his speech tailed off, he seemed disappointed at not getting an immediate response, and so he tried again.

"Then we're leaving early in the morning to head up-country, so to speak. Could you? Would you mind? You've got a charger unit, for this sort of thing I suppose?"

Beth was now feeling somewhat uncomfortable herself with this strange little man's behaviour, it was such a strange encounter she wondered how deliberate this chance meeting may have been. Looking to Matthew for support and some form of confirmation that he felt the same, she realised that he was so annoyed as to be dismissive of the whole situation. Disappointed by his apparent lack of support, standing slightly apart, she reluctantly conceded that they could and would help.

"Yes… I should think that will be alright. We do have one of course."

Then as if relieved to find there was nothing obviously difficult in the request, she perked up and smiling reinforced the offer.

"No, really it will be no bother at all. Perhaps we can pop it back to your hotel for you when it's ready. I presume you are staying at the Auberge?"

Disenchanted with the morning and clutching the man's bulky battery pack, Matthew walked on disconsolately, having left Beth abruptly to finish the conversation and extricate herself.

Finally, hurrying after him, she caught up in the shadows at the end of the street – where she fell in silently beside her husband. It was difficult to explain but the intrusion into their reverie had affected them both and though outwardly it appeared innocent enough – they couldn't put a finger on it – they both felt something was wrong. Rather than talk about it however she sensed it was better to leave well alone and remain silent. Walking together, each wrapped in their own thoughts, they passed through an ancient passageway or tunnel. It ran under a crumbling gatehouse which connected the centre of the village and a labyrinth of inter-twining lanes. They realised now how it was that the man had first appeared out the shadows in a seemingly dead-end junction. Continuing through further streets unknown to them both gave them time to clear the air, his annoyance calmed and her misgivings dissipated. Moving through the ancient, limestone passageway had provided some respite from the meeting, the carvings in the mildewed stone were of interest enough to stop and examine and finally emerging back into the square their mood had changed. Matthew had been rattled by the incident and until the battery was charged and out of their hair he would not settle easily.

Unbeknown to them the stranger had stood his ground and watched as their retreating figures moved from view; he followed their progress with interest until they were both out of sight. His eyes by this time were hidden blankly behind the silver screens of his dark glasses. There was something of a smirk on his face as he saw them enter the gloom of the cavity and passageway beyond. With their disappearance a thin smile of satisfaction formed in a crease at the side of his mouth to reveal a gleaming gold canine tooth; it seemed to flash at the pleasure of his encounter.

Chapter thirteen

Brotherhood

At some distance from Matthew and Beth's village in another rural setting, close to the border with Spain, a rough-hewn table echoing the rusticity of the oak-beamed hall had been prepared for a meeting. Not a grandiose building, in fact quite the contrary – the whole edifice attempting to assume parity with its neighbours and merge into obscurity. Its compact form sat quietly at the end of a cul-de-sac marking the edge of the village, where the relatively flat landscape of inter-linked streets could contain the horizontal inclination no longer. Adjacent to the village an impassable wall of mountainous rock cloaked in thickly wooded sides soared upwards, rising sheer into the mists above. On a clear day, the summit – visible only from a distance of several kilometres – revealed the castle ruins silently brooding on its summit. Sitting impassive, hugging the rock that spawned it, the castle omnipresent from all approaches and now a symbol to the martyrdom and a cause for which the group existed.

The group met when needed in the building used solely for that purpose. The exterior of the mellow building, concerned as it was with higher ideals, was unobtrusive.

With small, deep recessed arrow slit windows, just above street level and beyond the prying eye, it sat as a curiosity. Dimpled glass set back into the recesses further withheld the inner image, maintaining an aloof detachment from the casual onlooker. Inside, generally unknown to the casual passer-by, a subdued gathering had assembled, sitting formally around the table. The hushed nature of the group, who were awaiting one particular member, further expressed its secrecy, which was the way of the 'Brotherhood'. There were always twelve seats placed equidistant around the table and on this occasion all but three of them were occupied. Patiently the assembly waited, remaining seated until the missing members joined them.

Creaking hinges turned heads towards the door, raising hopes that the reason for this unscheduled meeting would soon be disclosed, enabling them to resume their normal occupations. Immediately following was a low rumble as the great studded entrance door moved slowly and dramatically, shattering the expectant silence. After hitting the top of its halter, the latch clattered noisily back down again to complete the drama as the door swung aside. Light flooded into the inner gloom of the vestibule, throwing a shaft of bright light which dramatically engulfed the cloaked figure that stood for a moment in its opening, bathed in the rays of the sun. All the members of this select band were similarly attired in cowled habits but of a uniform bland grey; the newcomer was dressed resplendently in a scarlet cloak, which gleamed as he approached the table. They stood acknowledging the opening of the door, standing in respectful silence ready to receive the Grand Brother – as he was known – who responded appropriately by bowing low to them. The community hovered before their seats watching him now stride positively to the head of the table. Once in position they followed his example and lowered themselves – as one – back into their seats, in a disciplined move, as part of ritual.

He spoke to them in a quiet voice, emanating the gravity of the message, the manner in which he spoke showed a weariness and disenchantment.

"Brothers!"

With a voice resonant yet grave, he addressed the assembly. They sat straining with intense concentration; twitching with unease, the assembly sensed all was not well. Obviously their gathering was incomplete, two members of the group were absent and yet Grand Brother was present and the meeting had begun.

"I have distressing news to bring to you… It will not have escaped your notice that two places are empty at our special gathering today."

His delivery, purposefully slow and deliberate, was effective as a murmur ran around the room. The speaker in red allowed time for recognition of the fact to permeate around the table, he wished to use it to his advantage. Raising his hand to assume authority once more the group fell silent: his authority was not questioned.

"One of our number has strayed and played the game of deceit! He has it seems withdrawn from our circle, from our once in a lifetime chance to cherish and remember our ancestors; more seriously, by throwing his hand in to consort with others. His purpose would appear to contradict all that we stand for and also deprive us of a valuable commodity."

172

He paused.

"I am informed that a find of the utmost importance in this year of the 'Hundred' has come into his possession. I may add by diligence and scholarly research, which when we first knew of it thought the brothers had a member in their midst who would make this year truly memorable. I have reason to believe however this is not to be. He plans to steal that which we are the guardians of and at a time when it is our good fortune that our celebrations for the 'Hundred' are nearly complete."

There was a distinct gasp from the assembly, identities were not sought, and only the Grand Master was the holder of this information. The cowls and bowing heads, although preventing any stray or accidental recognition, in fact knew each other, though cared not to speak of it: it was in reality a secret society. The cause was not sinister as such, with the group dedicating itself to the memory of the martyred Cathar Knights and their dead kinsmen. They met intermittently and on such occasions, questions of history and the 'Hundred' celebrations occupied most of their meetings. Many groups would never see a celebration but this was the year – according to dates – when one fell. Sometimes national fervour spilled into the arena, matters treated in a more guarded fashion, because they affected regional aspirations for autonomy and could be frowned on by the authorities, there was good reason for strict secrecy in these matters.

"It has long been my desire, since assuming this position as 'Grand Brother', to forward our cause in any way possible. I hoped that during my term of office we would be rewarded with a find of relevance connecting us with our past. This would be of major importance and give fresh impetus to our cause... in this year of all years. We are blessed brothers with the reality of living in a once in a lifetime situation, celebrating the 'Hundred'. It appears that we have indeed been blessed with good fortune. A find of immense importance would seem to have been unearthed by one of our brothers; surely a wonderfully dedicated act after all this time? But no! It appears that he has strayed with weakness and covets these items as his own, making a pact with the devil – one believes – to sell his soul and our birthright. There are two gaps in our numbers at this table today, the other belongs to a tireless friend, who is at this moment considering our interests in this matter as he watches, listens, and records this treachery. This could not have been achieved without devoted help of a woman."

A murmur rippled around the room at this exposure of deceit and of the fact that among their number was a woman at work.

"Our society has not found the need in recent times to extract penance from any miscreant or – though I own it was born out of a bloody age – found the need to take drastic action or commit violent acts. But I stress to you all that it may now be the time when we have to stand together resolutely in order to deal with these indiscretions appropriately. One of our brothers, whom I shall merely refer to as 'le traître!' has been seen and overheard discussing monetary matters with an unknown foreigner, we believe, English, and we know it concerns a find of great importance to us and our 'raison d'être'. The Englishman has visited his premises, making an initial contact."

Seeing their response as their cowls lifted questioningly and hearing the dismayed murmurs he commented, "Patience! We have friends!"

He paused and looking around the room elaborated on his statement, there was a note of pleasure in the admission.

"Although women, as you all know, are by tradition not permitted to join the brotherhood, many of them do work tirelessly towards our mutual benefit and one such has found herself duty bound to alert us early and furthermore is passing us information about this matter. It is necessary therefore to discover how far this canker has spread – so for the time being we shall observe and when the time comes decide on the appropriate action."

One of the group raised his hand, indicating he wished to speak.

"Yes, brother, you have something to say on this matter?"

He rose slowly from his seat, troubled and concerned by the implications, then clearing his throat nervously, for it was not easy to stand in present company and perhaps to even dare to criticise the directive of 'Grand Brother', "I understand this is a grave matter most dear to us all and to the memory of the 'Chosen Ones'. It is after all what they held sacred and gave their lives for, why we are assembled here in reverence today. Is it therefore 'Grand Brother' that you are suggesting we break with Christian… ermh… ideals, held dearly since the fourteenth century, and then maybe to commit the gravest sin of all?"

"Please! – Go no further."

The arm swathed in heavy red of leadership waved to the speaker to resume his place.

"It is with a heavy heart that I speak, we shall of course attempt to travel a non-violent path, or at least use nature to cause the turn of events in our favour. I would remind you all, however, there are wider issues. In the beginning, the Albigensian movement meant a land, a culture and a way of life worth defending, and I would add, die for!"

Chapter fourteen

A taste of the sea

The coastal strip – once an area of infected mosquito swamp – cleared by the order of an enlightened president in recent history, now stood as an example of what was possible with the will and necessary resources. Clinging to the azure blue of the Mediterranean – this belt of gold - skirting, virtually unchecked, the whole seaboard of southern France; had become a playground for European tourists and nationals alike. Coveted each year by the returning naked flesh flocking to its shores for 'les vacances', these mellowing centres had over the years matured from the clean sea and sand of conception to become outcrops of sophistication and originality. Harbour towns graced by 'Haute couture' and 'chic' restaurants mingled amongst alleyways with bistros and 'objets d'art'. Surprisingly within their midst, giant Mediterranean ferries hailing from the mysterious North coast of Africa, berthed incongruously in the midst of streets of fashion and play in the Venetian, surreal landscape. Other centres offering freedom to abandon the restrictions of dress and go as nature intended lured unabashed flesh up to ultraviolet inspection and be damned.

After driving around one such neatly manicured sea front, Matthew and Beth found themselves travelling along a small slip road. By now heading away from the main nudist beaches they followed the moorings of the marina used by the smart set's sailing fleet. Deciding earlier on fish for the main course of the day and having entered the exclusive harbour side, they were delighted to find a row of open air specialists offering a multitude of freshly caught *fruits de mer*. After assessing the restaurants for local approval, checking menus and table cloths and the like – it became obvious by the heavy patronage, which was the preferred place to eat. So they settled happily into lunchtime, one of unabashed gluttony at their chosen venue. It was not long in coming and seated contentedly amidst clattering implements, discarded lids and a large silver chalice from which they savoured the flavours – subtle and thought-provoking. They both relished the moment in noisy aplomb as the silver bowl filled with licked clean mussel shells; all that remained of the moules marinière. They battled on until the rich cream and wine liquor, sporting fine parsley pieces, was spooned, mopped and finally totally consumed. Both experienced this fine occasion of gastronomic pleasure, totally absorbed and in complete harmony. There was no need for words to pass their lips until the contents of the big red cast iron pot had expired.

Matthew, finally looking up as he adjusted his belt, gave her a broad smile, his now tanned face showing a healthy enjoyment of the good things of life; the holiday he felt was finally succeeding.

"That was one of the best. I don't readily appreciate mussels, as you know! Not to put too fine a point on it I find them somewhat rubbery. And the smell sometimes offends me with a convincing 'niff' that I'm right. But today things – well, it's different. There is something special in the subtle blends, a well disguised fine mix of cream, wine, herbs and whatever else, it was well worth the effort and I liked it very much!"

He stretched his arms out in a public display of satisfaction, totally relaxed as he combed his hair back with his fingers and leaning back on his chair he rubbed the other hand mockingly across his stomach.

"I'm totally blown and I regret to say it Beth, but there's absolutely no room for a naughty today! Coffee only I'm afraid."

He looked at the empty plates with contentment for a while and mused on a meal now gone, considering the debris and his empty bowl with mirth. Looking up to his wife opposite, expecting her to display a similar pleasure, he realised that she was looking intently towards him, but not actually at him. Her attention was held elsewhere, she seemed to be studying something over his shoulder and beyond, it was such a deep concentration that it worried him to see her face with its marked concern.

"What's wrong? Is there something upsetting you?"

Beth appeared agitated but continued staring at something by the marina.

"I'm not sure… at least I'm not dead sure… it's just that I had a funny feeling when I realised the car, that white one across the street, the one like ours. I felt that I had seen it before; it drew me back to the night when we arrived. I had a feeling that it could easily be the same one that nearly collided with us at the airport… you know? – When we landed in Girona."

179

Matthew looked across the road at the vehicle, it was as she said similar to their car, but then there must be thousands of the self-same small white cars. Sympathetic to his wife's concerns – and understanding the unfortunate experience at the start of the holiday – he still found it difficult from that distance to make a sensible judgement or even believe that she could be right. His feeling of wellbeing and the recent over-indulgence bore heavy on him, leaving him contented and unwilling to move or even take a look at the vehicle in order to reassure her. So despite Beth's obvious concerns he refused to be drawn; believing that the incident in Spain was just too far away from where they now sat, he turned back to her with an expression of scepticism on his face.

"Oh I shouldn't think so… it's too far from where that happened. The coincidence would be too great for it to appear at the same destination as us in France. Besides there's lots of these similar cars around… all hired from the same company I should imagine. It's funny that it carries Spanish plates though and is parked next to ours – just a coincidence I suppose."

Shrugging it off dismissively he turned back to relax in the sun and nurse his coffee, but the situation remained in his mind as he thought on the circumstances.

Relaxing on the terraced frontage of 'Les Copains d'Bord' they were aware of a strong breeze now blowing inland. Beyond the substantial wall on the foreshore, a sudden squall whipped across the waves, as they crashed, producing a fine sea mist of spray that drifted across the yachts at anchor. Small flags decorating the masts flapped noisily tugging at the support wires. Across the mass of expensive pleasure seeking craft in the marina, taut wires hummed loud to the incoming wind. The restaurant's sign – a model of a boat and lighthouse – sitting astride the polished brass fronted 'La Carte' menu case caught the same breeze. The featured propeller spun precariously, causing the small mechanical cut-out boat to head perilously close to the rocks below the lighthouse. Despite this adjacent drama, Matthew sat as a contented diner, musing sleepily over the view. On their table the discarded shells and remains of mussels, prawns and langoustines, the dregs from two plundered wine bottles and two very empty bright red cast iron pots. Beth, in contrast, remained sitting with furrowed brow in silent agitation, whilst continuing to contemplate the white car opposite. Although he had been totally dismissive of it, she remained uneasy, still convinced that it was the vehicle implicated in their near collision at the airport.

o-O-o

Mark Gower, having completed his business with less than a satisfactory conclusion at the village curio shop, had returned, reuniting with his now very angry travelling companion. She had expressed herself more than adequately for his piggish behaviour and abandonment. Though sore at the treatment handed out by him she had willingly agreed to accompany him again, especially this time with the promise of a coastal visit on his lips. Reaching the coast had been relatively uneventful and, as he had some time to spare before further negotiations, he decided to indulge her. Parking their white car by the marina he finally gave in to her needs for sea, sand and freedom and was suitably rewarded by her lifted spirits and girlish antics. Walking to the shoreline and crossing between the piles of cobbles excitement gripped her, at last they were by the sea; her eyes glistened in obvious pleasure as she scrambled over the remaining rocks and climbed the sea wall. He watched as first – amused at her child-like qualities – she walked and then ran towards the surf, hurriedly discarding her clothes as she went. She hastened to the inviting waters with a display of leg-hopping and disrobing en route, for fear she should miss a moment's pleasure. It kept him mellow, not a romantic by any stretch of the imagination, but her image was both amusing and pleasing and for the moment a useful distraction.

Emily finally reached the pounding surf, by which time she ran totally naked, squealing into the welcoming waves, apart from themselves the beach was totally deserted. Watching her gambol girlishly in the foam, her petite frame and rounded breasts lifting in the swell combined to raise his awareness of possibilities. He did not easily give way to diversions or submit to the will of others, for his life had been complicated and at times extremely dangerous. The dog-eat-dog mentality had left its damaging mark on him. He liked to be in control, a survival mechanism and for that reason there was little place for intimacy and attachment. But there was something different about this one however, a nomadic girl of nature who made demands of him, sometimes unnerving even with his demonstrative sexual appetite. *'What the hell!* He thought, *'in for a penny in for a!'* His clothes, unlike hers, were placed on a rock in a neat pile. He was a creature of habit and his way of life demanded constant awareness, always the need to recover quickly and change course, if events so dictated.

Despite his initial reticence he finally ran self-consciously down to the waves to join her, their two heads bobbing in the swell and gradually the heads moved closer until they were one, moving in rhythm with sea touching each other intimately. There was a smirk on her face that changed to the laughter of devilment as he succumbed and they locked limbs. Then the brushing lips tipped with laughter ate hungrily at the sensual pleasure, giving way to serious demand as they enjoyed each other's responses. Below the surface in the swirling waters, their entwined bodies pulsed in the excitement as they rose on each crest and benefited from the rushing waters' descent in the flowing rhythm of bodies and waves.

Chapter fifteen

In the halls of dreams

The small car had managed the drive up the twisting incline from the coast and onto the broad rock-strewn plateau, a wild scrubland of gorse and ochre stone. Across the wide expanse of scrub, in the middle distance, stood the first of Matthew's desired destinations, Monségur, perched on its own and quite separate across the valley. Framed by a backdrop of high mountains it perched on its own hilltop, bleached white and crumbling at the extremes. The remaining stones of the edifice were time-worn and shored up recently with newly-hewn rock. In the late morning sun from a distance the repairs were obvious; they would never somehow match their hosts but the building had been saved from deterioration. On closer inspection two arched doorways and a rise of metal steps were the only other concessions to the modern world, just enough to encourage the visitor and would-be conqueror to enter; it was a necessary embellishment to reward the curious after such a flight of rock-strewn hazard.

Matthew and Beth had enjoyed the drive, the changing scenery from course scrubland to foothills gave its reward, although it took somewhat longer than they had imagined.

Two-fingers' distance on the map had in reality extended to become two hours of considered driving; perhaps a formula they ought to remember. Parking at the base by the tourist sign they had coped with the polished boulders, made shiny by countless passing feet, but it was not easy. Scrambling inelegantly was the mode of ascent necessary to achieve the summit, but the reward for such a concentrated effort was a view that surpassed description for its isolation and grandeur. The hill lay at the foot of the Pyrenees, jostling with the mighty crags and to Occitan eyes uncomfortably close to the Spanish border. From within the shell of the chateau, a sanctuary of calm remained that replenished breath and gave adequate moment for a pause to contemplate. The awesome realisation of the symbolic nature of this structure and its position held on a thrusting escarpment spoke much of the needs of those gone before. Seen from below this lonely portal, symbol of historic resistance to the corruption of state and church alike, still moved the emotions. To those who continued in their beliefs for autonomy the hewn stone still lit the skyline, beacon-like, with a fiery vision that raised their regional fervour.

Matthew stood for a moment; both distracted and in deep thought, the images of their previous journey came flooding back to him. He muttered his thoughts to himself, under his breath, for fear of upsetting his wife.

'I can't understand what's going on. I've been plagued. No… that's not true… not so much plagued, more… I don't know, it's as though I had been invited, even, to witness something.'

Though the thoughts were not morose on this occasion, he had turned away and was completely wrapped within himself, to the extent that he was unaware of Beth's approach. After studying him for a moment she picked up on his mutterings, as she believed them to be, and registered her presence.

"Oh! – When was this? – Since you've been out here you mean?"

The interjection with her flippancy had not even registered with him. Matthew did not respond to her comment but continued trying to pinpoint what it was that niggled him, considering when and how the feeling had originally come about. He spoke out aloud, slowly and deliberately, attempting to analyse events as he went and as if to answer her.

"It started when we were flying over the mountains. Yes… that was it! The most detailed and complete dream I've ever had. But was it a dream? No… Not so much a dream, it was more real than that; I was encouraged as a witness to look on. Really that was it! It was more like a vision having been invited to enter as an onlooker to a series of real events. But even that's not very explicit and more to the point it's not the sort of thing I would normally own up to!"

He looked over the wall, having wandered absentmindedly up the grass slope to the battlement edge. There were different birds of prey and vultures circling above and as they lifted upwards, floating on the thermals, further reducing his status, 'So what does it all mean?' he thought.

She attempted to smile, quipping cynically, wishing to make light of what was to her an irritating and irrational conversation that she had now begun to dislike intensely, even to the point of finding his distraction unnerving in such a remote place.

"You want to be careful, 'St Joan' confessed in open court that she heard voices and look what happened to her!"

Matthew, standing at the wall's edge, shook himself out of his reverie and fixed his attention on Beth's cynical comments, he was displeased with her attitude over something that was troubling him. Matthew, distracted by thoughts and his wife's lack of understanding, retorted,

"Please! – It's not like that – on the plane; it was a sort of mood. I know you questioned the tablets and quantities! But it doesn't explain the subject matter. There were images and yet it was more than that. I couldn't shake the darn thing out of my mind… then again when we landed, and afterwards at the villa; it's…"

He turned to face her.

"I know you find this very difficult and unacceptable but to me it's all very unnerving. Yet at the same time, in a macabre sort of way, darkly compelling. I seem to have a permanent dreamlike state connecting me with the past. Somehow I feel I'm being seduced, willed towards something beyond my control, I know it sounds daft… it makes little sense to me and I don't know what to think. Someone or something out there wants me to watch and understand, at least that's how it appears to me."

She turned away from him, hiding her obvious alarm and disbelief, his purpose was not clear and his preoccupation with this strange subject and its influence on their holiday had become untenable. When they planned the holiday in early spring it had seemed so straightforward. A break from England and its uncertain summer weather, going to a part of France that they both knew so well and loved, but now in such a short time the mood had turned very sour. It had been a difficult year for them both, leaving many unanswered questions. His involvement in matters that were no longer his concern, after heralding his retirement, had left Beth wondering as to his true intent towards a new life together and her involvement in it. The violence that had embroiled them both had threatened their very existence, leaving them strangely susceptible, even after the enquiry into the horrific murders had been completed. The images were not as yet completely excised from their minds.

Retirement itself was also problematical, the events they had both witnessed, along with peculiar behaviour from some ex-colleagues had influenced Matthew's attitude towards the advantages of it. In fact, quite to the contrary, he now believed retirement to be a waste, having so much on hand still to offer.

The expression on Beth's face displayed both her displeasure and anxiety as she turned away to look down across the surrounding valleys, she hoped the view – for it was indeed a beautiful sight – would blot out this strange moment. Continuous rolling hills in all directions, but to the west, where wave after wave of lofty peaks bit the sky. Feasting on the romance of it she felt her spirits lift slightly and whilst the feeling of unease remained, she attempted once more to close the matter and rescue what was left of the day. She chided him brusquely for affecting her mood and dampening the day.

"Look at all the reading you did before we came away, knights in armour, crusades, Cathar rebellions. My God! You were brooding for weeks on the terrible inevitability for those peoples and their sufferings. What do you expect when you fill your head with such images and now we're here at the very spot where it happened. The whole thing, the castle, its location; I readily concur that strong atmospherics exist and are probably playing tricks with your mind!"

He kicked something loose on the ground, it flew towards the solitary stone staircase that rose up to the battlements and then, looking through the open doorway down to the path that wound back to the car, he said,

"I'm not sure I understand any of this either, I know you mean well, Beth."

His voice rose, but he was hurt by her response and spoke out loud with emotion.

"But on the plane it was horrific, you don't know how real, and yet strangely surreal, I was both a part of it and apart from it at the same time. I watched the whole darn thing unfold in front of me! It was like being on a film set, being shown every part of the production, every movement and detail was fascinating, dropping in to see how it progressed. But this was so real, the fires burned, and I could feel heat, even hear the screams from those wretched people, with all the bodies burning I could almost sme..."

She cut his speech dead before he could say the ugly word, and angrily rounded on him.

"ENOUGH! Stop it, Matthew! I'll not listen to any more, you are getting carried away. If you are not careful it'll completely spoil our holiday and more."

After snapping at him, she attempted to change the subject.

"Look! Look across at the view. The trees and the ruins; there's a sense of Tennyson, even Rossetti about it, a sort of bygone romantic mysticism; it's very evocative and above all romantic. Come on, let's just go enjoy it!"

Attempting very hard to change his stubborn mood, she extended a hand and moved towards the staircase.

"Come on, let's explore!'

"But Beth, I'm not prone to dreams or..."

His morbid fascination was irritating her beyond belief, she wanted only to lay the dust once and for all; sighing with exasperation she challenged him head-on. Calling across to him,

"Matthew, there are simple explanations for most things. It was more than likely the tablets that set you off in the plane, along with the heat; it was very uncomfortable, far too hot. Why you took the tablets I don't know. You never have before… you took far too many of the dammed things and it's obvious you had a nightmare. Being drugged you couldn't wake up properly, so it just continued on and on, a recurring dream that's mixed with reality and it has frightened you! Then when I swerved at the airport, it gave you a sudden start that compounded your misgivings, and left you with an uneasy troubled feeling ever since."

He listened to her reasoning and remained silent, absorbing the amazing view across the valley far below whilst attempting to comply with her wishes. The thin vein of a small herd of white cows made their way slowly along the grass slope towards the forest, they appeared so small as to be indistinguishable from sheep, only the clanging of their bells as they ambled slowly along the hillside identified their species. His mood, far from changing, drifted back and forth between the reality of present and strange complex images of the past. Muttering on – careful to keep it to himself now, sensing her deep frustration – he felt her lack of understanding puzzling, and in his unease, distinctly unhelpful.

"I'm sorry, but it's something more than that, I watched people die. It was here at the foot of Monségur; I saw the whole thing, I believe I was meant to... This is the first time we have ever been here, you know that, and yet if you asked me about the place, anything, I could relate every detail of it to you. It all happened here! And in my mind is still happening!"

Realising there was no response from Beth, he looked around and saw she had moved well away and was now at the foot of the grassed slope; and that he had been speaking to himself for some time. She was now walking across the bare ground of the lower hall after climbing down the slope from the wall. He grunted to himself over her lack of understanding, and continued muttering without actually moving for a moment whilst looking around at the empty shell of a once large baronial hall. Sighing deeply and focusing his mind clearly on his wife's whereabouts he descended the steep flight of narrow stone steps, in preference to the slope, in order to catch up with her. He met her at the bottom and was pleased to find an attempt by her to change the mood, with light-hearted comments falling from her lips, as she stood flipping casually through the pages of the guidebook.

"I'm trying to follow the guide, apparently in the early twelve hundreds they asked one of their lords to do some rebuilding. It's quite incredible that the place is still standing, but he had little idea of comfort. Fancy living up here, the logistics of it are scary, shopping, food, water all those steps it doesn't make much sense... Not much fun either I shouldn't think!"

Matthew, ignoring her flippancy, peered impatiently through the rear entrance gateway towards the thickly wooded slopes below; he still felt sore and aggrieved by her attitude, feeling inclined to correct the details now as though it was his moral duty.

"That was the problem of the day, you had to pay twice. Once for the supplies, then again to keep the paths secret; it was a form of blood money. Most of their treasure was used up in this way to survive, this was after all the main Cathar centre towards the very end of their existence. They had been forced into a corner; with the mountains to the rear there was nowhere else for them to go."

Matthew, sensing her silence, stopped speaking for a moment, he waited for a positive response, but she said nothing. Beth remained impassive as she stood looking at him, not wishing to show how alarmed she was at his dramatic outburst in claiming the situation as his own. Eyeing her first to confirm he had her attention, then again surveying the remaining shell of the walls, he spoke quietly and with a degree of sadness.

"It was here their cause was lost."

She shivered a little, concluding that it must be a change in the weather, what else. With the sun now dipping behind the mountains their shadows cast a chill layer of air across the landscape. Pulling the collar of her coat up around the nape of her neck to keep her ears warm, she continued turning the pages of the guide demonstrably, with a fair amount of aggression, determined to ignore his outbursts. At the same time she was insistent on imparting the facts clearly and coldly to him.

"It says in the guide how many people were thought to have been living here at the time."

Casually, and without consulting the booklet or even looking in her direction, he responded automatically, continuing to quote the facts as though everyone knew such details.

"About five hundred, maybe a thousand, squashed into this small space at the end, coming and going at safe times and when it wasn't, waiting for the inevitable."

It was a statement made as much to himself as to her and she felt distinctly uneasy by his apparent grasp of such obscure details and his obvious deep involvement in this period of history.

"Yes! How... I suppose."

She looked at him disconcertedly.

"You must have read about it! – Before we came here I mean."

Matthew was no longer listening, but totally absorbed within his own distractions, talking to himself, going over the salient points and querying his own conclusions.

"It was the last one, well nearly, 'Queribus' was last, but the cause was lost here. Not just religion but a way of life, a culture and this region differed from the rest of France; it was their own nation state not identified with mainland France. Both the king of France and the Pope at that time were power hungry, one for souls and the other for land – it was a fragmented France at that time – so in the process they slaughtered thousands of their own people in the crusades. All in the just name of religion with the Pope's blessing and God's understanding in what had to be done!"

"Matthew!"

She growled loud at him, emphasising his name by accentuating the syllables; it was her way, and he answered appropriately.

"Okay! Okay! – Don't get so worked up. It was I know a long time ago."

He made his way to the top of the steps of the approach path and looked down at the stone slabs, they reminded him of something so he called back to her.

"There were no steps then you know, secret paths in amongst the trees and the undercut of the hill with a cave here and there where the route became obscured... safety for those seeking isolation above."

She walked back towards him and grabbed his arm insistently, before making her way down the hill in his company. It was slippery, the marbled rocks on the path of their descent gleamed from the constant buffing of passing footwear. Before guiding her down, her ill-chosen shoes included, he ventured to discuss more of the past with her.

"You know it's ironic... the people fighting for the cause of independence all those years ago were betrayed by a band of mercenaries, the Basques."

Beth looked sceptical, but shrugged her shoulders, knowing full well she needed his support on the sloped descent and as such she would have to endure the conversation on hand. She sighed.

"Oh yes, they scaled the cliffs with ropes – it was their forté. They had been brought in especially for their skills – and because of this, the attackers had the element of surprise on their side, and as a result the defenders above were overwhelmed."

Standing together Matthew and Beth looked down onto the roadway below as it snaked its way around the hill to the village. Across the green slope and the lay-by beyond they could just make out the shape of their car, she joked about it in a cutting way.

"It looks even smaller from up here. It would have been nice to have had a bit of comfort, one day we might even be able to afford to hire a bigger impressive car… you know!"

Mocking him, she walked back again – changing her mind now about the immediate descent. Crossing the interior courtyard once again and then out through the rear archway, she went to see the view from the other side. His nerves being on edge, made him unnecessarily sensitive at that moment and he found himself hurt by her quip as to the size of the hire car; he remained standing where he was, brooding on his own. Matthew, his mind elsewhere, stood mulling things over whilst he looked down absent-mindedly at the car in question for a second time. He realised there was now another vehicle parked alongside it and unnervingly it was also white, looking remarkably like theirs. From where he stood some four hundred metres up he could just identify that there was a figure leaning into the driver's door of the second car.

o-O-o

Gower's great frame stood hunched over; leaning awkwardly at the driver's window of the vehicle he was busy instructing the occupant, his tone was insistent but matter of fact.

"Em! Have a wander will you? Look around a bit, I've got one or two things to do. There's not enough time to climb up there, not right to the top anyway, go and have a

195

mooch, will you? There's a good girl. There're some seats, information boards and things up there to have a look at."

Emily huffed and scowling in mock resentment did not move but instead remained, obstinately sitting where she was in the car. She wanted to be back in the sea again, he was more fun to be with there and the sea was very much to her liking. Emily now becoming bored, even with the mountains, reasoned out that they never seemed to stay long enough anywhere – to have real fun.

"Where are you off to then?" she quipped.

"What are you up to this time, bit of French fancy is it then?"

Her face creased into a smile as she pulled his leg, pretty sure he didn't know any French women, well certainly not up in the mountains. She wasn't really angry with him, in fact she was now much happier in his company and the sea had been a good mixer for them both. A light tan had replaced the white pallor of arrival, it gave her dark eyes a new meaning, and she looked quite the 'Latino'. The trip to the sea had given them both fulfilment, '*haven't done it in the sea before*' – she thought, – it was... good. She watched him collecting some bits from the boot, his broad back taking the strain as he lifted, and smiled to herself, reflecting – '*he is a big bloke – in every way.*'

He called across to her.

"I've gotta have a leak. Then there's a box of something to collect from a man in the village."

"Food?" she asked expectantly.

"No – not exactly. Anyway you can keep your sticky fingers out of it! Sit in the car if you get bored and listen to the radio."

"Oh sure, all that gabble, I can't understand a word they're saying, double Dutch or what?"

"No it's..."

"Okay French – don't be long though."

She pouted.

"I'm getting very hungry again for food and?"

He looked hard at her, allowing a glimmer of a smile to show through for once.

"Again!"

Emily pulled herself out of the vehicle and watched him for a while as he made his way around the bend in the road and out of sight. Managing to drag herself up the grass slope, she wandered as far as the foot of the steps leading up to the chateau, then slumping herself down on the wooden bench she was pleased to find it quite warm. At the foot of the hill it was peaceful and she realised amazingly beautiful. Looking around the scene she thought, '*Yeah it is kinda nice here.*'

Mark meanwhile followed the curving road down, dipping out of sight as he dropped down onto the hairpin, walking briskly to the village below. The roadway lay strangely silent and empty but the solitary figure standing in the shade of the wooded high ground above the village church had been waiting for such a moment. Viewing the empty scene, he paused for just a moment more, hesitant and unsure. Then as beads of perspiration broke out above his top lip, he gripped his precious cardboard box decisively, tucking it firmly under his arm he made the decision to break cover and move out. The walk for him was interminable – a nightmare – much preferring the obscurity in the tree line. Having reached the two vehicles in a state of nervous apoplexy, he was immediately confronted with an unforeseen problem, pacing uncomfortably he found himself between two identical vehicles.

The expression on the man's face was a mixture of confusion and panic, two white cars, both the same make and model, which one was which and how could he tell the contact vehicle. Anxious to avoid being observed for longer than was necessary, he carried the box that he held so reverently and placed it carefully down on the grass between them and ahead of both the two vehicles. It was not as he intended and muttering expletives aimed at English ineptitude he shrugged and accepted that was all he could do. He looked back once at the box, shaking his head doubtfully and finally slunk away, wiping the sweaty palms of his hands on his trousers as he went. His ill-formed moustache and hanging moist mouth accentuated his distress. He looked back apprehensively, but only the once, before climbing away over the grassed slope above the lay-by. The man moved stealthily in the opposite direction to the village, dropping down into the next valley where his vehicle was parked under the trees out of sight.

Emily now bored and fatigued by a lack of food and drink, and somewhat unnerved by the persistent silence of the place, trudged dejectedly back to the car. It was unlocked and pulling her door open she slunked down dropping back into her seat inelegantly to await Mark's return. Her purple tee-shirt – appearing to have shrunk – finished high above her navel, exposing tanned young flesh in the gap above her travel-worn bleached red jeans. Sprawled in the seat she fidgeted around to get more comfortable. It was still quite hot in there and restlessly she threw the doors open, hers and the driver's door, switched on Radio France and was pleased to hear music familiar to her. It seemed that they were playing a lot of English pop that day, so settling down, accepting the foreignness of the programme she was content to listen and wait for him.

After a while, looking around distractedly – her boredom threshold took hold – her gaze wandered aimlessly about the vehicle, then out through the door to the car parked next to them. It being the same make and colour of the car she was sat in amused her. It was then that her eyes alighted on the package lying on the ground outside; it was a cardboard box, tucked quietly to the front, exactly between the two vehicles. On its side in big letters was the word 'Miel'. *'Urh! What the hell is that?'* It rung a bell. *'I've seen it before somewhere!'* she thought. Slipping out of the vehicle and walking around to the other side, curiosity overcame her; bending down to the box she slit open the tape along its top with her nail and lifted up one of the flaps to look inside. *'Of course!'* – Suddenly remembering where she had seen the word in the villages, *'Honey! It's French for honey.'*

Pleased she had identified the package and its contents she excitedly she pulled back the flap and there they were – six lovely new jars of honey. It was all too much for her. Thinking aloud, she murmured, *'That man must have brought the parcel Mark was waiting for.'* She lifted one of the jars carefully out of the box and unscrewed its lid. Then wandering slowly back to the car she climbed in and leaned back into her seat. Emily extended her arm to adjust the knob on the radio, just so the music hit a volume that bit into the silence, suddenly it filled the air with a buzz and she smiled. Having removed the lid on the jar, she looked down into the golden liquid and seeing the honeycomb

199

portion floating inside she eagerly stuck two fingers into the open pot. Giggling, she hurriedly plunged her sticky fingers into her mouth; it was warm, very runny and sweet. Laying the pot in her lap, she toyed with the golden liquid, holding her arm above her head and letting it run down her fingers into her mouth. It also began running down her arms and as she started to lick herself wherever it fell, she became very sticky; the honey was golden nectar. After some more play, Emily tired of the game, and leaving the pot unopened on her lap, pulled the door to a little, and rested back to doze in the now very warm sun.

Slouched down in the seat and feeling drowsily comfortable – with the music throbbing softly through the speakers set in the doors – her hand beat out the rhythm as she slowly succumbed to the mood of music. As the warmth of the day and sweetness on her tongue produced a feeling of contentment her hand stopped its twitching. The combined soporific effects of sound and heat caused her eyelids to flutter then close; relaxing, her body sank back as she gave in to sleep. Visions of festivals and musical dreams filled her senses, dulling her survival mechanism.

She was now blissfully unaware of the padding feet that made their way stealthily around the opposite, hidden side of the vehicle. Through the open front passenger door – unnoticed by Emily, who by now had totally submitted to a euphoric state of wellbeing – a hand slid into the car well and carefully glided over the seat, seeking communion with the hand brake. After a slight hesitation, whilst seeking the control characteristics, the hand continued on its journey without further hindrance or observation; its deadly purpose being enacted as the release button was carefully eased off and the lever lowered: very slowly. Silently the figure moved on to the front of the vehicle; remaining unseen and ensconced by the radiator, the crouching figure exerted pressure to the front, pushing hard against it. Very slowly – imperceptibly at first – the vehicle responded as the wheels pushed slowly through the grass to an increasing momentum backwards. The changing sound, now from grit on the road, that normally would have alerted the vehicle's occupant, went unheeded as its progression gathered pace. Music obliterated any sounds, natural or otherwise and the car continuing its course diagonally across the road now picked up speed; moving without disturbing its slumbering occupant. The smooth road and empty parking lot on the opposite side allowed it to gain pace rapidly. From there it left the tarmac, mounting the grassed bank and taking the immediate plunge towards the steep downward slope. The velocity of the vehicle increased as it rampaged through the grass tussocks in its downward motion then with a sudden elevation lifting it off the ground the wayward metal box leapt a span of several yards before dropping back to hit the earth with a thump; slamming both doors shut, this time noisily.

Emily, jolted by the noise, was now fully aware of some kind of movement; she pulled herself upright, confused and frightened, not knowing what was happening. She had no opportunity to gauge the moment or understand what had occurred before the car connected with two large rocks, hidden amongst the hummocks of grass on the sloping bank; they protruded through the grass like a launch pad and pointed directly across the valley. The vehicle bouncing violently onto the ramp of stone was hurled skywards, veering into the air across the greensward. Continuing its death-defying flight, the dented vehicle cleared the stout wooden-posted fence that marked the edge of the field below. An even steeper field of lush green grass received the flying object after its completion of the five-metre drop; the vehicle, miraculously, still remained upright as it bounced onwards, gathering speed.

Inside the vehicle Emily, terrified, fully awake and now very aware of her desperate plight, sat mesmerised, gripped by the horror of it all. Her white knuckles showed the terror of her situation as she clutched hold of the seat edge, then pulling herself into a ball she curled down into the pit of the seat. Knowing she was taking an unwilling part in a nightmare, all she could do was just watch in pitiful disbelief. Unable to influence the rapid descent she looked on wide-eyed, cataloguing the action as it flashed past in the windscreen. The embattled vehicle hurtled backwards from the road above; she saw it receding rapidly from view. The horror of what was happening shook her to the core and a chill demented terror consumed her whole being, as she realised her fate. The jar of honey having fallen into her lap, lid-less, was busily emptying its contents that ran freely down into the crotch of her jeans. The sky and the world outside tumbled crazily through her vision, as the vehicle, careering and bouncing violently on its way, descended the slope beyond the reach of human intervention and totally out of control.

Emily's dark attractive eyes now widely set acknowledging her plight, screamed. It was a long haunting note that wailed her distress and helplessness to an un-listening world. A world that failed to respond as it echoed around her containment. For a moment, silence, then she swallowed hard and screeched her demented despair over and over.

"My God! – Help! – Help! – Help!"

Emily screamed on and on at the top of her voice, as though it would somehow stop this nightmarish dream. Radio France, oblivious to her distress, beamed without respite its songs from home that no longer registered in her ears. Desperately, she clamped her hands hard to her head cupping both palms over her ears and with her eyes tight shut; she attempted to obliterate what was happening to her. The honey ran freely down her temples, which in turn met tears of anguish on the point of a dimpled chin. Now no longer feeling a part of the violent passage, only aware of the spinning surreal world outside as a bad dream, she retreated into her despairing mind. The car, as if to answer her pleas, suddenly and unexpectedly hit a huge rock with full force, one that marked the lower perimeter of the field. It broke the vehicle's back and hurled the spinning, contorted metal into space, high above the hairpin bend, the last before the village came into view.

The force of the blow shook Emily's small frame violently and pounded out what little air she had left in her lungs, as though she were a rag doll. With her disbelieving face terror-struck and hard pressed against the glass of the windscreen, her open-mouthed scream was stifled by the savagery of the blow. Wedged, frozen and unable to get away or affect the flight of crumpled metal, she lay captive to the web of a spinning vortex. It spun over and over, a balletic aerial display of whirling, whooshing air, cutting sounds, showing the passenger all aspects of flight. Then just as suddenly the whole carcass descended with full gravitational force, dropping the last ten metres to embed itself hard into a rock pile at the side of the road. Emily's frozen scream set the moment her neck snapped; blood oozed out of her broken head from mouth and temple, mixing with the sticky amber nectar that coated the inside of the windscreen. The vehicle, trapped in the vice-like grip of the rocks, wavered back and forth in a springing, creaking, motion. Easing itself ever downward until the battered metal settled into a crevice, where it locked; brazenly displaying all for the world to see, its last tail-high pirouette. The wheels spun for a while remembering the journey taken, then grated and rumbled to a halt. With the car's heart dead, only the babble of the French presenters could be heard blaring from the radio, their egocentric discourse wafting into the ether, with their unwillingness to interrupt talk with tune.

Chapter sixteen

A deathly hush

Far above the tarmac bends Beth, pricking up her ears to the wind, felt sure she had heard something, a noise, something different to the natural sounds.

"Matthew! Did you hear a noise? It was a tune or maybe grinding metal. I think it came from somewhere down below. Listen!"

Standing on a knoll together at the rear of the chateau, the land dropped suddenly down to the valley floor and a wide spread of grassed common land in between two woods. Matthew made an effort, turning his head in the direction Beth intimated, in order to concentrate.

"No I didn't… wait a bit though… there is something… yes… look, I can't quite make them out oh! They're probably cows, it's a long way down. I think it's the cow-bells you can hear. I suppose it's difficult to find your stock around these parts, so sounds are important."

Beth shrugged, not totally convinced by his explanation.

They made a careful descent, noting the changing weather pattern, as clouds traced the line of the hill opposite and then kissed its crest. The best part of an hour was needed for the return climb down using the same single pathway, the only one to Montségur. Emerging from cover on the boulder-strewn hillside and out of the tree line, Matthew and Beth both reached base together. Although tired, they were able to smile at one another; they were very satisfied with their achievement. They both felt pleased with their achievement, especially so looking up at the height and the craggy rock strata where they had stood viewing the world from the castle wall. Beth, with her nose once more into the guidebook, was anxious as ever to keep the day light-hearted; she quoted some further facts.

"Do you realise the guide says it is twelve hundred metres or more to the top, that's as high as Snowdon?"

Having experienced the last refuge high up on the crag, they found themselves at its foot quietly reading the words that described the event where some two hundred brave souls had perished. It was somehow more pertinent seen inscribed on the 'Stele' cross. Nestling peacefully below the tree line the dignified cross and floral tribute from an anonymous modern day believer became even more poignant. Beth made to compromise with her husband accepting the strange effect the place was having on them both.

"It's… very moving!"

She looked up in awe at the sheer height of the mount, its obscurity and obvious commanding viewpoint chosen by those believers from so long ago.

"The temerity of such a small group of people who wished only to worship in their own way. Contrary to the state and the power of the church in Rome but they were passive and alarmingly unaware of the avarice of the King. I mean… is… is that what I mean, or is there really a special atmosphere about the place? Do you think it's possible for such things to linger?"

Beth shook her head, full of uncertainty.

"I don't know. To believe in something you're... willing to die for? Not just die, but to die horribly by walking into a raging fire. I don't see anyone with that kind of fervour today. Surely they would just walk away, a cause, any cause wouldn't justify such a terrible end." She dropped her to a whisper. "All those people... it's beyond belief. It's truly horrible."

She bit her lip, dwelling on history was causing her disquiet, she turned away distressed, the mists of time seemed to hang heavily in such a remote place. To her mind the whole atmosphere was highly charged and oppressive. Matthew, heartened to hear her openly discussing the plight of those peoples, noted her obvious distress to which he made a conciliatory effort to be less emotional and more factual.

"Yes it seems too horrible to contemplate – but you know – they had spent ten months of uncertainty, getting steadily weaker, it was a torture of sorts, to the mind anyway. With the waiting and physical deprivation they... would have been very weak, when they were led down. It seems they were given the choice to recant – well, some choice. A large angry mob of war-hardened veterans, who cared little for their prisoners, more aware of their homeward journeys with impending winter setting in. I'm not sure they were able to make rational decisions or consider anything; even their own welfare anymore."

She flared at him for a moment, not liking his casual response to such a sad moment of history, intent on reminding him of the power of belief.

"Oh Matthew! You are not considering their faith. That's what took them up the hill in the first place!"

Beth made her way gingerly down the remaining slope in his company, being forced to hold on tightly to Matthew's supporting arm. The path was very uneven at this point; the only other thing for support was a dilapidated wooden rail of a fence long gone. They soon completed the descent down the steep grass slope and were now talking freely as they went. On reaching the bank backing the road and parking bays Matthew, boyishly, jumped down and walked across to the car, leaving his wife to struggle down the sloping path on her own.

His first sight of the cardboard box was insignificant; eyeing the cloud formation swirling around the crest of the mountain opposite caused him wonder and nothing else entered his mind. The wind picked up and whipped around the knoll, managing to raising up the flap of the brown box which caught his attention; the movement opened the flap sufficiently for him to glimpse at the contents inside. He called across to Beth as she approached.

"Was that box there... when we arrived?"

It was less of a conversation and more like voicing his own thoughts out aloud, by which time Beth had joined him and was questioning what he said.

"Matthew, what are you talking about? I can't even see a box."

He persisted,

"I can't remember it being there when we arrived... can you?"

Now, standing next to him, she had to admit that it was something she had not noticed when they drew in with the car. The problems of a cardboard box however, that had probably blown down the hill in the wind, seemed somewhat insignificant and remote to her, especially after a good climb that had promoted a really healthy appetite.

"Matthew Rawlings! – You promised me a meal at the 'Auberge' restaurant in our village tonight. With the coach party and our friend missing, we'll get personal service all evening. It will still take us two hours to get back, even if we go now. It might even still be open when we arrive, if we put our skates on!"

Matthew muttered distractedly,

"Yes… okay!"

He was bending down, examining the inside of the box, as he murmured further to her, agreeing to whatever it was she was saying. For his own mind was racing with a mystery in the making, which was just up his street.

"I don't understand it, the box is full of honey jars… well not quite, there's a gap. It seems possible that one is missing, umh!"

He pondered over the find, making noises which denoted both interest and a growing compunction to intrigue.

"According to the box there should be six and one's gone! – I wonder why they've been left here?"

"A passing lorry, perhaps?" his wife suggested, anxious to be going.

"No… I don't think so."

He dismissed her suggestion out of hand, much to her annoyance, the light was dropping and she would have much preferred to be have been elsewhere.

"No! I don't think so somehow, if that had been the case the jars could quite possibly have broken, at least some of them. You know, I think they have been placed or put

209

here for a purpose. The question is what or why? And where's the one that's missing?"

"Oh! Matthew! Come on, it's probably a dropping place for a remote farm or something; they'll come down and collect them at some time. Or perhaps it's from a farm waiting to be collected by the villagers… We'll answer questions later, I'll do anything later."

A saucy smirk crossed her face.

"But at the moment I'm very hungry – for food that is and the sooner the better!"

He nodded absent-mindedly in agreement, missing the offers along the way but having made a decision regarding the mystery box he bent down to pick it up.

"Okay… but… I think we'll take the box with us. I can hand it in at a police station, should we find one."

She screwed up her face quizzically at the '*Good Citizen*' bit; pulling the seat belt noisily around her Beth waited now somewhat impatiently for the off. Whilst he carefully placed the object of mystery into the boot, she also found herself musing on the puzzle, then angrily she shook the distraction out of her mind in order to consider fine wine and food; after all it was the reason for their French holiday.

Chapter seventeen

An unexplained accident

Pulsing blue light bounced urgency at every corner as the road dropped rapidly down through a flight of 'S' bends skirting around the 'Massive', from the grassed plateau above – known locally as the 'Pog' – to where the village nestled complacently at its foot. Police vehicles parked strategically glowed in fluorescent livery, symbolically controlling any would-be approach of traffic. The display of authority was somewhat irrelevant at this spot and at such a time, there was so little in the way of passing traffic, even in the full height of summer. Those that came, curious for the history and anxious to explore the chateau perched high above, did so happily until nightfall. But the atmospheric nature of the place, amplified by the gathering gloom, caused them to steal away quietly without chancing a backward glance. The foreboding twilight affected even the stout-hearted; those who professed to admire mountain solitude and the high citadel amongst the remote crags. The roadways, never abused by mass traffic, would become strangely quiet as visitors fled back to the civilisation of town.

The testing nature of the road – passing as it did through mountain terrain – was such that the slender resources of the local gendarmerie and emergency services were sorely stretched with such an incident. The few vehicles and those curious enough to approach on foot – inquisitive villagers – were hailed down and questioned by police officers. Clipboard notations were made in an effort to seek witnesses. But it would seem from their comments that the vehicle had just appeared – from out of the blue so to speak – despite their sadness and a deal of chin rubbing and head shaking, nothing of consequence had apparently been seen; only the final dull thud had been heard by a few of them throughout the long day.

Powerful arc lights had been put in place which lit the hillside, throwing the twisted metal sculpture into sharp relief – placed as if by some giant hand bizarrely nose down into the rocks. Surreal shadows cast by the lights across the bank echoed the presence of officers moving about their business, encircling the scene like giants in attendance. The stark whiteness of the car's remaining paintwork cast an ethereal glow across the roadway. In such a macabre position the vehicle and its occupant remained seemingly unnoticed and strangely detached: aloof from the mêlée. The group of officialdom, preoccupied with designated tasks, was milling about in the narrow roadway below. The metal pile swayed unnervingly as if seeking attention, its instability giving the structure an appearance of having been placed carefully in the position for effect. To an onlooker it was almost a film set, surreal and unaccountable, as though it waited for cameras to roll and action to commence.

A thin line of liquid oozed rather than trickled down from the front nearside wing of the vehicle, it dripped very slowly but continuously out of the void through the shattered windscreen; bloodied matter of steadily draining life forces that would remain forever France. Two officers from the main gendarmerie at Quillan – stood for the moment perplexed as to the best course of action – pondering the whys and wherefores of such a hideous mess. Whilst absorbing the carnage of the scene they attempted to comprehend and make sense of what lay before them; anything that might lead to a justifiable explanation. Making their way warily around the wreck – they ventured as close as they dared, in reality it was a dangerous predicament. With an increase of dramatic sounds emanating from within the heap of grinding metal; closer inspection was hampered. Cautioned by the noise, as wind, licking across the embankment, chased circling gusts around the upright obelisk, they paused, staring up at the swaying pile. The instability and creaking of twisted metal proved enough for the enquirers to visibly falter, the senior of the two in command hesitated; he quickly conferred with his colleague then called out to the general gathering of officers grouped below.

"Clear the ground directly below and one of you! Yes, perhaps the two of you over there, bring up the large emergency lamps, there are more of them in my car!"

Astutely he realised that their personal torches were not equal to the task in hand; more light was needed to check the interior for passengers, in what was a potentially dangerous situation. There was an impatient moment as they stood waiting for the lighting units to be put in place; dissatisfied by the lack of knowledge they realised they were not in possession of the whole story. Visible relief was expressed when they were able to play beams of light across the remains of the car. Crushed and contorted the extra lighting clarified what remained of the vehicle and also helped distinguish the sole occupant of it, as it reflected starkly back to them. Those closest to the vehicle swallowed hard seeing the image of the girl pressing down hard onto the shattered windscreen. After the initial shock, their mood passed to one of sadness for yet another victim of the road. One or two muttered, making comments on the waste of youth, seeing Emily's young and once attractive face squashed hideously against the glass. The two senior officers, hardened by life and case work, visibly flinched at the sight of the young girl. Her mouth remained wide open with its bloody scream – unheard and trapped within her throat – her dark eyes, so redolent of the south, staring in wide-eyed terror.

The sight that greeted them was disconcerting to the officers, despite life's experiences and the violent confrontations of human-kind. They generally found the torment of women and death of children difficult matters to contend with; emotions were running high. One of them, the most senior – Inspector Fougare – stood in the harsh light on a rock nearby; he held a clipboard containing some initial notes. With the authority of rank he then gauged what had to be done and what needed to be achieved. Raising his voice to compete with wind and the babel below he shouted down to his men in the road. The orders were given in a voice marked by emotion and were directed to the sombre group in a series of short but succinct commands. Turning his head as he spoke to ensure that his words reached the necessary ears and achieved the desired effect, he watched as the scattered assembly both above and below him moved off to comply with his wishes; finally adding.

"I want a crane! There's a breakdown vehicle in the village… perhaps it is big enough… hein, it will have to do on this occasion. There is a young girl in the vehicle… she is dead unfortunately… I want pictures, plenty of them, as many angles as possible. It's quite probable she is not local… the car is registered from across the border! Get a photographer here pronto! Understand that means now! I will not allow the vehicle to move without pictures being taken."

Several officers below grouped as they consulted each other, discussing and delegating the commands as they were dispensed. After a pause to see the effect he continued,

"And I need a doctor fast! Find me one, I know there is such a person in the village."

He looked questioningly at his men, who stood disheartened by the scene but remained listening in silence.

"It is obvious, I know… unfortunately the young lady is… but only the doctor can pronounce it and write it down. Then she can be moved from this wreck to another place of decency and calm."

The speaker finished what he had to say and turned away from his audience dismissively, to consider his next task. The group, fully cognisant of what was needed, dispersed quickly to set about organising things.

There was much manoeuvring as vehicles were rearranged in the narrow roadway to enable colleagues to run their urgent errands. The officer who had directed his men was back amongst the debris, feeling distinctly unconnected to the root cause as yet and in need of a closer examination. Although it was obvious the young lady's life had been extinguished, he still felt the pressure to satisfy himself that the reasons for it were straightforward and did not implicate the involvement of a third party. Did she die in the accident? If that is what it was? He needed someone else to utter the words and be decisive on his behalf, for there were distractions of another kind, which were equally important for him to conclude. For a moment the administration of detail and command of the scene was less relevant to him, something else now controlled his enquiry which needed his complete attention. The moment was at hand when he needed time and discretion as an individual.

The dead girl's eyes, unnervingly, seemed to follow him each time he passed the windscreen; he looked in from the other sprung doorway. Acknowledging sadly that she was far too young to die, her eyes carried a frozen appeal, accusing the world for its lack of protection; the sight of them worried him. His colleague, taking a closer look at the bonnet and wing of the vehicle, called for his attention. The Inspector, preoccupied, was busily examining a point near the bottom edge of the glass, paying particular attention to where running liquid had collected. The pinpoint of his own interest was picked out as his inspection torch hovered over a gleaming pool. His colleague called out to him again.

"There is something on the screen – see! Here and here."

He appeared excited by the find, relaying his thoughts to the Inspector.

"It has run down the glass, I don't know what it is – I don't understand, I thought some fuel or even oil… but no!"

Inspector Fougare looked at the place indicated beside Emily's head and tentatively dipped a finger in; he rubbed his two fingers together, feeling its viscosity. Sniffing his extended sticky finger back and forth under his nose he began moving the finger towards his mouth, appearing to be about to taste whatever it was. His colleague, dismayed by the possible danger of unknown liquids, quickly leaned forward, grabbing hold of the Inspector's arm, before the offending finger and its amber covering could be sampled. At the same time the man waved a disapproving finger towards his boss.

"No! – No! You mustn't!

Then, perplexed by his boss's rash behaviour, he scratched the back of his head considering the possibilities, whilst continuing his disapproval,

"We really don't know what it is!"

Fougare, with very sticky fingers and a face that contained a wry smile, gently mocked his colleague openly, dismissing his concerns.

"It is 'miel'! Enriched with some of her blood no doubt, but 'miel' all the same, simply that. It is all over the screen and of course her body."

He sighed at the wasted life. "Poor girl, she was obviously not the driver… so where is that person, that's what I want to know? More to the point how the hell did she land up here?" He surveyed the bizarre spectacle in front to him. "It's such a hideous way for a young person to die."

The light was fading into early evening gloom, made more resonant by the surrounding escarpment casting shadows, all of which foreshortened distance and height. The Inspector checked his wristwatch, it was a little after 7pm, as he moved in to continue a closer examination; he was – despite having made light of the sticky substance – deeply preoccupied by its existence within the crushed vehicle. Whilst his colleague scrambled through the opening at the back as far as he was able, Fougare stood quietly listening, paying particular attention to where the rest of the team were placed; hoping their preoccupation would hold, whilst he fished around in the well of the vehicle with an extended arm. As his fingers probed, stretching to the limit exploring around the floor, he recognised the position of the pedals – which were also well coated with the sticky substance. Then with an assertive thrust of his hand and a look of satisfaction that spread across his face he made contact with a rounded object in the pool of liquid: it was anticipated.

Fougare ran his finger over the small, loose object, carefully squeezing it between his thumb and forefinger as he lifted it up gingerly. The minute object meant much in other circles but here it could be an object of concern and possible threat to himself. Appraising where his colleague and other officers were situated he was relieved to note that they were for the moment occupied. It was an observation that gave him confidence enough to extract the small parcel from within the well of the car and quickly place it into the folds of his pocket-handkerchief and thereon unnoticed into his inner coat pocket.

His clipboard lay idle, making no reference or observation as to what had just taken place. He gazed thoughtfully around the busy scene and was reassured that his actions had gone unnoticed. Turning his powerful halogen lamp away from the crash site, Fougare aimed the beam up to the bank above, partly to detract from his recent activities but also to counteract his strong urge to move on. Calling across to his colleague, who had seen the light move and was following the beam expectantly, they turned to face each other briefly and nodded, without words being uttered; though their train of thought implicit.

"Yes... I think we shall find some answers up there." He pointed up to the rise above, then called for his colleague to join him.

"Come on!"

The two men grabbed tussocks of grass to aid themselves as they slowly climbed up the steep bank. Crossing diagonally above the bend of the road the scene was soon lost from view, with just an eerie glow of blue reflecting on the trees. They found themselves standing at the lay-by, adjacent to the 'Pog' of Montségur! Both sighed at the empty roadside where they knew something devastating had happened and at this stage could not rule out foul play.

Chapter eighteen

Guilty knowledge

There had been little custom all day; the village appeared deserted so to the proprietor it seemed pointless to keep the premises open solely on the pretext of a chance passing visitor. The likelihood of anyone popping in to make a last-minute purchase in such a remote location stretched the imagination. In reality the merchandise proffered was hardly a line that provoked an urgent need. Tarot cards and incense were, to put it mildly, of a specialist nature; items which one addressed thoughtfully before purchase, or as more usual, acquired at last minute, tourist gifts bought to amuse families on the return home.

The village itself was off the beaten track and perched on a knoll, set before the vista of the Pyrenees lifting majestically skywards as a backdrop. Despite its isolation there were interests in the village closely allied to the nature of the shop's business, which from time to time encouraged curious motorists to climb the slope and enquire further. Centrally positioned was a strangely decorated church belying all explanation; its bizarre painted scenes and inscriptions gave rise to speculative intrigue and the suggestion of ungodly practices. In the interest of the shop's business one could say it was a 'God-send', involved as the shop was in mysticism, such a location was invaluable. Even the garden of rest to the rear of the church held unusual memories, along with the bodies of those who had taken mystical secrets to their maker.

Henri Douchez should, he knew, have already released his young assistant, who was unusually distracted. Aware of her restlessness, which he found irritating, customers were not after all in abundance. Why was she so preoccupied on this particular day, the girl looked continuously out to the road beyond, almost as if anticipating an arrival? After watching her for a time he dismissed her behaviour as something connected with boredom and youth; surmising that she would prefer to be doing what young girls did somewhere else. Deníse Pineau was one of only two girls now remaining in the village; Henri employed her because she came from a family whose ancestry, like his, stretched back to the time of legend and the dawn of Occitan pride. She was a slightly-built, quiet and, to his mind, insolent creature, who spent most of her free time frequenting the terraced seats of the cafe in Ansach, three kilometres away. The spa town, only in reality a stone's throw from the shop, nestled directly below at the foot of the hill.

To Henri's mind there were matters of a more tenuous nature at the cottage that needed pursuing. An inspection of the site was overdue, it had been a rather hurried withdrawal having realised his goal, in the excitement things could well be out of place: difficult questions might be raised. With a good deal of sighing and shaking of his head attempting to dismiss these matters he fixed his mind on the needs of the business; checking stock, re-ordering and such like. Certain books and charms were the mainstay of summer trade; he knew well that visitors liked to be fanciful and even perhaps unnerved when faced with an element of the bizarre. Religions, mainstream and obscure were featured on his shelves, along with incense, tarot cards and candles. All of these items needed to be reordered, although the latter fell into the category of dressing but they had proved more than useful in tick-over trade; he felt the need to cloak the shop with an air of mystery.

He had high hopes of an improvement in his fortunes. The long hours spent poring over old manuscripts had seemingly paid off, although as yet the monetary rewards were elusive, he had indeed literally struck gold. The deal with the 'English' however was slow; he felt a cold chill on his neck at the manner of the exchange and how unwise he had been to agree to it. Realising his membership of the Brotherhood had given him privileges and, on occasion, sight of priceless documents. They had all at times been at his disposal, this element of the society was considered a worthy enterprise by the community, researching their rich and tragic history as a worthwhile ideal. Henri however, saw the venture quite differently, not as an historical research project which might eventually provide a treatise on the misfortunes of their Cathar forebears, but more simply, a route to prosperity: a method of obtaining untold wealth. There was a problem however – there always is with self-aggrandisement – his deliberations had been observed. Quite naturally in such a close-knit community, connected as they were with the Brotherhood, trust was paramount. Other members and friends within the locale had become uneasy at his behaviour. There was an awareness that he had been furnished with privileged information, an earnest wish prevailed for him or someone amongst their number to produce something remarkable with which to celebrate 'The Hundred'. Naturally to their minds, anything discovered in the form of artefacts linking with that proud period would be presumed to belong to the Brotherhood and subsequently to the whole community. This was where Henri disagreed in principle and practice with their beliefs and aspirations, indeed a matter where he lacked a definitive compliance with community spirit.

Was it not as a result of his hard work and excavations within his own house – property that had been in his family for centuries – that the items had come to light, any advantage must surely be rightfully his? He appreciated the difference of opinion was one that might lead him into difficulties with others; but now that he had stored the said items in containers and they were about to journey to England, no-one would be any the wiser. Of course he was not too sure of his ground with the 'English', but having kept back a number of items as surety to tempt further negotiation, he surmised the integrity of payment might be intact. The Brotherhood would be unaware of these delicate transactions and no harm would done, he thought.

Denise interrupted his preoccupation, she had been hanging about by the window all morning, half-heartedly dusting. He was always surprised she still worked for him, imagining that she would someday leave and find employ or get married in Ansach, a town of opportunity. Despite her quiet manner and sullenness he was happy with her work, the arrangement suited him very well and with no other tangible employment in the village it meant he could pay her scandalously low wages.

"Monsieur, I was wondering, I know it is short notice… but as you see we are not overly populated with customers… I would like to go to town this afternoon, if I may be excused my duties?"

"Well," he hesitated and shrugged his shoulders, just long enough to make out that it was inconvenient; magnanimous gestures were not his forte.

"Just this once… in the circumstances. Things are as you are fully aware, not good here today!"

He watched her leave – somewhat abruptly he thought – as though she had a prearranged appointment. Perhaps a young man, he thought, if so, the young man had obviously made quite an impression on her for she left the shop in much haste. He watched as she ran along the lane to disappear quickly from view, her family home, a smallholding at the crossroads, was only a matter of yards away. They kept just a few animals and vines, certainly not enough income to support a daughter. His gaze returned from the window, the lane was absent of people and therefore devoid of potential customers. Dismissing her quickly from his mind he sighed whilst fiddling with the sign on the door, reversing the message to 'Fermé'. Finally sliding the bolts across the top of the door he turned away with relief, for he too had finished for the day.

Slightly lethargic with the lack of custom meant that he had retreated into the shop's interior, obsessed with papers and other matters; so doing he missed the car that glided slowly and quietly past the window, its movement discreet but deliberate; although the road was narrow at that point it was being driven with more care than was necessary. The brown-grey Citroen saloon, a nondescript vehicle with colour to match, blended naturally with the soil and could usefully be described as a farmer's car. Beyond the locked and bolted shop door, oblivious of the world outside, Henri busied himself collecting together a bundle of bargain offers recently supplied from the wholesalers. Relaxed and in reasonably good spirits he made his way through to his living quarters, anticipating a tipple of his favourite wine. Last year's wine was particularly good; the region had at last been accepted as Appellation Controleé. He passed the glass under his not inconsiderable nostrils to savour the subtlety of the raisin. Mellowed by the seasons and temperate climate the result was indeed very favourable. He moved his wrist playfully, swirling the liquid around the glass as he admired its colour then, anticipating his first sip, he slowly raised the glass to his lips, only to be rudely interrupted. For coinciding with his pleasurable anticipation came a harsh knocking, which reverberated through the building and emanated from the front door.

The sound of the thudding echoed through the dusty gloom, curtailing his good humour and a moment of pleasure, what on earth could it be, he wondered, who would be interrupting the afternoon's revelry? But more the urgent demand of the continuous harsh knocking now alarmed him and his annoyance was marked on his face. Placing his glass down carefully on the table with a reverence to the year, he rose from his chair and made his way somewhat apprehensively through to the shop. Pushing aside the woven screen Henri peered anxiously attempting to identify the source of the irritation that intruded into his private world.

There were two shadowy figures standing silhouetted in the entrance-way, one cloaked in a red garment, whose thickset outline and considerable height identified the man whom he knew only too well. The other a tall thin man, wearing glasses perched on the end of his nose and dressed in a sombre grey suit, whom he assumed to be one of the faceless ones in attendance. Henri, jarred by the apparition, was concerned, his angry face changing immediately to one that reflected a deep agitation. With his mind racing seeking to provide him with an explanation, he pulled back the bolts, released the lock and finally beckoned solemnly for his visitors to enter the premises. Henri remained at the door whilst they entered and then peering around furtively in both directions from the front step, to appease his anxiety, lest someone should have noticed his visitors' arrival. Then returning blusteringly to their presence – his servility intact – he made much of encouraging them through the shop and into his own private parlour beyond. He pulled the screen quietly back into place that separated his living quarters from the shop, aware of the need to secrete this visitation from the world's prying eyes, whilst attending to the needs of an unscheduled meeting, for which he had not as yet not formulated a purpose. He was nervous; it was the first time such an event had occurred at his little shop. Normally he would have been honoured by such an esteemed presence at his home, if notice had been served or he had been aware of the impending nature of the visit. Truth was that although ignorant of the purpose he conjectured much as he stood fidgeting nervously, worrying about what they might know.

Henri, unable to contain his misgivings any longer, expressed his anxious state by attempting a cordial welcome.

"I... I... I am honoured by your presence Grand..."

Before completing the statement however, he was directed by a raised hand to cease acknowledging the rank of the man whom he addressed, who in return waved his fingers in mock humility. Noting the recognition that he should fall silent, Henri ingratiated himself and tried again this time with a little hospitality.

"Please... gentlemen, I would be honoured if you would accept a glass of wine with me?"

The red-caped visitor sat himself down on a large chair – Henri's favourite chair. It was throne-like and imposing, with faded red leather pads and ornamental barleycorn twisted legs; the other chose to walk about, taking account of the abstract nature of the artefacts and generally surveying his surroundings in the room. Despite its clutter it was obvious to the seated visitor that the room contained material wealth in the form of fabric and furniture which all bore the imprint of age and style. He remained silently contemplating, nodding to himself at the obvious comfort of the place and every now and then looking up and frowning towards his restless companion, who was agitated, pacing silently up and down, looking for something that apparently wasn't there.

Henri licked his lips nervously, waiting for a response to his offer of wine and a possible forthcoming explanation for the visit. Apprehension held Henri rigid, their considerable presence made him almost too frightened to consider purpose, believing they might conceivably be able to read his thoughts. He watched their faces, surely his recent activities had not come to their notice, nothing was to be seen in the shop of his foreign intrigue, quite to the contrary, an exchange rather appropriately he thought, at the foot of Montségur. Had something gone wrong? The cars, it had been so confusing at the time, they were so alike. Perhaps the parcel had been overlooked, mislaid, the stupid 'English'.

His thoughts were interrupted as the seated visitor, clearing his throat noisily, spoke for the first time. By contrast it was a quiet voice, but one which spoke with authority. The intonation showed a familiarity with command as at the same he put forward a hand in acceptance to the offer of wine.

"Yes, we shall accept your kind offer and take wine with you, Brother Douchez – please."

Henri swallowed hard and, with a smile to conceal his discomfort, carefully poured some of his favourite store. Not a local vintage but one from Provence, an expensive tipple, guaranteed, he hoped, to soften the hardest heart. Presenting one glass to the seated visitor with due deference, he, looking perplexed, placed the other onto a table being passed continuously by the pacing stranger. The continuous movements back and forth across the room were adding to Henri's increasingly nervous state, he was now quite beside himself, bubbling with anxiety. So moving a chair into view, intercepting the pacing figure, he beckoned for him to sit, but to no avail for disappointingly the striding continued with renewed vigour, only now it included circling the chair as well.

"And?"

Henri left the word hanging nervously in the air, hoping the prompt would extract a reason for their visit. He tried again, aware that they were studying him intently; he was unnerved by this personal inspection.

"What do we…?"

Henri attempted once more to elicit the reason for the visit, for Grand Brother was not known to make casual visits; it must be for some significant reason, he thought. In his heightened state of agitation Henri had not long to wait to understand their purpose.

"We are drinking to absent friends, Brother Douchez."

The speech was slow, not without warmth but delivered with solemnity.

"Our meetings are sad without your company."

Henri attempted to intercede,

"But I have only missed…" The red-cloaked figure interjected once more with a raised right hand, commanding silence.

"All the Brothers are sad, it seems that bad blood, the type that sold our cause so long ago, flows yet again."

The seated figure, though hooded, held Henri in his gaze and raised his voice from quiet mediation to one of assertive command.

"Brother Douchez, I need not tell you, of all people, from such an esteemed ancestral lineage, that we deal in trust; our symbols from that time long ago granted audiences, opened doors, and elicited help, whenever it was needed. The symbols, you know, have sadly eluded us for centuries. Imagine our joy when we discovered, yes, knew that one of our brothers, blessed with the necessary knowledge and equipped with the means, had the good fortune to rediscover these most precious of commodities. Miraculously the treasured ones – we can only regard them as such – have once more emerged, and to unaccountably reappear on the slopes of the sacred mountain?"

Henri froze inside. He was undone, all was known; the jars had been discovered. There was a silence, a long deliberate pause in which Henri inwardly panicked, feeling the heavy presence of both visitors who were now studying him closely.

"It is a puzzle to us all why these symbols should appear in such a vessel, in such a place, at such a time? However, we are not unjust and feel perhaps an accident could account for such an indiscretion!"

The voice was lowered to a menacing cynicism.

"Nervous fingers, perhaps! Whilst looking at the noble beasts, who can say. Such beauty to see the light again... confusion and one could imagine a careless slip over the pot, it would be easy to forget such an incident and remember where such an item had gone... being so small!"

Henri, shivering uncomfortably, with beads of sweat freely running down his temples betraying his deep-seated fear, now absentmindedly licked his top lip, making the corner of his mouth obviously very moist. Remaining seated, he was aware of his sagging eye; it twitched uncontrollably, disclosing the uncomfortable nature of his interrogation and there was little he could do but listen obediently. It seemed to him that they knew too much and as a consequence denial was pointless. The seated figure continued,

"Alas! It would seem that a stranger from another land has stumbled into our domain and been encouraged to become familiar with property that bears ownership." He waved his hands widely to indicate how important the matter was. "The value of which is beyond any individual."

He paused for a moment to increase the gravity of his next statement.

"For her, it brought bad luck... such a pretty girl in life, a needless waste!"

He looked at Henri in a disparaging fashion, then continued,

"But we were confused as to where this amazing revelation had appeared from. In this, the year of the Hundred!"

He sat, looking into the air, as if for heavenly inspiration, now ignoring Henri, who was squirming on his seat. He was so frightened by the nature of this inquisitorial meeting as to emit a strange low, dog-like whining sound of fear; it made little difference, nothing changed, he said nothing and the speaker continued unabated.

"We feel some produce from your shop, very special produce, has somehow gone astray, which must be of great concern to you!"

At this point the visitor produced a small, red velvet bag from the inner pocket of his matching cowl and with due reverence placed his finger and thumb inside to extract the contents. The man visibly grew in stature, affected by the small object that he was honoured to be in possession of. He held it between his thumb and forefinger with the reverential pride of centuries. His face, partially hidden, glowed with aspiration as he examined the minuscule golden object resting on his hand. Savouring the pleasure of the rare contact, it was some time before he continued to address a now subdued and demonised Henri Douchez.

"And we would like to help you retrieve it, before some other unlucky individual comes to harm. There have been far too many accidents already over this affair, so we shall keep a watch at all times... in order to maintain your wellbeing."

The visitor changed his manner of speech from the quiet inveigling tone and persuasive contact with the past to one of formal directive.

"Some notes have been prepared for you to follow and addresses for you to visit; it is necessary to sacrifice personal gain in the year of the 'Hundred'. So be diligent and successful." There followed a pause, as if to emphasise the gravity of his situation. "There must be no further doubts!"

The visitor fell silent and slowly rose to his feet, at which point he turned and moved menacingly towards the unhappy proprietor. He laid two folded sheets of handwritten paper on the table before him and brushed past, leaving in silence with his colleague.

Henri Douchez, curio specialist of 'le Chateau St Jean' was now engulfed in a mixture of fear and anger; left to his own devices he sat white-faced and openly trembling in the now-silent snug behind the shop. The cleft stick he found himself to be in was entirely of his own making; in turn it posed the question, health or prosperity, one or the other? Or was there a possibility of having both, manifestly complying with the Brother-hood's wishes, whilst still conspiring with the English for financial settlement. But the 'how' would tax even his devious brain; 'English' was not a man to be trifled with and improbity was not to the Brotherhood's code: to be caught in either camp might well be fatal.

Chapter nineteen

Minerve illusion

Mentioning the weather – an English trait habitually referred to in an attempt to construct meaningful intercourse – was an unnecessary preoccupation in the deep south, for one day was like any other day at that time, in that place; a balmy warmth pervading all. The far south did not carry uncertainty in matters of climate, plans could be made and arrangements kept, enabling commitments weeks ahead to remain highly probable. Such was the day, beginning with blue heavens stretching to infinity in all directions, with not a blemish to spoil the perfection, a day when the unexpected should not occur. The soft hum emanating from the pump house reassured the would-be bather that the temperature and 'Ph' had been catered for and as a result all would be to paddling perfection, as the waters oozed freshly processed from the vent, gurgling into the blue calm of the pool. Although the glinting sun temptingly flashed onto the water's surface it failed to lure the travellers seated in the car minded for a journey; preoccupied for vistas new they concentrated as it purred along the gritted track outward bound. The vehicle's passage teased the odd stone or two, propelling them sideways into the thick undergrowth, a demeaning statement in leaving such an idyll. A fledgling golden oriole, making persistent demands of its parents, sat secreted on the lower branches of a fig tree in the avenue. It squawked in annoyance as the car passed slowly by, interrupting its engagement with food, parent and its eagerness to resume feeding.

Well-laid plans could be undone so easily seeing such visions, but no, the day had a purpose and for once they were up early enough to be resolute and make good use of it. Another hour or two's delay would diminish their resolve and the soporific nature of weather, together with the tranquillity of their surroundings, would seize hold; weakening all but the strong-hearted into another day of oblivion by the pool. Last evening had provided the details, with them both poring over maps to find a route of interest and midday destination that would meet some of the expectations they had for this year's holiday. Once beyond the last remnants of the sleepy village with its fading shutters, the landscape breathed out its raw beauty to them as they skirted the river's edge. Outcrops of limestone and pine trees marked a jagged spine that edged the succession of small valleys as they passed through. The journey was one in which each turn was capable of producing a pleasing vista of undulating hills, distant mountains that now were only visible as indistinct blue shapes mellowing into the horizon. The sudden exposure of a hidden vineyard dotted here and there in quiet hamlets made the journey all the more intriguing.

Purposefully travelling away from main roads – using their well-worn expired Michelin map – they picked their way through a succession of villages, all tucked tight and secure into the hillsides. The journey was long but certainly not arduous, anything to be away from all but the curious traveller. Finally, after all the meandering, they passed beyond the silent and secluded commune of 'Mailhac', then dropped through a cutting to what appeared to be a long-forgotten valley. A new road curved in a wide sweep around the valley wall, hugging tight to where the rock face lay, scarred and still bearing evidence at the hands of intruding man and machine. The reward, for this violent incursion of rock and dust, gave travellers at this point their first ponderous view of history. Across the valley floor raised above neat vineyards and a dry riverbed sat 'Minerve', awash in sunlight and looking mystical, its yellow stone presence announced, but coyly cloaked by rock and market gardens at the same time. The ancient retreat bathed in the morning sun, sat proudly on its pinnacle of rock, elevated, but remaining a distinct part of its surroundings. It glowed golden and peaceful amid the neat, manicured rows of vine that lay resplendent, filling every corner of productive space on the valley floor.

The physical features, produced by forceful waters flooding through gullies over several thousand years, had cut streams, forged chasms and with resultant swirl had roared out of newly-hewn caves. The tortuous process had finally left its physical mark on the landscape, in the form of a deep gorge that ran for many miles. The marks clearly visible on both sides showed where swirling waters had undercut the cliff edge into strange formations, revealing the strata in jagged patterns of contortion.

"Oh Matthew… look!"

Beth's jaw dropped in awe; she was visibly moved by nature's palette as she turned to speak to her husband.

"Have we got the camera handy? Please say yes!"

Matthew, anticipating her possible request, glanced into his mirror, checking to the rear. As he much expected, the road appeared empty, it was the time of day he guessed. Pulling the vehicle off the tarmac and onto the rock-strewn edge to the new road, a planned wide space for a future viewpoint he imagined, he turned off the ignition. There was no fence or barrier before the drop, but the inordinate size of the boulders was sufficient deterrent to encourage motorists to stop in time. Matthew's response was somewhat less than enthusiastic.

"The camera's in the bag on the back seat, I think. I ought to say though, Beth, the view is more for the mind. Just remember the scene as it is, the camera's not really up to big landscapes, I'm afraid!"

Beth joined in word for word, mimicking him as he spoke. It was a statement he had made many times before and she still failed to see the logic in carrying a camera around on every trip, if it were not to be used. Why not buy a better model was her conclusion, it was justified in the cost of a holiday anyway.

"I'm sorry, I just don't think the camera will cope."

Matthew realised she was not convinced and tried to express that look of earnest entreaty whilst at the same time attempting to appear knowledgeable as he elaborated further.

"It's a big view – the light and the distance. Even the photos in the guide-book have trouble with this one… it's just too wide, too deep and the village blends in with the surrounding rocks!"

Beth gave him the eye and a look that contained an expression of mild amusement, tinged with doubt and an expression that said she was totally unconvinced.

"You always say that! But it's still worth a try Matthew, isn't it? It's so beautiful and full of mystery."

Matthew stood outside the car, propped against the door for support. He looked through the viewfinder, smiling to himself at the well-trodden conversations culminating in packs of unrecognisable distant views stored in their chest back in England. He passed the camera over to her and watched with amusement his wife's antics, as she attempted the impossible. Photographing a vision too great for the eye to comprehend, but uplifting for the soul, was, as he knew, quite beyond the abilities of their modest camera. Another pack of dust-collecting photographs stored in a drawer that would need a great deal of explanation when passed around for friends to view, he thought. Satisfied with her efforts, Beth climbed back into the car, dumped the kit onto the rear seat and sat happily waiting to continue their journey. Her husband kept his peace, smiling, somewhat too benevolently she thought, across at her.

"I know!" she said indignantly. "They probably won't come out. They won't show the place to its full advantage. But one thing's for sure, it's better than nothing. And it will certainly help me to remember the place, when we see our friends again and I tell them, as I will, about the holiday."

There was no need for further comment; he had a feeling that the resultant photos would probably feature the usual small, insignificant images, but then the enforced stop had ensured their full enjoyment afforded by this unique viewpoint. Instead, he sighed to himself, resigned to the ritual of holiday, then slipping the car into gear drove back onto the road and headed on towards the village. After the tight right-hand bend, the road lifted upwards on a slight incline to meet the entrance of the village at its bridgehead. A junction at the crest snaked into a small approach road, beyond which lay the tourist car park, marked by a boundary fence along its length. Against the fencing was a brightly coloured, detailed picture map of the village, placed there to identify buildings across the gap from the viewpoint. Matthew pulled in and parked their car. They immediately found themselves standing at the same height as the walled village opposite; it was an unusual and strange feeling facing the outer walls of this Cathar retreat across the deep cut of the dry river gorge. The greying yellow stone of the gorge gave a warm glow and the houses opposite, clustering tightly around the top of the rock, blended together by imitating the cliff face itself. The whole village sat at the centre on its pedestal above the river that had in earlier days swirled urgently past on three sides, before disappearing into a huge cavern. Minerve, separated from the passing world for centuries, had an umbilical link, forged in more recent times, forming a bridgehead to service its needs. The short walk across the elegant single span of the structure belied its significance, until viewing over the edge confirmed the depth of the gorge below.

Before crossing the bridge to reach the village, Matthew and Beth deviated for a moment, stepping out of the car park at the opposite end and dropping down through the rough scrub a few paces to see the vines below. He was moved by the moment, enough to offer her a small peck of affection on the cheek. Soon the hillside would hang richly adorned with purple-bloomed grapes as they nestled on the protected slopes: it all seemed so peaceful. Beth lingered a while in a dreamy state, musing over the view; when she finally caught up with him he was standing back at the edge of the car park frowning. His mood had obviously changed; she noted that his sunhat was pushed back onto his head and that he was scratching his head irritably.

"Whatever's wrong, Matthew? You don't look best pleased, I thought the trip was going well and to your liking… and back there?"

She coloured slightly at his show of affection.

"It's those…"

He didn't say it but she knew what was on the tip of his tongue.

"Londoners again. You know, that strange man we met in our village, it's his party."

Matthew was looking beyond the car park exit to where the sloping road dropped out of view. Beth followed his line of sight and could just make out the party of travellers who were disappearing over the rise; she nodded her understanding to him as he continued speaking.

"The strange thing is, he didn't even acknowledge that he knew me and we still have the wretched man's battery at the villa! I can't stand this, it might be better to find out where they're going each day – and then head off in the opposite direction."

Beth flared momentarily, red-faced, indignant that he was so intolerant of other people, she snapped back at him,

"Matthew, how could you?"

She found his outburst unsettling and was wary lest his morose preoccupation of their previous trip to Montségur should return and spoil yet another day. He was not normally so disenchanted with other people; completely the opposite in fact, he was a confirmed people watcher. Studying passers-by and their varying characteristics both amused and fascinated him, but for some unaccountable reason he seemed to have a 'bee under his bonnet' about this group of tourists and one of their party in particular.

"Come on love, it's only one silly coach. There's enough room in the village to absorb all of us, without the need to overlap or even bump into each other."

Beth's attempts to lift his spirits and change his outlook did little; he remained doggedly downbeat and groaned begrudgingly,

"Yes, but we shall probably hear them."

They walked silently on, passing the glossy show coach, with its pictures of exotic holiday destinations emblazoned on its side. The solitary occupant of the vehicle, the driver, sat hunched over his steering wheel totally engrossed as he read a copy of a daily English newspaper. It was confirmation to Matthew, as if he needed it, that the man seemed oblivious of his surroundings, being absorbed as he was in news from home, albeit two days old. Matthew turned away quickly, he had no wish to see it. 'God forbid', he was on holiday.

Where the road dropped away from the car park with its clutter of vehicles, the rise acted as a shield, retaining the quiet atmosphere of the village beyond, luring the tourist ever onward to cross the divide. Passing over the bridge with its single-track narrow roadway and peering over the ramparts to the floor of the gorge below produced a strange realisation of the insular nature of the place. Whilst welcoming visitors during high summer and the exchange of finance that it engendered, it still managed to retain a protective veil of mystery for its own survival. An

'Auberge' was the first substantial structure opposite, guarding the bridgehead, sitting solid above a flight of stone steps. Matthew and Beth decided it was the place to take the first break of the day. Climbing up the steps light-heartedly they found themselves on the terrace above with a choice of empty seats, and stretching out good-humouredly across two of them in the welcome shade of a mimosa tree, they waited to be served. By the readiness of the place, napkins, cloths and menus all in neat order, they appeared to be ready for early customers. The patron, aware of the approaching tide and possible trade, quickly bade them welcome and with quiet efficiency took their order.

Matthew ordered two coffees and a pine nut tart to share.

"Oui monsieur, 'dame, d'accord!"

He left to attend to the order as they sat mesmerised in the shade, 'people-watching'. It was a splendid elevated position for such an occupation, sitting in the shade above street level, comfortably observing, quite unnoticed as they watched the world ambling by in the sunshine below. From where they sat, the bridge – about three metres below – stretched directly in front of them. It was an advantageous position; every visitor could be scrutinised and subjected to conjecture whilst crossing the gap. Once across, they would disappear imperceptibly into labyrinthine alleyways that criss-crossed out of sight into the quiet and shady cobbled streets.

A tray of coffee and pine nut tartlets arrived, which received their instant approval, and during the light snack they enjoyed watching the continuous panorama of the passers-by. Below the balcony, the village road – after crossing the gorge – formed a 'T' junction, to the right it twisted in switch-back style to the village centre, to the left it dropped down to a small orchard of heavily laden apricot trees, with a huge crop of red-tinged, yellow ripened fruit; and beyond the orchard, there lay neatly manicured vegetable plots. This communal garden marked the end of the gorge, but along its route a smaller roadway snaked back on itself to drop down to the lowest road level. At this lowest terrace of the village, further restaurants lay secreted under the rock-face amongst art and craft displays, until finally petering out at a footpath to the gorge below.

Beth excitedly tapped Matthew on the shoulder, alerting him to the scene below.

"Oh! Matthew! Look! Have you noticed? – Over there, quick!"

She looked at him with a pained expression, whispering in despair, "Where's the camera?

There was a peal of bells from the church directly above them, sounding a regular three note trill as he looked across to where she pointed; he saw the approaching procession, now halfway across the bridge. A bride in white was on the arm of her proud father as they crossed the bridge sedately, being followed by an equally slow procession of guests, who stretched out of view around the bend to the main road. Using his own camera with a small telephoto lens, Matthew busied himself capturing images to feed Beth's romantic notions. In fact, it was quite easy from their discreet position to enjoy the opportunity, allowing him to take close-up studies, an array of very natural images without objection or affecting the disposition of the group. Beth just sat gooey-eyed, relishing the scene; the romance of the occasion and its setting was making a strong impression on her, with an almost carnival

242

atmosphere now unfolding. The very slow procession of cars immediately following the wedding party began making their presence felt by sounding car horns in celebration.

Whilst engrossed in the spectacle, neither of them had been aware of or even noticed the elderly, grey-haired lady – clutching a copy of 'Logis de France', as she climbed the steps to the 'Auberge' in great agitation, passing closely by them. She entered the building and spoke excitedly at the reception desk, just beyond where they were sitting. The manager appeared with an assistant, listened intently for a moment to what the woman had to say and then, together with his assistant, quickly descended the steps with her, the assistant clutching his mobile phone at the ready. They made their way hastily downwards amidst much animated conversation, finally disappearing into a recess below the terrace. The wedding guests meanwhile had crossed the bridge and were making their way down the second slope towards the restaurant. The entourage of vehicles that followed on behind – sporting lace appendages on their aerials – were confronted by a difficult turn and amidst much laughter were forced to shunt vehicles back and forth in order to enter the compound below.

An interesting display from where they sat, with the final vehicle bringing it to a conclusion in the form of a large police van with its blue-grey image and 'Gendarmerie' inscribed on its sides. It spoke of officialdom as it slowly edged forwards, rounding up straggling vehicles to restore some form of order. Matthew thought on the wisdom of holding such functions within the confines of restrictive places having no vehicular access – it was a police thought, which quickly passed – he shook his head at the ineptitude of it and smiled good-humouredly. The now empty street meant that peace and tranquillity appeared to have returned to the village. With the entertainment value diminished it was time for them to take a gentle turn and explore the narrow hidden alleyways themselves. Dropping down the steps from the 'Auberge', their attention was drawn to a staircase cut into the rock, only a matter of yards from where they stood. There were no obvious direction signs indicating the purpose of the steps and as such it intrigued them both. The invitation declared by this staircase of mystery was compulsive enough to encourage them upwards, to who knows where. After a short, but exhilarating climb they found themselves in an area above the 'Auberge'; it was the sudden evocation of stillness in the new setting that confounded them both, after the excitement and 'goings-on' below. They appeared to have reached a quiet corner of the village and were standing outside an aged, rough-wood church door, in a small courtyard. On one side of the courtyard was the church and on the other the 'Mairie'. Opposite where they had entered was a high wall featuring one small entrance, which gave considerable seclusion from the adjacent buildings. Edging the enclosure was a low retaining wall, at the extreme end of which, adjacent to the flag-bearing 'Mairie', a cross had been erected and at its foot, on top of the wall, lay a plaque.

It was the viewpoint over the gorge that first took their eye; with the rise of just three flights of steps the surrounding hills had now come clearly into play. For a moment, standing by the wall where the rock edge dropped quite dramatically into the gorge, they stood silently impressed by the breadth and richness of an uncluttered vista. But despite the richness of colour there was an overwhelming sense of loss purveying the air. Matthew's eye, gazing along the wall adjacent to the church – the centre of the village's religious beliefs – came to rest on the cross and its plaque. Wandering inquisitively over to it he inspected the rough-hewn simple stone more closely. There was an inscription on it, which he half expected and, despite his inadequate abilities to master the language, he found he was able to reconcile its message. The legend incised into the stone was simple but powerful and it left him drifting thoughtfully to bygone ages. The stone bore witness to the fallen ones, but unlike memorials found in most villages and towns – remembering the dead from conflicts past – this one, he realised, was much more poignant.

Matthew read the text out loud, it of course was in French but simple and understandable enough for him to comprehend. The words, exact and to the point, said much; they evoked images of a small group of villagers – ordinary folk – who happened to be caught up with the beliefs of others, which during their life-time was a perilous thing to do. He reread the inscription several times and knew exactly, even sensed, what it was about. For those mentioned anonymously had put their trust into following the 'Perfect Ones'; it was another Cathar tragedy played out exactly on that spot so many centuries before. The inscription referred to those who were called into the fiery furnace and burnt alive for their faith, words simple, even simplistic, that resisted any elaboration on the gravity of this sad loss. They encapsulated the basic, evocative nature of the moment that hung heavy in his mind.

So long ago, yet the facts were plain to see, one hundred and eighty people walking into the flames in the year twelve ten. As the text said – simplistically – they had chosen to walk into the flames, to die rather than renege on their faith; for that act they were still remembered with honour to this day in this small corner of France. Images that had troubled, even taunted Matthew since his arrival, flooded into his mind en masse. Moving shapes, flames, screams, all held together by a deep feeling of despondency and to him a sense of guilt, his merely acting as a voyeur instead of participant. He drifted with the conjured images, his mind locked in this nightmarish state, until,

"Matthew?" She waited, wincing a little at his drift but determined to break his train of thought.

"Matthew, what are you thinking about?" She was quite insistent.

"Where are you? For goodness sake come back here to me!"

She waited patiently, watching for a response, enough for him to comprehend her presence. Once she had caught his attention, and fearful his mood had changed irrevocably for the day, Beth smiled encouragingly and took him gently by the hand, guiding him away from the courtyard of silence. Beyond this enclosed square they dropped down into a small roadway that snaked past two brightly-coloured pottery and gift shops. Indicating the top of the slope beyond the lines of cottages she attempted to pull him back to reality by raising the conversation to a lighter vein.

"Let's walk to the end of the village, the gorge opens out at the top... you remember? It's really quite breath-taking."

She gave him the look that said conform or else... "Then we really ought to find something more substantial to eat. Well I think... don't you? We are both quite ready for a meal."

Focusing his attention onto the hillside above, to the wild physical nature of the place, and perhaps more importantly, his own more obvious feelings of hunger, did the trick. Despite their recent snack, if nothing else was learnt from the ways of the French, meal times were sacrosanct, late attendance was unforgivable. The gorge at the top of the village was untouched by man, its brush and grass banks with outcrops of rock swung wildly back and forth after the torrents of centuries had gouged the ravine deep around the outskirts of the promontory on which the village sat. Truly a remarkable place, the depth of the ravine cut by raging waters had left this giant single rock as the waters had encircled then dropped to the valley floor beyond. They gazed on the rawness of the undercut on the cliff above, still glowing yellow and below, where the scrub had taken command there now lay a profusion of wild flowers. The vegetation added soft light to the valley and a mysticism, suggestive of 'Rider Haggard' and forgotten African adventures.

Later under the canopy of limes they both felt, for the first time that day, at peace and visibly relaxed; realising that earlier concerns had, if not completely disappeared, certainly faded. Beth's observation that the coach party would not clash with their enjoyment of the village had proved right. The irregularity of the streets and alleyways had given all the visitors the space to enjoy without confrontation, with just an occasional fleeting glimpse of an odd visitor from afar. They were very taken with the place, this curious freak of nature with a tortured past that was so obviously a tourist trap, of which they were now happy to be part. The meal under the trees was taken at a modest café situated to the rear of the village, it rested against the outer wall with mesmerising views across the gap to the encircling banks of wild thyme, rosemary and berries, all of which added to the rustic charm. Despite Madame's lack of humour and initial curt manner, her culinary skills more than compensated, a quiet meal taken under the peaceful cool shade of lime trees out of the noonday sun. The 'maître de', not expressing a familiarity with the art of polite conversation, showed a curious mix of obvious irritation, which every now and then manifested itself by outbursts of loud plate clattering. The offerings of her kitchen were such that all could be forgiven, the food being devoured with relish. From 'Salad Niçoise' to game bird, well wined and seasoned, glazed to perfection; completed with a generous portion of the tarte de pinau, they felt truly mellow. The enjoyment of the local wine accompanying the meal had in itself been a pleasant surprise, its subtlety was greatly to their palate and because of it they found themselves unwilling, or unable, to move. Even a noisy farm vehicle failed to move them, quite the contrary. The driver being troubled by the narrow curve in the lane below – and so obviously aware of his audience seated at the cafe above – had made umpteen attempts to take the corner in the heat of the day, which at a successful conclusion had extracted a strong round of applause for the entertainment value from the diners above.

Although the past was so obviously apparent in the village – indeed its 'raison d'être' – Matthew chose to make a determined effort not to dwell on historical misdeeds.

With atmosphere oozing from the very fabric of the place – especially its ancient stone, to deny its past was not easy. During their meal under the cool of the lime trees, Matthew commented briefly on the strange nature of the place. Then, struck with the realisation that perhaps a pilgrimage into another's faith and tragic past was less than desirable, on such a sunny and delightful day, he smiled across to his wife to reassure her and summarily closed the issue, erasing all reference to it from his mind. The rest of the afternoon moved uneventfully along as they visited the majority of attractions that the village had to offer, including the small museum housing artefacts from prehistory. Somehow these dusty, fossil-like remains – lying as if discarded in glass cases and not displayed with any intent – showed similarity to those collected in most towns and villages and were of little interest. So to complete the trip a little pottery was purchased, wine sampled and finally on reaching the extreme edge of the village, following the crude map supplied by the tourist-come-post office, they were somewhat perplexed not to have had sight of the crowning glory of the place. Minerve's very being was as a result of the forces of nature, which in the turmoil of swirling waters had culminated in a natural phenomenon, the village's special point of interest, known locally as 'Le Pont Naturelle'. Proclaimed in the leaflet to be 'an immense cavern', formally the underground bed of a river, it remained annoyingly elusive. According to the literature it disappeared from view into an enormous underground void which lured tourists into its dark, rock-strewn recesses. The map was quite explicit that it was to be found easily at the foot of the village, directly below the road bridge and described by coloured arrows on the walls of the houses marking the route down.

Descending hopefully towards the river basin in order to explore it, they both clattered happily past the gift shops and down the twisting cobbled street. After stopping a while to admire a well-potted frontage, with interesting décor and cascading floral displays, they found themselves confronted by the road changing into a narrow staircase cut from the cliff face. A high cliff face of rock on the one side and a row of cottages on their right and immediately to the fore the cliff face curved around and formed what seemed to be an impassable barrier. The archway that spanned the steps on a curve initially concealed any further view of the gorge, until quite suddenly they found themselves descending steps that clung to the cliff edge on the outside of the village defences. It was so sudden and unexpected it took them unawares, but left them feeling pleased with themselves that at long last they were standing in the gleaming sunlight in sight of the empty river basin.

At the bottom of the steps they could see the small roadway, that descended into the riverbed itself for some unknown reason. Finally reaching the bottom they crossed the road and dropped down small concrete steps, reaching the dry rock-strewn base of the gorge itself. Against the cliff face opposite were fruit trees; some boughs hung heavy with cherries and one tree, absorbing heat from the sandstone, slyly offered ripened figs, the first they had seen this trip. A short outburst of exuberance from Beth had her running on ahead; on reaching the cliff face she stood beneath the tree and feeling the excitement of the atmosphere acted as if a child again. She persisted in goading him with overemphasis whilst reaching up to pluck the full ripe seductive fruit. Beth's voice boomed across the gap, as she called back to him in a loud mocking voice, knowing full well he would be shy and reticent.

"Mmmm! Have one of these, they're perfect... they're so sweet and juicy... hurry up, come and try one."

Matthew was however in no hurry as he made his way carefully between the boulders. In fact, he hung back with embarrassment, never one to behave recklessly or act on impulse, and the squandering of someone else's produce fell into that category. Beth's deliberate taunting was compulsive, leading him to cast caution to the wind for once. Finding himself standing alongside her he eagerly broke open the secretive parcels to devour with relish their livid red interior. After consuming several of the fruits Matthew remembered the last time they had gorged on fig. It had been on a day the year before when driving through the mountains in autumn time to view the Vandage, figs of late season had been in abundance and very ripe. They had consciously plundered the trees, eating far more than was good for them, breaking open the sensuous fruit and stripping the livid flesh from its skin had been as compelling as it was competitive. He watched her as she continued looking for more, pulling excitedly at the branches and lifting up leaves. He felt self-conscious in the quiet gorge and embarrassed by her indulgence, which was becoming obsessive, so he walked on ahead. He imagined in such a close community – the trees and produce probably had a family name attached to them, meaning ownership. His dogged police reserve caused him to distance himself from the trees and Beth – for a moment leaving her out of sight – he wandered round the cliff base in his eagerness to find the cave entrance.

A whirl of dust whipped up around him suddenly and because of it he paused, confused by the unexpected movement on such a still day. Lifting his hand to protect his eyes he stood quietly watching loose debris lifted up into the air towards the upper reaches of the gorge. Aspens edging the dry riverbed – with their top boughs clear of the gorge – felt the squall most, as the wind gathered its freedom from the cliff wall. It was as if a hose had been turned fully on; the giant, golden leaves of the trees held their faces steady into the fierce gust of wind as it pounded and washed over them. Only moments before, the same leaves that had danced and twitched in the layers of warm air, gently dipping in the thermal movement, were now objecting to the violent rattling of their leaf edges. The freak wind continued for some thirty seconds or so as the trees suffered the indignity and change of mood. Matthew, for some unknown reason, felt uncertain, wary of the sudden wind pulsing through an otherwise silent gorge. It had appeared unexpectedly and without rational explanation. He felt uneasy, he could not explain it but it was as though danger walked abroad. The portents had a marked effect on him, a cold feeling ran through his very being; it was like a visitation, a ghost walking over his grave. The ancient stones, which had witnessed much over the centuries, seemed to hold court on their intrusion. There was eeriness within the confines of the towering silent walls upon which the village sat; it perched above and at his back, appearing to question their ethics. A feeling of hostility had replaced the earlier welcoming warmth; windows stared out from amongst the yellow sandstone cliffs above, glaring silently into the void. The dusty bowl, long devoid of water, assumed its vigil and all fell to silence once more, nothing else stirred in the heat of noonday. Just as quickly as the squall had started, so the leaves had fallen back into place, as the gorge resumed normality. The ethereal fluttering of an odd piece of paper high above, lifted and passed by an overhang. It held him mesmerised for a while, until a shaft of wood – dislodged by the same breeze, fell rapidly against the cliff, bouncing and clattering onto the rocks as it descended. The noise resounded in sharp urgency, penetrating his mind to snap him out of his trance-like state; he was suddenly aware of being alone.

Walking back to the tree line where he had left his wife, he was surprised to find that she was no longer standing there gorging herself on the ripened delights. For some unknown reason Beth had moved away, whilst he had been distracted by the coming prospect of cave discovery. He hadn't seen her go, of course, and had no idea which direction she had taken. Thinking she had possibly ambled on to where the two water courses met he walked, on hoping to meet her. It was confusing to him, she could so easily have wandered to the other side of the village beyond the steps or even simply climbed back up to the centre. For, unlike him, she was quite impulsive, but not having said anything to him of her intentions left him puzzled and annoyed by her absence. They had planned to visit the cave together where it would be cooler. He felt uneasy now as his concern grew and, perplexed by the situation, the village felt less charming. Standing with the cavern to his back, where he had a commanding view of the gorge in both directions, it was obvious there were no people within the riverbed, nothing moved, nobody to see and nothing to be heard. He felt both foolish and anxious at the same time and there was no justifiable reason for it, although the unease from the squall had not left him.

He moved determinedly across the dusty base – this time without delay – towards the flight of steps and, anxious to be reassured, he ran up the steps two at a time. The small roadway that skirted the gorge at the foot of the cliff was also empty. He glanced on passing at a poster stuck to the rock face, which finally explained why the road was there, a garish image of contorted guitars advertised a pop festival to be held in the cavern. There were no cars today though, or sounds of music from the cave, all of which would have gone some way to reassure him. Having made the roadway, he walked briskly on towards the foot of the main staircase that led back up to the village and the tourist shops above. He presumed she must have gone that way; it was after all how they had descended. Looking briefly back towards the cave entrance below, which he could now see across the gorge, he caught sight of, out of the corner of his eye against the skyline, the silhouette of a head and shoulders on the connecting bridge above. By the outline he felt certain that it was his wife Beth, both happy and relieved to see her – although a hundred metres or more from where he stood – he cupped his hands and shouted up to her with full voice,

"Beth! Beth!" Seeking reassurance,

"Beth! Are you okay? What are you doing?"

Before he could utter anything further, with his voice still echoing around the emptiness, she or the image that he thought was his wife had gone. The suddenness of her pulling back from view, after such a brief glimpse, caused him to doubt whether indeed he had seen her at all. Yet there was a distinct impression in his mind that she had initially turned her head towards him and had in fact looked directly down at him. For some unknown reason Beth had either pulled herself or been dragged back out of sight. He realised it was more than a silhouette, he had seen her face and her expression up in the daylight above, one of sudden surprise which quite clearly had changed to one of alarm before she was lost from view. He quickly considered what he had seen – already unnerved by the place, and its history, he sensed a more ominous situation in being. He knew things were not right; indeed, quite to the contrary they seemed very much amiss. Matthew now ran round to the foot of the steps, where he stopped and hoped in vain that she would appear smiling; descending back down the flight clutching two welcoming ice cream cones, a ploy she often adopted after a moment's absence; but the steps remained broodily silent, as did the bridge above. It was as if the whole village was holding its breath or was somehow complicit in controlling the moment; the blank, vacant windows all stared back at him.

With logic gone and panic setting in he pounded up the long, steeply sloping cobbled pathway. The climb was extreme – he felt a tight pain within his chest, but despite this he forced himself on; the adrenaline flow was serving him well. Having reached the top of the steps and the craft galleries he rushed on dementedly, unaware of the faces in the darkened interiors that followed his frantic flight with curiosity. He staggered on with aching sides beyond the tourist centre towards the span of the bridge where he had last seen her. The bridgehead that had sung with chattering and laughing voices of the wedding party now lay ominously silent and deserted. Similarly, the café at the 'Auberge', its shutters tightly drawn with a 'Fermé!' notice clearly displayed, now presented anonymity, an alien face to his distraught lonely figure.

Remaining doubled over, clutching his sides as his lungs heaved, he tried desperately to regain his breath and catch up with his violent exertions. Matthew, despite his agitation, sought an explanation, an understanding of what it was he had seen. Studying the roadway to the fore and over the bridge onto the opposite side nothing moved. From where it went to a 'T' junction bearing left to meet the main bypass above there were no vehicles. Looking across the gorge he could just make out the car park, partially hidden on the knoll where they had left their car that morning. For a split second he thought he caught the sound of squealing tyres and maybe a glimpse or flash of white from a car pulling away at speed. He was troubled by a second vision now, real or otherwise he was no longer sure of either. The searing light of the south played tricks on the eyes, shadows danced and the bright patches gleamed with shimmering movement. One could never be sure of what had been seen without the opportunity of a second glance. Looking down over the parapet of the bridge where he stood he realised that if it had been Beth she had been standing right where he stood now and had probably crossed the road out of sight just at that spot, but the question was why? Was it by choice or otherwise, he didn't know, but backwards was difficult to explain? Quite beyond rational explanation or reason, cold panic crept in, despite his training and years in the police force, he let go of logic and releasing his emotions shouted out her name in anguish, "Beth! Beth! Beth!"

He continued shouting long and hard, but there was no answer, nor in his morbid state did he really expect any; the passion of his emotions echoed around the gorge in a metallic ring as the call bounced up and around the houses above. Despairingly he sank back down onto his haunches the weariness now taking control. Crouched by the buttress of the bridge and putting his head firmly between his hands he covered his ears and closed his eyes to block out his immediate surroundings in an attempt to think logically. Sitting in the same position for some time, and unnoticed by him, a shadow appeared close by, accompanied by a nervous cough announcing its presence. The figure, which had approached quietly whilst pondering the huddled, distressed shape on the ground, stood patiently waiting for a response. The patron of the café above was a dark swarthy man, with a large moustache and tired grey, baggy eyes. He was still dressed in his starched white apron – now covered in fresh splashes of food and tied at the waist to protect his pinstriped trousers from the rigours of culinary art. He stood with his open necked shirt still drying his hands thoughtfully on a cloth as he drew nearer, then speaking gently in the deep soft patois of the region, he broke into the silence of thought.

"Pardon! I have been watching monsieur from my balcony – it is unavoidable you understand. One sees everything from up there. Monsieur is troubled? Il y a une problème? – Erh! – Something 'as 'appened! Something is wrong, monsieur? – Madame is here? Can I fetch her for you?"

Matthew looked up, suddenly hopeful, although confused by the silhouette that stood blocking out the bright sunlight. In his agitated state he picked up on and noted the last words spoken and latched onto what the man was saying. He wrongly reasoned that the man knew his wife's whereabouts, even indicating that she may be at his café. In response, Matthew's agitation amidst relief showed as he blurted out to the proprietor,

"You have seen my wife? She is at your cafe?"

"Non monsieur, j'ai pensé … mistakenly, I thought peut-être! … that madame, she was with you and I could get her for you."

Matthew realising the differences of language, rose dejectedly, the effort of the earlier frantic running having a marked effect on his ability to stand up easily. His cramped legs failing to respond caused him to move awkwardly, resulting in him slumping forward in a dramatic movement to look over the edge of the parapet. Suddenly the café owner, alarmed and thinking the worst, as he looked wide-eyed at Matthew, rushed forward to support this man whom he thought might jump. Matthew, irritated, shook him off, realising what the man must be thinking and pointed down to the river basin below, whilst at the same time repeating over again and again. "My wife!" The surprise and uncertainty showed on the man's face, Matthew realised at last his language was lost on the man and instead now repeated, "Ma femme! Ma femme!"

The Frenchman, shocked by what he imagined had happened, seemed to comprehend and pointing excitedly downwards, exclaimed, "Votre femme, elle est tombée?" expecting to see her body splattered below.

"No! No! Monsieur," Matthew retorted, loud and angrily, not relishing what the man had mistakenly thought.

"She is not there, that is the problem. I don't know where madame is!"

He struggled to find an appropriate short form to make the point. "Ma femme, elle est perdue!"

"Oh! Ce n'est pas bon, monsieur! Ici, ici, – come!"

The proprietor beckoned with a bent finger encouraging him to move, then aware of Matthew's difficulties helped him to his feet, taking him firmly by the arm. He did not object or resist – but allowed himself to be led meekly up the steps to the seated terrace above. An altogether different situation to one earlier in the day, where they had sat happily together, people watching. Matthew sank down gratefully onto the seat by the wall with the vantage point that overlooked the bridge. The patron, in his turn, bustled around, and then after a short absence – as if by magic – returned clutching two bulbous glasses and a full bottle of cognac. Whilst opening the bottle with due gravity, he surveyed its contents with a twinkling eye, openly relishing the pleasure of what was to come. The Frenchman chuckled to himself contemplating the bottle's contents, as if he knew it would change the mood of this troubled Englishman.

After pouring two generous portions of the amber liquid, Matthew's host sat adjacent to him, glass in hand. The man was encouraging him with a bravado display of raising his glass to his lips, willing him to take some of the liquor himself, if for no other reason than it was – necessary. After the first gulp, the liquid coursed down his throat taking the strain; Matthew coughed as the spirit bit his throat and he visibly relaxed, feeling its warmth take effect. His host, quick to see the change and pleased with the immediate results, took the opportunity to introduce himself.

"Je m'appelle Claude Bonnard, and what name shall you be known by, monsieur, during our conversation?"

"Monsieur, je suis désolé. Je m'appelle Matthew Rawlings, we are here on holiday, resting at a village only ten kilometres from here. En vacances pour deux semaines, a couple of weeks in the sun with my wife, Elizabeth … Beth!"

Matthew's face grimaced as he mentioned her name and then he continued to explain the facts as he understood them, in a mixture of garbled English and French, both of which became more and more confused as he struggled with the recall in two languages. Despite this, the patron appeared to listen attentively, nodding his head every now and then with serious concern and waving his hands in the air as if clutching at the nub of the problem. As the story unfurled he listened, stroking his chin and moustache in a thoughtful way, along with administering more liberal helpings of the very fine French spirit.

Monsieur Bonnard, patron of the Golden Vine Restaurant, finally rose silently from his seat, whilst extending his reassurance to Matthew by patting him on the shoulder in a kindly manner; amidst noises of understanding. At the conclusion of the story the Frenchman nodded; appearing to comprehend Matthew's dilemma, he made his way through to the bar, shaking his head with concern, to where his telephone sat on the counter. He made several calls, all of which were noisy and it seemed to Matthew deliberately so; during the course of these exchanges Beth's name was clearly discernible, 'Elle s'appelle Elizabet. Oui!' The phone finally fell silent and Monsieur Bonnard, making several guttural sounds of annoyance, returned slowly in a ponderous frame of mind. He lowered his frame down next to Matthew unabashed, whilst studying the face of this Englishman with a strange story to tell. Sitting next to Matthew and after a short pause, during which he appeared to organise his explanation in his own mind, the patron quietly detailed the nature of his calls.

"I have contacted my friends, neighbours and family in the village. It is only a small community, close... you understand... very small."

He bowed his head, looking under his brow and pressing his thumb and forefinger together as if to emphasise the point: the tightness of their society.

"You comprehend? As such it is necessary for us to know each other very well here. Anyway it was to see if anyone had seen a woman on her own, maybe appearing lost or taken ill, who may be the wife of monsieur. Unfortunately, it seems – I regret to say – no one 'as. I suggest perhaps monsieur waits here a little longer, she has been to my restaurant before, as you say, it is a good place to meet again. The view of the bridge will allow you to see her should... pardon! When, she returns. If not... well!"

He shrugged his shoulders.

"Then we shall consider what is to be done for the best, Oui! C'est bon?"

Matthew was grateful for the attention and now in a more ebullient mood – as the brandy's maturity became more invasive – he thanked the Frenchman for his kindness. The cheery patron, pleased with himself, now departed to the inner depths of his kitchen. After briefly consulting his watch along the way, he turned his attention to more pressing matters, for soon the evening meal would be needed by his customers. Lost wives were not the only problem for a busy restaurateur in a tourist haven. Conscious now of matters relating to his culinary art, he disappeared to organise the final arrangements for the serious eating of evening. Matthew sat alone with the bottle to hand, as a police officer he had often talked to people who had '*mislaid*' someone, temporarily that is. Reassurance, in the short term, was all that was required and normally all would be well, but he had no idea what to do in this self same situation he found himself in. He couldn't think straight, there surely had to be a simple explanation, a fall perhaps, or even maybe she had been taken poorly and the message had not arrived as yet. But what? How? And when?

The light of the afternoon had changed; a low bright sun replaced the glare of midday, now casting deep shadows across the gorge. During the two hours that passed Matthew had found several scraps of paper in his pocket on which he had made copious notes, trying to sum up the events of the day. The patron returned on several further occasions, checking on his distraught guest's welfare. Each time he appeared – and as a result of seeing the empty brandy bottle – he plied Matthew with black, and incredibly strong, brackish coffee. These small cups, all of which had been rapidly consumed, and the sobering nature of the plight of his missing wife; along with the deadly silence of no news, confirmed that nothing had changed. Finally, the patron returned; having commissioned his immediate arrangements for the evening and satisfied himself all was well in hand, his thoughts had returned once more to the troubled stranger. Sitting thoughtfully by, he eyed Matthew with concerned pity, for this Englishman was obviously much troubled as he sat dejectedly staring out across the bridge. Suddenly the patron, becoming somewhat agitated, leapt to his feet, about to become a man of action. Pursing his lips as if to speak and then changing his mind, he walked to the bar and returned immediately. Then, portraying someone who has seen the light, promptly sat down and with a benign expression of goodwill on his face once more addressed Matthew.

"Encore monsieur!' Tell me again 'si vous voulez', if you would like to?"

Matthew, who was by now exasperated by inaction and fear for his wife, tried again to recall the order in which things had happened. As he spoke he attempted to focus more clearly on the events – he was aware of the close scrutiny that followed his every word. The Frenchman this time distanced himself in a more formal manner for some unknown reason, whilst watching the stranger quizzically, as he elaborated on each of his answers. Matthew came to the conclusion that perhaps the patron disbelieved his story, or the circumstances that surrounded it. It both irritated him and confounded him to be disbelieved, but he felt compelled to go along with it, although he now distinctly felt he was under interrogation.

Monsieur Bonnard made careful notes; scratching the pad with a pen that that was drying out, he licked the nib incessantly in order to achieve the necessary continuity of words on the back of a menu card. As to exactly what was said, amid mutterings and pen licking he finally looked up and made a pronouncement.

"Monsieur, je pense. You are a little confused… peut-être, mais! I will call our police officer for assistance and maybe he can discover where madame is and what it is troubles monsieur – if this is acceptable?"

Matthew's fraught and exceedingly agitated state made him ready to agree to any action.

"Yes! Yes! Oui! S'il vous plaît. Hurry, vite! Vite! I am desperately worried for my wife's safety."

He raised his voice to protest and turning away spoke, not necessarily towards his host but more to the unjust nature of the world, it was not the best action to take.

"It's not normal for my wife to disappear."

The café owner, eyeing Matthew with nervous apprehension at his outburst, and concerned by what he had heard, moved away from the area to make the necessary contact with the police. Whilst walking away he made a point of looking back several times, muttering to himself during the process, finally hurrying out to an unseen telephone beyond whilst calling out, "Moment! Moment!"

The Frenchman retreated into the interior of the building by an alternative route, one which, Matthew presumed, had been taken in order to find a telephone which could not be overheard.

Both impatient and despondent, Matthew's state of mind gave little regard for appearances, as he quickly descended the steps down to the roadway, leaving the café in the ensuing silence that followed, before the patron could return with a response. His despair was not so great as to completely cloud his judgement and so he retraced his way back to the bridge where he found to his surprise – at the end of the rampart – a partially hidden flight of steps, covered by dense undergrowth. He had not noticed their existence earlier, but he could see that the steps – too numerous to count – dropped dramatically down to the river basin below. Despite the uncertain condition of the handrail, the unknown quality of the steps and their improbable angle - which would normally have made the prospect of descent daunting and unacceptably dangerous - he was too absorbed with concern for his wife; how dangerous, did not register. Having little idea of what he was doing or why, he scrambled hastily down the polished stone. Having reached the base, he crossed to a rock conveniently positioned nearby and sitting himself down awkwardly on it rethought the whole matter over again, examining every detail as best he could.

Staring vacantly across the gorge he became aware in his peripheral vision of people peering over the parapet above, looking down to where he sat. Their shapes were indistinct, all he could assess was that they were human figures and he could just identify their gender, but more than that remained obscure. Perhaps he had after all been mistaken, had the atmospheric nature of the place planted a suggestion of menace – playing tricks with his mind – when the truth might be much more straightforward and simple? Despite the time, now several hours, what if Beth had simply returned to the car and was waiting for him or had gone off trying to find him and was herself fuming at his absence? He chided himself, but surely she would have returned looking for him by now. Setting himself to think the former was more plausible and indeed more acceptable, his spirits lifted greatly, indeed he thought, why should it be otherwise? They were on holiday in the south of France, for goodness sake; there could be no other reason.

He ran towards the steps now somewhat lifted, imagining her to be waiting for him and very annoyed by his absence. Their steepness was not in itself an obstacle to his buoyant mind, for he was eager to prove how stupid he had been. Of course, she would be in the car reading, snoozing or more likely getting angry, as his absence had spoilt their day out. As he cleared the last step, wheezing, with the strain of the steep climb that suddenly gripped him, he felt a heavy pain surge through his chest. Bending double and panting hard, he was overcome with a feeling of nausea, then after a moment or two pulling himself upright and turning at the same time – intending to return to the car park – he almost collided with the stationary figure standing directly in his pathway.

"Monsieur is in a hurry?" After a thoughtful pause the voice continued, "He has perhaps, seen or remembered something of interest?"

Matthew stopped in his tracks, realising the man who stood blocking his path was in the uniform of the gendarmerie and was probably waiting for him. The officer continued,

"I was watching the agitation of monsieur and thought to myself it must be the Englishman I have been told of, who has, we are told … mislaid his wife!"

Matthew's urgent concerns were put to one side for the moment in order to placate the interest of the police officer. Whilst his agitation was obvious, for the car was foremost in his mind, Matthew held back and spoke to him,

"Look, I'm sorry! Je suis desolé. Parlez-vous Anglais, monsieur?"

"Oui, parlez plus lentement, s'il vous plaît! I speak a little – if you can speak more slowly. please." He waved his hands to indicate that he was listening and for Matthew to continue.

"I may have made a big mistake, my wife is probably sitting waiting for me in the car in the parking lot across the gorge."

He pointed, indicating to the officer the car park opposite, near the entrance to the village.

"I will walk with you to the car, monsieur, then we will both be reassured."

Together they crossed the bridge in silence, Matthew, with a determined expression on his face, forcing the pace and anxious to prove his fears were unfounded. It was now dusk and as they climbed the slope approaching the car park his initial enthusiasm was replaced by nervous apprehension and he began to talk inconsequential gabble, embarrassed by the possibility of being mistaken.

"I think the atmosphere of your village is very strong… it… clouds one's judgement… I think I may have panicked and got things out of all proportion."

On reaching the car park only two vehicles now remained, a camper van in the far corner and one other vehicle, parked centrally, facing across the gap; it was his white Peugeot. From the camper excited children's voices rang out amid the clattering of crockery and a faint whistling of a kettle; much to Matthew's relief the Peugeot was exactly where they had left it earlier in the day. As Matthew ran ahead to check his vehicle, his despondency returned. No obvious reassuring silhouette was visible from the interior, either sitting reading or slumped sleeping as he had hoped, the vehicle sat silently empty in the gathering gloom. The policeman, having caught up with him, now stood nearby watching with interest. He noted Matthew's frantic display and was curious to see his reactions; then interrupting Matthew's despondency he spoke,

"Monsieur is mistaken? She is not 'ere! – Perhaps she is unwell in the village or resting somewhere?"

The officer pausing, "Ladies you know, have minds of their own!"

He smiled as if knowing only too well the vagaries of the opposite sex.

"We must look to see what is possible?"

Matthew searched his mind urgently as the officer droned on with formality; he needed to divorce himself from the niceties of polite conversation. Reliving every moment and incident that had occurred to them since their landing in Spain, he attempted to provoke an explanation. Confused by the circumstances in which he found himself, the policeman's words were as a muddled echo in his mind – of course, what the man said was possible, she could be anywhere in the village, waiting for him to find her. He found himself peering across to the village, now in its darkened form, considering the feasibility of what was being suggested. His experience of life and its possibilities weighed against a rational explanation, he felt compelled to reject the hypothesis that she was just across the divide waiting for him.

Turning away from that line of thought his eyes alighted on a piece of white folded paper, lying on the dashboard inside the vehicle. He could not immediately remember its presence, could it be something from Beth, a message to say where she was and what she was doing; he desperately wanted it to be so. Walking around the car whilst arching his neck, he tried hard to seek a clue from this unrecognised image, lying where he knew none had been before. The policeman, who had been observing his behaviour since their meeting, realised that something had caught Matthew's attention and as a consequence to his reaction, felt it needed further explanation. He picked up on the moment and questioned Matthew closely.

"Monsieur has seen something, that is perhaps different?"

Matthew responded in a sentence of confused, mixed language.

"Oui! Il y a une lettre, dans la voiture… it wasn't there when we parked!"

The officer moved closer.

"Alors! It is interesting. N'est ce pas? Let us see what it says?"

Patting his pockets and then realising the spare key was still in the glove compartment, he hesitated from moving forward to retrieve the object, now feeling rather stupid. His key remained firmly locked inside the vehicle, and not on his fob as he had faithfully promised Beth it would be. She of course, he remembered, had put the keys for safe keeping – the driving set that was – into her handbag.

"I'm sorry the key… my wife has… there's another in the car!"

His voice trailed off to become indistinct, as he realised with embarrassment that he was again wrong-footed in his dealings with the gendarme. The policeman to his credit remained outwardly calm and dismissive of the perceived difficulty and made a move to enter the vehicle.

"Pas de problème, monsieur! I can open the window, je pense! It is not difficult with such a car. Monsieur, attention s'il vous plaît!'

The policeman moved forward – urging Matthew aside with a casual wave of his arm – then standing closely, leaning to the door, aligning his eyes on the catch, he grasped the door handle putting his full weight against it and pulled hard. To his great surprise it fell open easily, he turned and eyed Matthew keenly, questioning the inconsistency.

"Mais! Monsieur, the door. It is not locked! Without a key it opened?"

The surprised officer stepped back a little watching for his reaction, he could see the Englishman had expressed puzzlement. As Matthew made a move towards the car he interjected through the open door.

"Moment, monsieur!" exclaimed the officer, just as Matthew reached in to retrieve the paper.

"Je voudrai voir la lettre!" nodding authoritatively, "I, please, first!"

Leaning into the vehicle the officer picked the folded sheet up carefully by its edges and withdrew his arm. Holding it to his face for scrutiny, he opened the single sheet with great care.

"There is some writing, monsieur! It is in English. Please! If you would be so kind… read for me!"

Matthew saw the words, assembled them quickly in his mind and instantly froze. He felt the blood drain and a dull ache spread across his temple. There it was; his fear, his sixth sense, having served him so well all those years in the force, had again proved capable of prediction. His mind raced as he re-examined the simple message.

'YOU HAVE COMMODITIES BELONGING TO ME
WE CAN EXCHANGE IF YOU WISH
DON'T BE STUPID
BOTH THESE ITEMS CAN BREAK AND
EXPOSURE WOULD BE CRITICAL
JUST GO BACK TO YOUR VILLA
I HAVE YOUR WIFE
ARRANGEMENTS WILL BE MADE
TO EXCHANGE THE FIVE SOON!

Reading the words as unemotionally as he could – despite the message jarring his mind – he was thankful the uniformed officer's comprehension of written English was limited. The acrostic nature of the message within the letter meant little to him, but to Matthew it bit deep. He now knew – clearly corroborated by the message – that because of a bizarre twist of circumstance and his insistence on propriety, his wife's life now hung in the balance over his possession of five jars of honey. The policeman, impatient to procure helpful information, interrupted Matthew's thoughts with a question.

"You do not recognise this writing?"

"No!"

"Or perhaps know why your wife has seemingly been abducted… or what these commodities referred to could be?"

Eyeing Matthew warily, at first hesitating, then moving in closer, voiced angrily with vitriol, it was obvious that he assessed the situation differently and believed the Englishman to be lying. The officer, expelling a great sigh, openly expressed distrust towards Matthew's attitude; already assessing this Englishman was holding back on information, he probed again.

"You seem to have something these people want… and they want it so badly your wife is some kind of pawn, until whatever… is returned."

Matthew shook his head in denial, refusing to divulge information to someone who he did not necessarily trust, especially with the life of his wife. He reasoned, quite irrationally, that he alone should pursue whatever course of action was necessary for her well-being. The Frenchman felt his patience tried as he watched and waited; the officer was well aware that he was experiencing obstructive behaviour, it suggested that matters were far more serious than had been admitted. The officer, looking on, puzzled with concern, was well aware that Matthew in his morose state, would not be helpful with the enquiry. The Englishman leaned wearily against his car for support, realising that too much time had slipped by, enquiries needed to be made and soon.

The sun was dying bloodily on the horizon, his mind drifted; if Beth had been here he knew her enthusiasm and the camera to her eye – my God he wished she was. Matthew turned back to the officer who was now examining the paper again and briefly checking the interior of the car with his flashlight; the shadow of the hill now cloaked the area where they stood in semi-darkness. The Frenchman tried yet again without enthusiasm.

"Is there something that you know? Enough to cause these circumstances?"

Somehow the officer knew that he would not get a change of resolve from this man. Matthew, nodding his response of denial, confirmed the officer's misgivings. Inwardly Matthew was questioning his own motives and behaviour now, but how could he relate earlier incidents to this officer with today's happening at Minerve; it all made little sense to him, who after all had been a Detective Superintendent until very recently.

"Monsieur, I will need information to assist me. Please close your vehicle and lock the door, then come with me; there's much to do."

Obediently Matthew locked the door with his spare key and then belatedly acquiesced to Beth's wishes. It somehow kept him in touch with her, fiddling with the key

272

fob as he sat morosely beside the gendarme in the police vehicle. He listened to the officer's excited and demanding discourse over the car radio, whilst conferring with a number of his colleagues. Matthew understood little of what was said, his name of course, and that of his wife, then quite unexpectedly he distinctly heard the word *'Montségur'*, it startled him – how could the officer know of the honey jars or connect them with that place? Matthew bristled when noting the word 'mort', a significant word and not one he wished to hear in conjunction with his wife's name; to speak of death was beyond the pale. When the communication over the radio fell silent, the handset was replaced on its support and for a while the policeman sat quietly, saying nothing. He appeared to be taking in the gravity of the situation and comparing whatever information had been forthcoming from colleagues. Turning towards Matthew with a concerned look, he shook his head and started the car engine, the police officer drove his vehicle slowly back over the bridge towards the village. Here and there he left the car and visited several addresses. The little blue car bobbed up and down the narrow sloped, single track lanes and as doors were held open, shafts of light spilled out into the early evening darkness. During the babbling intercourse that ensued with every call, curious occupants tried hard to gain a glimpse of the policeman's English passenger with a strange tale to tell.

Finally, they returned together in silence to the now solitary vehicle in the car park. Completing the form with Matthew's holiday address and personal details the officer sat quietly pensive, awaiting a response from his passenger. He knew full well that the recalcitrant figure seated beside him in the vehicle was a retired senior police officer from a British police force and was going to prove to be difficult. The unusual circumstances the officer found himself in required careful consideration but there were enquiries to be made with or without this Englishman's approval. After some moments had elapsed he broke the silence, now with a growing sense of frustration he no longer made any attempt to hide; his angry voice tinged with exasperation as he spoke forcefully,

"Monsieur Rawlings, I know your background and how you must be feeling at this moment! I think it would be fair to say that if I were in similar circumstances, seated next to you in England, there would be an expectation of assistance from me to help you, would there not? And naturally you would in return do everything possible to help a fellow officer."

He stopped speaking to allow the point to sink in and, after a cursory glance out into the darkness across the gorge, he suddenly turned to face Matthew. This time somewhat menacingly, he held his face uncomfortably close, perhaps to induce fear but more likely in an attempt to get into the Englishman's mind.

"There are matters that occurred yesterday, some distance from here in the mountains, which I believe may have a bearing on today's events. It is my belief also that you are aware at least in part of what happened there. If you have any knowledge of what happened or suspicions as to what it means, I too wish for you to help us!"

Following the silence of several minutes the policeman folded up his pack and clipped the roll tightly onto its stud, he slipped out of his car and opened Matthew's door, standing again intimidatingly close by as Matthew emerged from the car's interior.

274

"I am not happy with your explanation. I believe you know much more than you are willing to say. Whatever the reason for your silence, again I urge you to help. Your wife's welfare is in your hands; we need your co-operation, she could well be in great danger. Consider carefully, please leave your frustrations out of it and remember you are in a strange land where you need help from others. It is our job as serving police officers to solve this problem! We know our country and people well enough to be successful, so for your wife's sake, please be sensible and extend a hand of friendship to help us."

Matthew gazed forwards tight-lipped, underneath he was uncomfortable at this plea for common sense; he was under the officer's gaze and the ensuing silence as the police officer granted him time for a response was difficult to bear. The gendarme shrugged his shoulders, but despite his protestation there were no words forthcoming. Climbing back into his vehicle, angry at this man's pig-headedness, he called with some reluctance across the car through the open passenger door window.

"I advise you to keep in touch and for the moment I do not expect you to leave your holiday accommodation, you understand? Okay. À bientôt, monsieur! Until we meet again, and we shall meet again, I assure you. Unless there is something else?"

His comment died on the wind; frustrated the officer turned away.

Slamming the passenger door noisily to vent his anger, the officer then threw his pack onto the rear seat in frustration; the Englishman's behaviour was insufferable, which annoyed him intently as he settled back into the driving seat. The disgruntled gendarme started the engine and drove out into the black night without further comment or even a glance in Matthew's direction. Matthew, on the other hand, remained standing numbly by his car, fully aware of the futility of his own position. The officer had quite naturally not believed him and he had not volunteered to help the officer in any way towards the rescue of his own wife. He was confused and racked with doubt as to the competence of a brother police force and now out on a limb, partially due to his own parochial attitude and ego of knowing best. Matthew's guilt rose to a pitch believing that he only was blameworthy for getting his wife into danger in the first place. Feeling desperately lonely and scared, not for himself but for Beth, after a lifetime of job demands and separations inflicted because of it, he was terrified he might now lose her: permanently. What had to be done was unknown, but whatever it turned out to be, he knew that all local help had been recklessly rejected. From now on his wife's safety was solely his affair and as such he must co-ordinate thought, word and deed to see her through the nightmare.

Chapter twenty

The long night's silence

The villa rested strangely quiet on his return, the frogs, as always sitting sentinel by the pond, made their retirement obvious in one synchronised leap, entering as one into the murk for the night. For once, this moment passed Matthew's notice, as he dejectedly swung the little car (his wife's description) around to the front of the house. The tight turning circle caused the headlamps to flash across the wall as he turned, picking out the now livid, cerise heads of bougainvillea. The framed darkened windows within the illuminated outer wall confirmed the obvious lack of occupation: it felt abandoned. Switching off the car's ignition, a simple action that also eclipsed the light, changed the darkened tree line of the garden into an encircling presence that morphed into something less friendly. His deep unease increased with the realisation that he was ill-prepared for what was to come. Preferring for the moment to remain seated in the car as he continued to contemplate both his and his wife Beth's predicament, the uncertainty of purpose and strangely unreal isolation now bit deeply into his psyche. With a reputation – in his previous life – for positive action he felt strangely inadequate, knowing full well that the time for decision making had arrived and was paramount to such an enquiry. But, as yet, there was nowhere identifiable to go and nothing tangible or obvious to be done.

Dwelling on the recent past, prestige and process were spheres he knew well and could manage; in another time and place, his command would have instilled a positive and unswerving loyalty from a team dedicated to success. Regretting at that moment the obvious absence of such familiar comradeship, he could only mourn their passing. The irony was that under his command the team would normally form a methodical approach capable of solving even the most bizarre of crimes. In such company he would have identified both the path and direction to enable them to pursue their chosen target and with their stubborn willingness to work all hours, everything would have felt more positive.

He was in reality without command, without position and, as Beth would probably have said, floundering in a soup of his own invention, waiting to do another's bidding. The truth was that he was in the hands of an unknown protagonist who held all the cards in a game for which the rules were as yet unknown. Hope, he knew, was all that one could cling to in such situations, having witnessed at first hand many people experiencing the same. In his ignorance he had always believed he'd known how they felt; now shaking his head and muttering 'absurd arrogance' to himself, Matthew bit his lip and wanted to lash out in regret at the reality of life and his own stupidity.

Surveying the darkened, lifeless frontage of the building advanced his feeling of isolation, sending a cold chill right through him. He prayed that the trade-off would be accomplished purposely, leaving the car door unlocked – for a quick retreat, should the need arise. The sound of his footfall resonated loudly across the yard as he crunched distractedly on the pebbled drive towards the garden store. Reassuringly the switches for exterior lighting were conveniently positioned just above the gossip-door and with one flick of the master switch the darkness on the vast plot was instantly transformed. This simple action raised his spirits for the moment, a memory of better times, as the lanterns that hung about the garden at strategic points now glowed warmly. A welcoming light that reminded him of the early months of summer, it was then that he and Beth loved to sit and watch and, most remarkable of all, listen to the nightingales as they flitted through the boughs, busily setting up home together; his reflections bit deep.

He cuffed his eye with the back of his hand and sniffed, wiping a moment of emotion away; Matthew shook his head in disbelief at the absurdity of both their predicaments, not knowing how to react sensibly and appropriately when the most important person in his life was in mortal danger. To dispel the mood, he purposely used action instead of words by fiddling about, moving plants in the potting shed, determined to keep his mind clear and alert for whatever was to come. Thorough immersion in the immense task of watering the three-acre plot would hold him he knew; steady enough to deny any panic from setting in. The task would normally ensure total submission, moving pipes, sprinklers and junctions about the site required great physical expenditure. Thought processes were held in suspension until the garden, harried by dozens of fine jets, would lie glistening under the deluge.

They were at the villa ostensibly on holiday, but predominantly mindful of their obligation to care for the garden – a bartered chore – that they had accepted gladly. Friends longstanding and owners of the site, who were now faced with failing health, had been encouraged by Matthew and Beth to return to England, albeit briefly to reacquaint with family and old friends, also to gain some respite from the heat of the south. Hauling pipes and changing connections in order to force water from the river below to refresh the giant plot, may not appeal to everyone's sense of holiday abandonment. It was however proving to be a particularly useful therapy for his agitated mind, and the surprisingly robust demand on his physical being left little room for self-pity or despair. However, neither the garden nor his preoccupation were completely at one during the process and with the daily drench commissioned – as best he could in the middle of the night – there was little more that could be achieved usefully on his own account, or to reward the garden, until daylight returned.

After such an exertion the reward would have been self-indulgence by the pool and a chance to curl up and read under the canopy of palms in the warmth of a lazy day. But self was irrelevant in such circumstances and the timing obscure to indulge in anything other than his wife's demise. He knew from the experience of others there would be extremes, moments of despair, periods of exaltation, mixed with large consignments of soul searching and self-recrimination. During the long night ahead he would have to wait – as others had – in the game of chess, in which he knew he was merely playing the pawn. Everything hung on the receipt of instructions by a hand unknown for his next move, an anonymous contact who would try to control his every thought and action. Clinging to the known facts, he felt the letter left in the car had at least affirmed that Beth was, though captive, alive and hopefully well. He tried to dismiss the alternative possibilities from his mind, as it was by no means a proven fact. In simple terms the facts of the matter were that Beth, his wife, was being held against her will, as hostage to fortune until an exchange could be arranged.

He had seen 'kidnap' at close hand before, it was unpleasant and on occasions fatal to the victims and always agonising for those personally involved, as it played spitefully with their emotions. Matthew did not want to be pre-emptive, hoping he would be able to rationalise and separate his innermost feelings in order to make the necessary fine judgements that were to come. He knew full well that this test involved emotions and a degree of exposure of feelings, which he had not experienced in open court before. Fearing his abilities would elude him at the crucial moment, Matthew, although moderately calm, knew he could so easily funk the call when it came. He knew well that under duress there was a possibility of careering off, following illusory ghosts in a wrong direction. Beth, he conceded, was totally reliant on him, he alone would do all he could, but he feared it might not be enough and failure was not an issue to be taken lightly as it would leave her without support, abandoned to her fate. These doubts crowded into his mind and his cavalier attitude towards local help now left him full of regret.

Needing to enter the silent villa in order to prepare for whatever came next, and mindful he was on his own, engendered an unaccountable unease, a tangible feeling of fear. It was immediate and worrying, for he previously thought he would, when the time came, control such emotions. It was not the physical fear of facing his antagonist; no, it was the disadvantage of the unknown, placing a face or voice to who that adversary might be. To one whose emotions were heightened – with nerves pitched to an acute edge, the mere switching on lights, banging of a door, or the creak of a floorboard, could all conspire to produce dangerous illusions. The cold, clammy realisation, exacerbated by sounds from an unknown source, formed the beginnings of an unpleasant and to him unique experience into the agonies of the mind. Feelings of inadequacy flooded in, even to the extent of reassessing his role in the lives of others, considering with regret the perfunctory nature of his dealings.

Many times in the past, contact had confirmed the worst fears; a parent's abhorrence that their child was in the hands of an illogical, perverted stranger. Their unremitting self-recriminations and tears of reproof remained all too vivid in his mind, as did the sadness and remorse of the final inevitable discovery of a body, whose young life had been squeezed out of existence. A family reliving the child's final moments of despair rebelled at the unfair nature of life. Dwelling on the child's terror and isolation, without their comforting hand, only compounded a multitude of precipitous questions, all firing imagery of a bizarre, unsavoury kind. Did they? Had they? Words and questions that provoked answers, which always would be better left unsaid. Then the incongruous moment when thanks had been meted out, grateful thanks for his and his fellow officers' assistance... for what! A dead child; there was little comfort in that. The ineffectual outcome, which left a bitter tang for both him and the team, merely gave voice, a pronouncement, on their inefficiency and failure of purpose. Their detached involvement in matters that destroyed families left him with a sense of futility and of justice that had failed to be served.

So it was – heavy-hearted and despondent – that he finally entered the house, locking himself into his own destructive cell for the night. On moving through the rooms he almost failed to recognise the object which was the cause of their predicament. The simple and, in normal circumstances innocent, shape of a plain cardboard box that sat smugly on the table. It was after all just a cardboard box; but its existence was the cause of his present anguish and the reason for someone unknown to abduct his wife. The box was nondescript, without obvious colour or decoration, it had just one large symbol in black decorating the exterior. Although in French, it was not difficult for him to understand, it simply translated as *'Golden Bee' honey X six'*.

Though, obviously he was very aware that it was not just a box, it was to someone an object of value and involved unprincipled behaviour from some unknown factor; he was confounded as to how such a simple commodity could suddenly threaten their very existence. Very much awake to the value of this package, its strange unidentified and, as yet, obscure message that held a meaning yet to be solved. Whatever else it implied, his wife's safety included, he knew he must guard it well. Concentrating his mind – resorting to type – he checked the exterior thoroughly in minute detail, but there was, disappointingly, only the simple printed label, the brown card sat mute and unresponsive. Then annoyed by the initial lack of detailed description he prodded and tapped the top flap absent-mindedly with a red capped Biro, in his frustration remembering it was the one that Beth used for making out the list of their barbecue needs.

A sudden movement of the box lid surprised him as it flapped upwards and stood briefly open to reveal its interior; releasing the probe, it dropped immediately back down into place. He repeated the action several times as if willing a message to leap out and tell all. The reality was that each time the aperture closed the contents within were spirited away from his prying eyes, it acted as if playing hard to get. Leaning forward he pushed at it again, angrily, this time with a finger. Prodding it accusingly, as if the inanimate object was controlling the situation, and just lying there, gloating at him. This time the flap stayed vertically to where he pushed it, he was not going to be fobbed off by a box, the French police, a madman, or anyone, when it came to Beth's safety.

He pulled himself up to hover over the package, although exhaustion was setting in, he knew this container must hold the key somewhere within its recesses. It did however, look just like any other cardboard container. Matthew muttered his thoughts whilst turning it around to view all sides; 'drugs, small items, could be hidden in the seams of it' … 'LSD dots on the label, no surely not'. 'They, or he, had mentioned jars, five of them, so they all must have a purpose, but what?' He did not initially disturb the packages but remained studying the contents, eyeing the individual items with deep suspicion, desperately attempting to understand where the code might lay. The jars sat inside the box – he felt – mocking him from within their split card separators. There were five neatly labelled jars of translucent golden honey, capped with bright yellow lids and labelled Le Château St Jean, Produit de France. 'What in heaven's name makes them different from English honey?' He couldn't comprehend the significance of it. Recalling the message left in the car and retained by the police officer, he could remember it word for word.

'YOU HAVE COMMODITIES BELONGING TO ME
WE CAN EXCHANGE IF YOU WISH
DON'T BE STUPID
BOTH THESE ITEMS CAN BREAK AND
EXPOSURE WOULD BE CRITICAL
JUST GO BACK TO YOUR VILLA
I HAVE YOUR WIFE
ARRANGEMENTS WILL BE MADE
TO EXCHANGE THE FIVE SOON!

Although the message was clear enough he was still mystified as to the meaning or relevance. 'What makes them worth risking a kidnap and toying with the life of my wife?' Frustration at the unseen message and his lack of comprehension made him increasingly angry at his own incompetence.

Removing the jars individually and with care, he examined the exterior of each one, in particular the labels and lids. It appeared to be the same thick amber liquid that sat in each of the clear glass vessels, he could see straight through the jars to the rear of each label, apart from where the small section of honeycomb sat at its centre. Not being an apiarist, he had no clear concept of what a honeycomb should look like close up, but to his mind it looked distinctly realistic, the comb with its six sided recesses appeared authentic. Of course there could be drugs, diamonds, or who knows what in there, but the complete package, undamaged, was his wife's insurance and salvation; so the examination, at best, could only be surface, anything else would face scrutiny in another place. Matthew replaced the jars each to its own division, in the same positions from where he had taken them. Then clutching the box firmly under his arm, with an overwhelming tiredness controlling his step and thoughts, he made his way sadly up the stone staircase. Leaving the ground floor lights ablaze to act, he felt, like a beacon, should his wife be free to return.

Falling across the bed – sleep was no passing friend – he turned the day over and over in his mind. She had chided him for trying to get brownie points, handing in lost property, how stupid he'd been. He was no longer a paid officer of the law; it wasn't England; who knows what arrangements had been undone by his interference.

Would the phone ring?

A knock.

A call.

Anywhere, any time, now!

Beth was everything to him; they had no children in their marriage, one of those physiological non-baby-making problems. It had not been such a problem to him with all the distractions of detective work. Beth however was a different story, she had her own circle of friends who all eventually had babies or were associated with children. Baby clothes and baby talk were the order of the day and she had taken part in their lives, where she could; finally becoming godmother to one of them. It was not that she was made unwelcome in their family circles, but in truth the children were not hers or her responsibility. That unsubtle difference caused a cooling in friendships, the pang was hard, but since his retirement things between them had improved, Beth and he had established a greater understanding of each other's needs.

He considered the details over again and over again but to no avail, it still made no sense to him; the box stayed by his side where he willed it to talk. Finally giving in to exhaustion he closed his eyes at somewhere near two in the morning and despite the fact that it was unbearably hot, the air conditioning was off, so any movement in the house or grounds would be heard. Volleys from the glowing tennis court across the river were not cutting the air – it was strangely quiet, the only sounds were the hooting and crying of nature. Nightmarish images flitted through his mind as his sub-conscious state veered towards strange imagery, horses, soldiers and a great column of white-robed people with bowed heads. He had seen them all before, ever since his arrival on Spanish soil, and they had in turn followed him into France. So far their actions had been repetitious, always walking slowly past him towards the fire, but tonight one significant detail had changed, every face he now saw was made in the image of his wife Beth. Even more disquieting to him, he realised that for the first time since the visitations had begun, an air of acceptance reigned; there was no plea or play on his emotions for him to help. He was purely a voyeur, as the procession of spectres floated continuously across his dream-like vision, retaining a quiet dignified resolve. No screaming, crying, or protestation, as they glided ever onwards into the insatiable flames.

-oOo-

Near the end of his service in the force, he had been called to a house in the middle of the night. It was for him, one house too many, a body too often; the cold slabs and lifeless forms, such sights he had hoped to avoid in the last months of his career. Now in the heat of night he seemed surrounded by death. As fitfully he walked yet again up the same staircase and came face to face with a young girl strangled. Her face pained and contorted from the struggle with the halter around her neck as it had stealthily choked her spirit out. The pressure of command had been heavy on him, the need to make a decision, take charge and react with calculated skill. Faces watched for his reactions, waited for his orders, images multiplied and flashed before him. A roadside body, another woman surreally exposed and skimpily dressed in a lurid red Basque and thigh boots. Her hideous mascara-streaked face from the overnight rain, still taunting from pained expression on the spot where she had been dumped. They crowded in on him, bodies, questions, where were you?

What did you do?

Where is she?

What are you doing now?

-oOo-

Panting hard, and tossing back and forth, the world closed in on him, his body shook with the enormity of it; suddenly he struggled free from the vision, sitting bolt upright he found himself sweating in a darkened room. Half awake, he screwed up his eyes and shook himself again to break out of the circle, the surreal imagery, that had taunted him with its frightening faces, now fading. He looked across the room at the clock, the bright green digital numerals told him it was four in the morning; somewhere a bell was ringing, somewhere in his mind, no, it was the door. Quickly throwing back the covers, he threw himself out of bed and crossed the room, descending the stone stairwell full of apprehension. In front of him through the ornate glass of the front door was a solitary figure, silhouetted black against the glare of the security light.

"Who… who is it?" Matthew blurted out.

A quiet voice came back in reply, timid in sound, as though not wishing to wake the occupants, but quite distinctively the voice was one he recognised, there was a strong London accent. Matthew slipped the bolt and turned the key to find, incredibly at four in the morning standing on his doorstep, the diminutive Cockney tourist who had confronted them in the village. Matthew, disbelieving his eyes, was left speechless, but rallying to the absurdity of the situation realised that anyone could or might be involved with Beth's disappearance. He struggled hard to control his rising anger, refraining from outwardly showing aggressive behaviour. The game could be commencing and not wishing to jeopardise his wife's safety he responded, but finding an inability to be civil to the man, his response was curt.

"Yes? You rang the bell! Is there something?"

Everything beyond the figure facing him across the garden remained quiet, with the darkness absorbing all other shapes. The man stood in a pool of light emanating from a harsh spotlight above. His eyes were blacked out in shadow; he appeared quite uncomfortable, shifting from one foot to the other self-consciously, or was it a failing nerve? He seemed aware of his intrusion and the lateness of the hour, speaking quietly and succinctly about the purpose of his visit; Matthew listened intently yearning to gleam information, anything, some small detail that would be helpful in getting to Beth.

"I have called to collect something you have of mine, I would like to make the exchange now."

He wasn't the brash, loud-speaking tourist of earlier that day, but a quiet, thoughtful dealer in commodities.

"Sorry for the hour old man, you see we returned late... only an hour ago in fact and in two more hours we're off again. So you see I'll need to take my package to England with me."

It was all negative, Matthew had no proof of good intent, where was Beth, was she outside in a car maybe. He struggled to understand what it was the man was trying to say and more importantly what he wanted Matthew to do.

"I have your property and it is safe. Is mine in the car?"

The Cockney scratched his forehead and looked puzzled, remarking,

"Why yes... I... I don't understand?"

Matthew climbed the stairs in a melancholy frame of mind in order to collect the box from where he had put it for safekeeping. He was confused, it was not happening as expected, there was no pattern that he could decipher or any information as yet, to be helpful. Returning quickly to the door – he was over-anxious and it showed – he looked around panicking for a moment thinking the man had gone. Then, hearing the metallic clunk of a car door as it shut nearby, he was relieved to follow the sound of feet returning across the loose stones on the drive. Bracing himself to receive instructions, which would surely be the next move, he waited expectantly for the man to return. Suddenly appearing in the pool of light by the porch, the man, his bright white suit gleaming, was disappointingly alone. Matthew spotted that the man held something and on reflection realised it was being offered to him. For some unknown reason the stranger seemed to take delight in what was on offer, his face carrying an obsequious golden smile.

Matthew hesitated to pass the cardboard box and its contents across to him for checking; after all there was no mention of his wife and no guarantee she was still in the vicinity. The little man looked across to Matthew and was clearly puzzled further by the box that he was holding.

"What's this? A rather large box, old man, just for the battery that is! It's not necessary you know."

Was the man leering at him, or maybe he was being tested in some way. trying to establish whether Matthew knew its contents.

"There's no need to bother, I can manage a small package in the suitcase for the journey home."

Matthew couldn't believe what he was hearing, was this man for real at four in the morning? His agitation grew, as frustratingly the man remained placidly quiet standing before him on the doorstep. There was no sense of clarification; nothing was being achieved, his wife's incarceration remained obscure and remote. Matthew needed more and in his curt response pushed the man for more information.

"I'm not sure what it is you want or require me to do, but have you really come here… just for your battery at four in the morning? Is there an exchange? You mentioned it."

"Oh that!" He smiled and in a matter of fact manner pushed the videotape he was holding forward for Matthew to accept.

"A little present for your kindness. I took the liberty of taking some pictures of your wife, I hope you like them."

The peculiar nature of his speech, totally out of context and yet very close to what he had expected, left Matthew floundering. Was the man genuine or did he note an edge, maybe concealing a threat; he felt strongly that there was a connection. These two messages, a tape of pictures showing all was well so far and a request for commodities seemed to fit the pattern. They flowed towards him, around his brain and collided but neither making sense. Surely the contact would not be so brazen – even in a foreign land – as to expose an identity and show involvement so openly. Matthew was decidedly confused as to what he was witnessing and how relevant the bizarre meeting might be. It was hard to believe that this was the contact, it seemed both absurd and surreal, but there was something strangely unnerving in the quizzical nature of the man's personal comments about Beth.

"You know she is a fine-looking lady, your wife. Very photogenic! I'm very sorry about the timing, I really am, but our coach is on the move again… I tried all day, really I did. I popped round twice to see you yesterday, but each time you were out. And as I drove past I saw the lights on so I took a chance." With his head cocked to one side he appeared to study Matthew's face intently for a reaction before concluding,

"If I could take my battery with me? Hope you don't mind?"

There was a long pause in which Matthew felt something must transpire, something tangible was about emerge, a glimmer of information on which he could cling, something to work on and gain purpose.

Then just as suddenly this strange little man concluded the meeting, without directions or commands or anything that would further his cause.

"Well, must be off."

That was it; he was no closer to securing Beth's release or wiser as to what had happened to her or more to the point how to proceed. Carrying the precious box back into the house, he returned shortly with the wretched man's battery. The little man smiled with obvious delight when he received it, making a short comment.

"Thanks for that. Hope all turns out well for you both!"

There was a distinct pause as he turned away, then, glancing back over his shoulder, he called out,

"Toodle-pip!"

He then made his way back down the drive, leaving Matthew standing open-mouthed in disbelief. Watching incredulous as the man wandered away into the gloom, he was still suspicious, unconvinced by the little man's performance. Making a mental note of the car's registration number (probably hired under a false name he thought) the battery incident he felt sure must be a ruse. It was far too much of a coincidence; if this was the expected approach it was a damned strange one. Saying nothing more he sadly closed the door, his exasperation blocking out the image of the retreating vehicle.

It was light when Matthew finally dragged himself out of bed; there were sounds of a strong downpour outside. He was surprised as it was totally unexpected; there had been no rain for several weeks and if anything good could happen, it would certainly be a downpour. Several hours of intensive watering no longer necessary, no need to stretch and pull the green pipes around the plot, if anything good was happening this was it. Pulling himself up to look out and check the strength of the rainfall he realised that the sound wasn't right, it was hitting the shutters recurrently as the many garden hoses and fancy sprays might. Through the shutters he could see below a single hose by the front of his car, the outpouring jet of water had been aimed at the bedroom window as it circled relentlessly round every few seconds, taking in the pond, garage and upper section of the house. Matthew, still dressed from the day before – in case – hurried from the kitchen into the garden in order to attend to the troublesome hose; turning it towards the pond he stomped into the garage and switched off the tap. He stood by the garage door puzzled, his incomprehension at what was happening defeated logic, he knew everything was off when he closed down for bed: of that he was certain.

Crossing the patio to go back into the kitchen, a white object caught his peripheral vision and turning his head to understand what it could be he realised an envelope had been pinned to the upright post of the carport; obviously positioned for him to see with the playing water left to draw his attention to it. Rushing forward he snatched it from the securing pin and headed indoors, away from prying eyes. It was a square white envelope and inside it he found two similar coloured pages addressed to him personally. Initially this jolted him, seeing his name written there, then he realised of course Beth would make absolutely sure that anything named was correct and would reach only him. He read and reread the instructions, *'Go to Montségur, to the spot where you found things that belong to me, and wait'*, there was more but the message contained no demands only precise directions and timings. Of greater concern to Matthew, there was no mention of Beth other than if he did as directed, she would not be harmed. Realising the game was on at last; it would clearly be a long day ahead, with no exchange mentioned until nightfall. It meant a long hard drive and an even harder climb, but it seemed that all this was a prerequisite before any exchange could happen. Anxious and bewildered he considered the words again; it would appear that he had to reach the foot of 'Montségur' where the package was originally found, but why! What the hell was it all about?

Gathering up some items of warm clothing for his wife he buried his head into the wool and sensed her presence, touch and perfume. He dwelt for a moment as memories came flooding in, the reality of their situation clarified his potential loss, each item he handled was charged with powerful memories. Sighing despondently, he finally placed them into the flight bag and quickly collected anything that might become useful as the day wore on. With a torch, map and some food packed, he left the villa and crossed to the car, carrying out a final mental check as he went. Almost as he climbed into the vehicle Matthew cursed his own stupidity, he'd forgotten '*THE BOX'*. Returning to the car holding the wretched container as though it were unclean – yet he knew it to be priceless – he placed the box securely down onto the floor in front of the passenger seat and wedged items around it for safe keeping. Sobered by the immensity of the task ahead he settled himself into the vehicle and attempting to remain calm turned the key in the ignition; he was grateful for the engine's positive response as it burst into life. The small white car bit the road perkily as he turned left off the stony remnants of the drive, his face set with grim determination to above all else find his wife and set her free. Obsessed with his quest, he was too engrossed with matters in hand to notice a vehicle that pulled out a hundred metres or so behind him. The nondescript grey-brown Citroen, a colour that blended with the earth of the lane, seemed intent on mirroring his every turn.

Chapter twenty-one

Sacrifice

Matthew's journey lasted for more than three hours as he drove determinedly though the arduous terrain of the Pyrenean foothills. Previously the views at every corner would have provoked exclamations of glee from Beth, a memory that now haunted him, with the twists and turns making him both angry and frustrated. The journey however, although tedious in the extreme, proved uneventful, a blessing in itself with so much else taxing his mind. Approaching the rock stack from the east up the gradual incline, he could see shadows already hanging over much of the vertical face; the concealing woods at its base lay strangely quiet. He intended to steer into the lay-by last used when he and Beth had visited days before. He was perplexed and annoyed to be confronted with a long run of blue and white striped tape, strung between tripod posts, which blocked his access. The area had been cordoned off, for whatever reason, and stakes driven into the ground on the bank above. There were notice boards, which he presumed would give information concerning the restriction. A message in formal French was not something he cared to be bothered with just at that moment. Choosing to ignore what the notices might say, also the direction arrows indicating the route to a lower car park; he shunted his vehicle back and forth until it was as far off the road as the cordon would allow, then finally he applied the handbrake. Taking a moment to glance up towards the chateau above – the castellated top was just visible – he imagined the climb to come; disheartened by the prospect he groaned as he vacated the vehicle. With his right arm gripping tightly around the ill-fated box, he gritted his teeth and trudged despondently up the grassy slope towards the steps beyond; where the true assault would begin.

The rough-hewn steps rose steeply, quickly telling on his capacity to continue after a sleepless night; the effort was proving expensive on his reserves. The psyche of physical achievement relies heavily on mental well-being in order to regulate breathing and match pace to achieve a given task, both of which eluded him. The initial effects of climbing were painfully obvious, with a loud rasping sound emanating from him at every gasp, he knew he was terribly out of condition as his chest heaved whilst gulping for air; in such circumstances a silent approach was nigh on impossible. The box was both cumbersome and crucial; in his other hand he carried the bag with torch to the fore. With the rapidity of breaths failing to fulfil their purpose, he found himself hyperventilating as the tension of the task increased. A pain was seated deep within his throat, his head swam and ached with giddy nausea, there was a feeling of being immensely heavy and incredibly tired. Matthew combined with tensions experienced through the last hours was burdened by his own vulnerability. Having little or no sleep and deprived of rest from anxious phone watching – had eaten into his stamina, he felt morose;

whilst still fostering a strong feeling of anger that such a thing could happen to them.

Climbing had been reduced to a crawl, whilst he dragged himself forcibly up the last few cumbersome blocks of stone. Attempting to contain the exertion, he tried to free his mind to consider events and matters that had affected him personally, ever since arriving on French soil. The messages, a mixture of surreal dream-images that had clouded his normally secure and balanced judgement, had left him psychologically weak. Wearied by these dark visitations, that had called into play emotions not experienced by him before, all plunged him into self-doubt at the wrong moment. Debilitated, he did not know or care to trust his own judgement and in turn the judgement of others. Including, with belated realisation, that of brother police officers, he cursed himself again for his own arrogance.

His now rasping chest forced him to a standstill on the last step before the summit; he hung his shoulders as deep-seated melancholia crept in, the whole of his being ached from the exertion. His desire for individuality seemed now quite played out and support from any quarter would have been seized upon with both hands. Dramatically the light had dropped, the mountain shadows were cast and any glowing ember from the fading sun had long dissipated. His body warmth after the strenuous climb was chastened by a chill wind making its presence felt. So many twisted and contorted stone steps, all conspiring to form a staircase of trepidation, had proved to be a challenge even in daylight but come evening were capable of producing nightmares. Only days before he and his wife had helped each other to make the same ascent. It seemed a lifetime away; they had both hailed the ascent of the precarious escarpment along the path of polished marbled slabs as an achievement, especially so when they arrived safely back down at the base.

Her disappearance in the gorge had brought the safety of their world into question. The world of crime – one which, professionally, he had toyed with for so long – had touched dangerously close to home, something that had not occurred during the whole of his police service. Confused by the events, Matthew even considered the possibility of a past malcontent being involved: a revenge factor. As a player he found himself unable to assess clearly what action to take, but the letter nailed to the carport door had been quite explicit; there was no room for negotiation or manoeuvring, simply a command to bring the article required at a given time, to where he now stood. Having been governed by a plethora of dictates throughout his long successful career, he found himself faced with a situation without the framework of constraints and his ability to 'free-think' had all but left him. To make any decisions unhindered by procedures was proving difficult, emotions had seized his usually productive, well-ordered mind and constrained it into some kind of time lock, constricting any decisions he might have made elsewhere.

He rearranged the aching fingers on his hand, clutching the box of jars more firmly under his arm – their precious bartering moment now approached – wearily he climbed the last, loose shale slope with the five jars, his total insurance for Beth's longevity. Confused, but not stupid, Matthew was not naive enough to believe such arrangements were trustworthy, fool proof, or likely in themselves to be an end to the matter. Unfortunately, in hindsight he had taken a course of action that excluded the local police, so now reprehensibly he had to rely on his own judgement, the deal taking place and a large percentage of good fortune.

'Follow the path through the castle and across the courtyard. Go out through the archway to the rear of the building. Turn left and make your way to the grass bank by the keep.' The letter had been most emphatic, no deviation was allowed for. *'Put the box by the large rock, it's on your left. Walk along the ridge and you will see your wife across the gap, she will be safe, if you deal well.'*

It was a long letter, more than he had imagined would be used. It had intimated that he would arrive before dark and be down again in daylight in safety; he knew from his own recent experience this was more than optimistic, leaving him doubtful of the outcome and what their intentions were for 'the after'. Only the wind broke the silence, obdurately picking on the rough scrub and bushes then the rocks to produce strange vibrating moans. Not normally given to nervous apprehension – his placid calm and professional acumen had truly deserted him – feeling inordinately tense and uneasy, the distressed spirits of the past circled and closed tightly in on him. With what little light remained, the walls of the ancient structure looked down on him in abject dismay, as well they might.

He climbed the metal staircase linking rock to wall, with nerves pitched, straining to hear the slightest sound. Placing his whole weight awkwardly on the structure, the metal bridge responded with a sudden movement. The whole construction swayed and suddenly sagged in a sickening drop. He held on tightly to the rail, awaiting any further movement and daring not to breathe, then just as suddenly its motion reversed. The steel supports clanked back into their embedded recess deep within the rock, accompanied by a low thud; it registered with him as a sharp intake of breath followed by a strongly expressed expletive to relieve his tension. The staircase needed maintenance and before dismounting, it swayed once more, causing him to scramble hurriedly up the last few steps. Jumping clumsily to the rocks above, jolted by the incident, his nerves were at a dangerous edge. After climbing to the wall and pausing for breath, he cautiously crossed the courtyard, checking his way carefully in what little light remained. Intending to make the final approach as quietly as possible proved to be somewhat pointless as his footfall echoed with every step.

A harsh resonance from his well-shod feet, the leather soles reverberated around the empty shell, whilst above, the wind continued its weeping over the battlements. He could neither see nor hear his adversary, nor did he know where he or they might be hiding; but felt sure that his approach was being watched. Matthew was totally disadvantaged; passing beyond the courtyard and onwards through the rear archway he looked immediately left straining his eyes, trying to seek an advantage. Peering through the gloom towards the grassed slope at the foot of the castle keep, he searched the area where he was told she would be and hoped and prayed that she would be unharmed.

He had a torch with him and after retrieving it from his pocket switched it on, it had not been necessary until this crucial point of contact. The small pocket torch – quite inadequate for the task – but nevertheless lit a pathway through the falling light and its beam was a reassuring sight. Shining the torchlight beyond the wall to a small rock enclosure it was possible through the weak beam to identify the prominent rock mentioned in the note. He was just able to pick out a figure beyond in the gloom that he knew would be his wife; she was sitting hunched awkwardly on the ground. He was sickened by the sight and realisation of what he had put her through, he feared for her safety and wanted to rush forward in order to comfort her, but something held him back. He stood static, mesmerised by the situation, not knowing quite what to do next. From his position it looked to him as though her hands were tied together at the front and stretched across her mouth, he realised, was a strip of ugly white tape. Facing the showdown was not an unknown experience to him, but it had always been as a third party. Acutely aware of his wife's demise and not knowing the game play, or the opposition, was far more dangerous than anything he had ever experienced before. With caution no longer a part of the game play, it was his Beth and nothing else that mattered, other than to get her as quickly as possible away from this place.

He cast his eyes down disconsolately at the parcel and wondered how such a plain cardboard box, with its insignificant and seemingly innocent items contained within had become alarmingly obsessive to some unknown, unseen assailant. How on earth such a small commodity could commission all this pain and anguish was beyond reason. Then attempting to sense for a presence, for watching eyes, he reasoned that the box would occupy whoever it was out there, just long enough for him to get to Beth. Following the implicit instructions, he moved slowly across the uneven ground, anxious should he drop the precious cargo, until finally placing the box and its commodities carefully down on a grass tuft by the rock as demanded. With no obvious alternative he staggered onwards across the rock strewn narrow ledge, with nothing else but Beth's welfare and freedom in his mind. He felt her eyes on him with every step as she watched his approach but unable to speak or move in any way for some reason. The torch beam bounced up and down wildly as he tried to maintain balance crossing the rough terrain. Although the torch cast only a thin beam of light he was now close enough to see her outline and make out her facial features.

After straining to see her face he realised with horror that only her eyes were visible above crude wrappings of tape that ran across her mouth and around the back of her head. Her nose and ears were also covered, leaving her to look strangely mummified. But it was the glint in her eyes which held a look that he could not initially comprehend, a look of anguish such as he had never seen in Beth's eyes before. Alarm bells rang as he stumbled towards her, it was not what he had expected; an ecstatic reunion with his freed wife. Failing to comprehend exactly the dramatic message relayed through her eyes, he nonetheless moved forward, paying little regard to caution. Halfway along the ledge – Beth was now only fifteen feet from where he stood, close but not touchable; he realised the path was partially blocked by a large obstruction. The narrowing of the path by two immense upright rocks, both standing at twice his height, was enough to cause him acute anxiety in the frustration of trying to reach her. Matthew was forced to negotiate his way around the obstruction; the path was friable and dangerous with only inches from the edge left for footfall. It took considerable effort as he held onto the rock as best he could, with only a toehold for comfortable contact with the ground below. Beth remained a constant in his viewpoint; nothing else mattered to him as he squeezed by in the narrow space. About to pull clear of the rocks he failed to realise why she was shaking her head dramatically from side to side; he was so very close now that he could almost touch her but the wild horrified look in her eyes made him freeze to the spot.

A sudden and unexpected blow struck him hard on the left side of his lower back, the power of which hurled him instantly off balance, causing him to trip, stumble and fall outwards from the pathway, into the black of night beyond. Whilst continuing his fall into the void, above a drop that he had seen and respected before in the daylight, he thrashed out with his limbs wildly, panic-stricken at what his fate might be. Abject terror of the impending descent now gripped him; knowing it could be at best injurious and, at worst, fatal. With both arms and legs flailing uselessly, they cut the air without response as he fell confused and terrified into the blackness. Falling alongside, but not attached was his torch as it tumbled down aimlessly, he was mesmerised by the beams of uncontrolled light. Aware of it hitting the ground as he continued his strange surreal falling motion, its light twisted and jerked, catching the world in its beam as it bounced and buffeted onto the ground.

The tumbling world was revealed to him, the inky black above and great tufts of grass suddenly and frighteningly broken open by outcrops of sharp rock then just as suddenly a clatter and blackness as the torch's beam was extinguished against a rock. Having comprehended the nature of the ground as it rapidly approached, he braced himself, grateful that it was soft grass on the bank, which would absorb a degree of the initial shock of impact. He still met the ground with a sickening thud, letting out a sound of pain through his expelled air. With his breath dashed by the initial impact, he wheezed and struggled for an intake of fresh air to fill his lungs, the need was great but hampered by the accompanying pain from damaged ribs. He found himself panicking with all things conspiring against him, having great difficulty in drawing in air, considerable pain throbbing in his ribcage and the knowledge as he continued on his rolling descent down the steep slope that he headed towards possible oblivion.

Falling chaotically everything seemed to flash by, in his mind he questioned how he could possibly have tripped and quickly realised that he had been pushed, purposely and with meaningful venom. Having failed to mark sufficiently his wife's warning he had arrived as was planned into the path of an unseen assailant who, after biding his time, had gained all the advantage of cover. Beth had been desperately trying to warn him, but having failed to comprehend the message he was now suffering the consequence. Horrified by the possible outcome of his rapid descent he thrashed out with his limbs in all directions, hoping against hope to make contact with something and halt the downward fall. He kicked out at rocks, bushes, everything protruding as he tumbled by hoping to find a brake, even willing a broken leg, anything rather than his neck. Bewildered – he hadn't expected an attack – Matthew rued his loss of concentration, his complacency in lowering his guard leaving him vulnerable. It was obvious the push had been a calculated act and no accident and he had lost his balance as intended immediately. Beth's muffled cry, her dim shape ahead of him, the trauma of recent days, had all betrayed his normally cautious, calculated manner, to leave him plunging down the embankment. Her stifled scream had been lost in the wind as he continued apace rolling on and on down the steep grass slope, all the time the frozen mask of her face piercing his mind. Finally throwing out his arms and legs in one last major effort, sensing it was all or nothing, he contacted with a rock amongst some bushes. Hitting it hard with his foot he jammed his boot into the crevice, there was a crack as his body jolted to a standstill swinging round like a rag doll.

Groaning with intense pain, winded and badly bruised, he now suffered the ignominy of disorientation, exacerbated by his lack of understanding as to whether or not he was seriously injured. He could no longer assess the damage because of the throbbing pain he now experienced. Very grateful at that moment to have stopped the descent, all he could do was lie still; wincing with pain he attempted to recover his wits and take urgent stock of his situation. Since being violently pushed to an uncertain end he knew there was a serious game change on hand; the assailant obviously wanted no witnesses, so both he and Beth were fighting for their existence. His desire to secure Beth's release had certainly clouded his judgement, for somewhere amongst the rocks an unseen aggressor had taken the opportunity to try to cut the odds in their favour. Initially sensing success, the assailant must be hanging back out of sight, hidden in the dark shadows. For Matthew there was a pressing need to gain the upper hand in this deadly game of survival, and his awareness of a cold shaft of wind funnelling up towards him, left him in no doubt that the cliff edge was now perilously close.

Gingerly testing the ground, he attempted to pull himself upright and gauge where he was and the possibilities. Despite wincing with pain he managed somehow to turn over onto his knees and carefully raise his head. There was an uncomfortable sensation of lacking support underfoot; it was too soft and quite suddenly the grass under his right foot sagged ominously. Recoiling quickly from the unknown danger his instant impulse for survival caused him to lift the offending foot off the ground and move the total weight of his body onto his pained left leg. Panic-stricken he threw himself sideways, his arms flailing at the emptiness, his fingers twitched and clawed in the black abyss, desperately seeking contact with anything substantial enough to grab or hold on to. Something brushed against the back of the knuckles on his left hand; it focused his mind immediately onto the point, quickly sweeping his hand back and forth to locate the object again. His fingers touched it then it was gone, frantically he tried to relocate, grasping and clutching at dirt, rock and plant, until finally his extended fingers returned to the first point of contact and making no mistake this time the fingers wrapped, locked and held on tight.

It was the trunk of a small tree jutting straight out from a cleft in the rock; Matthew gripped his fingers tightly around the gnarled, wizened projection. He anchored himself, clinging on desperately knowing both their futures depended on his firm grip. Clamping hard to the trunk he braced himself for the force of gravity as his feet finally slid away from under him, his legs dangled free out into the void. The dead weight of his body swung loose as his arm took the full brunt of it and extreme pain bit deep into his shoulder; Matthew stifled a cry, biting hard into his lip to hide the acute pain and horror of it. Hanging in the wind he purposely rocked his body back and forth several times before his dragging left foot successfully reconnected with the ground again. Dubious that it may not be good fortune, he stretched full length whilst cautiously testing the foothold to see if its purchase was sound. His grip onto the tree was firm but the continued balancing of weight on his arm was proving to be excruciatingly painful. Nervously searching with his foot for hard rock, as opposed to tussocks of loose grass, he eased himself forward as far as possible without actually letting go of the stump. He was able with this move to allow his leg to take some of the strain, thereby relieving to pressure on his damaged arm.

Below him was – his imagination began to run riot –a void of nothingness for hundreds of feet, the horror of daylight vertigo was mercifully absent but it did little to relieve his horror. Realising his plight and knowing full well he now hung over that very precipice, Matthew attempted to reason as best he could on the peril he was in. Having gained a foothold, he felt somewhat reassured, the bush appeared to be holding firm; the ground also seemed good. Luckily for him in the darkness, height was not an immediate problem but he had no conceivable idea of how to get out of his predicament. With an aching shoulder and panting fiercely from his exertion some of the other feelings returned to his limbs, his shin retold the painful collision with the rocks and he felt both miserable and desolate at the same time. Whilst looking down depressed and forlorn into the dark abyss of nothingness below, he caught his breath and thought – or did he imagine – he could see lights. Blinking hard to readjust his eyes, which were now watering profusely, proved to be a problem under such a strain. There were now lights, he was sure of it, the vision was too consistent to be an illusion, he could see a strange illuminated trail unravelling far beneath him. A singular line of glowing torches was approaching from two directions where they joined to sway in motion in a dual column moving slowly towards a point, exactly beneath where he hung. The flickering flames held his attention, mesmerising him and despite the danger of his situation, he attempted to reason and imagine what it meant. No noise was apparent, nothing filtered up in the fierce breeze hitting the cliff face, which made the ethereal procession all the more extraordinary. He watched as the two columns finally reached the cliff face below, their thin line of flames stretched back over the approaching knoll to where the village lay beyond. He gritted his teeth at the irony of it – there must be hundreds of people down there he thought and they don't know how very much I need their help up here. Both distracted and fascinated by the swaying line of flickering lights advancing to the hill, he had all but forgotten his aggressor, who using this deceptive distraction was now closing quickly in on him.

What must have been initially a check by his attacker to ensure that gravity had done its work and saved him the need, now in turn confirmed to him – seeing the hanging form over the drop – that matters needed stronger persuasion to complete the task. His aggressor concentrated on the job in hand and the power and movement of his enemy moving through the darkness with stealth and obsessive purpose was not lost on Matthew, for whom all alarm bells now sounded loudly. He braced himself for the final assault; there was no escape from where he desperately hung on as he waited in fear for what the aggressor would do to him: survival, though unlikely, was all to him. Aware of the sounds of creaking leather from his aggressor's coat as it approached and rattling zips and buttons, he could locate the movement and prepare for contact. A shadowy blur came closer, as Matthew tensed himself and clung on for life, whilst leaning precariously backwards to gain something of a purchase for thrust. Not knowing who the enemy was, or why indeed he was an enemy, left Matthew's mind whirling. There was no doubt about the desired outcome; it was obvious from his aggressor's actions that it was exactly what he intended. As the attacker closed in on him Matthew's response was intuitive, though in the circumstances positively reckless. Having subconsciously tested the strength of the tree by bearing hard on it, he now prayed his judgement was sound as he pushed off from the rock launching both feet into space. Propelling himself away from the rock foothold and hanging on with both arms, his dangling legs parted from the land and once again swung wildly free, narrowly avoiding contact with his aggressor's fingertips. The hunter stood confused, swaying on the ledge, his hands left clutching thin air as he groped at nothing, his face blanched, drained with disbelief as Matthew hung on grimly a foot two beyond his reach.

The man, who had travelled so far and done so many devious things, wanted to conclude his commission from the solicitor with the leather-topped desk, if it was the last thing he did. He stood angrily cursing into the wind, unaware of the happenings below as the torch light procession came to a halt at the foot of the cliff by the 'Stele' cross. Unseen, one by one they began hurling their lighted torches into a huge mound of tinder wood and flames burst forth instantly from the stack, sending crackling sparks leaping up into the blackness above. The smoke from the stack rose to where Matthew was grimly hanging on. Gower, his attacker, seeing the situation as one in his favour, stood watching, realising that maybe there was no need for him to soil his hands further. A cruel smile formed at the corner of his mouth as he saw the flames start to climb ever upwards, towards its hanging victim; but Gower, not content with its progress, twitched with impatience as Matthew remained hanging on. He realised the fire was not quite strong enough to dislodge this persistent man, so edging along the rock slowly, now clearly defined in the light of the flames, and testing the ground as he moved, he gained sufficient distance to be able to reach Matthew in order to finish the job; once and for all. Ironically the fire's ferocity was now sufficiently bright as to guide him safely in his approach to the hanging victim. Then confident he was close enough to extract maximum effect, he leaned forward, lunging at Matthew with his big fists. The aggressor rained blows down hard, beating on Matthew's arms to make him release his hold on the tree. Grimacing further with the extreme pain, Matthew could only hang on without responding, suffering the abuse at the hands of his tormentor as the pain increased with every blow. As the punishment continued Matthew tried to make peace with himself, there seemed to be no help and no escape, he prayed that Beth would somehow survive.

Suddenly, for no accountable reason, the blows ceased; he was aware of a sudden preoccupation on the part of his aggressor, whose attention was focused on something or somewhere behind him. The bulk of the man remained ever present, standing near Matthew, but no longer looking at him. For now there was fear in his voice as he looked with alarm over his shoulder and appeared to be addressing someone or something beyond. Dust from the ledge spilled out in the paused moment, falling into the void and circling freely outwards into the air until, caught in the swirling heat, it shot upwards with great velocity into the heavens out of sight. A great glow now lit the cliff face and the huge crowd circling the glowing mass of fire chanted in unison to a repeated drum roll, the sound increased in a steady rhythm to reach a high crescendo, then suddenly as if orchestrated: silence. Gower stood for a moment hovering on the edge, everyone seemed to be holding their breath until finally his unbalanced form fell slowly outwards, as if in slow motion tumbling backwards through the swirling smoke; he twisted once to face his destiny, screaming a long "No!" into the funnelled smoking air. The word caught the wind and a screaming note that followed charted the whole descent, as everyone watched silently. The scream ceased abruptly as the body hit the flaming mass below, 'WHOOMPH!', momentarily dousing the fire's ferocity. Flames, smoke and sparks scattered amongst the assembled throng, who remained impassive, standing rigid and watching without comment or movement, accepting that all was meant to be. Gradually the whole assembly smiled as one, as if God had answered the prayers of the persecuted throughout the centuries. Today an offering of sacrifice had marked this special day of the 'Hundred'.

The flames drew back to the centre and returned to shoot with increased vigour high into the night sky, as if in celebration; they licked and curled up the rock stack, to where Matthew remained grimly hanging on in silence, numbed, coughing and choking in the acrid rising smoke.

He was too far from the crowd to see their satisfied faces, or indeed register their pleasure at how well the celebration's finale had gone. Horrified by what he had witnessed he was resigned to his own fate until suddenly he became aware of many raised voices; close by this time and calling, moreover shouting down to him.

"Monsieur, please, hold on very tightly! We are nearly there, you will soon be safe!"

He was vaguely aware of flashlights and several shadowy figures moving about on the rocks.

"Please, if you can make one big effort to swing backwards and forwards, we will attempt to catch you. Continue to hold on, monsieur, until we tell you to let go. Ça va? Okay? Okay?"

No longer seeing or understanding, his hands clinging on, desperately locked around his tree of salvation, Matthew complied with voices and swung his legs as best he could. Initially he felt unseen hands touching him then nothing; 'God, they've missed me,' he thought, 'I can't hang on for much longer.' Then on the second swing their attempts were successful and with great relief he felt a tug as someone gripped his legs and quietly issued instructions for him to let go.

"Okay we have you secure, please release your grip, you are safe now!" There was great reluctance to let go of his saviour, but the quiet voice persisted,

"Please, let go monsieur!"

It was not easy to release his fingers after such an ordeal, they had been locked together tightly and the blood supply locked in with them. They finally responded after great effort and gave in to his will as he managed to part from the lifeline tree stump. Sliding gratefully into the arms of unknown help, Matthew having let go drifted into half-consciousness.

His exertions had taken their toll, the effect was to make his body like jelly, he shook from head to toe and lay back, seemingly unable to control the movement of his limbs. A quiet voice came to him through the night air, speaking with reassurance, at first in French and then English, the words came through like nectar.

"Monsieur, lie quietly for a moment to regain your strength, you have been through a great ordeal. I have here with me, your wife! And don't worry, she is well. I will leave you together for a moment, then we must make our descent."

Beth knelt at his side, her grimed tear-stained face glistening in the torch-light, she was both smiling and crying at once; she gripped his hand and laughed dementedly, holding on tightly as if intending never ever to let go.

Chapter twenty-two

Troubled calm

Gazing absentmindedly through the bowed foliage of the palm, he found himself dwelling on its symmetry, each frond aligning implacably against the uncluttered blue of the sky; how neat and tidy nature was, he thought in comparison to life. Matthew felt grateful that the weather had held; the sun shone constantly since their return to the villa. The heat of the day, however, did little to dissipate the chilled atmosphere he now experienced, keenly aware that the rift between them was growing; silences now contained thoughts that held a dangerous edge to their relationship. The cooling recriminations had long since lessened the euphoric joy of their salvation on the mountain, now falling into the realms of cynicism and blame..

The reluctance to acknowledge each other's presence had stifled the atmosphere in the villa beyond reason; more than a local skirmish, it was likely to develop into a war of attrition. In his heart he knew he was on the thin end of the wedge, accepting she would and should blame him, but he hoped she was not going to allow him to drown. 'The runes' said otherwise, his feelings were that he would certainly be left to tread water for a considerable length of time. With little enthusiasm or desire by either party to engage in the obvious – the missing consent to a period of introspection – meant the icy silence would remain. Though he readily accepted she had a right to point fingers and blame him for exposing her to such inordinate dangers, her first outburst had been, although expected, more damning and aggressive than anything he had ever experienced from her tongue before. Accusing him of blind self-willed stupidity, which totally lacked consideration, he found he had no answers; the remedy for such an impasse remained elusive. A simple apology was just that, too simple and totally inappropriate. He understood little could be achieved in the long term without conciliation and as the belt of silence bit deep into his psyche, he kicked over the traces with only a faint degree of hope that matters might be resolved. The weather's calm countenance was proving to be the only constant companion of any worth, allowing them both to remain outdoors; the internal walls of the villa by contrast would have become interminably close. In such a large garden there was scope for freedom of thought, the space to give vent to personal grief and anger and expunge the traumas that had passed, a process that in itself – because of distance – caused further deterioration in their relationship.

Matthew turned his attention back from marital disharmony for a moment, to avoid the obvious and concentrate on his thoughts on why; nothing was clear-cut or obvious to him. He had always been adept at the minutiae of life during his career, able to assess situations and solve the intransigence of others, but he accepted that on this occasion he was too close and unable to function correctly. Matthew's attentive eye lingered on the plant in front of him, his analytical mind considered each individual segment. They clung regimentally to the long stem sweeping up from its bulbous base in curved elegance; when it reached the very tip of a pivotal arc, nature was both exotic and mysterious at the same time. His observation provided the curiosity factor necessary, a deviation to alleviate the difficult pause in his relationship: a distraction most welcome. As he observed the plant, its segments twitched and sprang as if manoeuvring to avoid the breeze, each segment reacting in its own manner. His first consideration of individuality was firmly put to the test, realising that the movement was part of a harmonious pattern seen on the rippling frond, the segments bore the brunt of the wind together and as such they dissipated its strength.

The splashing water nearby caused him to break his reverie and turn his attention away from the fern and back to the pool, where its lone occupant, his soul mate, carried a look of total dejection on her face, as if the world would implode. He screwed up his face, grimacing, studying his wife's forlorn figure in the far corner of the pool, whilst anticipating the difficulties to come. Frowning in the knowledge at the sight of his wife bobbing up and down to the inflow of water from vent, he knew in his heart of hearts had the area been larger she would have made the effort to distance herself further from him. Beth, desolate and lonely, her silhouette contrasting obtusely with the brightness of day, remained silently static in the shallows of the pool. Matthew felt an overwhelming desire to go over and wrap his arms around her, blocking out the hurt of a troubled world, but somehow lacked the moral courage to do just that.

He watched as she laid her hand on the water's surface, absentmindedly stroking lightly with the bent fingers of one hand, the other, troublingly, held at her mouth – revealing her anguish. The fingers pinched and kneaded consistently at her bottom lip in a state of punished turmoil, this small detail revealed her troubled state. Although Matthew was not in her line of sight, he felt sure her preoccupation included him in an angry, almost vengeful spirit. This total immersion within herself precluded anyone and everything, including him. He was shut out of her world and the rejection was hurting but he knew she was experiencing something far worse. The effects of recent events had demoralised her more than anything they had ever known in their married life together. But then, he had never knowingly crossed the divide and allowed the extremes of his work to expose her to such danger before. He had always remained silent in difficult and sometimes dangerous situations, never ever involving her personally.

Matthew looked up as the wind-lifted upper branches of mimosa swayed in the gust, but despite this obvious display of the physicality of nature, Beth remained impassive and oblivious. She appeared unable or unwilling to give in; if only the obvious tears that hovered would fall he conjectured; then a release would surely follow. He longed for the moment when the break would come. Yellow balls of mimosa blossom fell to become flotsam, riding the ripples of a changing sky, as the mirrored clouds of expectant rain blew grey across the pool's surface. Beth stood statuesque, with water gently lapping around her waist and, despite the warmth of the day, the sudden squall had her thighs in rebellion as goosed skin appeared with her inactivity. Her motionless form occupied a corner of the pool that heralded an avenue of dark green cypress trees, the beauty of the colonnade on this occasion passing her by. She continued her silent vigil, hiding her face from scrutiny under a wide-brimmed straw hat. The hat, an earlier statement – still encircled by chiffon and a flamboyant bow – spoke volumes of the carefree pleasure she had anticipated at the start of their holiday. The deafening silence goaded Matthew in his continued painful observation of a troubled wife and did nothing to alleviate his guilt, or cure the deflation he felt.

Following their ordeal and release on the wild mountainside of Montségur, Beth had clung to him desperately for comfort, understanding and reassurance. On their return to the villa, they had continued to seek sanctuary in each other's arms behind closed shutters; the anonymous shutters, that remained shut for all of the day following, suggested more than the reality within. The villa that appeared to the outside world as both defensive and defiant through the midday heat cloaked the cool darkness of its interior, where the two damaged inhabitants had found only brief respite together. The reassurance of familiar touch as they experienced the first natural easing of trauma, in the confines of their secret room, did much initially to relieve tension. Caresses, willingly given and received, did much to comfort them both. As they lay together responding to the therapy of touch and as always exploring anew the smooth glide of tender flesh that brought heightened pleasure; they fed on each other's warmth. Yet despite their urgent need for reassurance, fulfilment or plain sexual pleasure, they were faced with obvious failure. The distance was too great as they both remained locked wretchedly in their own solitude of self-doubt of both mental and physical pain. Her traumatic abduction and his physical abuse by his attacker both played a part: physical was defeated by psyche.

Finally, dissatisfied and keenly self-aware they had parted abruptly, both of them felt the barrier of rejection descend; their unlinked bodies assumed separate identities with a cold immediacy. Beth's long lithe back acted as a wall, blotting out any physical contact, leaving him further confused by the rapidity and querulous nature of her changing mood. The cold silence of distancing herself from him had been instantaneous; a singular preoccupation of judgement, her accusing finger had metaphorically pointed blameworthiness at the world and in particular towards him.

In the silence that followed, whilst deeply troubled by her desolate mood, he found himself analysing the whys and wherefores; brooding over the possibilities of what might have been. He was confused by the imprinted professionalism of his previous career and the strength of human response required to console his wife in her hour of need. Beth's innate lack of communication made it nigh on impossible to piece any concise facts together, it was only supposition that he held at present. Preconceived ideas – gleaned from his experience of the *'cause célèbre'* – mixed with the resulting soup of what little he knew, now inevitably resulted in a heady brew of uncertainty. Images flitted in and out of his mind, as they churned over vivid, disturbing suggestions, which also unnerved him. This mélange of distorted, disjointed images formed fears of the worst kind; it frightened him, and observing her obvious distress, he found great difficulty in shaking the thoughts from his head in order to reject their implications. Somehow he had to be sure of what he was dealing with and how to approach her without further antagonising the situation. Matthew, not imbued with infinite patience, found his emotions stretched to the limit as he battled with himself to assume a calm persona and at the same time remain sensitive to her needs. For the time being they were safely back in their residence, in a trusted village they both adored, cosseted in the confines of the villa. A safe haven where in the fullness of time he hoped she would finally respond and tell all; he could not truthfully say at that moment whether it would be for her benefit or his.

Beth, coldly aloof, immersed in her own private thoughts, with water lapping around her thighs, left him inwardly anxious and wary; he decided to gamble on making the first move. Pained and somewhat indignant – emotions not useful for reconciliation – and still wary of rebuff – he made a positive move to post his intentions. Bending down on his haunches by the poolside, with one eye warily watching her for acceptance and idly playing his fingertips in the water at the outflow, he hoped somehow to encourage the water to make the first communication. Matthew remained crouching down for a while, more than a little cowed and all too aware of the outburst that was possible; keeping a nervous eye towards her space, he had no wish to breach it. Beth remained locked into deep feelings of hurt, contrary to her normally placid and outward going nature; it was an obstruction to any positive improvement. Matthew desperately wanted '*a bloody good reaction*' – as he would put it – an expensive row even to the point of destruction. Feeling he could take the blame, anything to clear the air, he longed for her to shout the roof off, curse, even mouth expletives. He wished she would jump out of character, do something wild and be aggressive, anything but silence; something to free up the emotions and move on.

Matthew trod where angels fear to tread, he spoke to her with words that were irrelevant, stupid and totally inept, he droned on with oblivious persistence. He was drowning in verbal ineptitude, the words echoed around his head, which he knew to be embarrassingly obtuse. Her personal space was clear-cut; unspoken, yet clearly marked he could feel the barrier surrounding her. He used words and phrased them with a deal of hesitation, showing a reticence as if they had never spoken together before.

"Beth… I know things look bad between us… and probably are I suppose; in fact never been more so. I did something really stupid… unforgivable and that I could have lost you forever! I also know and accept you may not be able to forgive my stupidity… I'll understand if you cannot forgive or forget. But whatever the outcome I want you to know I care and love you deeply… I mean… I'm going to continue to care and love you whatever you feel towards me."

He paused, there was no response and he became clumsy again, over-anxious, saying silly things.

"You must be getting very chilled in the water… now the sun has gone down, please come out! Being ill won't help Beth… you must be very hungry; I know I am. If we eat something it may help a little… a favourite meal or just something to warm our insides, please come back to me, Beth, please try!"

He paused, not daring to breathe, and in the moment's hesitation was overcome with emotion himself.

"Will you come with me to the village… or… beyond, if it's easier that way?"

The subject of food was not difficult or contentious, quite to the contrary. It was one they had always revelled in together, both enjoying a healthy appetite for the good things in life; sometimes in provocative conversation and on other occasions sampling the sheer bliss of a new tasting experience. It was during such stolen moments that pleasures heightened as they conjoined with personal need, away from prying eyes to complete the satisfaction of indulgence. He checked himself and tried speaking more gently, hoping to avoid anything that suggested control or command, but she remained stubbornly sullen, preferring to keep her own counsel. He looked up to the sky as if seeking divine inspiration in order to make his next statement more worthy and relevant, but failed, only to lose his way and blurt out a banal statement of mediocrity. Not really speaking to her this time, his one-way conversation was tinged more with self-pity.

"I think it's likely to rain… I felt a drop or two earlier on! At least it would let us off the hook today… from watering the garden I mean!"

He took a sharp intake of breath; struggling with the effort and reigning himself back into trying to improve his attempt at communication. Matthew looked around the grounds searching for inspiration and, realising that it was an eternity since they had considered the needs of the garden, he muttered aloud to himself. Uttering a sigh of relief, just hearing his own voice again was proving difficult.

"Oh!… The tomatoes… they're in a mess!"

He saw the normally tanned, smooth skin of her back, on which droplets of water glistened, the globules which now reflected the final glint of a tired sun. The skin in turn matched the water in small points of goose flesh where the chill had been sensed from a dipping sun and her long inactivity. Observing the change Matthew moved with purpose across to the poolside chair where Beth had left her towel draped across the arm. He seized the opportunity by carrying it over to her; risking a rebuff in the process he crouched down purposely, moving in as close to her as he dare. Although fully dressed he also felt the change in the atmosphere, the chill air crossed the pool and looking skywards he realised that rain was indeed possible. In an exaggerated gesture he pulled the soft pink towelling gently across her shoulders, hoping the contact would soften her resolve, whatever that was. Matthew remained crouched by her side gently patting on the towel to dry her, silently waiting; although hopeful for a response, none was forthcoming. Beth continued staring blankly at everything and anything and yet nothing. She was either unaware or unable to acknowledge his presence and, from where he now crouched, her red-rimmed eyes were a painful sight to him, the drying stains of tears on her cheeks saying much of her anguish.

Waiting quietly for a response, he was both surprised and disturbed when, without warning, Beth rounded on him verbally. The sound of her voice was loud as it barked harshly out into the silence. He was shocked by its tone, there was a hard cutting edge to it. With no physical movement other than her lips repeating over and over, it was as if she communed with another world. The outburst unnerved him as she continued speaking accusingly; the anguish of which was tinged with aggression.

"Why? Why? Why me?"

Her sobs were deep and now, in what he had hoped in moving closer to her would be a comfort, he found instead that his close proximity had trapped him into receiving her fury, as she turned and glared, focusing her aggression more acutely straight at him.

"Where were you, when I needed you… you always managed to look after everyone else! When it was your blasted job! For once, when I… your wife!"

The jerky intake of breath relayed the sobs of betrayal that now emerged in profusion.

"I can't understand you, Matthew! You! Playing policeman with those damn jars! They were nothing to do with you… or me. In a foreign land… on someone else's patch! It's all a game to you. Only this time it bounced dangerously close to both of us! .W-e… A-r-e!" She stopped. "W-e… W-e-r-e…. O-n… Hol-i-day!"

She spoke the sentence slowly with a crescendo that rose in pitch, emphasising every syllable with fervour that clearly defined her anger and confusion over his lack of understanding. She spat her words out with venom, "For God's sake! We are not in England; it's not your patch! And where's this 'Brothers in Uniform Camaraderie?"

She gesticulated with clenched fists and made a sharp hissing noise of despair through her bared teeth.

"What happened to the glorious exchange of information, where were the local police then? – Are you so pig-headed to believe you can do everything on your own?"

The final outburst had been thrown into the air, as if he were not even there. Until – sensing her strength – she turned quickly towards him as if acknowledging his presence and face to face she glared at him with such vehemence he felt the cold chill go through him. It was some time before she spoke again, collecting her thoughts of times gone by and dwelling on a life that she hoped had changed, dismissing forever the connections with 'a way of life' that everyone euphemistically called it.

"I thought the past was gone! The fear. You've no idea, have you? Worrying, not knowing what was going on, what was happening to you, and now this!" She spoke scathingly at him. "How could you?"

Her stress echoed in the strained voice – unrecognisable to him – pitched strangely high and tremulous, with a suppressed sob as she blurted out,

"My God, Matthew, I've spent a lifetime waiting for you to come home… from… from, heaven knows where or what. Involved with people who were less than pleasant. How did they put it in your office? No, don't tell me *'Scum of the earth!'* Then… you, who have retired, who knows about retribution, revenge and the strange minds of cranks… should have exposed us… me… your wife! To such despicable people?"

She stopped and stared at him showing her disdain and disbelief, as if seeing him for the first time.

"Do I… have I ever counted for anything in your life? Do you care?"

She stopped and gave in to a deep melancholy, sobbing, with all sophistication abandoned as she wailed like a child.

Despite his alarm at the vociferous nature of her outburst, he inwardly felt a deep relief from it, knowing her

327

outpourings were a necessary step in clearing the air for better things to come. Matthew, despite everything, had remained crouched at her side; silently administering his concern by adjusting her towel and tentatively with his arm now around her shoulder, supporting her as she wept openly. Beth looked up; suddenly aware of his presence again she turned on him, flaring briefly whilst attempting to brush him away and shake off his hold; but this time he persisted. Matthew countered any resistance, until finally she gave in to his insistence and allowed herself to be led weakly up the steps and out of the pool. Crossing the terrace, she visibly faltered; then walking slowly onwards she held his hand, for a moment gratefully accepting his support as she steadied herself over the steps upon entering the villa. Once inside, speechless and shaking, she remained standing limply in the centre of the room whilst water dripped from her onto the polished ceramic floor tiles. Her pent-up emotions and the cold dripping water – now encircling her feet on the floor – left her shaking violently. He unfastened the shoulder strap and peeled her out of the wet garment as quickly as he could. Standing naked before him she felt self-conscious, no longer in charge and tried with a futile effort to turn away. She had no wish for him to see her naked in that vulnerable state. He ignored her embarrassment, intent only on towelling her down to raise her temperature as the convulsions of her body slowly dissipated. Busying himself with her physical needs blanked his mind from what she may or may not say or feel towards him.

There was a bottle close by and he poured a liberal helping of the strong local Grenache, handing it carefully to her; the glass was greeted lamely by her fingers and without comment. After an initial gulp – consumed too rapidly for her own good – she stood convulsed in a fit of violent coughing. Catching both the empty glass and his wife before they fell, Matthew warmed to the task as he held onto her firmly, he realised the precious nature of this woman and what she meant to him. Carrying her limp form towards the bed, he eased her gently between the sheets and was grateful for the touch of her, making him able to be part of her world again.

Closing the door, he retreated quietly, leaving her to rest and, on passing through the lounge, lifted an opened cognac bottle and glass. Gripping it by the neck, he wandered thoughtfully over to the poolside. The last embers of glinting sunlight shimmered along the base of the pool, reflecting the rippling waves above, as he fell back heavily into the easy chair, exhausted. His pained, tired body now reminded him of the abuses he had received over the last few days. The whole of his shin was deeply discoloured by severe bruising and the contusions generally were causing his leg to throb, the consistent pain in leg and wrenched shoulder were proving difficult. His mind was also awhirl with the accusations thrown at him by Beth. Of course she was right. Beth, through the cathartic process of purging her trauma, had managed in the outburst to challenge the ghosts of the past, the pomposity of his career and even the very premise of their life together. Feeling battered physically and mentally he opened the bottle, seeking comfort in another form; the underlying truth was that he had not truly considered her in any way. There was a deep element of unspoken history brought out in her unguarded outburst; it was hurting him to acknowledge the fact, but he knew the blunt truth had

329

correctly exposed his failings. His inability to communicate on the many occasions when embroiled in a complex enquiry had only ever been lightly alluded to by her. She had never complained directly and as a result he had overlooked any consideration of her needs. It had always been more a sin of omission, at the time being deeply embroiled in an enquiry very often complex and sometimes dangerous. Finally brought face to face with the fact and by such vehemence, he regretted his abject failure in not being more understanding. Shaking his head over the questioned, dubious loyalties allied to the job, which he had held in reverence above all else, he gripped the glass firmly as if it were his only friend. Concentrating on the rich liquor swirling around inside he clutched the bulbous glass of amber between his palms, watching the sparkle of light play on the waters of the pool, as he played the glass back and forth several times. Admiring its beneficial powers as though it would provide him with an answer, he completed the ritual by downing the syrupy liquid in a single gulp. Instantly he felt it glide on its beautiful journey, the warm glow flowing from his gullet to spread out across his being. For the moment the infusion left him more contented and able to suppress life's problems for a little while longer.

The frantic friction of calling cicadas sounded off into the Latin night, gradually rising in urgency as the sounds of the village stilled one by one; the laughter and clatter across the river were finally stifled by darkness. Matthew anxiously held his breath on entering the room; he listened in the dark to the uneven, stressful breathing pattern that filtered out through the open window. Nightingales somewhere beyond, down by the river, trilled to one another for reassurance and an individual bird sang stridently, giving a concert performance for audition. The lush, rich fruity notes rose in clarity near the window, there was a resonance and passion in the call, followed by total silence. Beth, as if controlled by the sudden silence, signalled the fact by sitting bolt upright; it was such a sudden movement that he was shocked and surprised by it. She spoke out as if mesmerised, there was an urgency of recall in her words.

"I waved to you – from the bridge…"

It was a strange single-note whisper, without emotion.

"It was too far to shout! In any case, he dragged me backwards… back to the… car?" She questioned her own statement. "No… no it was a van… Before I could shout again, or make sense of what was happening… I thought you saw… and recognised me?"

She paused, the sad ring in her voice revealed her disappointment.

After a long motionless wait – in which Matthew had hoped the moment would come, he scarcely breathed for fear of interrupting her. Wanting to reassure but fearful of stopping her outpourings he said nothing, merely placing a reassuring hand on her arm as he waited patiently. Her speech, a mixture of staccato and hesitant jumbled words, came out in sequences of erratic hypnotic utterances, she spat out the moments as if needing to purge the very thoughts by erasing them instantly from her memory, once told.

"I didn't see him… there. There was no-one on the bridge… when I looked over. No movement anywhere!"

For a while there was silence in the room, which seemed to amplify the call of nature; in the blackness of night creatures complained and challenged and beyond in the hills a lone fox barked. Beth broke the tension of the moment.

"I know... I ran on ahead without saying!"

It seemed to be an attempt to apologise, as if it mattered to her psyche.

"Beth, I didn't ..."

Matthew on impulse interjected briefly, then thought better of it, biting his lip to stop himself.

"I thought you'd seen me climb up the steps. I wanted something from the car. Ye-e-e-s, that was it, some of the gel... for insect bites... they were troubling me. I reached the car, then ran back to the bridge, thinking you would be panicking... Such a rush – I forgot to lock it... I left the car open! Suddenly... I was gripped by someone from behind... dragged backwards... and..."

Her body tensed; there was fear in her eyes.

"I was held very roughly and violently and pushed inside a vehicle... a very small van."

She looked to him for comprehension.

"Like the French farmers use, you know? With the crinkly roof! The man was very strong... I couldn't argue? He didn't speak. It all happened so quickly!"

She fell silent for a moment as if trying to absorb what she had said and feeling the need to check it for detail.

Matthew took a sharp intake of breath and realised he was thinking police again and needed to clarify the crossover between what happened to Beth and his own experience. He took a risk and posed a question.

"Did you go back to our car again? With that man I mean! Did you see him go to our car for any reason?"

"No! He didn't stop he just drove down the slope... to the vegetable gardens below the bridge and up the other side, leaving the village driving to the main road. Why… why do you ask?"

Matthew suddenly found himself on the spot; he was exposing his own ineptitude, the complete failure to aid his own wife when she was in dire need.

"When the police officer finally arrived… I… We… found a message on the dashboard. It was written on paper and folded over. I thought… I had hoped it was… you might have seen… I thought it was from you, I was hoping. But after reading it through, I quickly realised what it meant and went cold with the terror! My God Beth, I was very frightened… I thought I had lost you!"

Matthew slid his hand down to her waist and put his arm around her, pulling her closer to him as he spoke with emotion.

"Inside my stomach heaved… I felt sick… worst of all I didn't know what to do. For once I was helpless, you were in mortal danger and I could think of nothing positive to help."

Thinking through the events, piecing together what he knew, Matthew spoke quietly, with regret for his stupidity.

"I suppose we must have been followed? Watching our movements all morning… you going back to the car was a gift, it was perfect. He could leave the note and grab you at the same time. It couldn't have been better for him."

He realised she had fallen silent and that he had been speaking too long. In his desire to seek answers he had foolishly curbed her outburst; fighting the temptation to continue he fell silent to give her time. The quiet moment was what she had needed, a moment's reflection after so much anguish. Several minutes passed whilst she relived her nightmare inwardly without speaking, remembering the very smallest of details. The chronology of detail was somewhat difficult to piece together, but strangely she felt she had to assemble her ordeal, assembling the story in such a way in which she could dare to speak it out loud. The methodology of such thinking was ironically the result of years of detailed conversations they had experienced together, it had become second nature to her to clarify events.

"I had no idea what had happened or where we were going. I was aware of the vehicle; it was old and smelt strongly of oil or petrol. You know how I am with car fumes! I started to feel very sick, it was the journey, I suppose, and obviously the tension. He took the corners much too fast in his panic, the car bounced about on the road. The only thing I knew was that I recognised some of the areas we passed through, it was in the hills of the Corbières. There were no other vehicles, at least I didn't see any or recognise any of the villages… it was just one long nightmare. The most unnerving thing was – he didn't speak to me at any time. What he wanted, what his purpose was, all were a mystery to me. Without speaking or any explanation I started to imagine the worst, and watching the man's face as he drove along gave me the distinct impression that his desperation was tinged with acute danger. He didn't look at me for the whole of the time, it was as if I was just an object for him to use. There was something so dark and broody about him, I felt his fear and agitation, it frightened me as I didn't know why I was involved!"

She turned to Matthew for the first time in the darkness and he sensed her anguish and that she was making a plea for comfort. He enveloped her in his arms, holding tightly for fear of losing her, the response was enough; she nuzzled into his chest and released her pent-up emotions. He felt the moisture of tears that fell and her gentle sobs against his chest, but said nothing. Very quietly between sobs, she continued,

"Not much worries me normally – but I thought – this time – 'You're going to die!' I was terrified! Matthew, I think it was the strength of this powerful brooding man. I couldn't fight him and the ride to nowhere, and without reason; it was a journey to hell!"

Only the urgent rush of water pouring over the scattered rocks in the riverbed, which lay in a gully some eight feet below the garden, cut the apprehensive tension of his thoughts. During the preceding week, storms in the mountains had caused extensive flooding in the village and a barrage, where the children normally swam in the warm summer months, now lay in scattered piles of disassembled rocks. The continuous rush of flowing water formed a background roar in its rapid descent, but even this he no longer heeded. Remaining propped upright he was preoccupied, listening intently to the sounds of his wife as he cradled her, thankful that she had finally given way to sleep. When the first glimmer of light fell onto the window, marking a new day, he watched silently as the sun's rays cut a clear path in the quiet gloom, crossing rapidly to play across Beth's face, which in turn caused her to wake. Checking only briefly for reassurance as to where she was, Beth glanced towards him then quickly away. The intimation of her movement when she looked away was obvious, still wishing to distance herself from him. Remaining sitting where she was on the edge of the bed, Beth refrained from speaking, her red-rimmed, strained eyes told all. Once out of bed, however, and down the mezzanine ladder – before he could say a word – she appeared to assume the role of domesticity. The splash of water tumbling into the kettle, along with its clattering lid, gave him a sound picture of what she was up to. He could sense her movements as the click of a light switch and her padding feet trailed off into the shower room; he felt somewhat relieved at the normality.

He knew there a danger in listening to deep emotional experiences; when witnesses bared their souls, resentment usually followed. Private thoughts were too painful to expose to others and he guessed Beth was feeling much the same. He imagined that she was probably confused about him, his inability to help her and now being privy to her innermost thoughts and emotions; matters that more often than not caused the divide between couples. He slithered down into the covers of the bed and by the time his head contacted the pillow, his eyes had already fluttered and he was drifting off to secure his much needed sleep.

Chapter twenty-three

Spiritual peace

An uneventful final week in a foreign land, where relationships had been tested to the full, was the most they could or would wish to entertain after their recent brush with mortality. Beth remained pensive for most of the second week, not obstructive or difficult, but always avoiding contact where possible, still preferring her own company. He had been happy to wait around patiently in case she wished to talk, but the moment never seemed to materialise, leaving him harbouring doubts and still having no concise idea what had happened to her between Minerve and the mountainside of Montségur'. Matthew's first inclination had been to consider returning home early, leaving her space to mull on life and their place in it, but when he had approached Beth to seriously consider it, he was thankful that the suggestion had proved unwelcome. In theory at least there was little in the way of danger left for either of them and the thought of leaving a preferred second home of many years, so abruptly, was an unwelcome consideration. Whilst the sun shone and the pool beckoned, and their supply of the local chateau's 'Rose' held firm, why should they wander further.

Driving back to Girona was, as ever, straightforward enough and without incident, but for once their conversations were subdued. The normal chatty excitement on passing the glittering Étang below, and the long climb to the Spanish border through the Pyrenees, remained a reserved contemplative passage and it was the sea that held their gaze wherever possible, for in the opposite direction lay Montségur. After the customary two hours, Matthew, who had insisted on driving, pulled into the wide sweep of the 'Aeroport', an ungainly large square blockhouse of a building skirted by a huge car park. For much of the year, this charter holiday destination airport remained silent – until peak season – then bristling with suitcases, trolleys, cars, officials and mystified passengers, all the visiting expectant holidaymakers poured through its giant glass doors, endeavouring to come to terms with cramped travelling and night shifts. He swung the vehicle into the hire car reservation space – where the bays were designated to companies – and thankfully parked. They both looked at one another without comment as they saw the row of little white cars, all exactly the same as theirs, with just one bay remaining unfilled.

After boarding the plane he managed to doze, this time successfully without medication or visitation, the occasional interruption aside of course, as the obligatory trolleys of duty free and trays of instant packaged meals rolled by. He had always considered the presentation as some form of calming process, like humps in the road – it slowed everything down and made everyone more manageable. Food was rather a presumptuous title for a tray of cellophane-covered implements and labelled tubs sitting on the tray before him. It was more like a family quiz show,

338

or 'Kim's Game'; how to keep all the bits on the tray, once they were opened, and what on earth were the contents inside them anyway. It did pass the time of course, Beth seemed to manage quite well and even ordered an extra alcoholic drink of known vintage to accompany whatever else it was she had found.

A smiling hostess removed the debris, not too many accidents this time; the idea of travelling in a shell suit was more appealing these days, easy to wash and freshen up after food trays and sleepless journeys were over.

"More coffee?" Again the broad smile as the hostess stood in the aisle hovering with a steaming jug, both plastic cups held out in position were replenished. After the first sips he turned to her; amidst the whine of jets and the gabbling passengers they were after all, almost alone to talk.

"Beth! – Do you feel able to talk about what happened yet?"

She sipped some more of her coffee down as though it were her first drink in weeks, then turned and looked at him.

"Ye-es!" There was a proviso in her response.

"I wasn't harmed, Matthew, if that is your worry – physically I mean. I find it strange, it's not very easy to recall everything, it's in some way like a dream."

She stopped talking and thought about the events, trying to slot the incidents into sequence. Living with a detective for so many years had taught her one thing, to be precise when relating facts.

"I was walking towards the bridge… I knew you were dreaming history down there, that place was a bit weird…

near the mouth of the cave. Stupidly I thought it would be fun to run up to the bridge and wave down to you."

"Why not?"

Matthew looked thoughtful.

"You know in strange places, it's always nice to know where everyone is!"

She didn't respond to the rebuff initially, instead they both sat listening to the drone of the aircraft, locked into their own thoughts, then,

"I know love, sorry. When I reached the bridge to lean over and wave, I realised you were already panicking down there. I supposed you were trying to find me; so I shouted and lifted my arm to wave. And that was that, a hand grabbed my arm from behind and bundled me backwards into a car. The man was big, very... I couldn't argue with him; after all he had picked me up, literally with one hand. He told me to sit still and behave and I would not be harmed, he just pushed me into the seat and belted me."

Matthew prompted her.

"Not tied in or touched in anyway?"

"No!"

She looked at him in an enquiring manner.

"I was very frightened though. I knew you were in the gorge tearing your hair out looking for me… poor you. The man drove for hours; we didn't stop. He had amazing bladder control, but for me it was a most uncomfortable journey! We arrived in a village around nightfall, driving up a narrow lane. There was nobody about and very few houses, well I know it was in the mountains."

"The man wasn't French?"

"No! Not all. It was the only time he spoke to me, just those few words. Very English, west country, Gloucester, Hereford maybe!"

"Okay, okay, go on!"

"Well in the headlights I saw a small cottage near some trees; he extinguished the lights immediately, I imagined he didn't want to be noticed."

"Are you saying Beth, that when he put you in the car he didn't drive to the top car park where our car was?"

"No, why?"

"No matter. Did you get food and drink?"

"Yes!" She looked surprised.

"He put me in a very small room with a barred slit window, I think it was a food or fuel store. There was a chair and table only, some water in a jug, several packets of half-eaten sandwiches and things and leftover food bits everywhere."

"And?"

"He told me to sit and eat if I wanted and he would be back soon – then he locked me in – it went quiet – and I heard the car pull away."

"Were you very frightened then?"

"No, that's the funny thing, at that moment I wasn't. I was locked in by this man who hadn't spoken above a few words to me, he didn't look at me, he seemed distracted, preoccupied by events. I realised I was his means of doing or achieving something, but what it was all about heaven alone knew."

"Can you remember when he returned?"

"It was about four or five in the morning, there was little or no chance of sleep with just a table and chair in a bare room. Luckily there was a bucket in the corner

341

otherwise life would have been quite distressing. He didn't come into see me on his return. About midday, I was feeling pretty awful, he came into the room and forcibly dragged me out, putting me back into the car again without any explanation and then drove off. I just could not believe where we landed up, all those dammed steps again and that's where you found me, thank God!"

Matthew took the cue to speak, "I didn't exactly find you as such, he left a letter at the villa – overnight – it told me quite precisely where you would be, and what to do if I wanted to see you again!"

Beth looked intently at him; he knew it to be ominous and that a pronouncement was imminent.

"Matthew, it seems to me that since you retired, the job keeps dogging you wherever we go and this time it too close for comfort. When you see something unusual, turn away, leave it for someone else, you've. NO! We have earned our rest!"

They stopped talking as the plane dipped, it was nice to fly in during daylight, it was still early afternoon and the sun was shining over England. Below the busy arteries of commerce pulsed with life as the plane turned for its final approach run; it banked and the sun glinted briefly across the surface of the lake at the exhibition centre. Beth turned to him quizzically.

"You haven't said why? – Why I was kidnapped? – Why I nearly lost you on a cliff face in France. What the hell it was all about?"

There were only moments left before the plane touched down and they left the aircraft.

Matthew screwed up his nose before conceding the explanation and offering what he knew.

"Well it was a matter of honey! Five jars of it to be precise."

She looked puzzled.

"What do you mean – not just honey, surely – even the cost of living in France is not that bad."

"No… it's what makes honey that matters – bees!"

The red sign glowed and those at the back nervously pulled at the straps that secured their seat belts.

"Bees?"

"Yes but not live or dead!"

"Come on, what then?"

"Gold! Golden bees of history; part of a treasure that once belonged to the Visigoth kings who ruled that region of France, centuries ago. Buried in the village, their centre of government at that time and used subsequently by, yes that's right, 'The Cathars' as some form of trust symbol. When 'The Cathar' cause was lost they were buried again and there they sat, until very recently."

"Okay, honey, bees, golden bees, where? What? Answers!"

The plane bounce once on the tarmac and they looked at each other, then instinctively out of the window; a second touch glued the aircraft to mother earth and they both sighed with relief.

"A shop in the village – where you spent the night – sold clear, Golden Bee honey, containing pieces of natural honeycomb. The owner thought it would be a useful cover to export a few of the priceless artefacts to England, to a contact he had made; the man who eventually fell from the cliff!"

She shivered at the thought of it.

"He had come over from England to collect the package – he was on our plane with a girl friend. I'm not sure what happened up there, it's as if someone else was involved. I have no idea why the local police chief was wearing the attire of a monk... bright red. Very attractive!"

"What happened to the jars? Were they really worth it?"

"The Emperor Napoleon had three hundred of the little golden bees sewn to his coronation cloak, the answer is yes and they are very valuable. It seems that there is some kind of conservation society over there, who will look after them, that's how the police chief explained it to me."

Their aircraft had taxied into the bay while they had been talking and was now connected to the exit tube. The other passengers had removed their hand luggage from above and were making their way out to the customs hall. Loosening her belt off to follow, she quipped at him,

"In future, no good works – lost property – someone else's department. Especially honey, after all you don't even like the stuff!"

Beth threw her head back defiantly and walked on ahead of him. There was no hold-up on this occasion, the cases appeared on cue through the opening from the baggage handlers. Quickly strolling on, with nothing to declare through customs, left them standing at the barrier with their trolley. The tannoy playing its three-note phrase was demanding attention from the bustling mass of eager travellers. A voice of rounded female strains broke into the concentration.

'Would Mr Matthew Rawlings of flight BA 321 AC from Girona please go to the enquiry desk in the main terminal

hall before leaving the airport. Mr Matthew Rawlings. Thank you.'

A further three notes marked the end of the message.

Matthew finally caught up with his wife – who was by then looking back apprehensively awaiting his arrival and ready to be disappointed. She of course had heard and noted the announcement and, reasoning that it had much to do with their experiences on holiday, felt peeved at the imposition of it. As if to emphasise the urgency still further, standing at the barrier immediately ahead of them were two uniformed officers; he shrugged his shoulders with acceptance to her then to her amazement walked straight on through, without acknowledging either of them. She ran to catch him up.

"Matthew you didn't speak to them… shouldn't you… I mean… it might be urgent, surely you can't just ignore an important enquiry?"

"You know after all the things you said and I know how you feel… inside you are more committed to the system than I am."

"But it may be very important!"

"Not so as to disturb our evening together, or disrupt a quiet homecoming dinner at our favourite restaurant. Tomorrow, well that's another story. Let's just wait and see."

They strode out of the main hall together, he pushing the laden trolley and she, walking dreamily along with her arm entwined in his, looking forward to the comforts of home.